ONEPLUSONE™

oni
PRESS

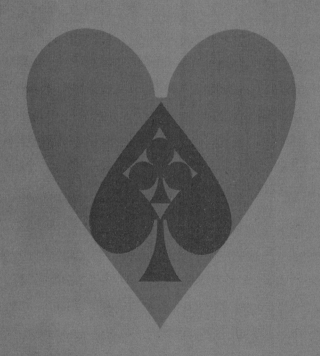

ONEPLUSONE

written by
Neal Shaffer

illustrated and lettered by
Daniel Krall

chapter breaks and introduction by
Michael Avon Oeming

gray tone assist by
Dawn Pietrusko

book design by
Keith Wood

cover design by
Daniel Krall

edited by
Jamie S. Rich

Published by Oni Press, Inc.
Joe Nozemack, publisher
Jamie S. Rich, editor in chief
James Lucas Jones, associate editor

This collects issues 1-5 of the Oni Press comics
series *One Plus One*, as well as a short story from
the *Oni Press Color Special 2002*.

ONI PRESS, INC.
6336 SE Milwaukie Avenue, PMB30
Portland, OR 97202
USA

www.onipress.com
www.spookoo.com

First edition: September 2003
ISBN 1-929998-64-3

1 3 5 7 9 10 8 6 4 2
PRINTED IN CANADA.

INTRODUCTION

by Michael Avon Oeming

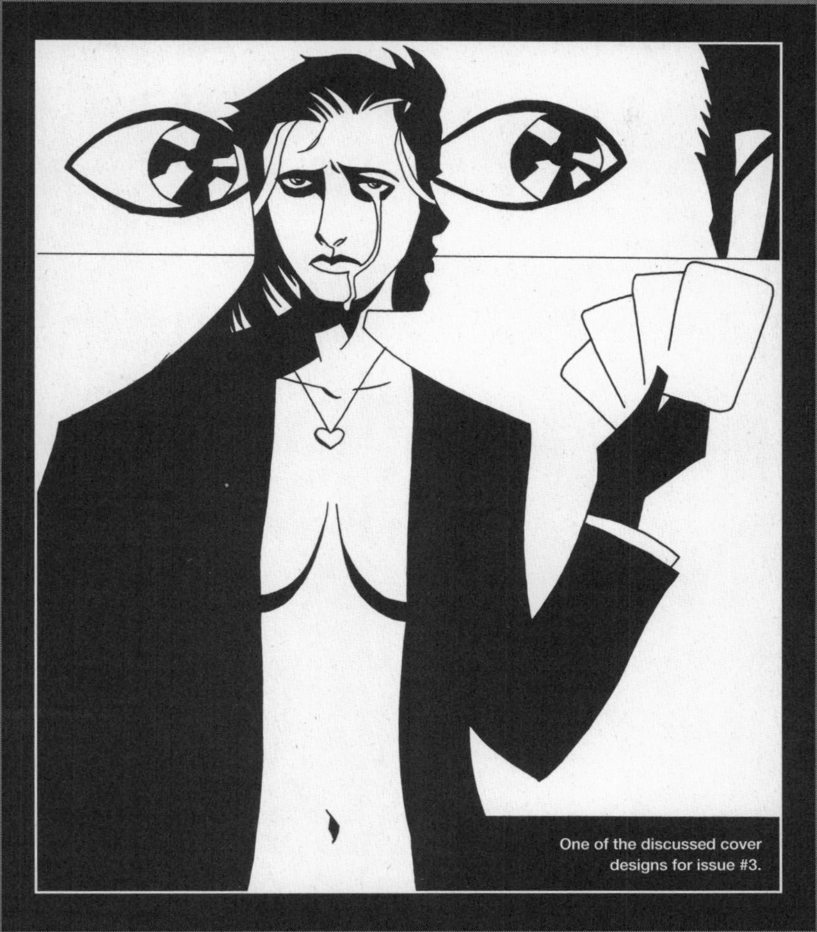

One of the discussed cover designs for issue #3.

I met Dan and Neal at the San Diego Comic Con in 2001. Dan had been working with Mark Wheatley at Insight Studios, and I was blown away by Dan's work. His portfolio was amazing and reeked of the best art training. There was color and design stuff going on there that was just beyond me. He and Neal were really cool guys, and they had this idea they were toting around called *One Plus One*. I don't remember if they had pitched Oni the project yet, but time goes by and they get the Oni deal and it's set. I don't remember how exactly the cover gig came up for me, if they asked me to do the covers or if I suggested it to them. It could be either way because I'm truly in love with Dan's work.

Also, I saw it as a great opportunity to do some really different cover designs, and to my great surprise, they were paying, too! Fools! I would have done them for free!

To do the covers, I asked Dan to send me plot summaries so that I could do something that reflected the story. I'll break the process down for you. Don't worry, I'm not giving any of the story away...though feel free to save this bit and come back when you're done if you're worried.

Issue One: This cover had to set the mood. Noir with a touch of Hell. The issue sets up our characters, and Leonard and David meet. We think this is going to be a story about either a dead man or a man who sees the dead...but wait, here comes...

Issue Two: My favorite cover for the series, so much to play with. I love drawing playing cards, although I can't play anything other than "go fish." We meet the other players, Eddie and Celeste. Eddie and Celeste are in a bit of a fix, but who is worse off? This story is really about them. David is the host of our world in a way, our dungeon master on a journey into the world of Hearts, Jacks, and Aces. Leonard is our witness. We also see the seeds of the Grift being set up—but who is setting up who?

Issue Three: I did about four or five different versions of this cover. I wanted to see an eye with an outline of a body and mix the two to be one. I think I got it down. Notice there are no faces on the cards—there's a reason for that, and you may be able to see why when you read the story. I won't say what, but think about it. The story asks you to think for yourself, there is meaning and plot hidden in character and motivation. Neal's writing is sublime and smart, so use your noggin or you may lose all your chips here.

Issue Four: There's no turning back for Eddie now. The hand has been dealt and the game is being played. People are being played, too. Who do you think is dealing the cards? Hopefully, the cover will spell that out for you...

Issue Five: Wow, this cover was fun. Cut off thumbs, threats, blood, and secrets. All the shit hits the fan here, all set up and spread throughout the story, and fate has taken its rightful path. I wonder if David is satisfied? His job is well done, and it's off to another city...

I just hope it's not mine.

Thank you, Neal, Dan, and Jamie for letting me be part of this incredibly hip and creepy book.

Michael Avon Oeming
August, 2003

As one of the co-creators of Powers—*a hard and clever amalgamation of the superhero and crime genres written by Brian Michael Bendis—artist Michael Avon Oeming is one of the top illustrators in independent comics. Not content to stop with one hit, he has also dabbled in his own creations, like* Parliament of Justice *with Neil Vokes,* Bastard Samurai *with Miles Gunter and Kelsey Shannon, and* Hammer of the Gods *with Mark Wheatley (all published by Image Comics). Additionally, he has lent his pen to such diverse projects as* Bulletproof Monk, Grendel: Red, White, & Black, *and* B.R.P.D. *He lives in New Jersey and watches lots of Hong Kong action flicks. The covers he discusses in this piece are used as chapter breaks throughout the book.*

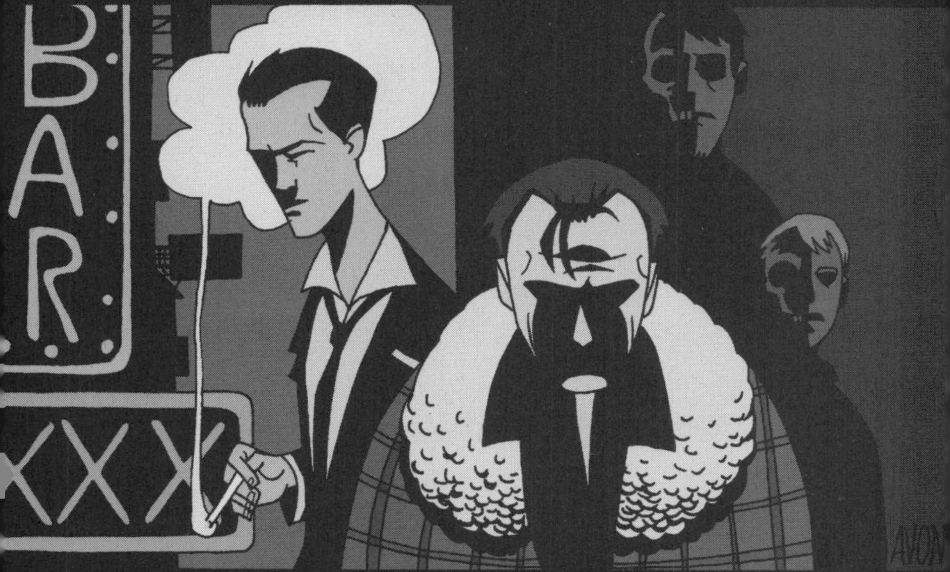
BAR
XXX
AVON

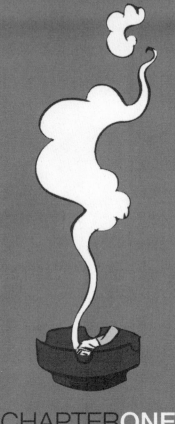

CHAPTER**ONE**

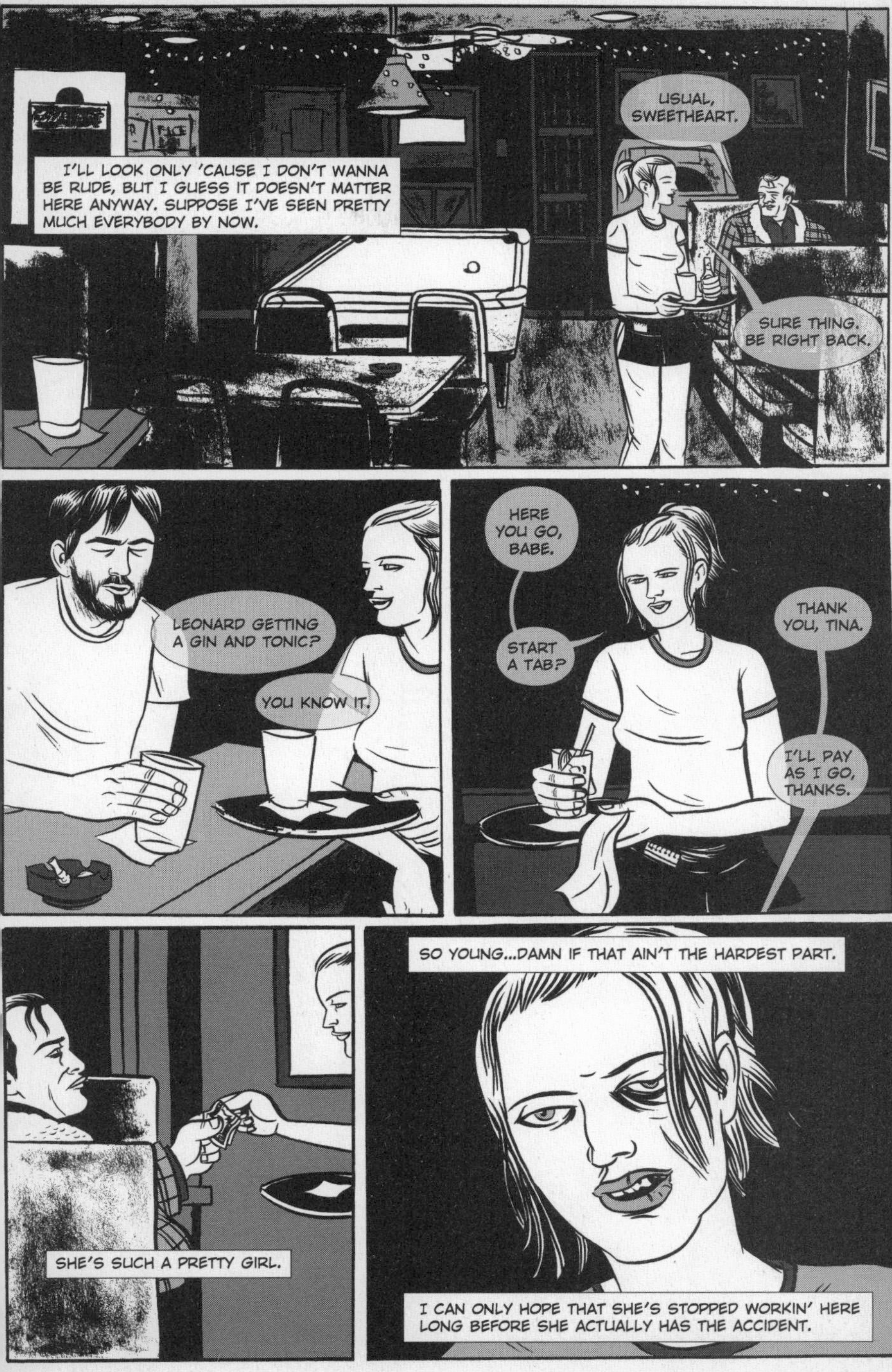
I'LL LOOK ONLY 'CAUSE I DON'T WANNA BE RUDE, BUT I GUESS IT DOESN'T MATTER HERE ANYWAY. SUPPOSE I'VE SEEN PRETTY MUCH EVERYBODY BY NOW.
USUAL, SWEETHEART.
SURE THING. BE RIGHT BACK.
LEONARD GETTING A GIN AND TONIC?
YOU KNOW IT.
HERE YOU GO, BABE.
START A TAB?
THANK YOU, TINA.
I'LL PAY AS I GO, THANKS.
SHE'S SUCH A PRETTY GIRL.
SO YOUNG...DAMN IF THAT AIN'T THE HARDEST PART.
I CAN ONLY HOPE THAT SHE'S STOPPED WORKIN' HERE LONG BEFORE SHE ACTUALLY HAS THE ACCIDENT.

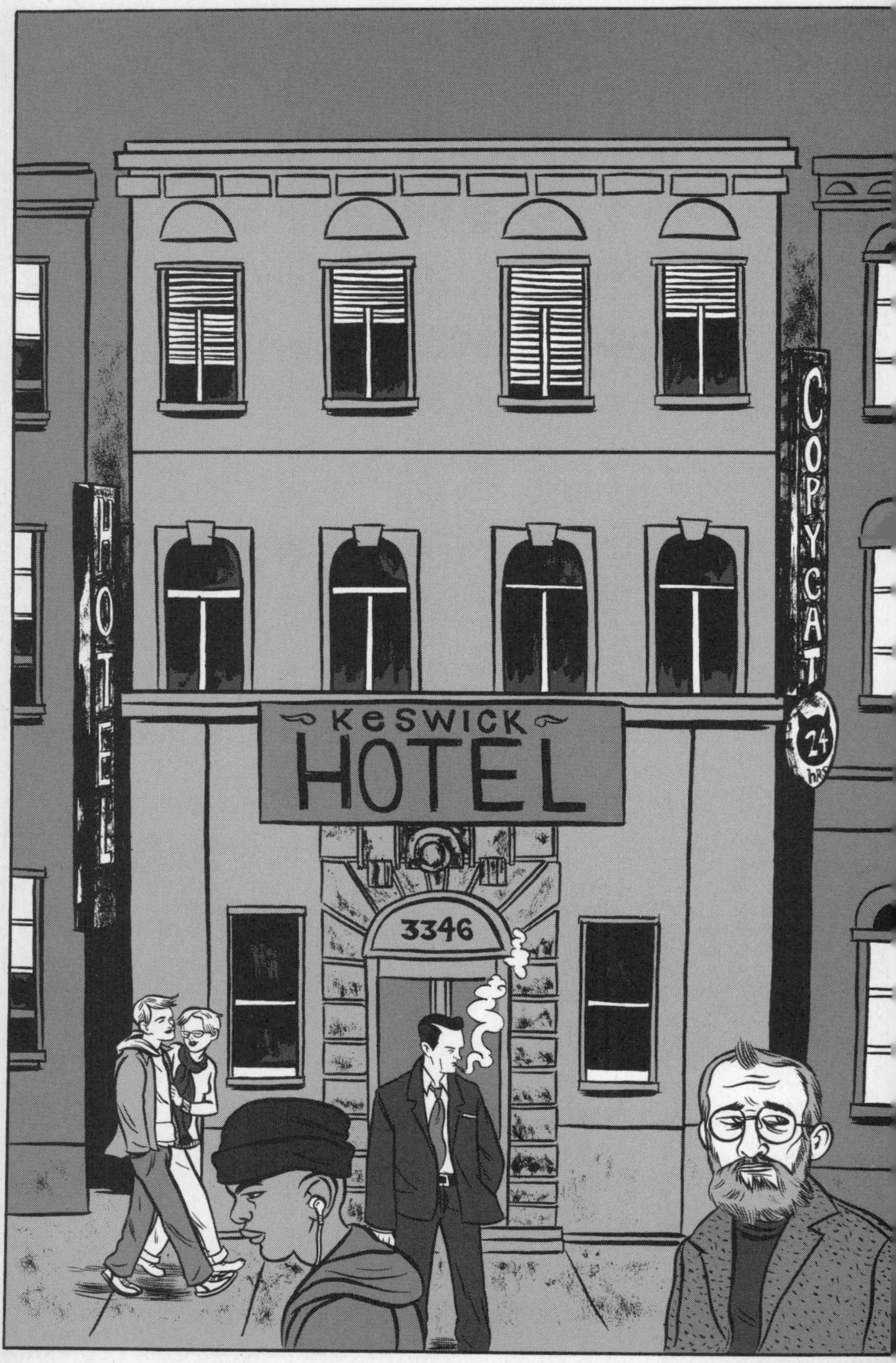
HOTEL
COPYCAT
24 hrs
KESWICK
HOTEL
3346

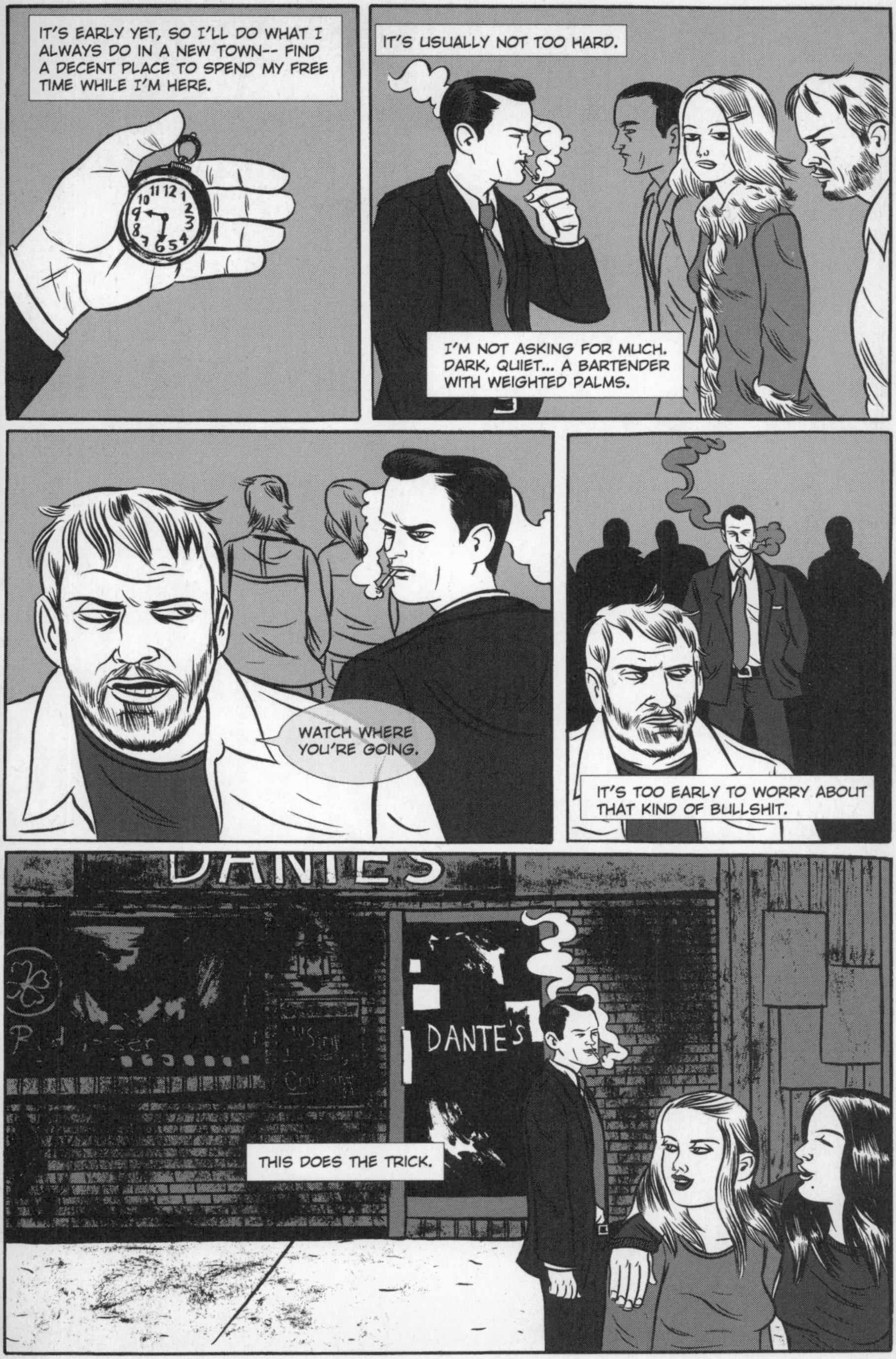

IT'S EARLY YET, SO I'LL DO WHAT I ALWAYS DO IN A NEW TOWN-- FIND A DECENT PLACE TO SPEND MY FREE TIME WHILE I'M HERE.
IT'S USUALLY NOT TOO HARD.
I'M NOT ASKING FOR MUCH. DARK, QUIET... A BARTENDER WITH WEIGHTED PALMS.
WATCH WHERE YOU'RE GOING.
IT'S TOO EARLY TO WORRY ABOUT THAT KIND OF BULLSHIT.
DANTES
DANTE'S
THIS DOES THE TRICK.

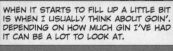
WHEN IT STARTS TO FILL UP A LITTLE BIT IS WHEN I USUALLY THINK ABOUT GOIN'. DEPENDING ON HOW MUCH GIN I'VE HAD IT CAN BE A LOT TO LOOK AT.

STILL, THAT'S WHY I ALWAYS END UP HERE. NOT TOO MANY NEW FOLKS WANDER IN, AND IT HURTS A LITTLE LESS EACH TIME I SEE SOMEONE.

LISTEN, MOTHERFUCKER, YOU LOST. YOU'D BETTER FUCKIN' PAY UP.

NAW MAN, YOU DON'T GET IT. I DON'T BE *PAYIN'* NO *CHEATER*.

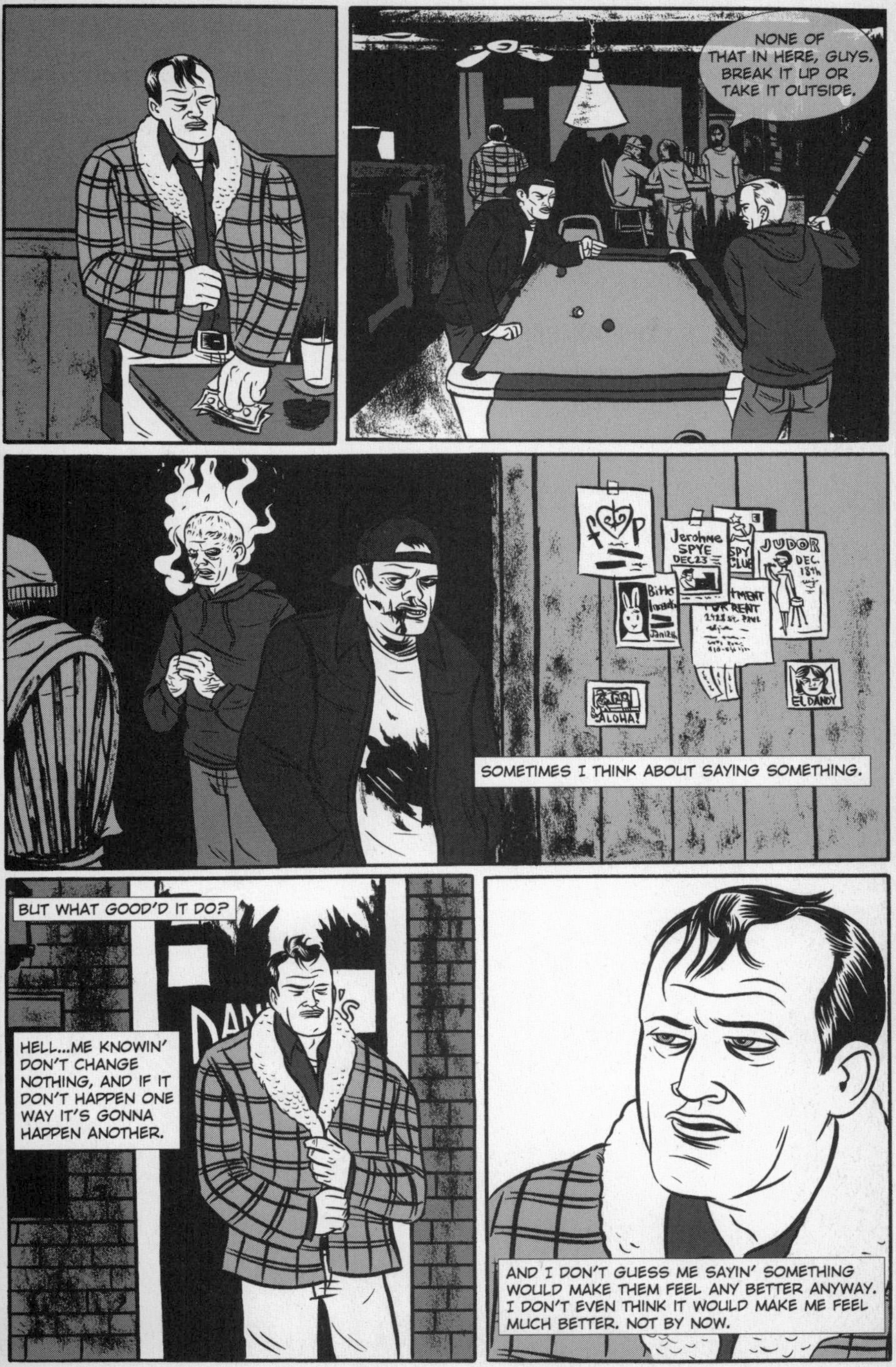
NONE OF THAT IN HERE, GUYS. BREAK IT UP OR TAKE IT OUTSIDE.
Jerohne SPYE DEC23
JUDOR DEC. 18th
ALOHA!
EL DANDY
SOMETIMES I THINK ABOUT SAYING SOMETHING.
BUT WHAT GOOD'D IT DO?
HELL...ME KNOWIN' DON'T CHANGE NOTHING, AND IF IT DON'T HAPPEN ONE WAY IT'S GONNA HAPPEN ANOTHER.
AND I DON'T GUESS ME SAYIN' SOMETHING WOULD MAKE THEM FEEL ANY BETTER ANYWAY. I DON'T EVEN THINK IT WOULD MAKE ME FEEL MUCH BETTER. NOT BY NOW.

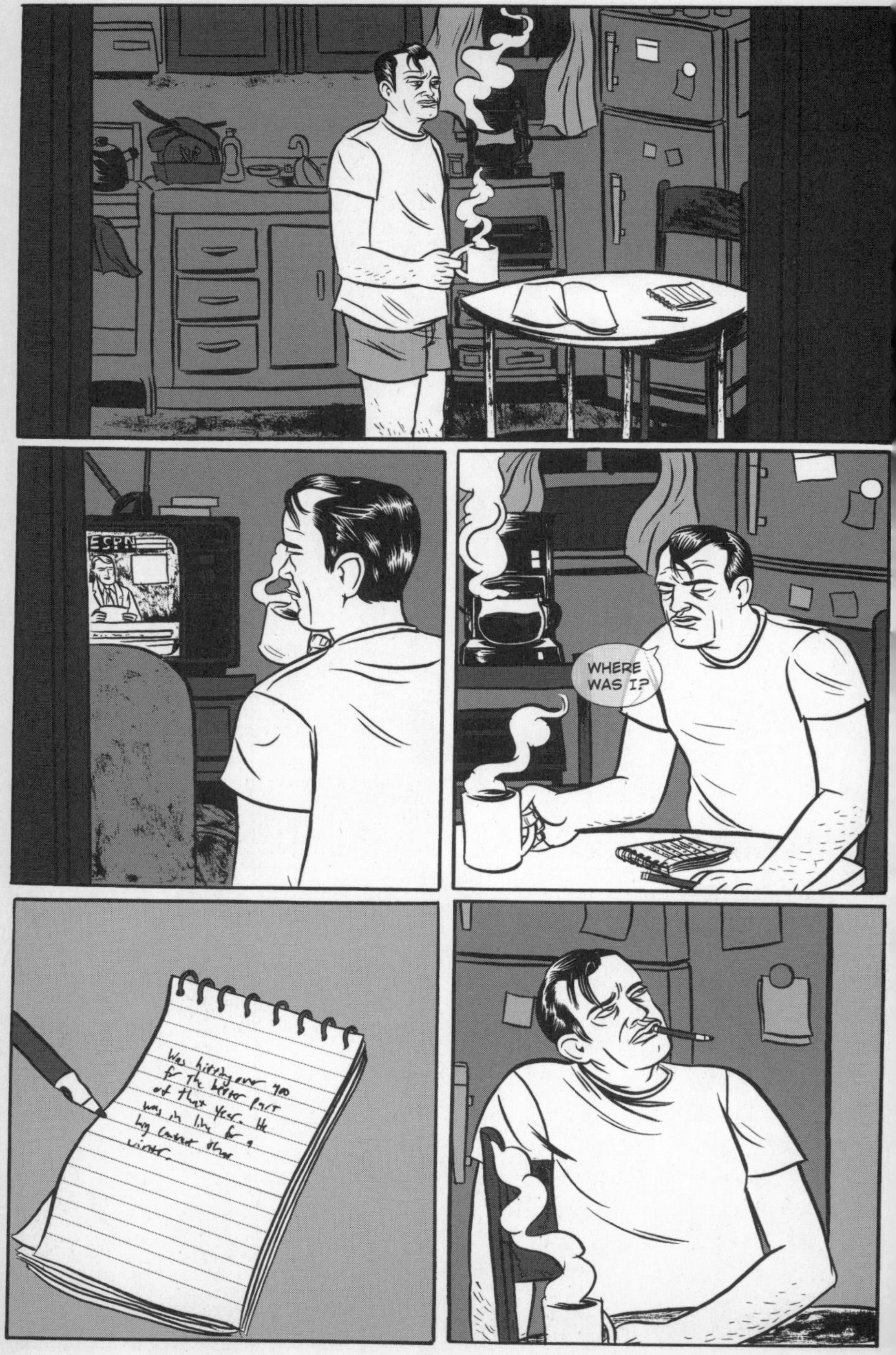
ESPN
WHERE WAS I?
for the better part
of that year. He
was in line for a
big contract that
winter.

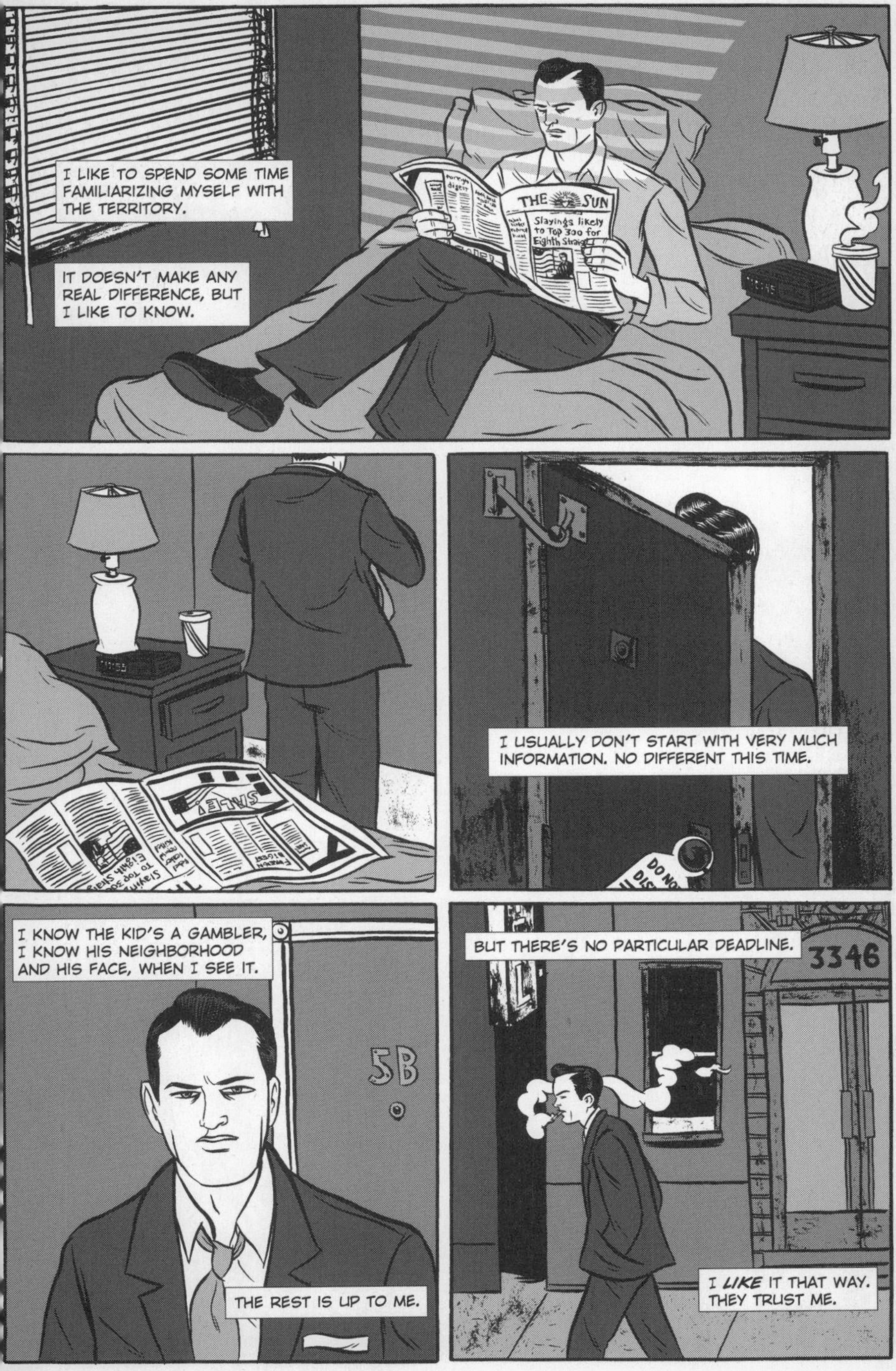
I LIKE TO SPEND SOME TIME FAMILIARIZING MYSELF WITH THE TERRITORY.
IT DOESN'T MAKE ANY REAL DIFFERENCE, BUT I LIKE TO KNOW.
THE SUN
Slayings likely to Top 300 for Eighth Straight
I USUALLY DON'T START WITH VERY MUCH INFORMATION. NO DIFFERENT THIS TIME.
I KNOW THE KID'S A GAMBLER, I KNOW HIS NEIGHBORHOOD AND HIS FACE, WHEN I SEE IT.
5B
THE REST IS UP TO ME.
BUT THERE'S NO PARTICULAR DEADLINE.
3346
I *LIKE* IT THAT WAY. THEY TRUST ME.

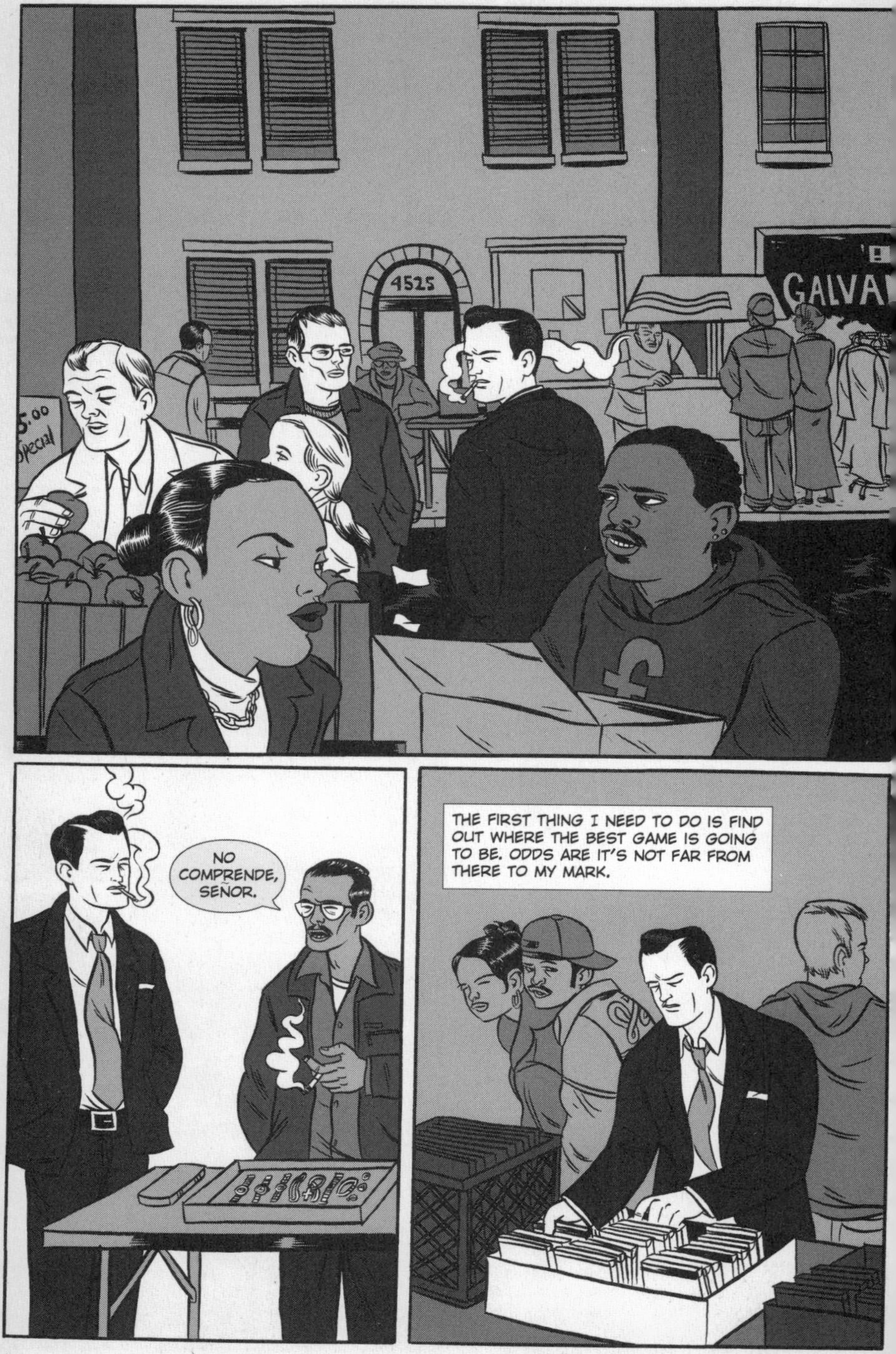
5.00
Special
4525
GALVA
NO COMPRENDE, SEÑOR.
THE FIRST THING I NEED TO DO IS FIND OUT WHERE THE BEST GAME IS GOING TO BE. ODDS ARE IT'S NOT FAR FROM THERE TO MY MARK.

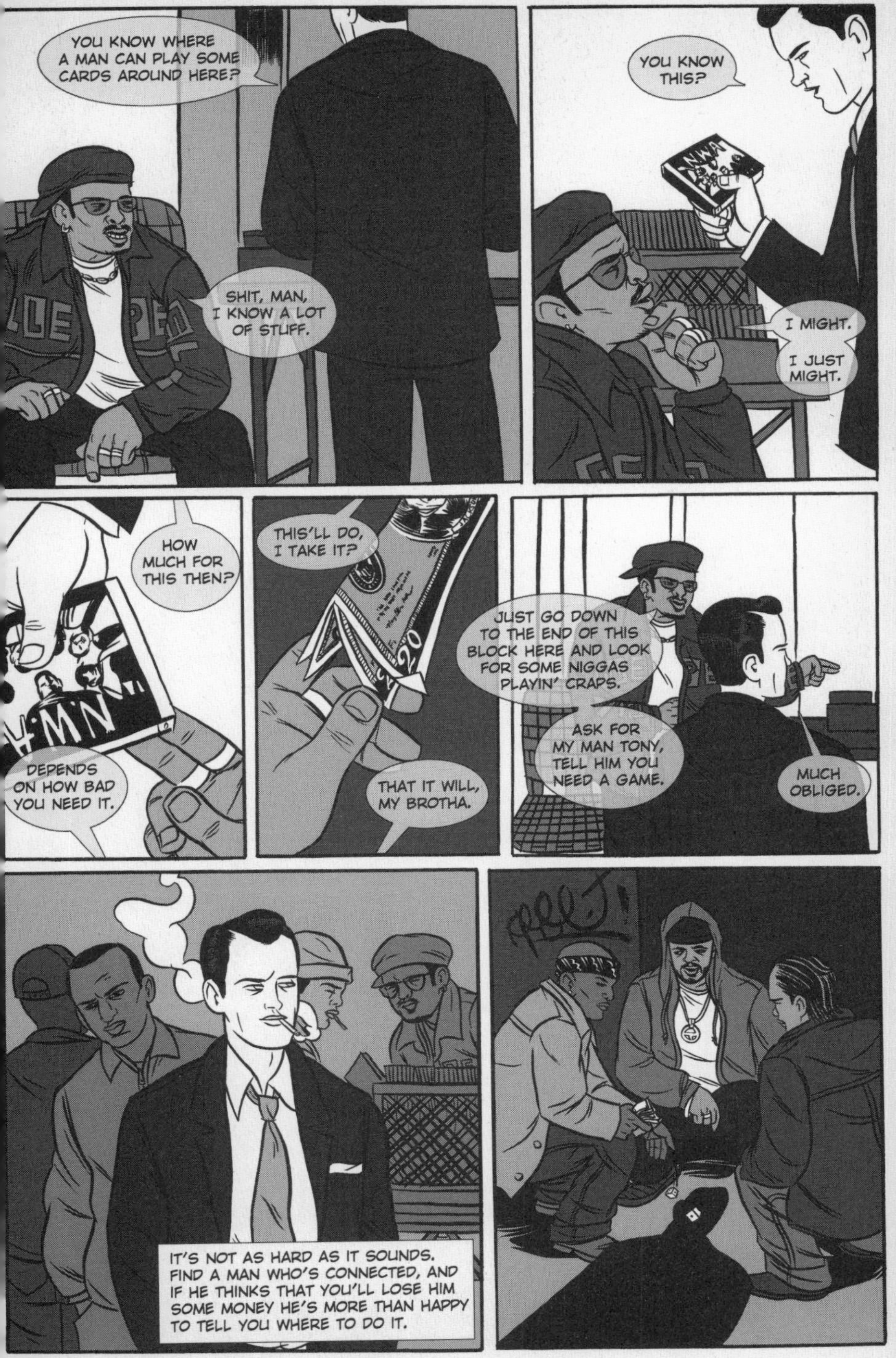

YOU KNOW WHERE A MAN CAN PLAY SOME CARDS AROUND HERE?
SHIT, MAN, I KNOW A LOT OF STUFF.
YOU KNOW THIS?
I MIGHT.
I JUST MIGHT.
HOW MUCH FOR THIS THEN?
DEPENDS ON HOW BAD YOU NEED IT.
THIS'LL DO, I TAKE IT?
THAT IT WILL, MY BROTHA.
JUST GO DOWN TO THE END OF THIS BLOCK HERE AND LOOK FOR SOME NIGGAS PLAYIN' CRAPS.
ASK FOR MY MAN TONY, TELL HIM YOU NEED A GAME.
MUCH OBLIGED.
IT'S NOT AS HARD AS IT SOUNDS. FIND A MAN WHO'S CONNECTED, AND IF HE THINKS THAT YOU'LL LOSE HIM SOME MONEY HE'S MORE THAN HAPPY TO TELL YOU WHERE TO DO IT.

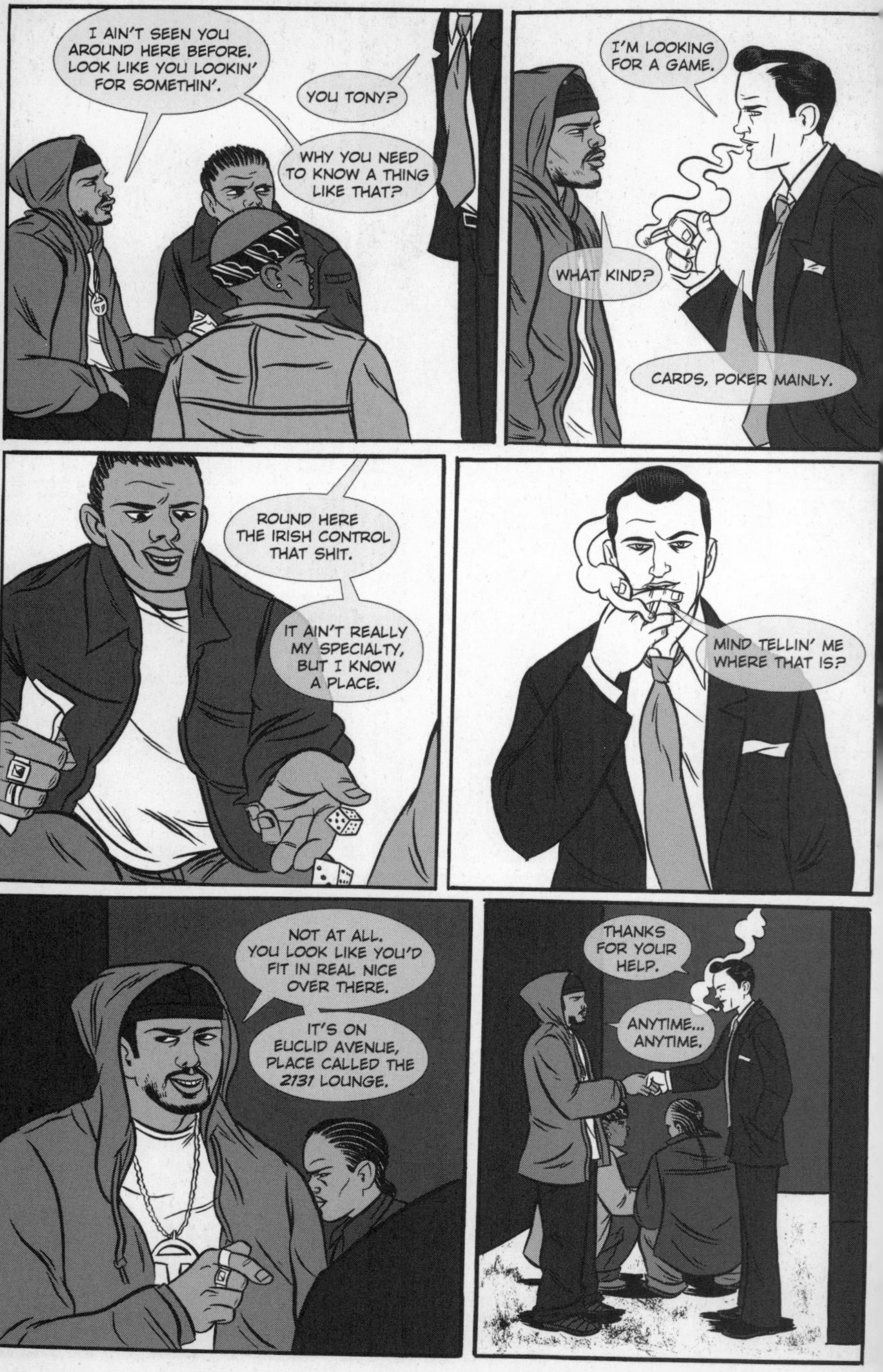
I AIN'T SEEN YOU AROUND HERE BEFORE. LOOK LIKE YOU LOOKIN' FOR SOMETHIN'.
YOU TONY?
WHY YOU NEED TO KNOW A THING LIKE THAT?
I'M LOOKING FOR A GAME.
WHAT KIND?
CARDS, POKER MAINLY.
ROUND HERE THE IRISH CONTROL THAT SHIT.
IT AIN'T REALLY MY SPECIALTY, BUT I KNOW A PLACE.
MIND TELLIN' ME WHERE THAT IS?
NOT AT ALL. YOU LOOK LIKE YOU'D FIT IN REAL NICE OVER THERE.
IT'S ON EUCLID AVENUE, PLACE CALLED THE 2131 LOUNGE.
THANKS FOR YOUR HELP.
ANYTIME... ANYTIME.

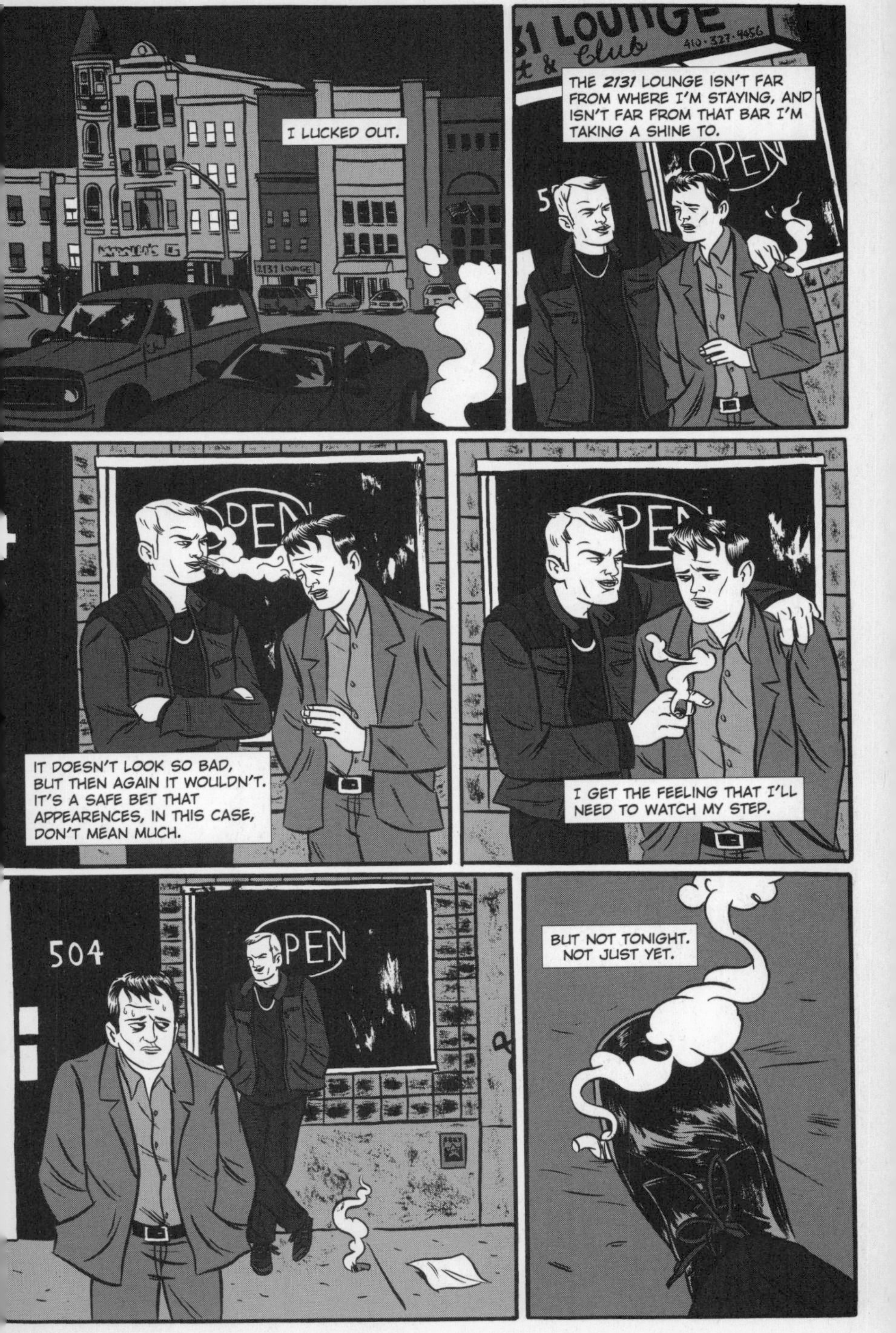
I LUCKED OUT.
31 LOUNGE
410-327-4456
THE 2131 LOUNGE ISN'T FAR FROM WHERE I'M STAYING, AND ISN'T FAR FROM THAT BAR I'M TAKING A SHINE TO.
OPEN
IT DOESN'T LOOK SO BAD, BUT THEN AGAIN IT WOULDN'T. IT'S A SAFE BET THAT APPEARENCES, IN THIS CASE, DON'T MEAN MUCH.
I GET THE FEELING THAT I'LL NEED TO WATCH MY STEP.
504
OPEN
BUT NOT TONIGHT. NOT JUST YET.

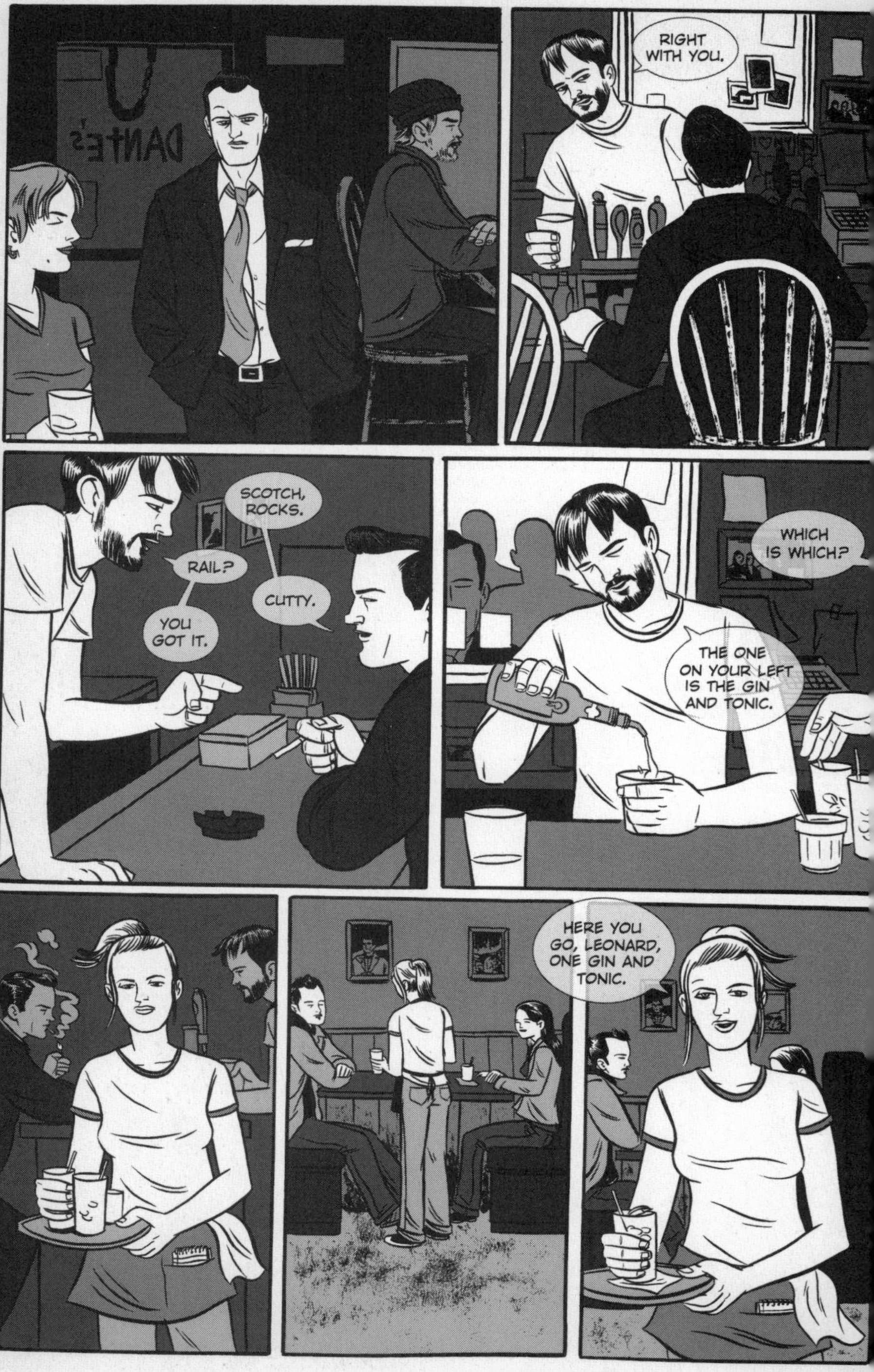

RIGHT WITH YOU.
SCOTCH, ROCKS.
RAIL?
CUTTY.
YOU GOT IT.
WHICH IS WHICH?
THE ONE ON YOUR LEFT IS THE GIN AND TONIC.
HERE YOU GO, LEONARD, ONE GIN AND TONIC.

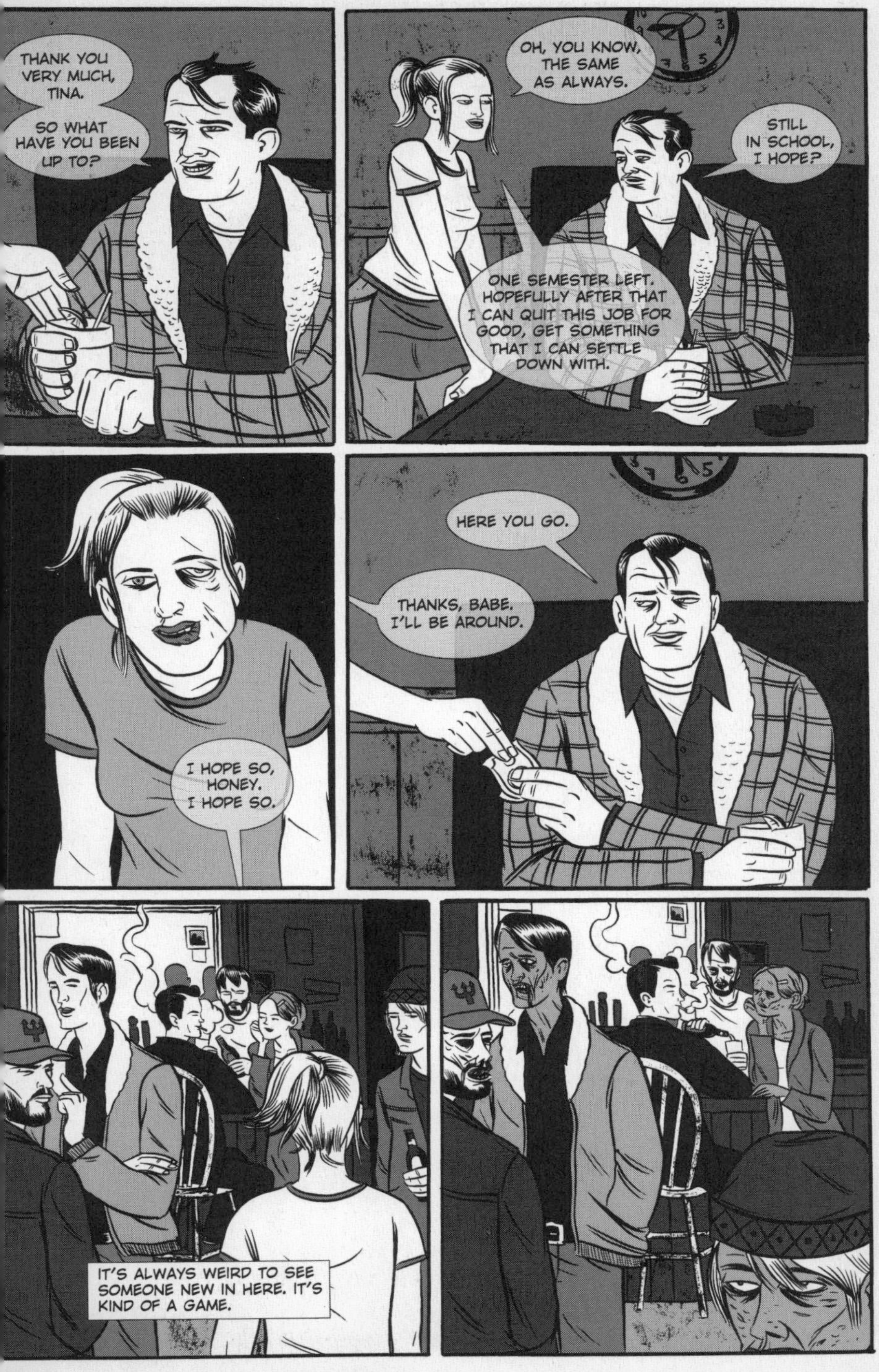
THANK YOU VERY MUCH, TINA.
SO WHAT HAVE YOU BEEN UP TO?
OH, YOU KNOW, THE SAME AS ALWAYS.
STILL IN SCHOOL, I HOPE?
ONE SEMESTER LEFT. HOPEFULLY AFTER THAT I CAN QUIT THIS JOB FOR GOOD, GET SOMETHING THAT I CAN SETTLE DOWN WITH.
I HOPE SO, HONEY. I HOPE SO.
HERE YOU GO.
THANKS, BABE. I'LL BE AROUND.
IT'S ALWAYS WEIRD TO SEE SOMEONE NEW IN HERE. IT'S KIND OF A GAME.

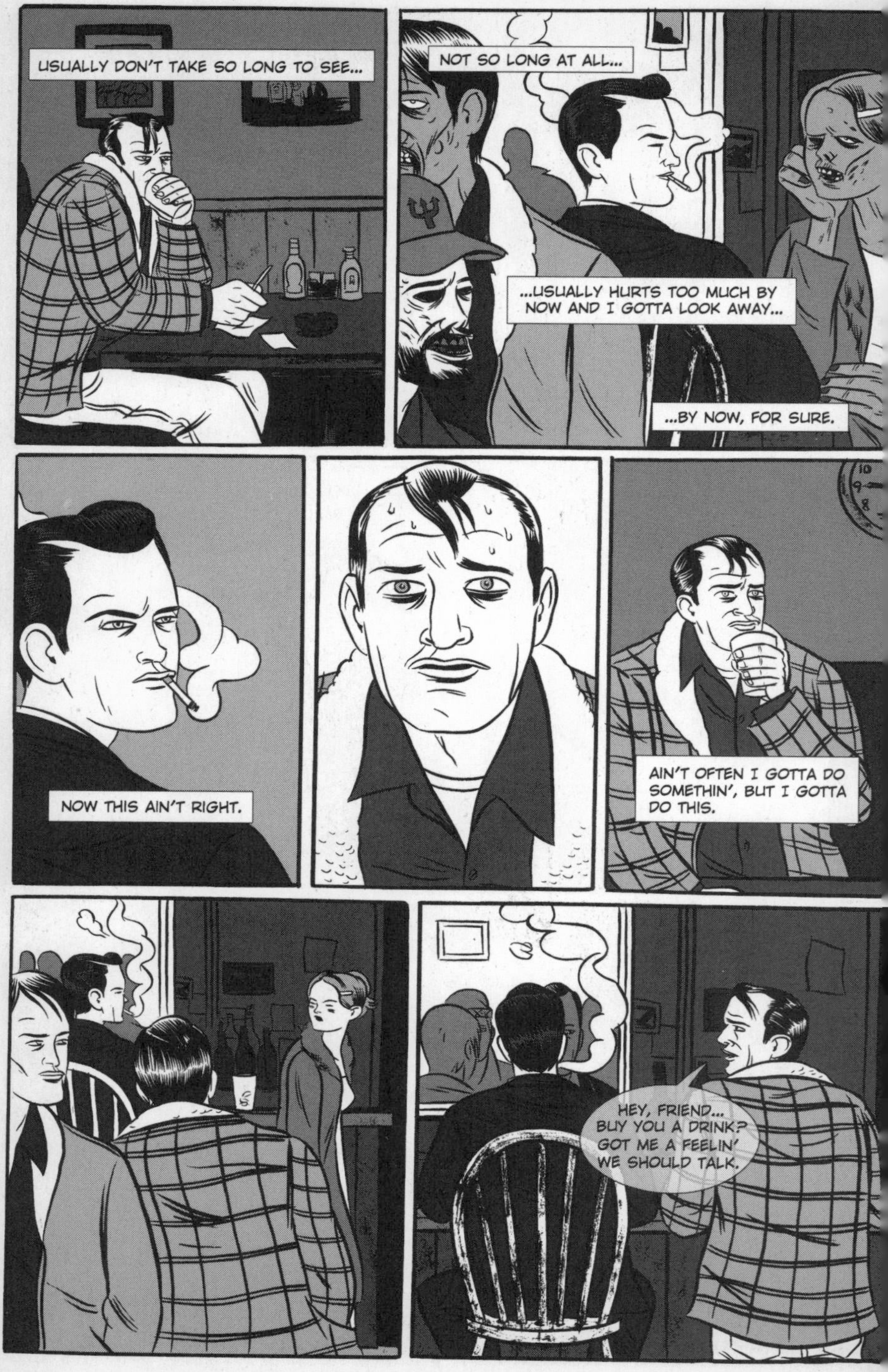
USUALLY DON'T TAKE SO LONG TO SEE...
NOT SO LONG AT ALL...
...USUALLY HURTS TOO MUCH BY NOW AND I GOTTA LOOK AWAY...
...BY NOW, FOR SURE.
NOW THIS AIN'T RIGHT.
AIN'T OFTEN I GOTTA DO SOMETHIN', BUT I GOTTA DO THIS.
HEY, FRIEND... BUY YOU A DRINK? GOT ME A FEELIN' WE SHOULD TALK.

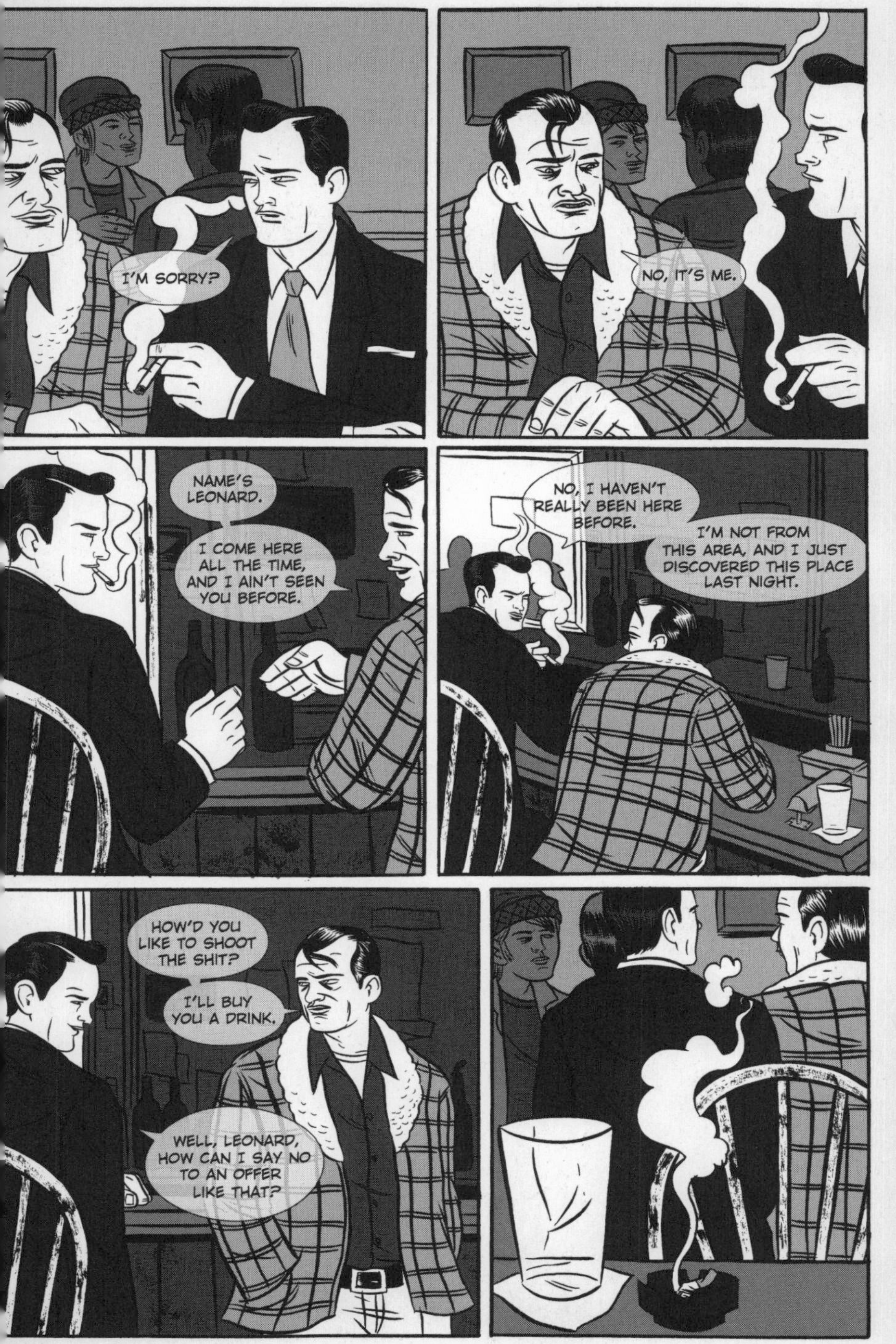
I'M SORRY?
NO, IT'S ME.
NAME'S LEONARD.
I COME HERE ALL THE TIME, AND I AIN'T SEEN YOU BEFORE.
NO, I HAVEN'T REALLY BEEN HERE BEFORE.
I'M NOT FROM THIS AREA, AND I JUST DISCOVERED THIS PLACE LAST NIGHT.
HOW'D YOU LIKE TO SHOOT THE SHIT?
I'LL BUY YOU A DRINK.
WELL, LEONARD, HOW CAN I SAY NO TO AN OFFER LIKE THAT?

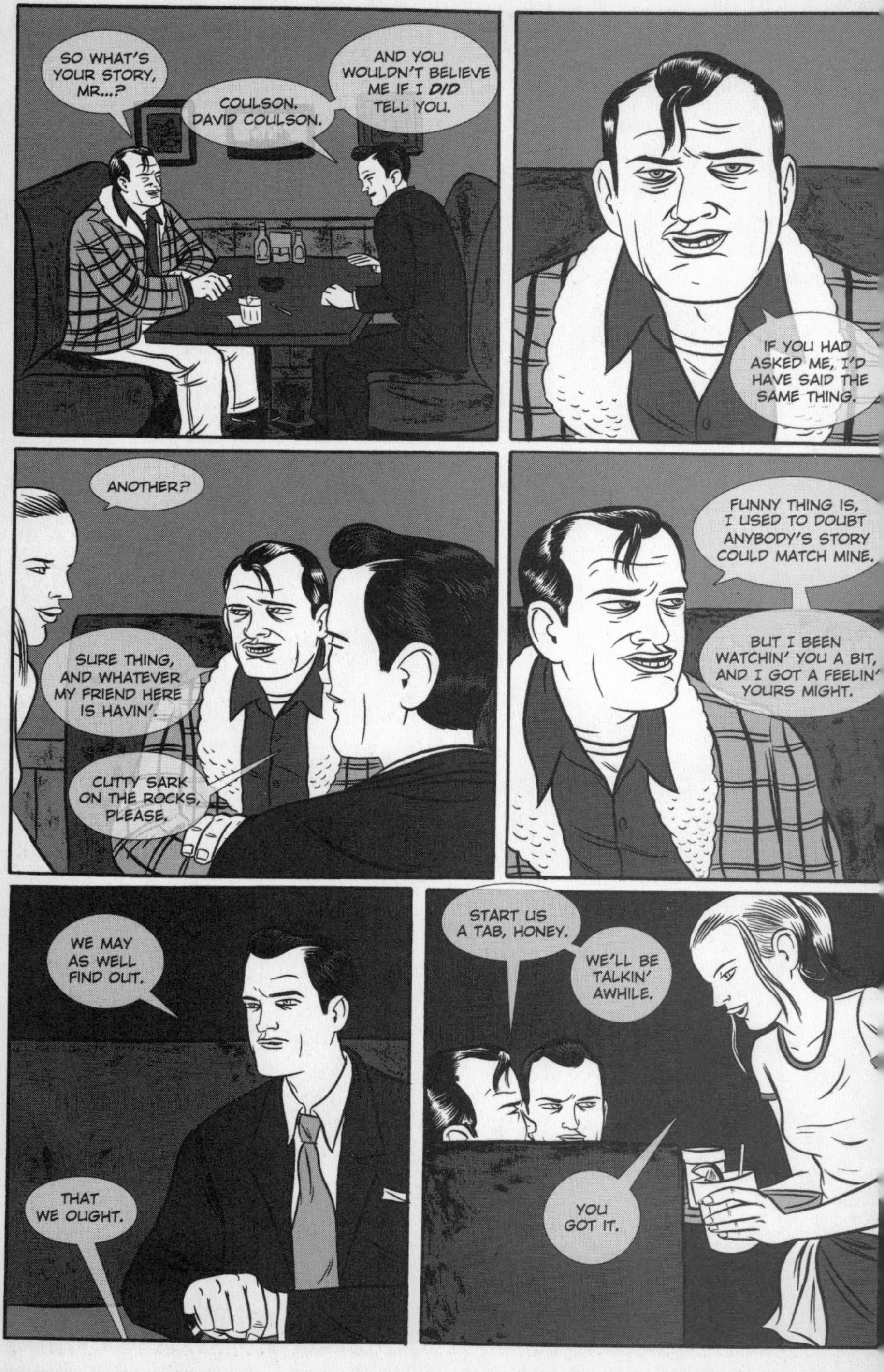
SO WHAT'S YOUR STORY, MR...?
COULSON. DAVID COULSON.
AND YOU WOULDN'T BELIEVE ME IF I *DID* TELL YOU.
IF YOU HAD ASKED ME, I'D HAVE SAID THE SAME THING.
ANOTHER?
SURE THING, AND WHATEVER MY FRIEND HERE IS HAVIN'.
CUTTY SARK ON THE ROCKS, PLEASE.
FUNNY THING IS, I USED TO DOUBT ANYBODY'S STORY COULD MATCH MINE.
BUT I BEEN WATCHIN' YOU A BIT, AND I GOT A FEELIN' YOURS MIGHT.
WE MAY AS WELL FIND OUT.
THAT WE OUGHT.
START US A TAB, HONEY.
WE'LL BE TALKIN' AWHILE.
YOU GOT IT.

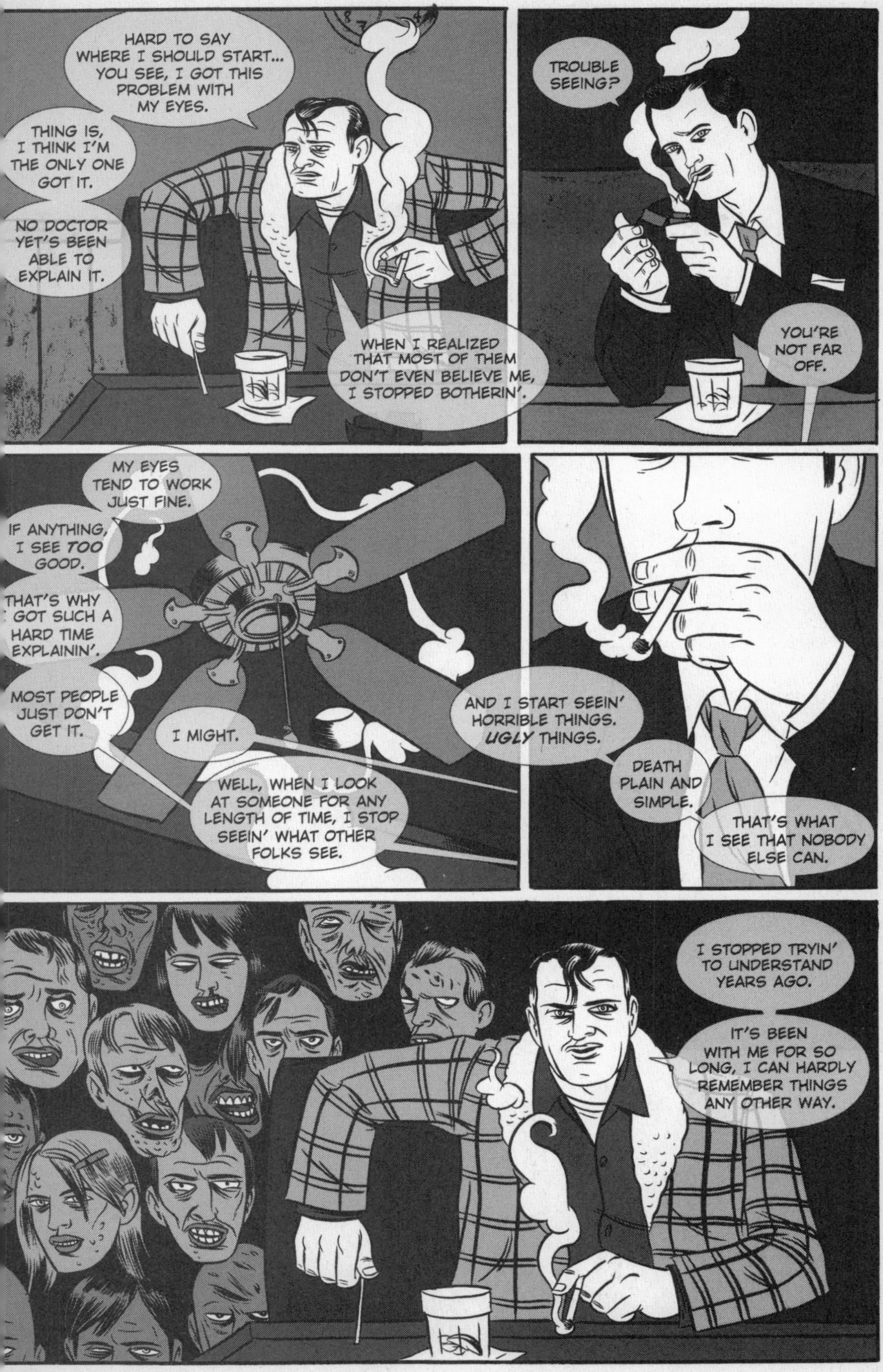
HARD TO SAY WHERE I SHOULD START... YOU SEE, I GOT THIS PROBLEM WITH MY EYES.
THING IS, I THINK I'M THE ONLY ONE GOT IT.
NO DOCTOR YET'S BEEN ABLE TO EXPLAIN IT.
WHEN I REALIZED THAT MOST OF THEM DON'T EVEN BELIEVE ME, I STOPPED BOTHERIN'.
TROUBLE SEEING?
YOU'RE NOT FAR OFF.
MY EYES TEND TO WORK JUST FINE.
IF ANYTHING, I SEE *TOO* GOOD.
THAT'S WHY GOT SUCH A HARD TIME EXPLAININ'.
MOST PEOPLE JUST DON'T GET IT.
I MIGHT.
WELL, WHEN I LOOK AT SOMEONE FOR ANY LENGTH OF TIME, I STOP SEEIN' WHAT OTHER FOLKS SEE.
AND I START SEEIN' HORRIBLE THINGS. ***UGLY*** THINGS.
DEATH PLAIN AND SIMPLE.
THAT'S WHAT I SEE THAT NOBODY ELSE CAN.
I STOPPED TRYIN' TO UNDERSTAND YEARS AGO.
IT'S BEEN WITH ME FOR SO LONG, I CAN HARDLY REMEMBER THINGS ANY OTHER WAY.

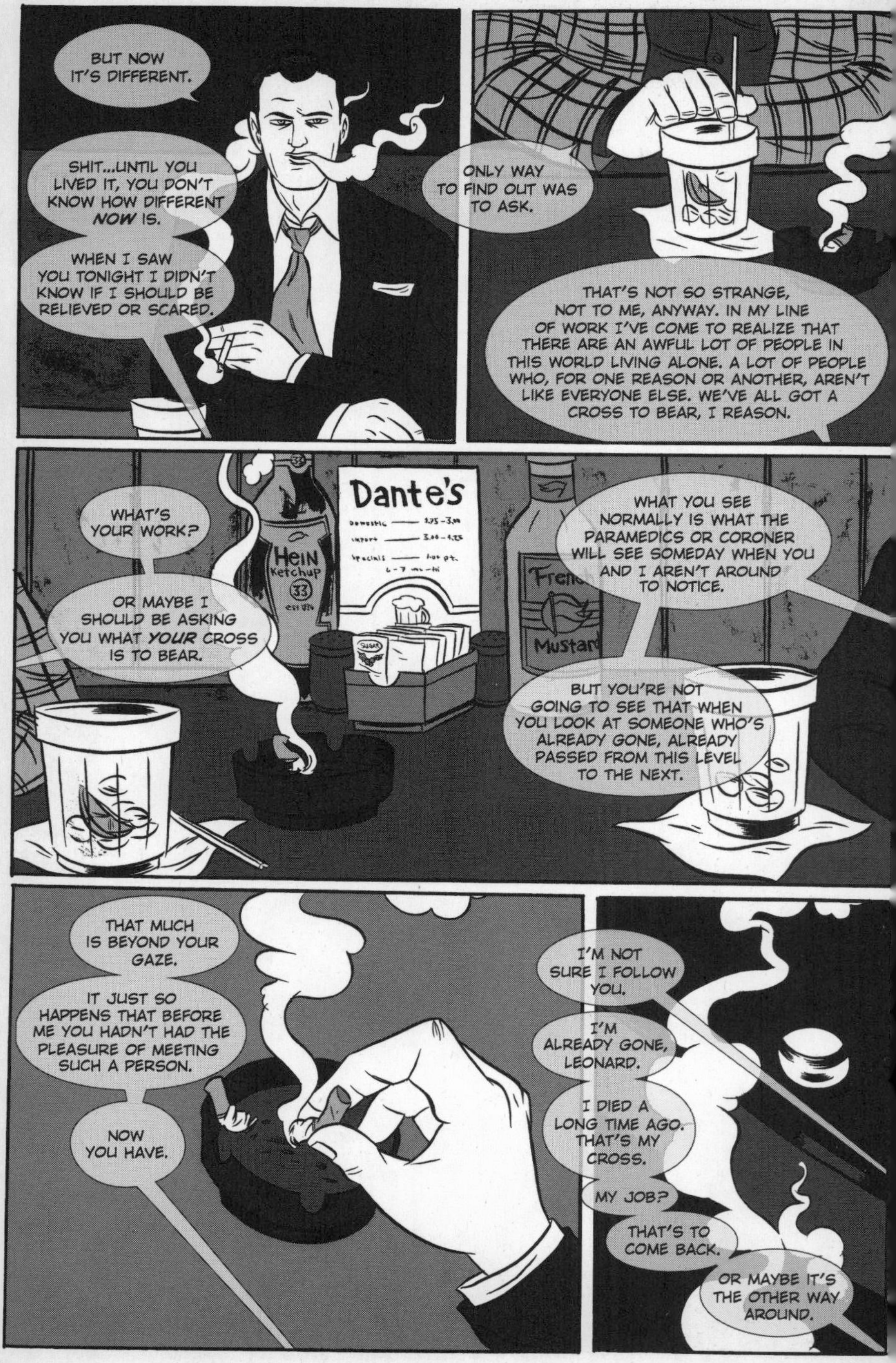
BUT NOW IT'S DIFFERENT.
SHIT...UNTIL YOU LIVED IT, YOU DON'T KNOW HOW DIFFERENT *NOW* IS.
WHEN I SAW YOU TONIGHT I DIDN'T KNOW IF I SHOULD BE RELIEVED OR SCARED.
ONLY WAY TO FIND OUT WAS TO ASK.
THAT'S NOT SO STRANGE, NOT TO ME, ANYWAY. IN MY LINE OF WORK I'VE COME TO REALIZE THAT THERE ARE AN AWFUL LOT OF PEOPLE IN THIS WORLD LIVING ALONE. A LOT OF PEOPLE WHO, FOR ONE REASON OR ANOTHER, AREN'T LIKE EVERYONE ELSE. WE'VE ALL GOT A CROSS TO BEAR, I REASON.
Dante's
Hein Ketchup
Mustard
SUGAR
WHAT'S YOUR WORK?
OR MAYBE I SHOULD BE ASKING YOU WHAT *YOUR* CROSS IS TO BEAR.
WHAT YOU SEE NORMALLY IS WHAT THE PARAMEDICS OR CORONER WILL SEE SOMEDAY WHEN YOU AND I AREN'T AROUND TO NOTICE.
BUT YOU'RE NOT GOING TO SEE THAT WHEN YOU LOOK AT SOMEONE WHO'S ALREADY GONE, ALREADY PASSED FROM THIS LEVEL TO THE NEXT.
THAT MUCH IS BEYOND YOUR GAZE.
IT JUST SO HAPPENS THAT BEFORE ME YOU HADN'T HAD THE PLEASURE OF MEETING SUCH A PERSON.
NOW YOU HAVE.
I'M NOT SURE I FOLLOW YOU.
I'M ALREADY GONE, LEONARD.
I DIED A LONG TIME AGO. THAT'S MY CROSS.
MY JOB?
THAT'S TO COME BACK.
OR MAYBE IT'S THE OTHER WAY AROUND.

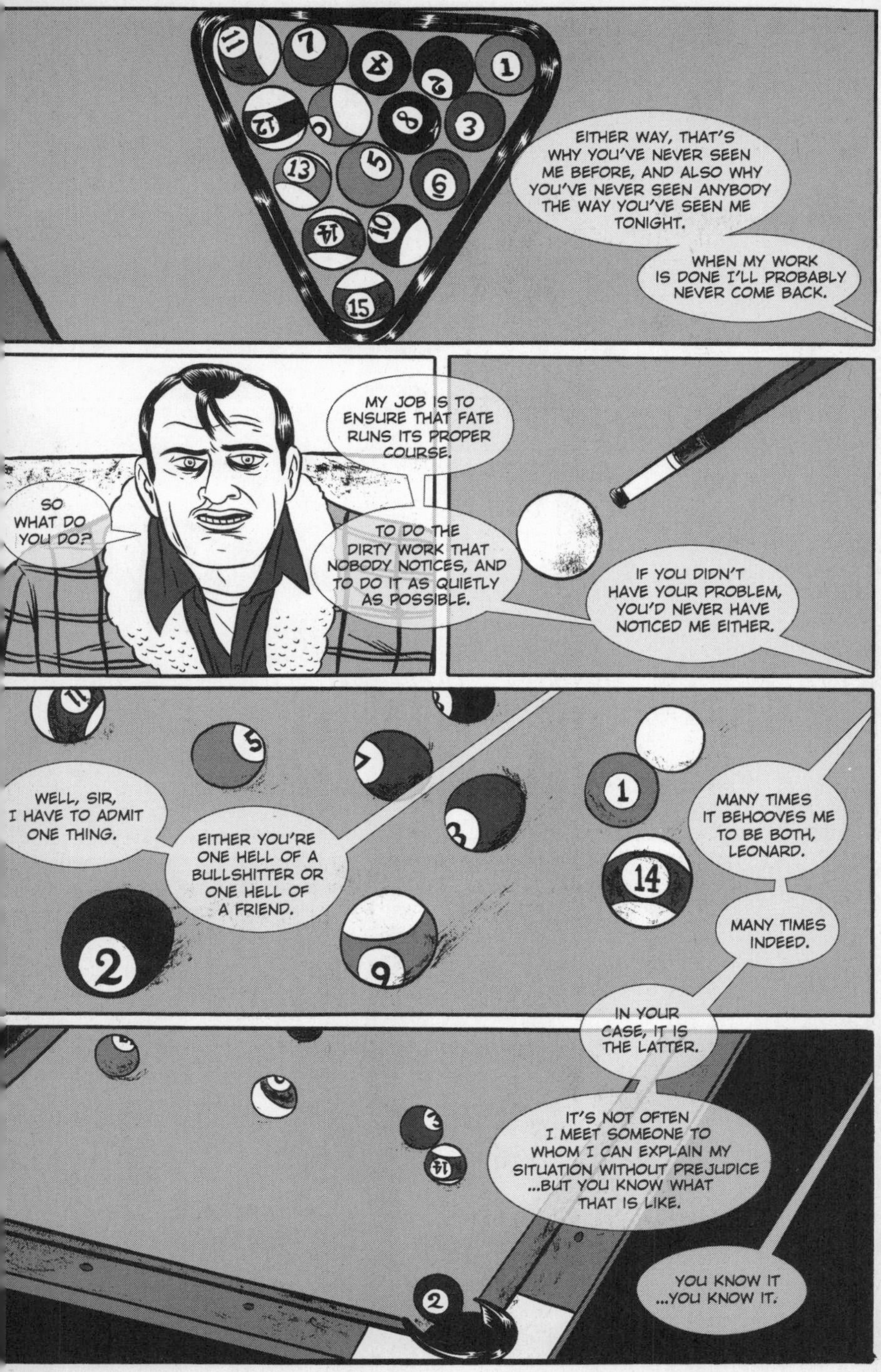
EITHER WAY, THAT'S WHY YOU'VE NEVER SEEN ME BEFORE, AND ALSO WHY YOU'VE NEVER SEEN ANYBODY THE WAY YOU'VE SEEN ME TONIGHT.
WHEN MY WORK IS DONE I'LL PROBABLY NEVER COME BACK.
SO WHAT DO YOU DO?
MY JOB IS TO ENSURE THAT FATE RUNS ITS PROPER COURSE.
TO DO THE DIRTY WORK THAT NOBODY NOTICES, AND TO DO IT AS QUIETLY AS POSSIBLE.
IF YOU DIDN'T HAVE YOUR PROBLEM, YOU'D NEVER HAVE NOTICED ME EITHER.
WELL, SIR, I HAVE TO ADMIT ONE THING.
EITHER YOU'RE ONE HELL OF A BULLSHITTER OR ONE HELL OF A FRIEND.
MANY TIMES IT BEHOOVES ME TO BE BOTH, LEONARD.
MANY TIMES INDEED.
IN YOUR CASE, IT IS THE LATTER.
IT'S NOT OFTEN I MEET SOMEONE TO WHOM I CAN EXPLAIN MY SITUATION WITHOUT PREJUDICE ...BUT YOU KNOW WHAT THAT IS LIKE.
YOU KNOW IT ...YOU KNOW IT.

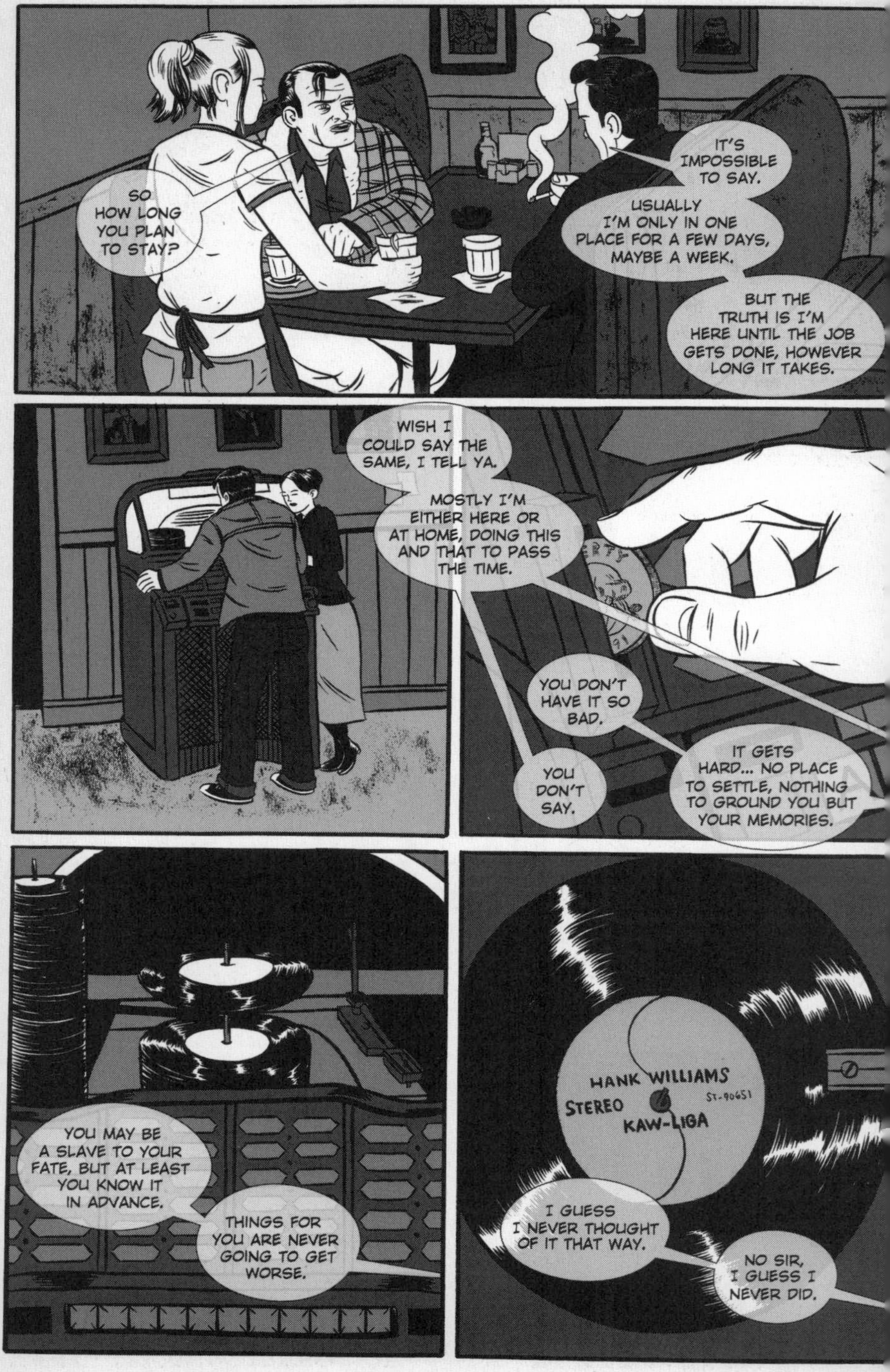
SO HOW LONG YOU PLAN TO STAY?
IT'S IMPOSSIBLE TO SAY.
USUALLY I'M ONLY IN ONE PLACE FOR A FEW DAYS, MAYBE A WEEK.
BUT THE TRUTH IS I'M HERE UNTIL THE JOB GETS DONE, HOWEVER LONG IT TAKES.
WISH I COULD SAY THE SAME, I TELL YA.
MOSTLY I'M EITHER HERE OR AT HOME, DOING THIS AND THAT TO PASS THE TIME.
YOU DON'T HAVE IT SO BAD.
YOU DON'T SAY.
IT GETS HARD... NO PLACE TO SETTLE, NOTHING TO GROUND YOU BUT YOUR MEMORIES.
YOU MAY BE A SLAVE TO YOUR FATE, BUT AT LEAST YOU KNOW IT IN ADVANCE.
THINGS FOR YOU ARE NEVER GOING TO GET WORSE.
HANK WILLIAMS
STEREO
KAW-LIGA
ST-90651
I GUESS I NEVER THOUGHT OF IT THAT WAY.
NO SIR, I GUESS I NEVER DID.

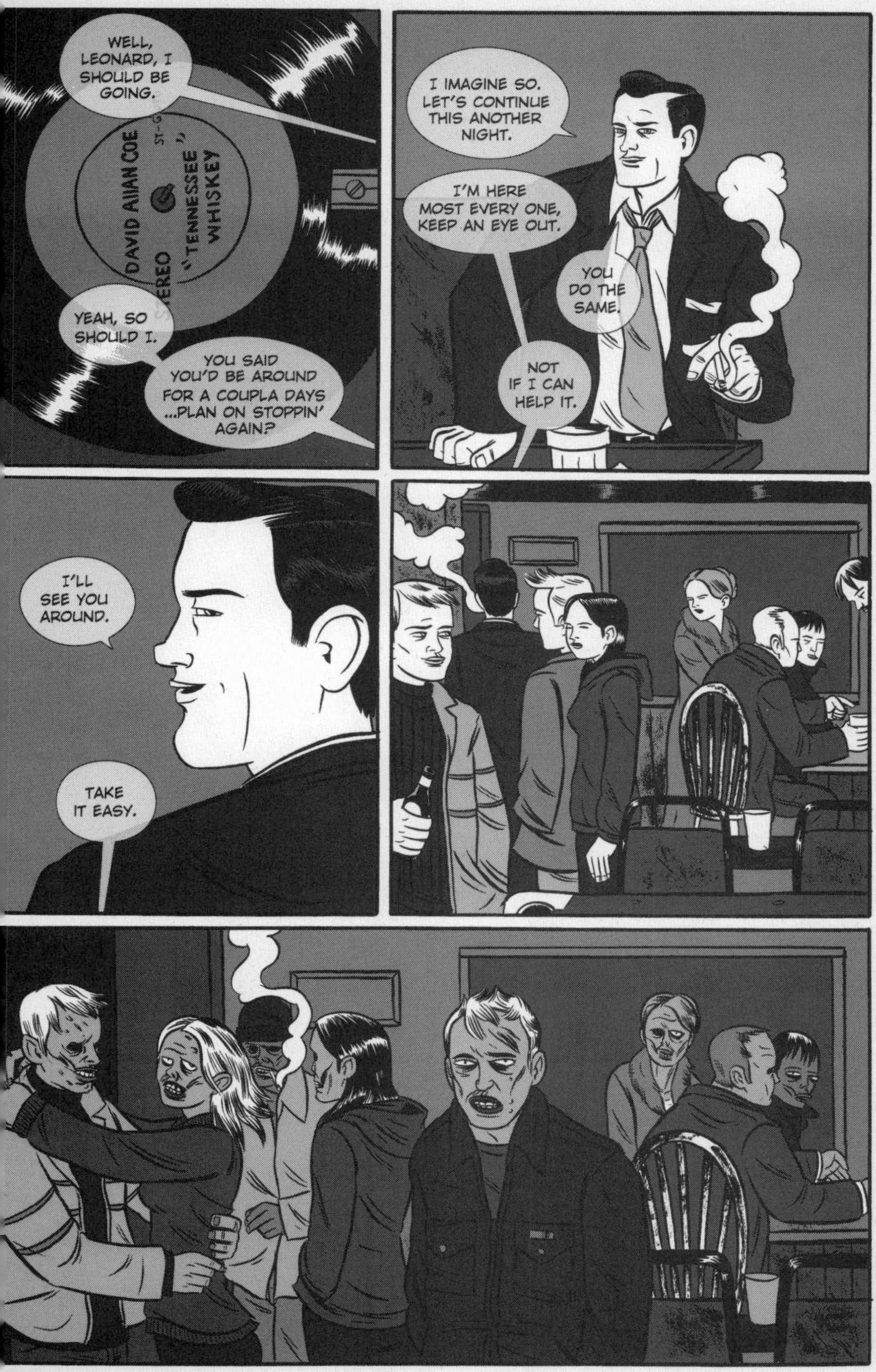
WELL, LEONARD, I SHOULD BE GOING.
DAVID ALLAN COE
STEREO
"TENNESSEE WHISKEY"
YEAH, SO SHOULD I.
YOU SAID YOU'D BE AROUND FOR A COUPLA DAYS ...PLAN ON STOPPIN' AGAIN?
I IMAGINE SO. LET'S CONTINUE THIS ANOTHER NIGHT.
I'M HERE MOST EVERY ONE, KEEP AN EYE OUT.
YOU DO THE SAME.
NOT IF I CAN HELP IT.
I'LL SEE YOU AROUND.
TAKE IT EASY.

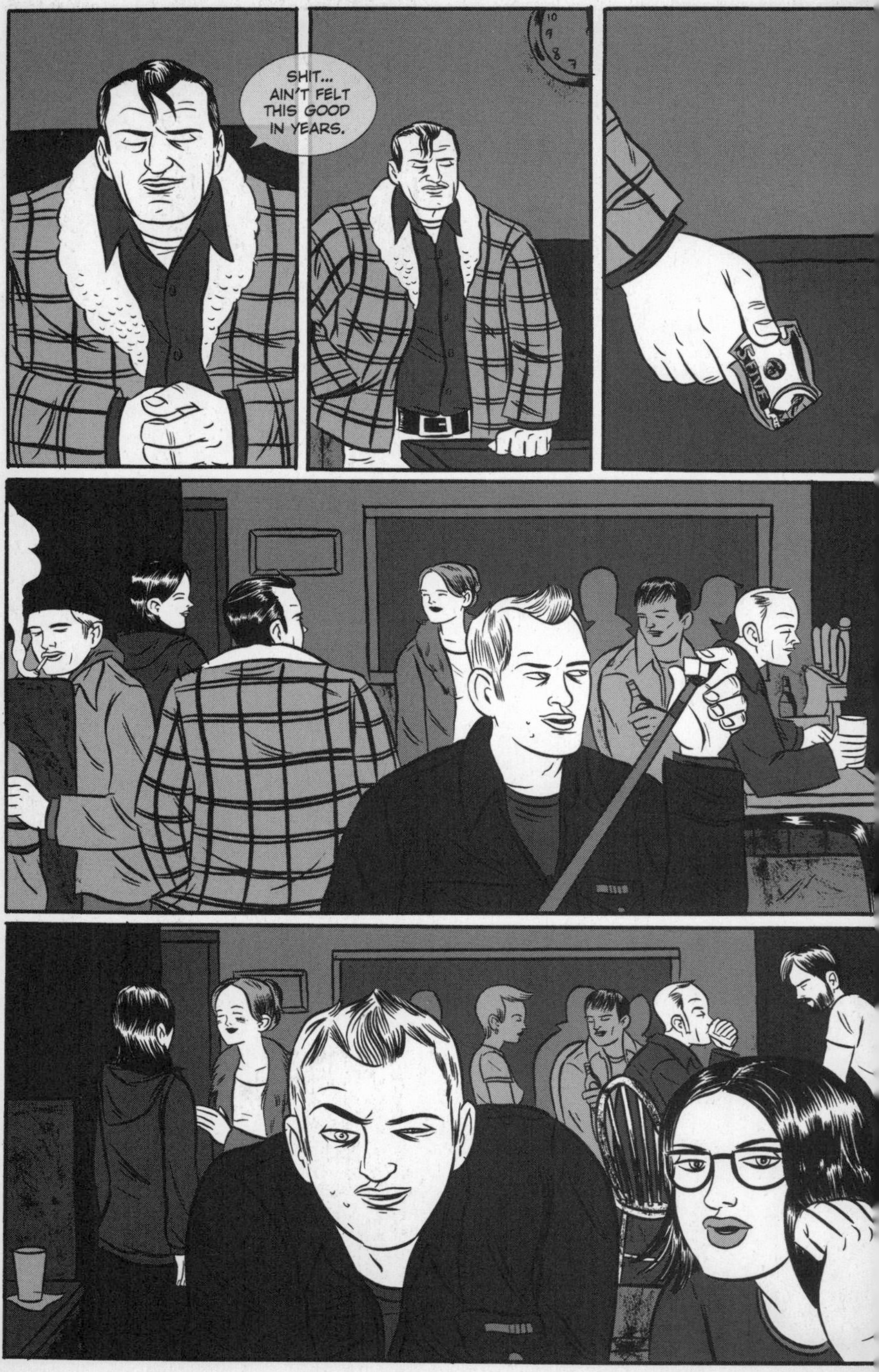
SHIT... AIN'T FELT THIS GOOD IN YEARS.

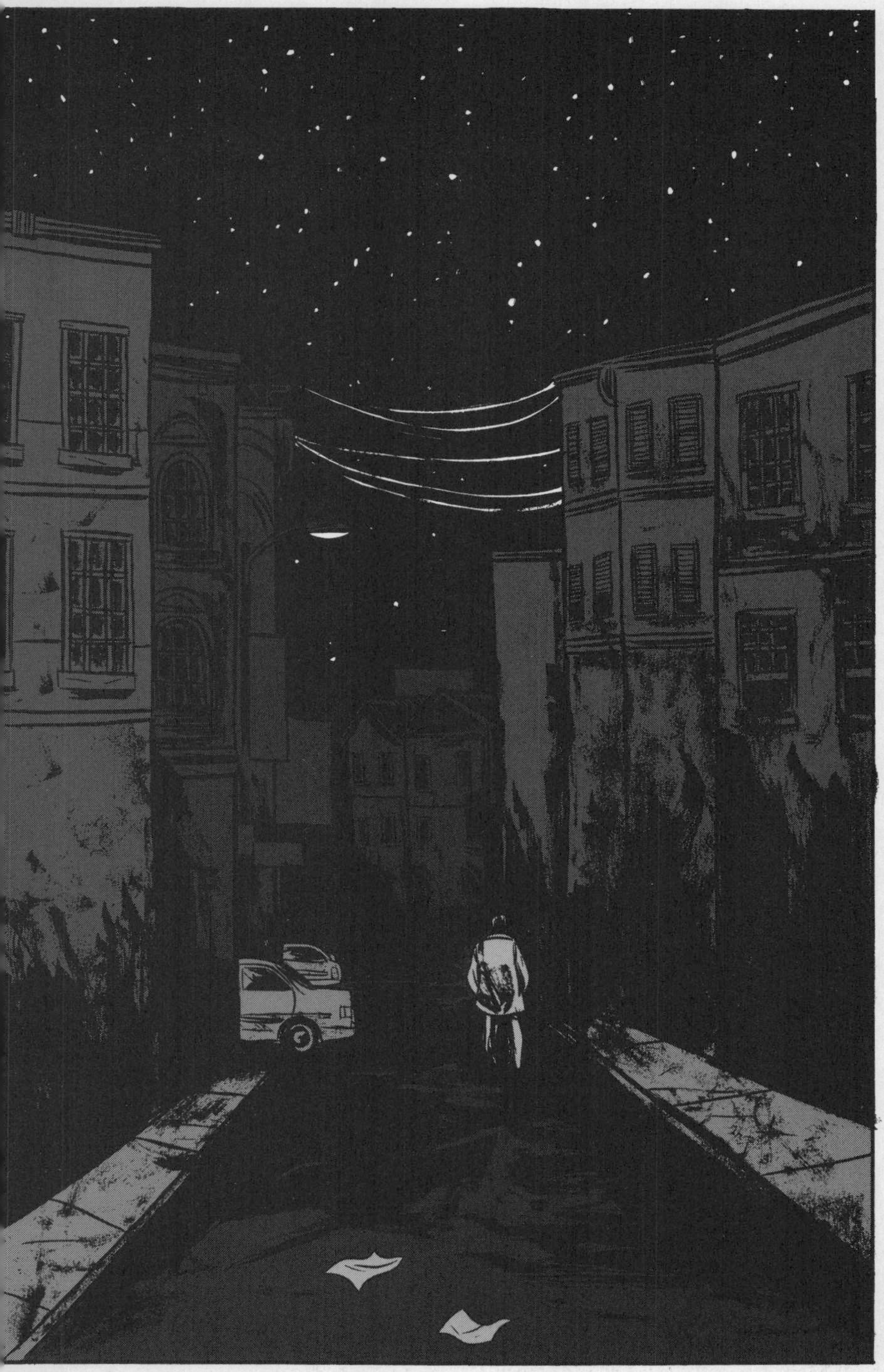

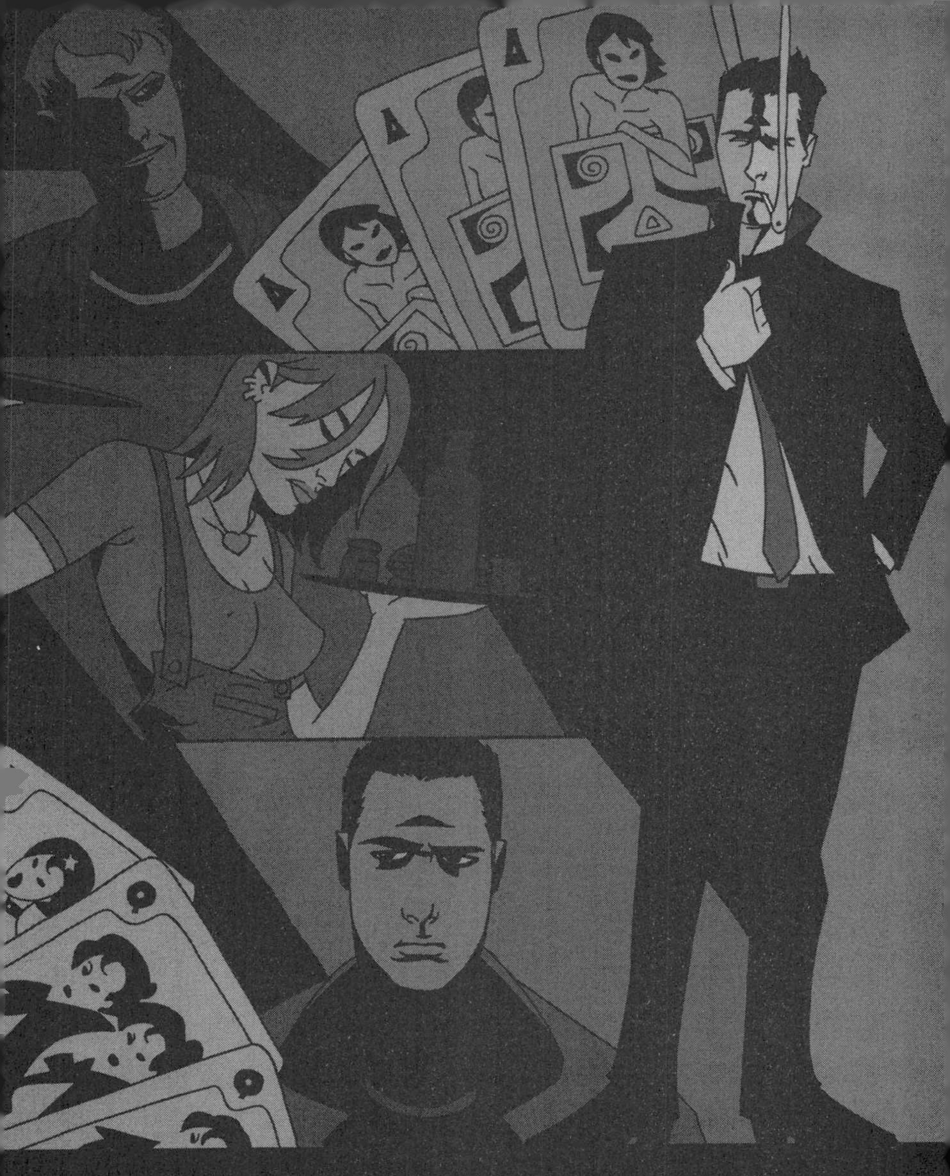

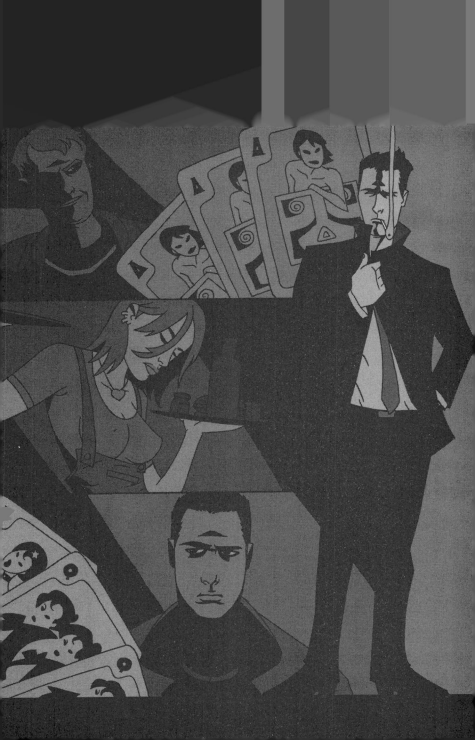

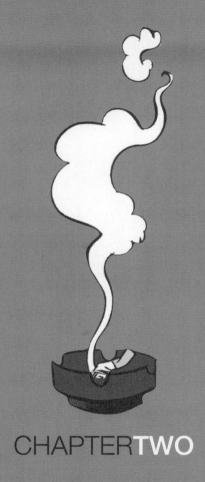

CHAPTER**TWO**

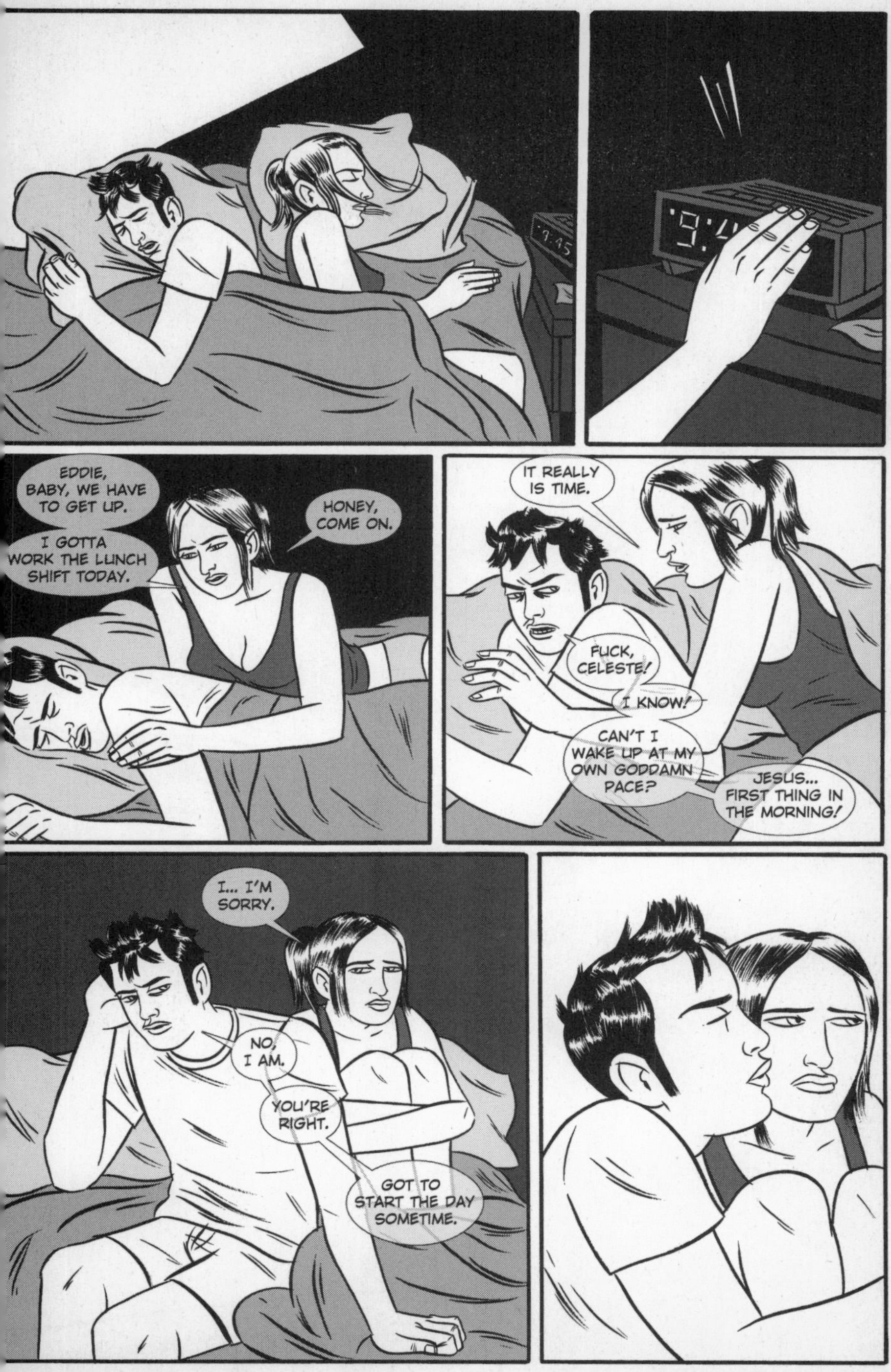
EDDIE, BABY, WE HAVE TO GET UP.
I GOTTA WORK THE LUNCH SHIFT TODAY.
HONEY, COME ON.
IT REALLY IS TIME.
FUCK, CELESTE!
I KNOW!
CAN'T I WAKE UP AT MY OWN GODDAMN PACE?
JESUS... FIRST THING IN THE MORNING!
I... I'M SORRY.
NO, I AM.
YOU'RE RIGHT.
GOT TO START THE DAY SOMETIME.

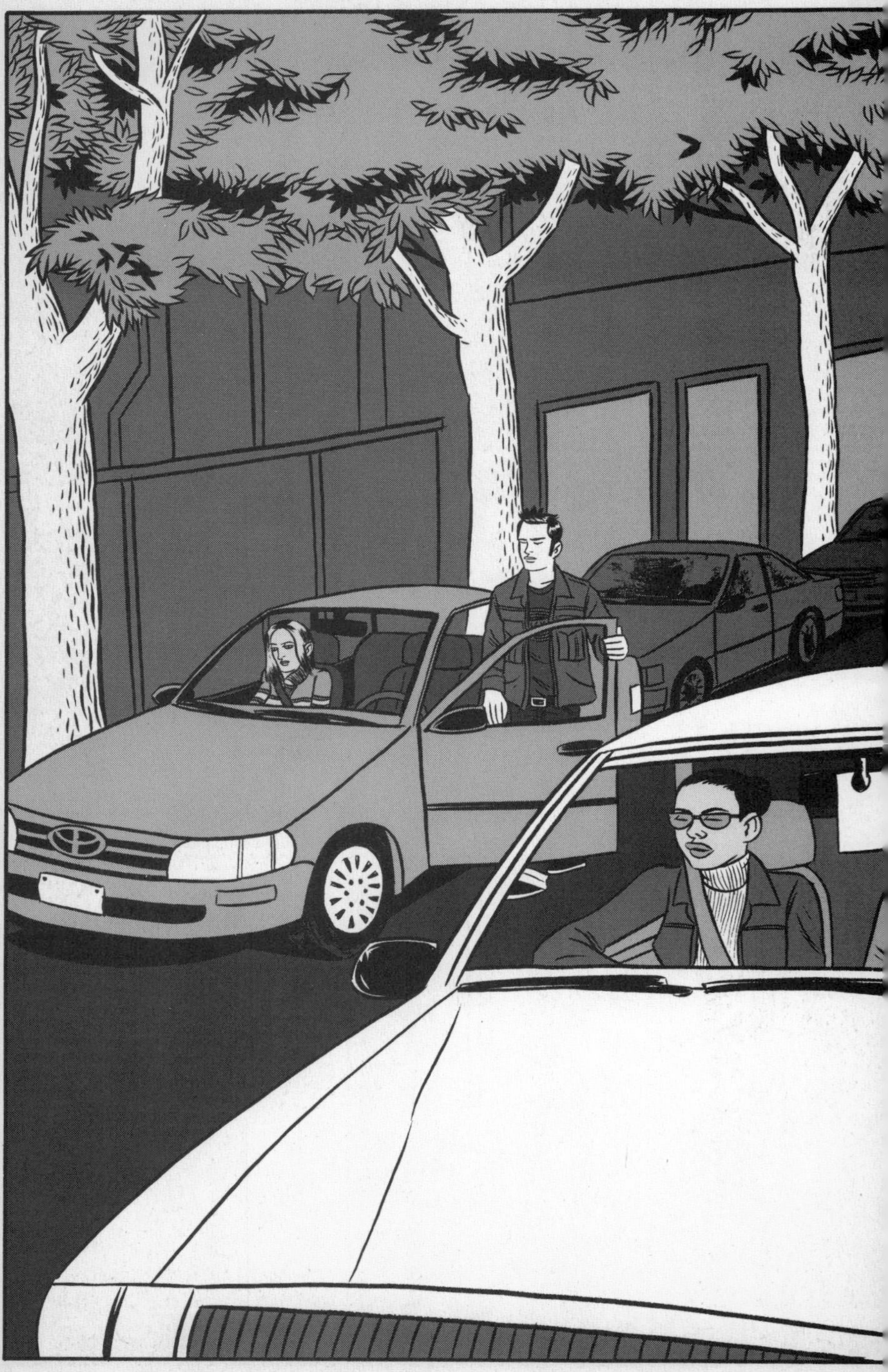

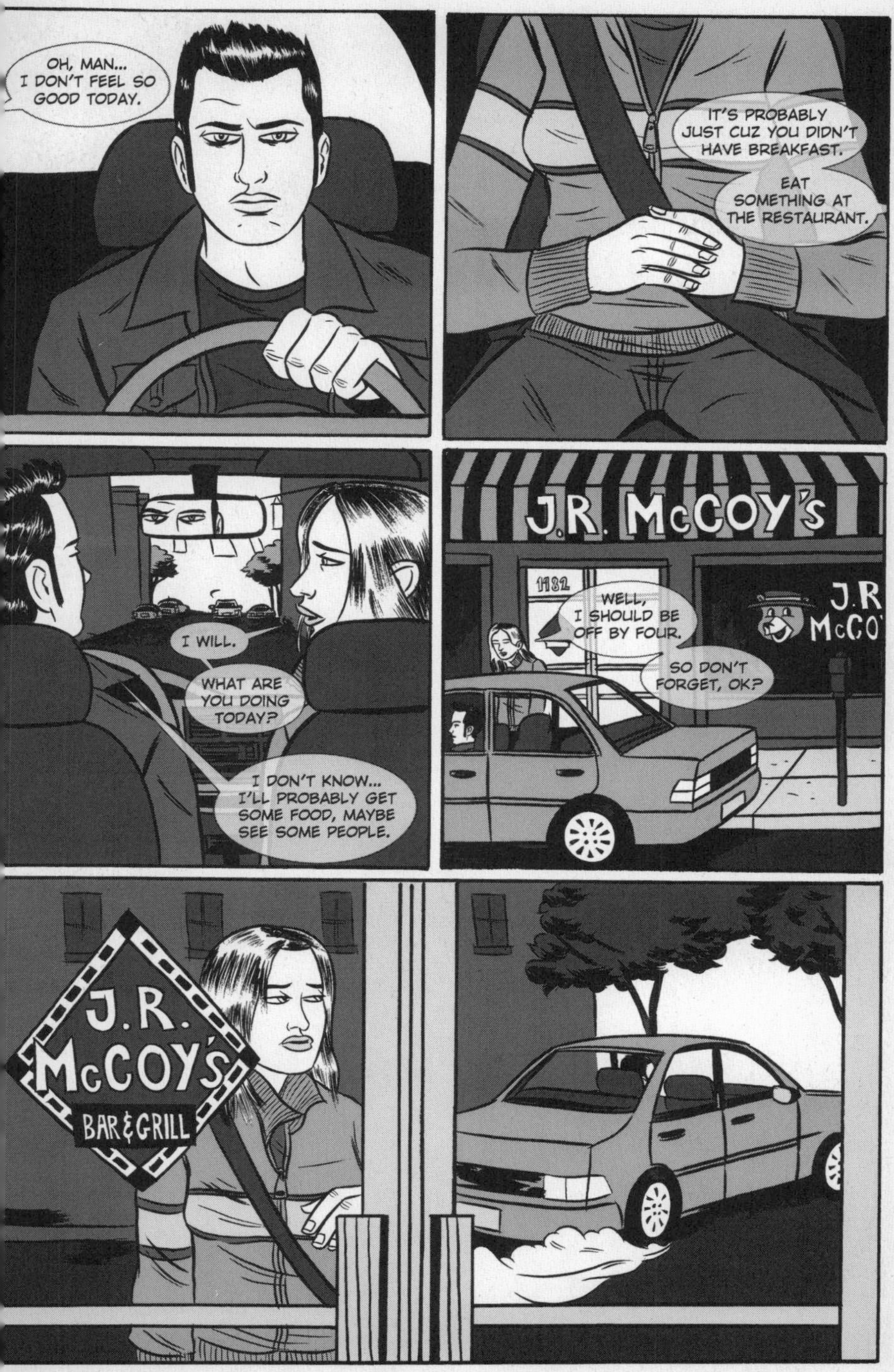

OH, MAN... I DON'T FEEL SO GOOD TODAY.
IT'S PROBABLY JUST CUZ YOU DIDN'T HAVE BREAKFAST.
EAT SOMETHING AT THE RESTAURANT.
I WILL.
WHAT ARE YOU DOING TODAY?
I DON'T KNOW... I'LL PROBABLY GET SOME FOOD, MAYBE SEE SOME PEOPLE.
J.R. McCOY'S
1982
WELL, I SHOULD BE OFF BY FOUR.
SO DON'T FORGET, OK?
J.R. McCOY'S
BAR & GRILL

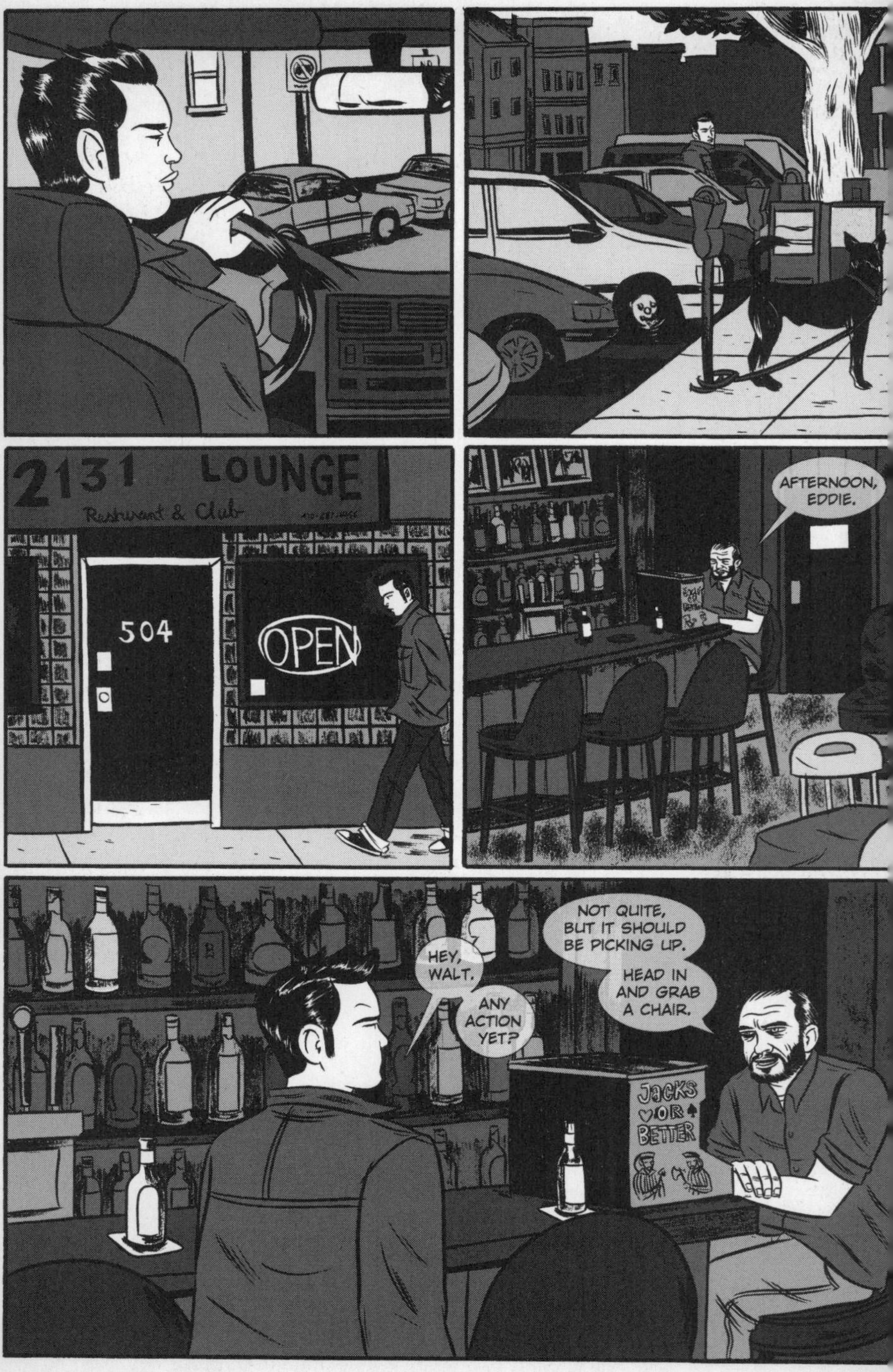

2131 LOUNGE
Restaurant & Club
504
OPEN
AFTERNOON, EDDIE.
HEY, WALT.
ANY ACTION YET?
NOT QUITE, BUT IT SHOULD BE PICKING UP.
HEAD IN AND GRAB A CHAIR.
JACKS OR BETTER

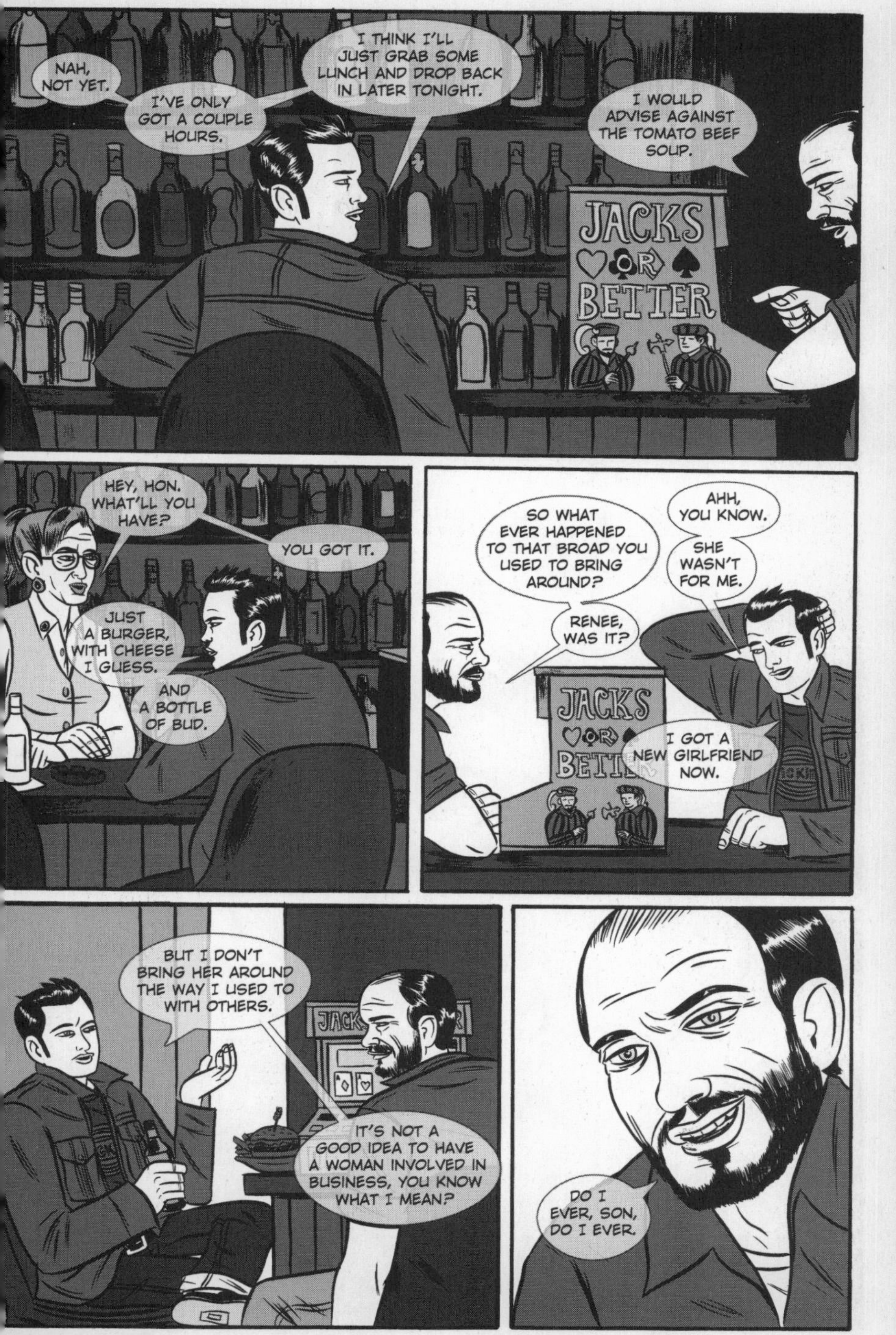
NAH, NOT YET.
I'VE ONLY GOT A COUPLE HOURS.
I THINK I'LL JUST GRAB SOME LUNCH AND DROP BACK IN LATER TONIGHT.
I WOULD ADVISE AGAINST THE TOMATO BEEF SOUP.
JACKS OR BETTER
HEY, HON. WHAT'LL YOU HAVE?
JUST A BURGER, WITH CHEESE I GUESS.
AND A BOTTLE OF BUD.
YOU GOT IT.
SO WHAT EVER HAPPENED TO THAT BROAD YOU USED TO BRING AROUND?
RENEE, WAS IT?
AHH, YOU KNOW.
SHE WASN'T FOR ME.
JACKS OR BETTER
I GOT A NEW GIRLFRIEND NOW.
BUT I DON'T BRING HER AROUND THE WAY I USED TO WITH OTHERS.
IT'S NOT A GOOD IDEA TO HAVE A WOMAN INVOLVED IN BUSINESS, YOU KNOW WHAT I MEAN?
DO I EVER, SON, DO I EVER.

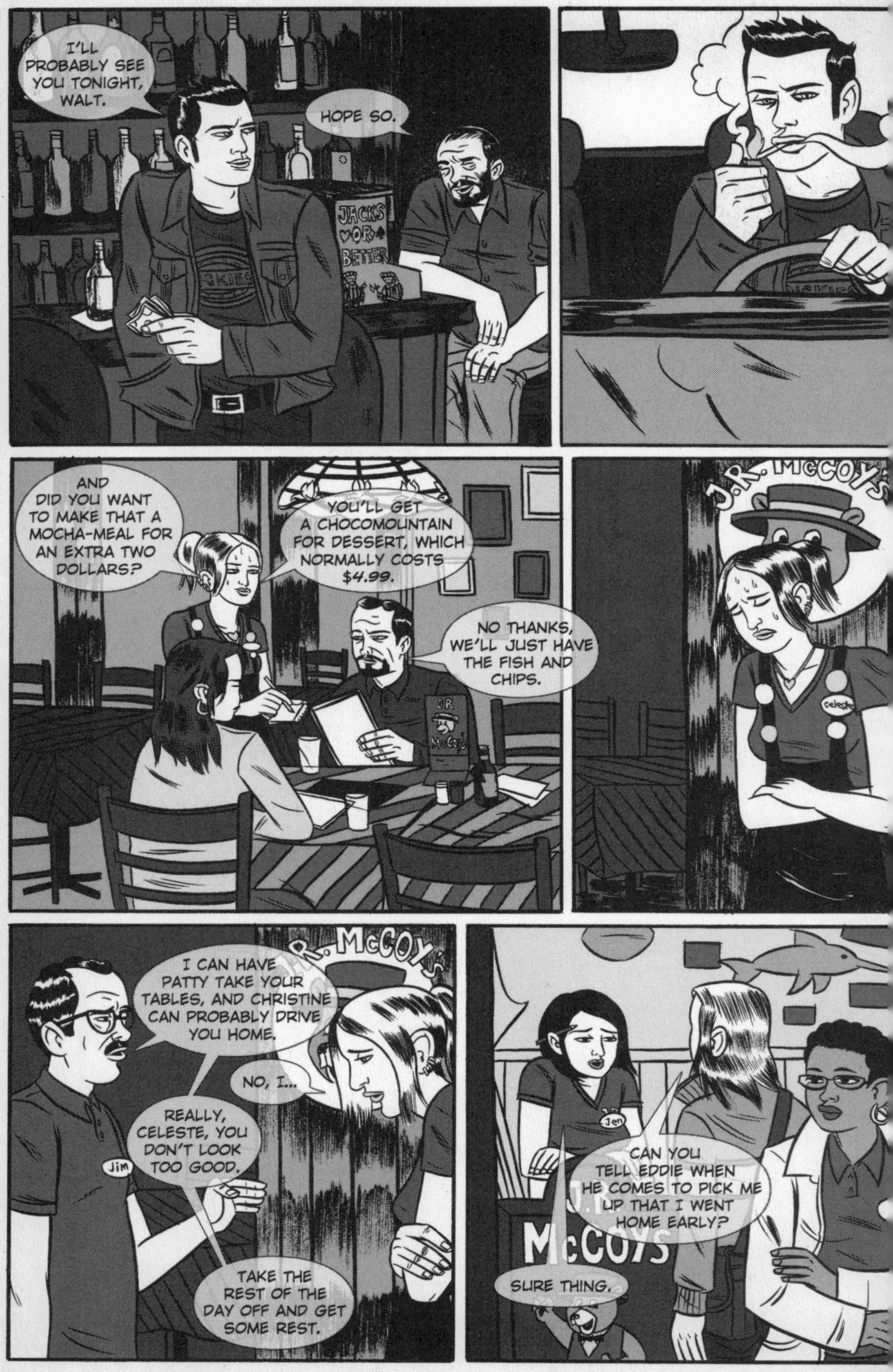
I'LL PROBABLY SEE YOU TONIGHT, WALT.
HOPE SO.
JACKS OR BETTER
AND DID YOU WANT TO MAKE THAT A MOCHA-MEAL FOR AN EXTRA TWO DOLLARS?
YOU'LL GET A CHOCOMOUNTAIN FOR DESSERT, WHICH NORMALLY COSTS $4.99.
NO THANKS, WE'LL JUST HAVE THE FISH AND CHIPS.
J.R. McCOY'S
Celeste
I CAN HAVE PATTY TAKE YOUR TABLES, AND CHRISTINE CAN PROBABLY DRIVE YOU HOME.
NO, I...
REALLY, CELESTE, YOU DON'T LOOK TOO GOOD.
Jim
TAKE THE REST OF THE DAY OFF AND GET SOME REST.
Jen
CAN YOU TELL EDDIE WHEN HE COMES TO PICK ME UP THAT I WENT HOME EARLY?
McCOYS
SURE THING.

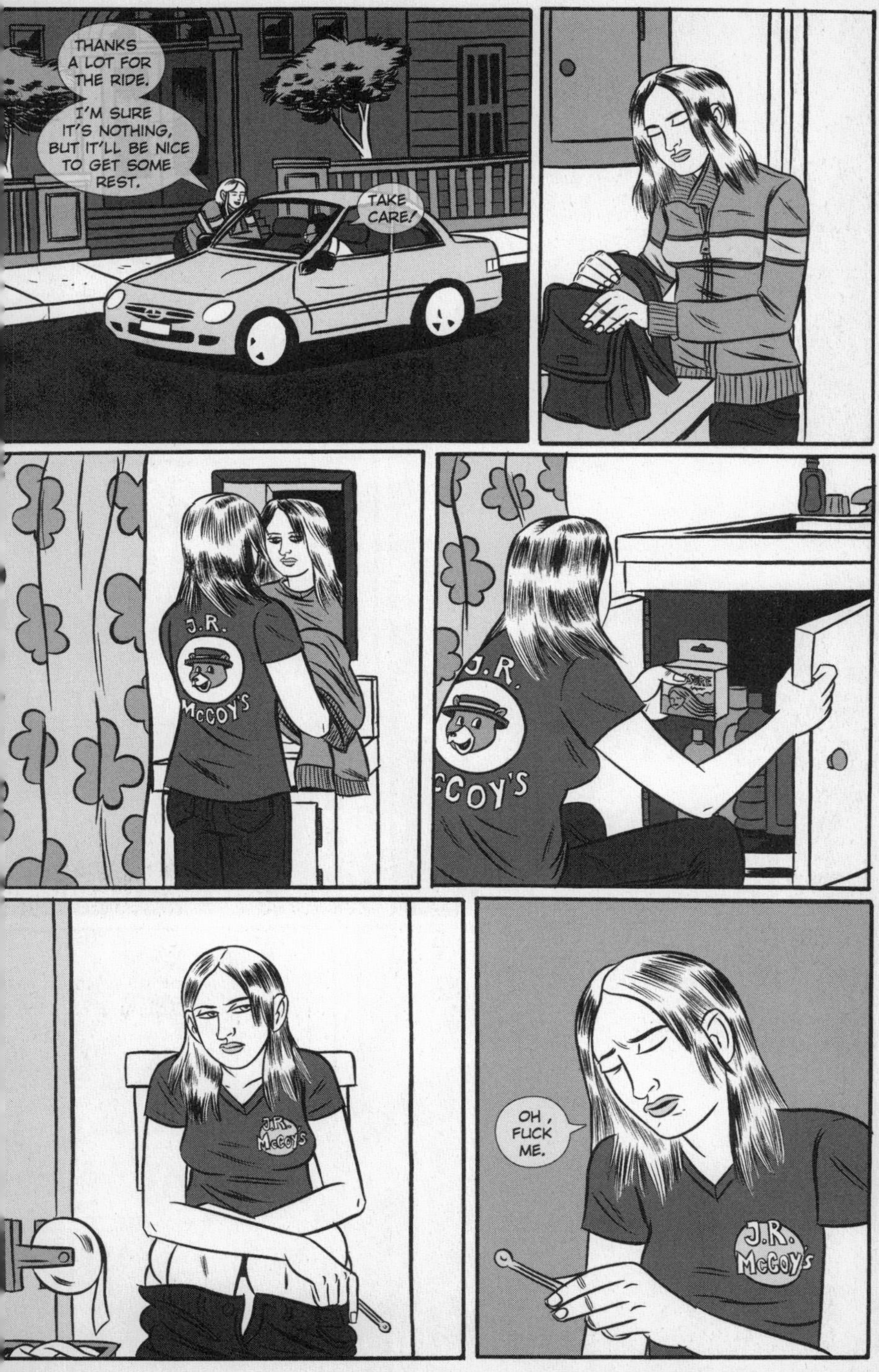
THANKS A LOT FOR THE RIDE.
I'M SURE IT'S NOTHING, BUT IT'LL BE NICE TO GET SOME REST.
TAKE CARE!
J.R. McCOY'S
J.R. McCOY'S
J.R. McCOY'S
OH, FUCK ME.
J.R. McCOY'S

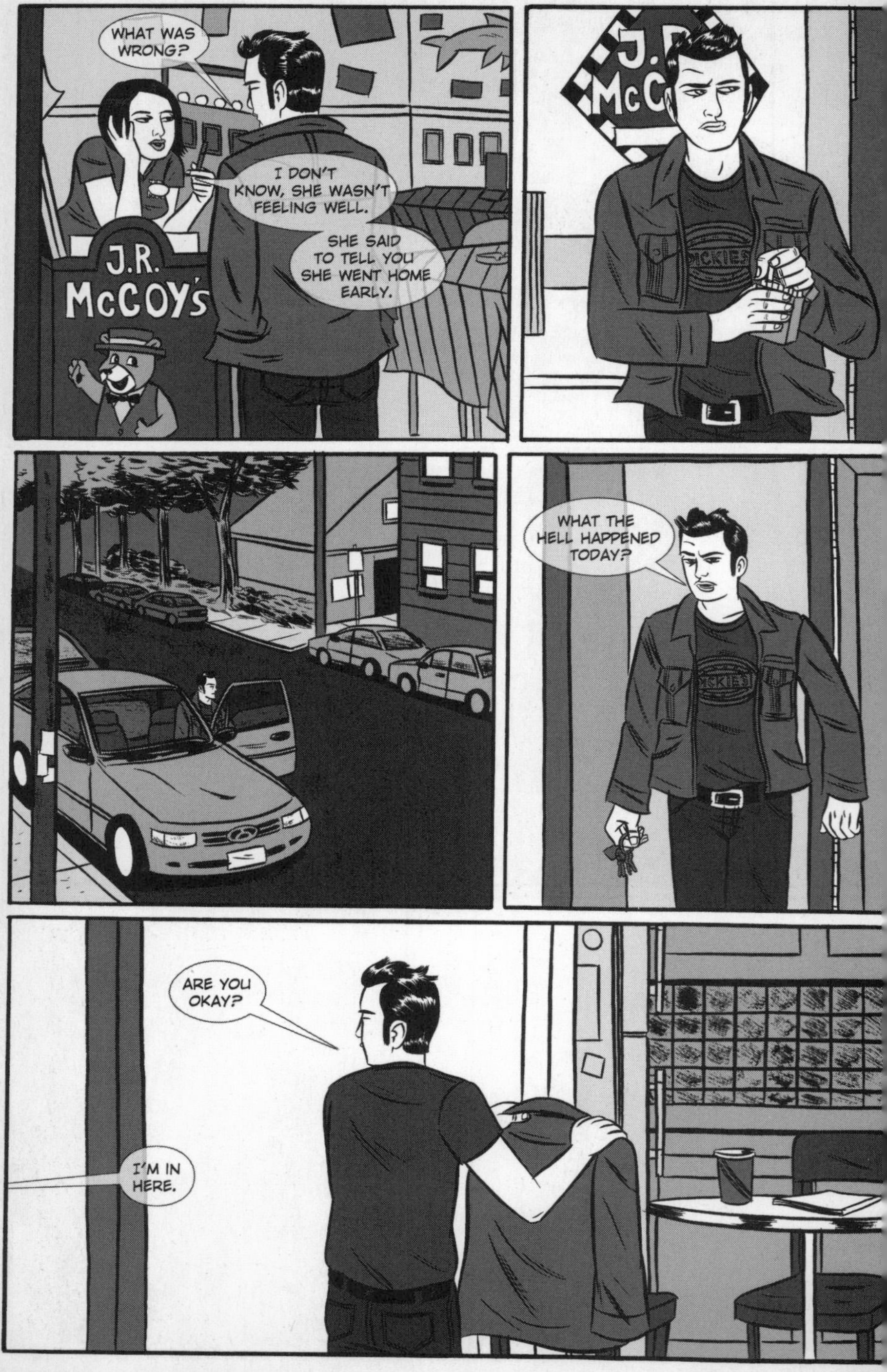
WHAT WAS WRONG?
I DON'T KNOW, SHE WASN'T FEELING WELL.
SHE SAID TO TELL YOU SHE WENT HOME EARLY.
J.R. McCOY'S
WHAT THE HELL HAPPENED TODAY?
ARE YOU OKAY?
I'M IN HERE.

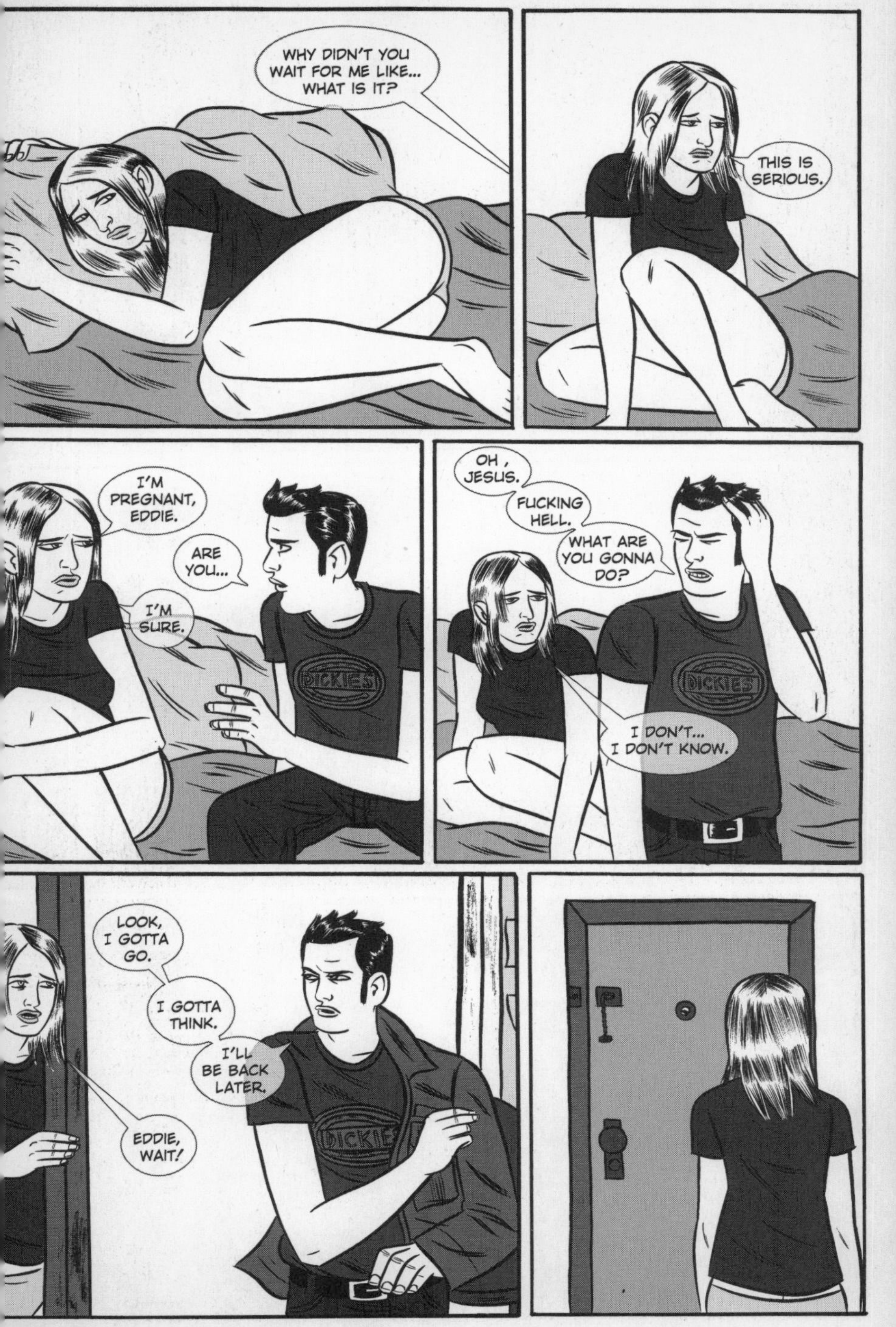
WHY DIDN'T YOU WAIT FOR ME LIKE... WHAT IS IT?
THIS IS SERIOUS.
I'M PREGNANT, EDDIE.
ARE YOU...
I'M SURE.
OH , JESUS.
FUCKING HELL.
WHAT ARE YOU GONNA DO?
I DON'T... I DON'T KNOW.
LOOK, I GOTTA GO.
I GOTTA THINK.
I'LL BE BACK LATER.
EDDIE, WAIT!

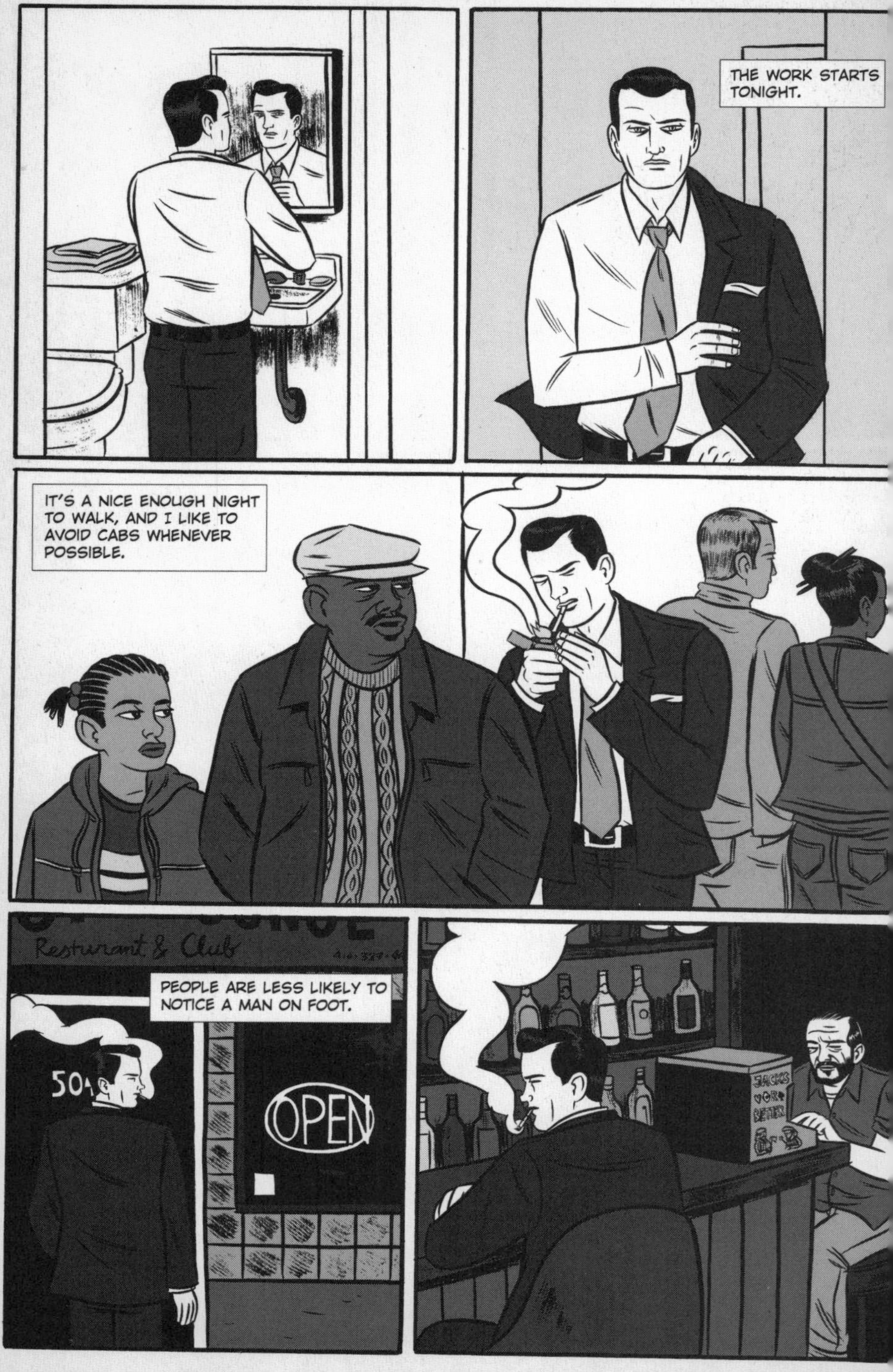
THE WORK STARTS TONIGHT.
IT'S A NICE ENOUGH NIGHT TO WALK, AND I LIKE TO AVOID CABS WHENEVER POSSIBLE.
Restaurant & Club
PEOPLE ARE LESS LIKELY TO NOTICE A MAN ON FOOT.
OPEN
JACKS OR BETTER

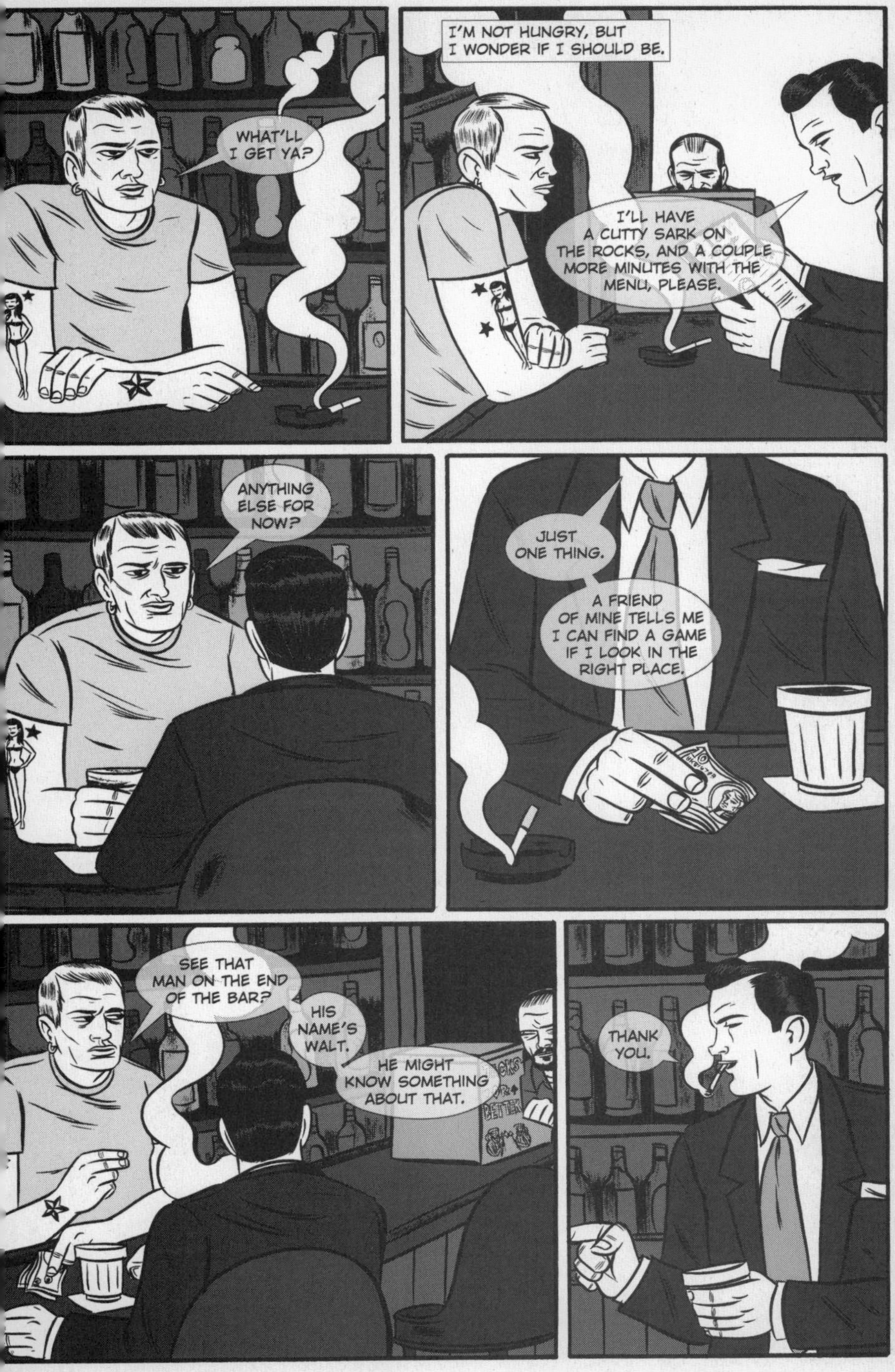
WHAT'LL I GET YA?
I'M NOT HUNGRY, BUT I WONDER IF I SHOULD BE.
I'LL HAVE A CUTTY SARK ON THE ROCKS, AND A COUPLE MORE MINUTES WITH THE MENU, PLEASE.
ANYTHING ELSE FOR NOW?
JUST ONE THING.
A FRIEND OF MINE TELLS ME I CAN FIND A GAME IF I LOOK IN THE RIGHT PLACE.
SEE THAT MAN ON THE END OF THE BAR?
HIS NAME'S WALT.
HE MIGHT KNOW SOMETHING ABOUT THAT.
THANK YOU.

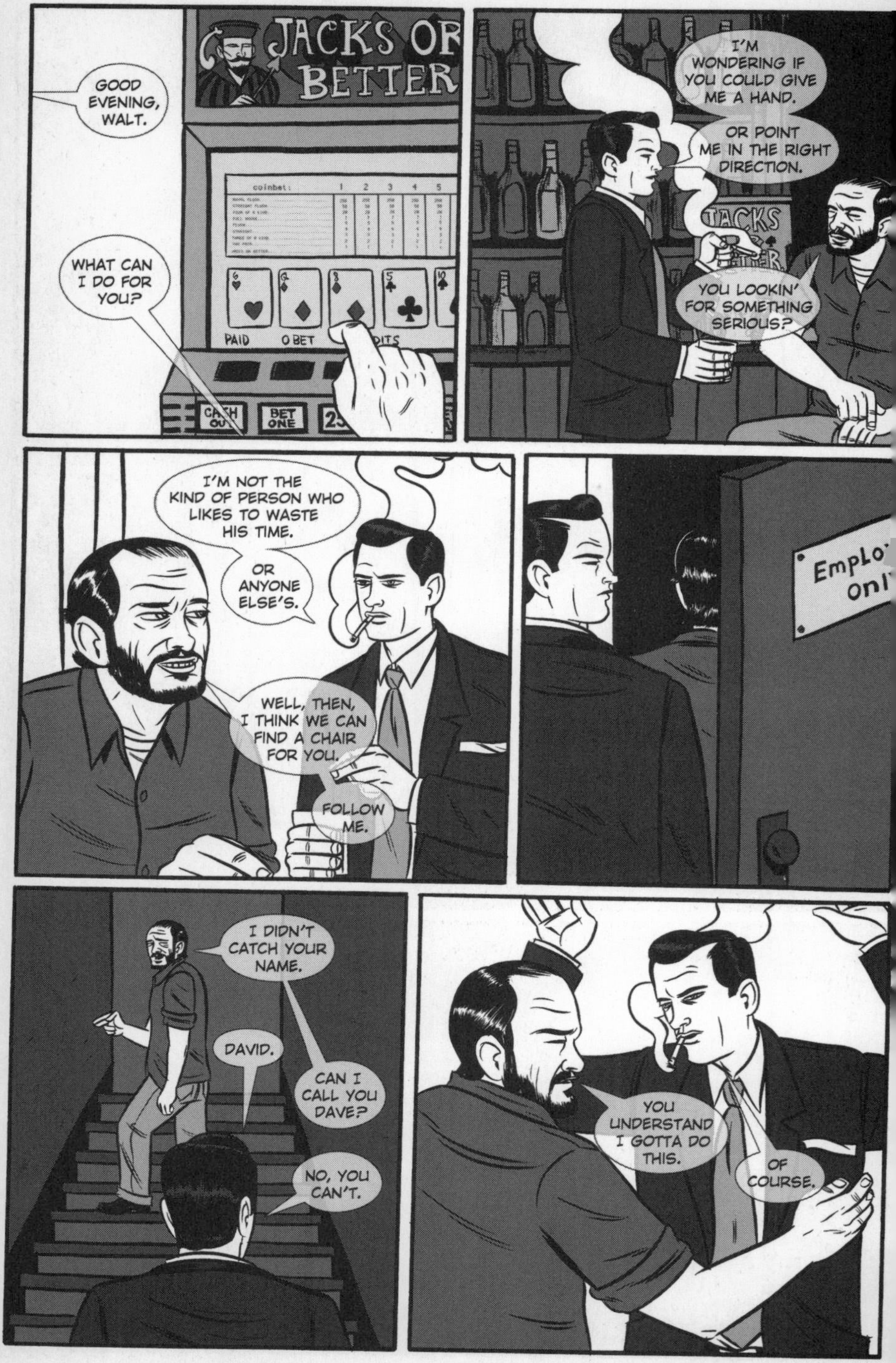
JACKS OR BETTER
GOOD EVENING, WALT.
coinbet: 1 2 3 4 5
WHAT CAN I DO FOR YOU?
PAID
0 BET
CASH OUT
BET ONE
25
I'M WONDERING IF YOU COULD GIVE ME A HAND.
OR POINT ME IN THE RIGHT DIRECTION.
YOU LOOKIN' FOR SOMETHING SERIOUS?
I'M NOT THE KIND OF PERSON WHO LIKES TO WASTE HIS TIME.
OR ANYONE ELSE'S.
WELL, THEN, I THINK WE CAN FIND A CHAIR FOR YOU.
FOLLOW ME.
I DIDN'T CATCH YOUR NAME.
DAVID.
CAN I CALL YOU DAVE?
NO, YOU CAN'T.
YOU UNDERSTAND I GOTTA DO THIS.
OF COURSE.

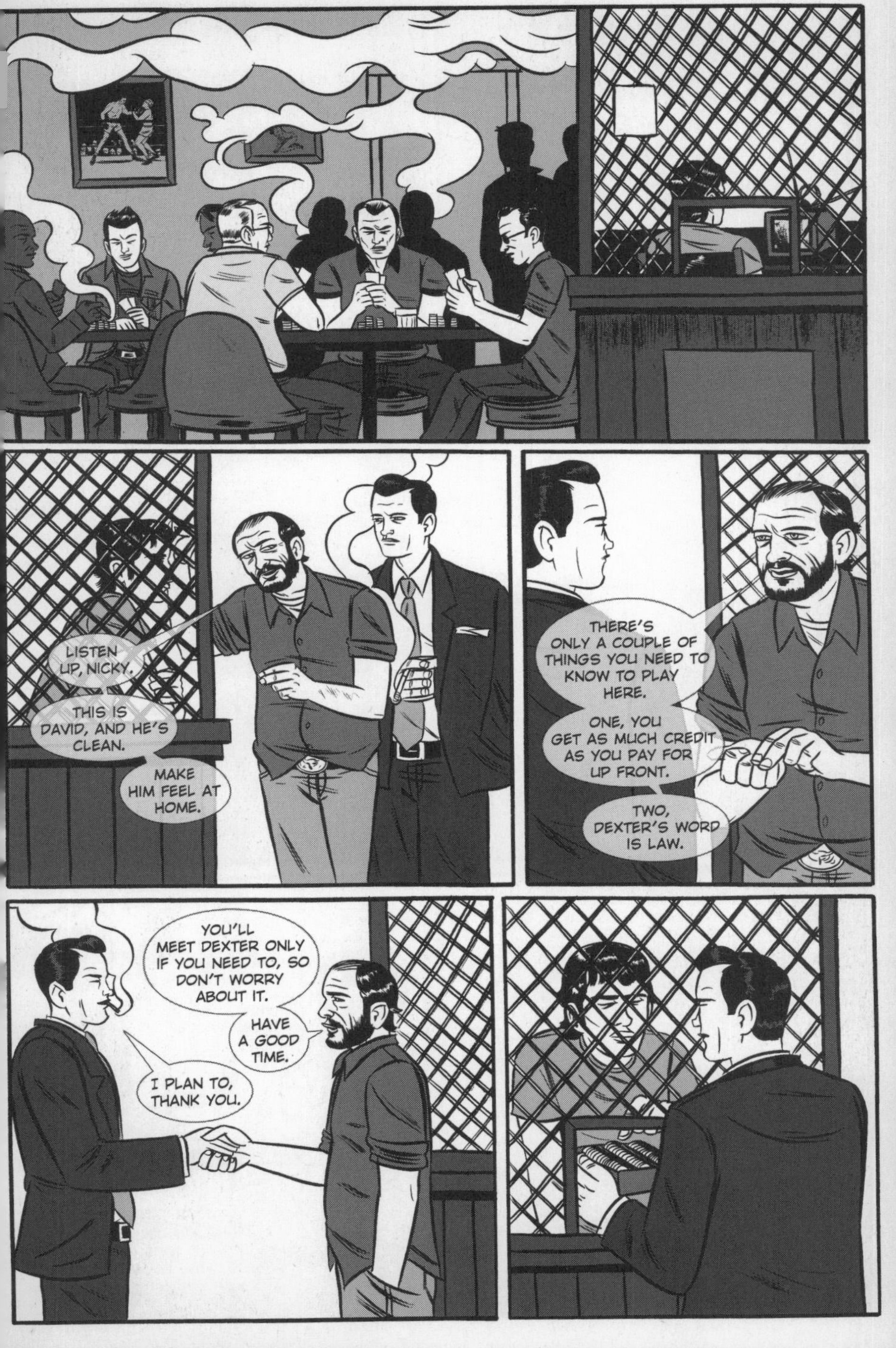
LISTEN UP, NICKY.
THIS IS DAVID, AND HE'S CLEAN.
MAKE HIM FEEL AT HOME.
THERE'S ONLY A COUPLE OF THINGS YOU NEED TO KNOW TO PLAY HERE.
ONE, YOU GET AS MUCH CREDIT AS YOU PAY FOR UP FRONT.
TWO, DEXTER'S WORD IS LAW.
YOU'LL MEET DEXTER ONLY IF YOU NEED TO, SO DON'T WORRY ABOUT IT.
HAVE A GOOD TIME.
I PLAN TO, THANK YOU.

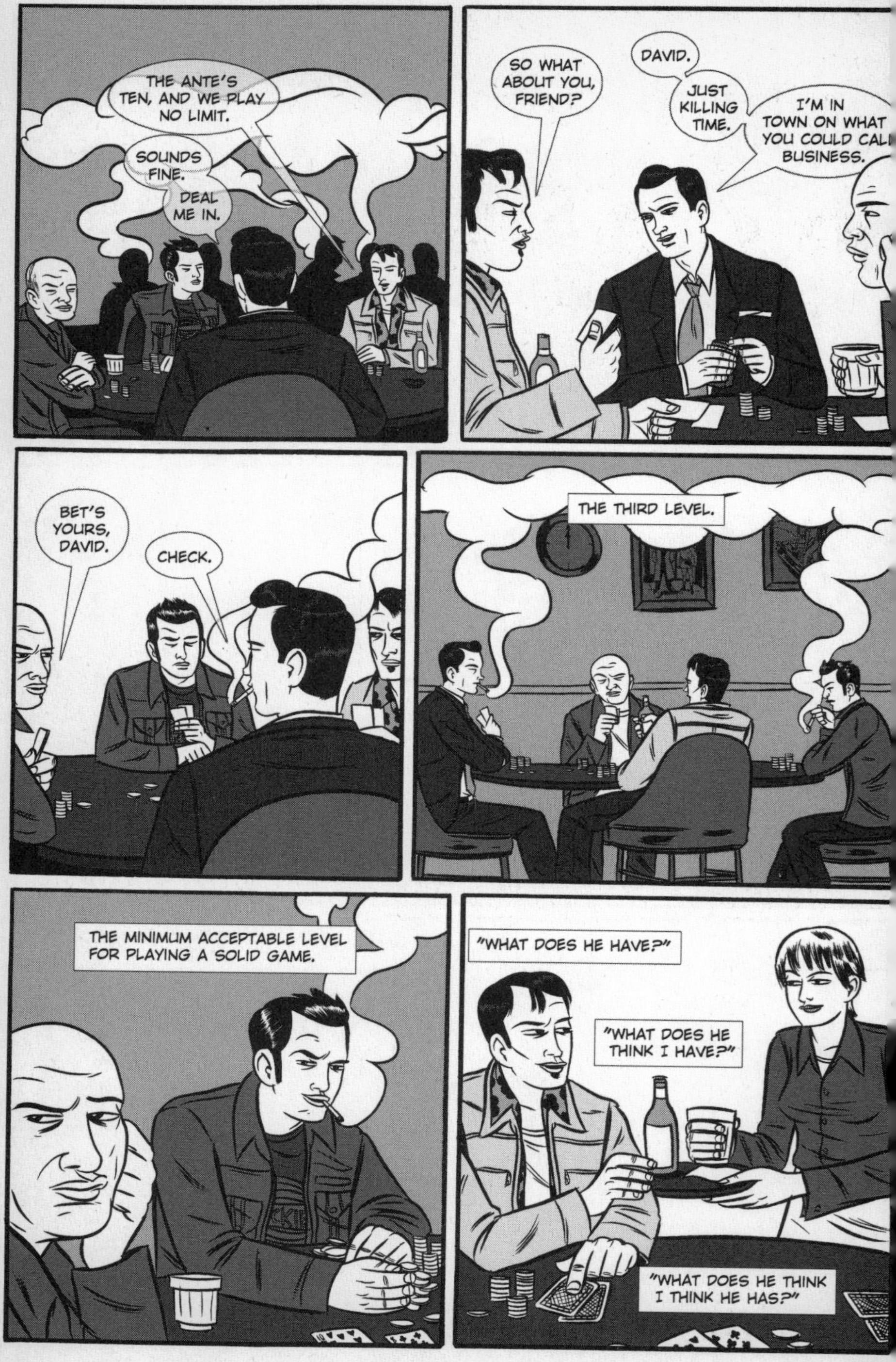
THE ANTE'S TEN, AND WE PLAY NO LIMIT.
SOUNDS FINE.
DEAL ME IN.
SO WHAT ABOUT YOU, FRIEND?
DAVID.
JUST KILLING TIME.
I'M IN TOWN ON WHAT YOU COULD CALL BUSINESS.
BET'S YOURS, DAVID.
CHECK.
THE THIRD LEVEL.
THE MINIMUM ACCEPTABLE LEVEL FOR PLAYING A SOLID GAME.
"WHAT DOES HE HAVE?"
"WHAT DOES HE THINK I HAVE?"
"WHAT DOES HE THINK I THINK HE HAS?"

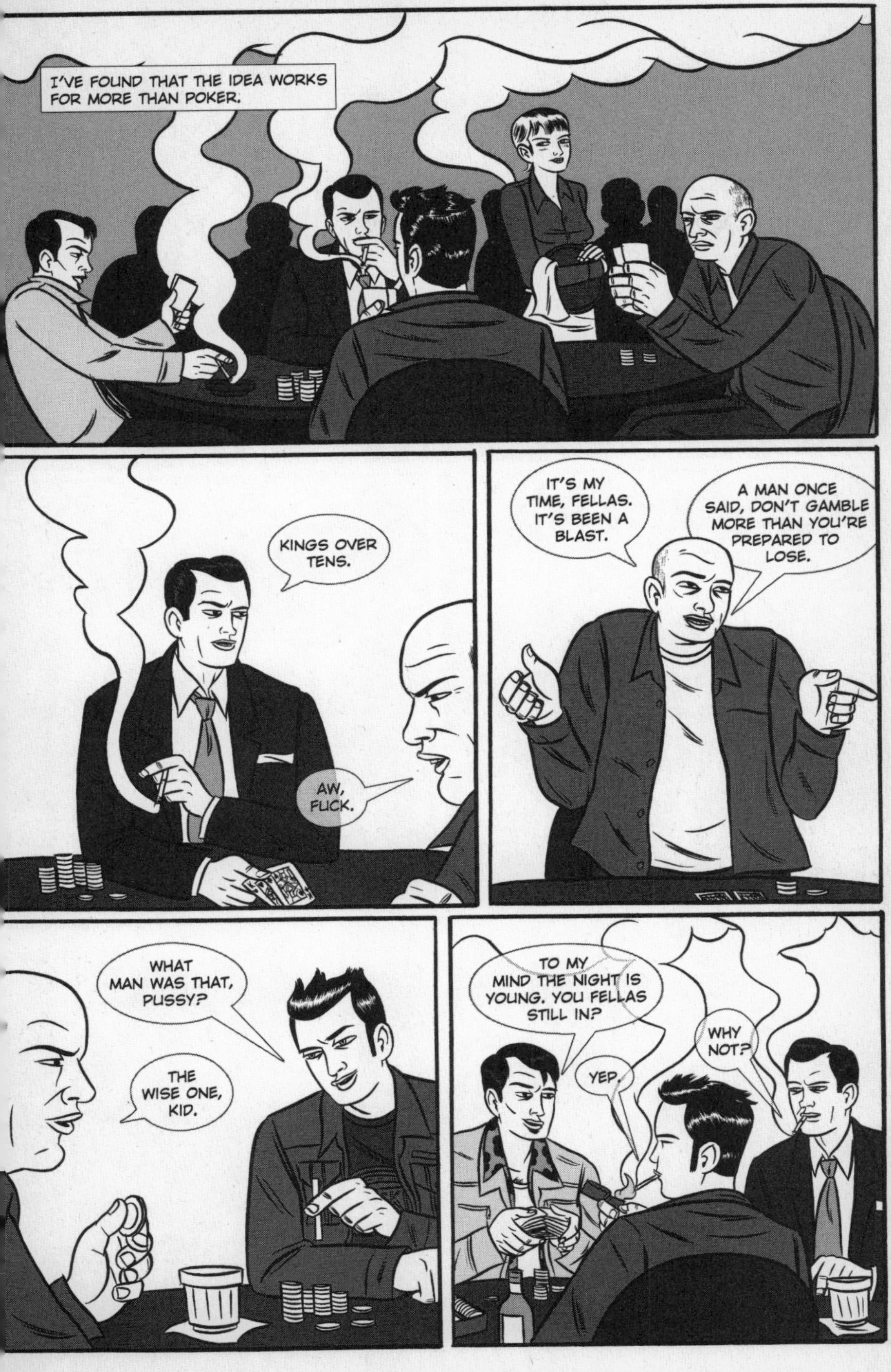
I'VE FOUND THAT THE IDEA WORKS FOR MORE THAN POKER.
KINGS OVER TENS.
AW, FUCK.
IT'S MY TIME, FELLAS. IT'S BEEN A BLAST.
A MAN ONCE SAID, DON'T GAMBLE MORE THAN YOU'RE PREPARED TO LOSE.
WHAT MAN WAS THAT, PUSSY?
THE WISE ONE, KID.
TO MY MIND THE NIGHT IS YOUNG. YOU FELLAS STILL IN?
YEP.
WHY NOT?

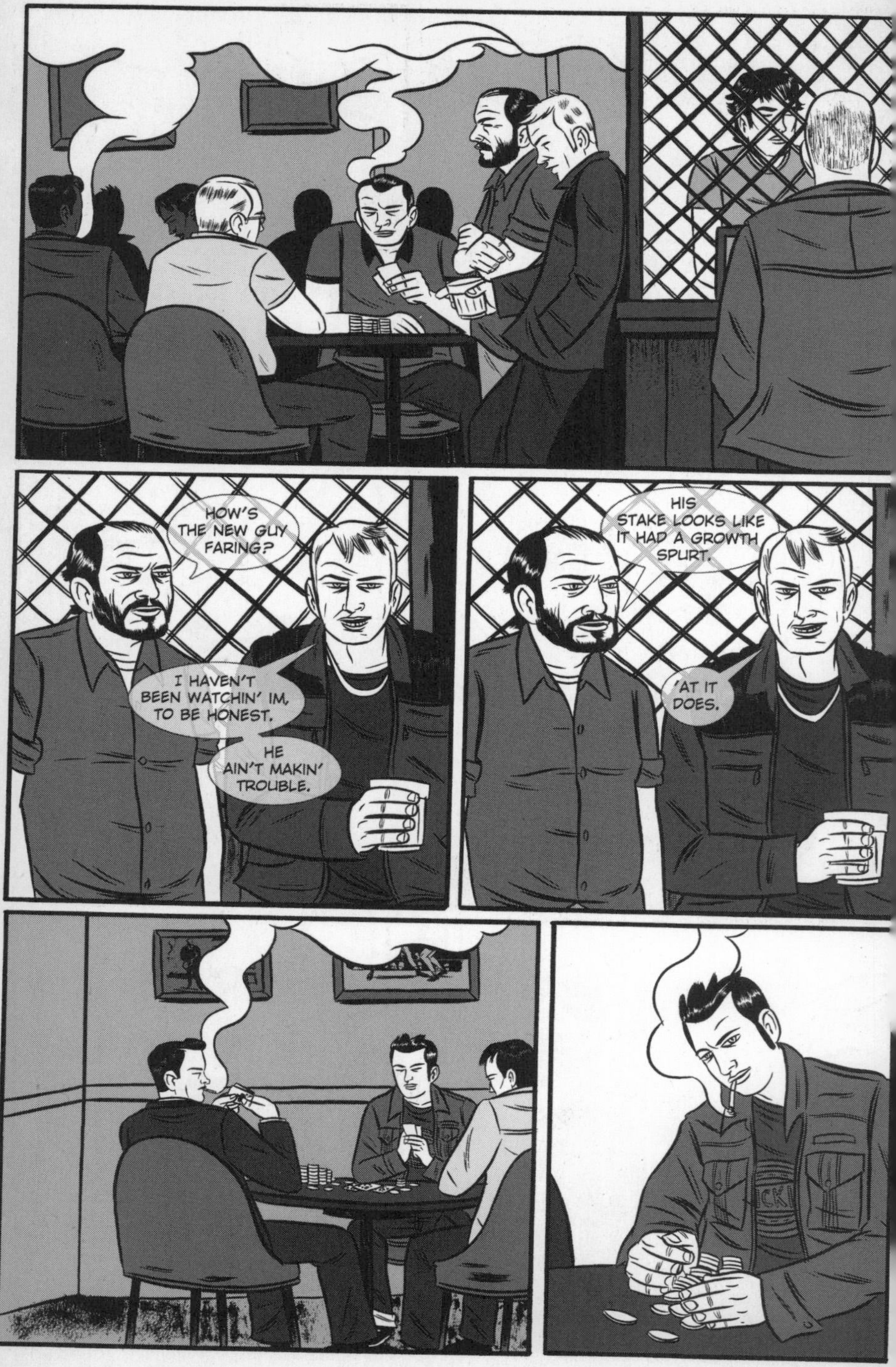
HOW'S THE NEW GUY FARING?
I HAVEN'T BEEN WATCHIN' IM, TO BE HONEST.
HE AIN'T MAKIN' TROUBLE.
HIS STAKE LOOKS LIKE IT HAD A GROWTH SPURT.
'AT IT DOES.

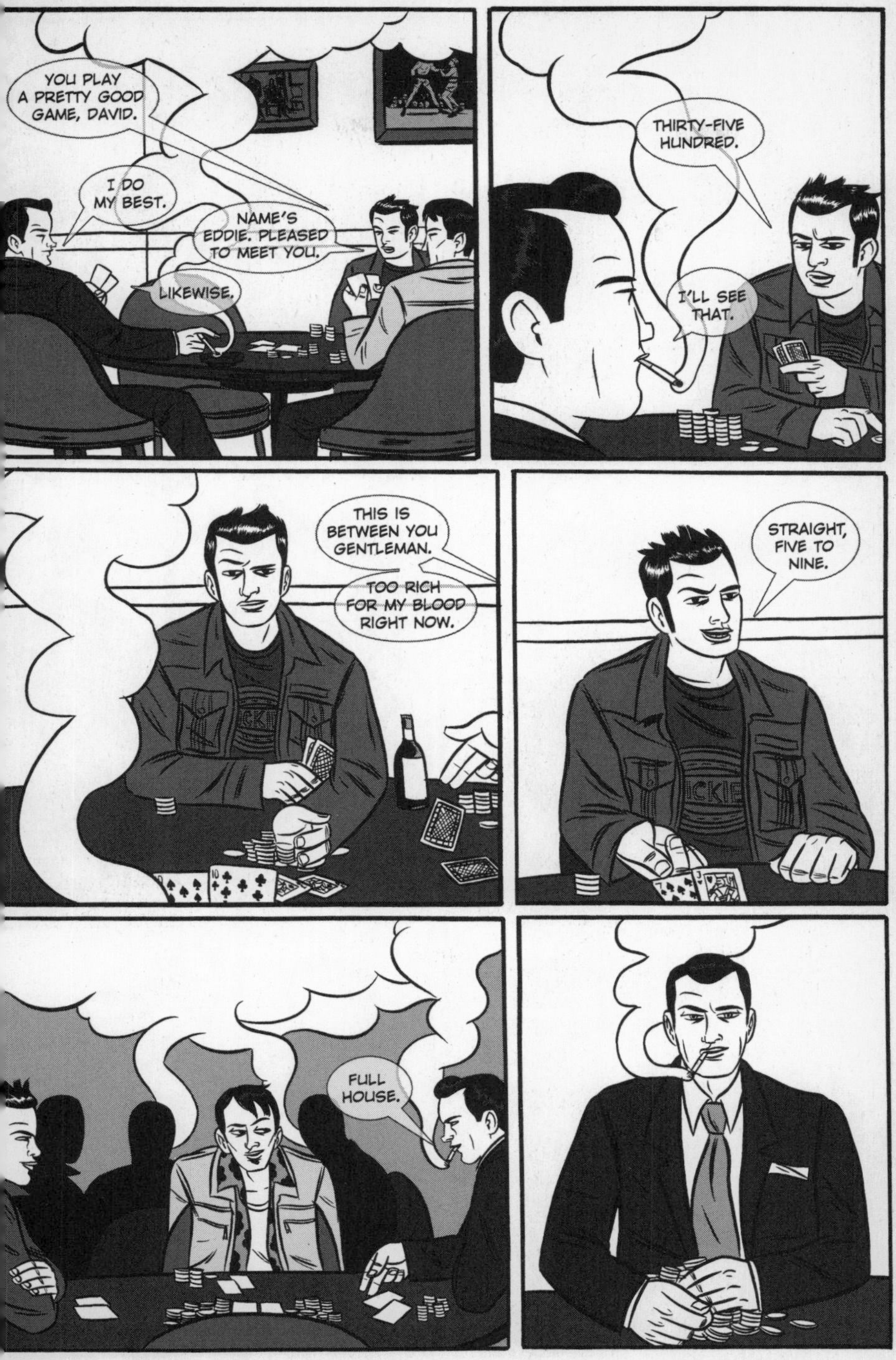
YOU PLAY A PRETTY GOOD GAME, DAVID.
I DO MY BEST.
NAME'S EDDIE. PLEASED TO MEET YOU.
LIKEWISE.
THIRTY-FIVE HUNDRED.
I'LL SEE THAT.
THIS IS BETWEEN YOU GENTLEMAN.
TOO RICH FOR MY BLOOD RIGHT NOW.
STRAIGHT, FIVE TO NINE.
FULL HOUSE.

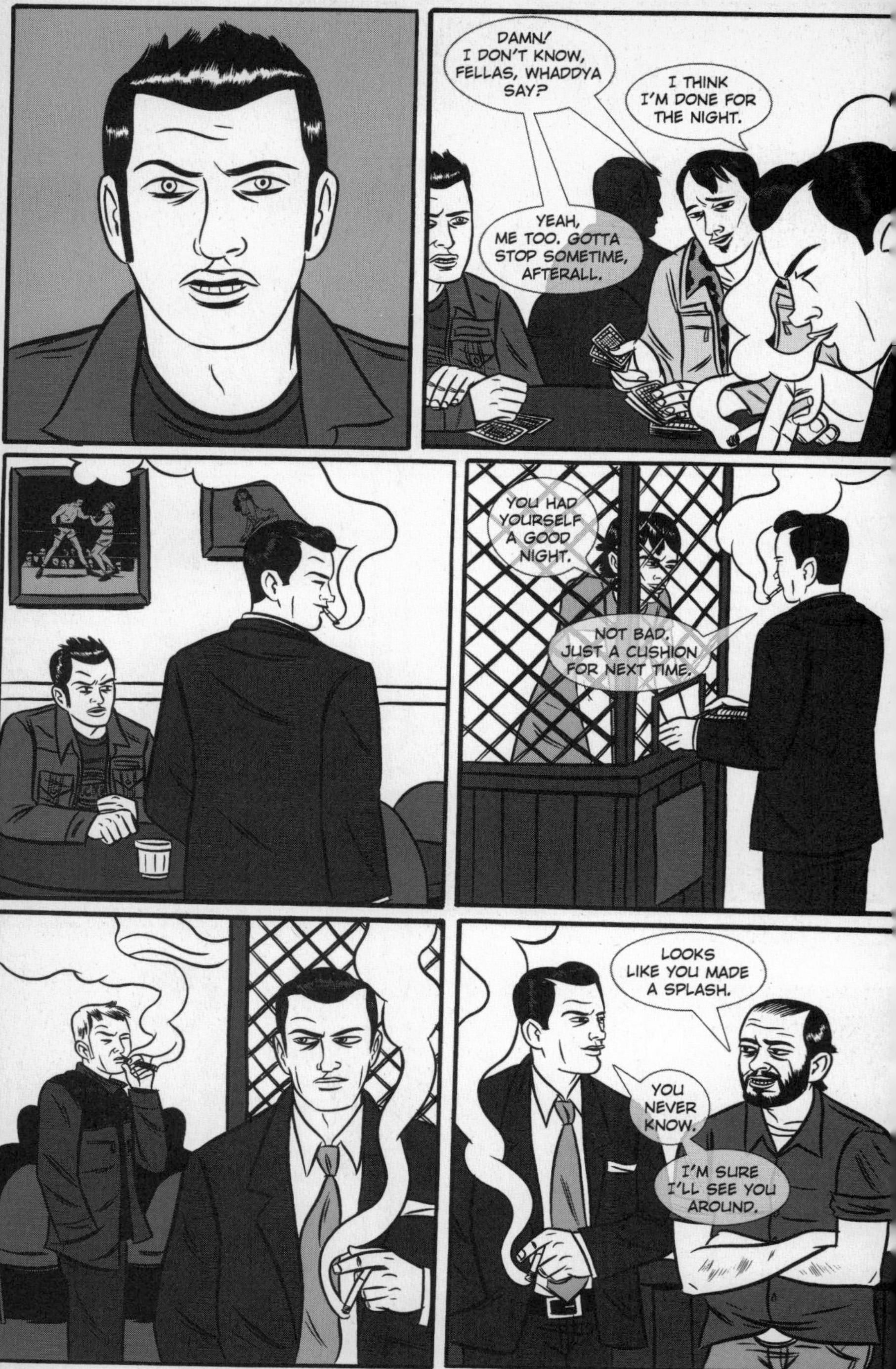
DAMN! I DON'T KNOW, FELLAS, WHADDYA SAY?
I THINK I'M DONE FOR THE NIGHT.
YEAH, ME TOO. GOTTA STOP SOMETIME, AFTERALL.
YOU HAD YOURSELF A GOOD NIGHT.
NOT BAD. JUST A CUSHION FOR NEXT TIME.
LOOKS LIKE YOU MADE A SPLASH.
YOU NEVER KNOW.
I'M SURE I'LL SEE YOU AROUND.

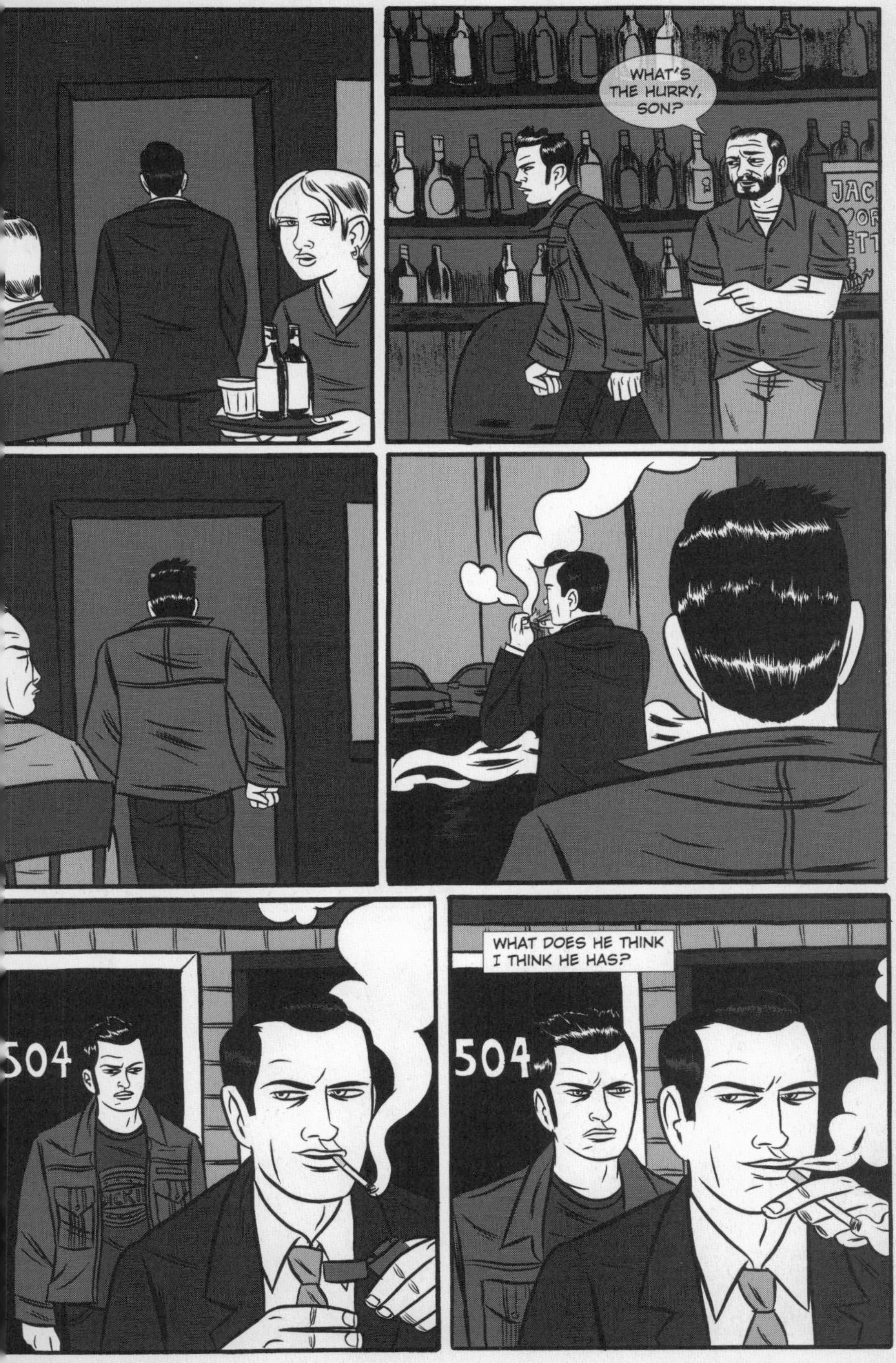
WHAT'S THE HURRY, SON?
JACK
WHAT DOES HE THINK I THINK HE HAS?
504
504

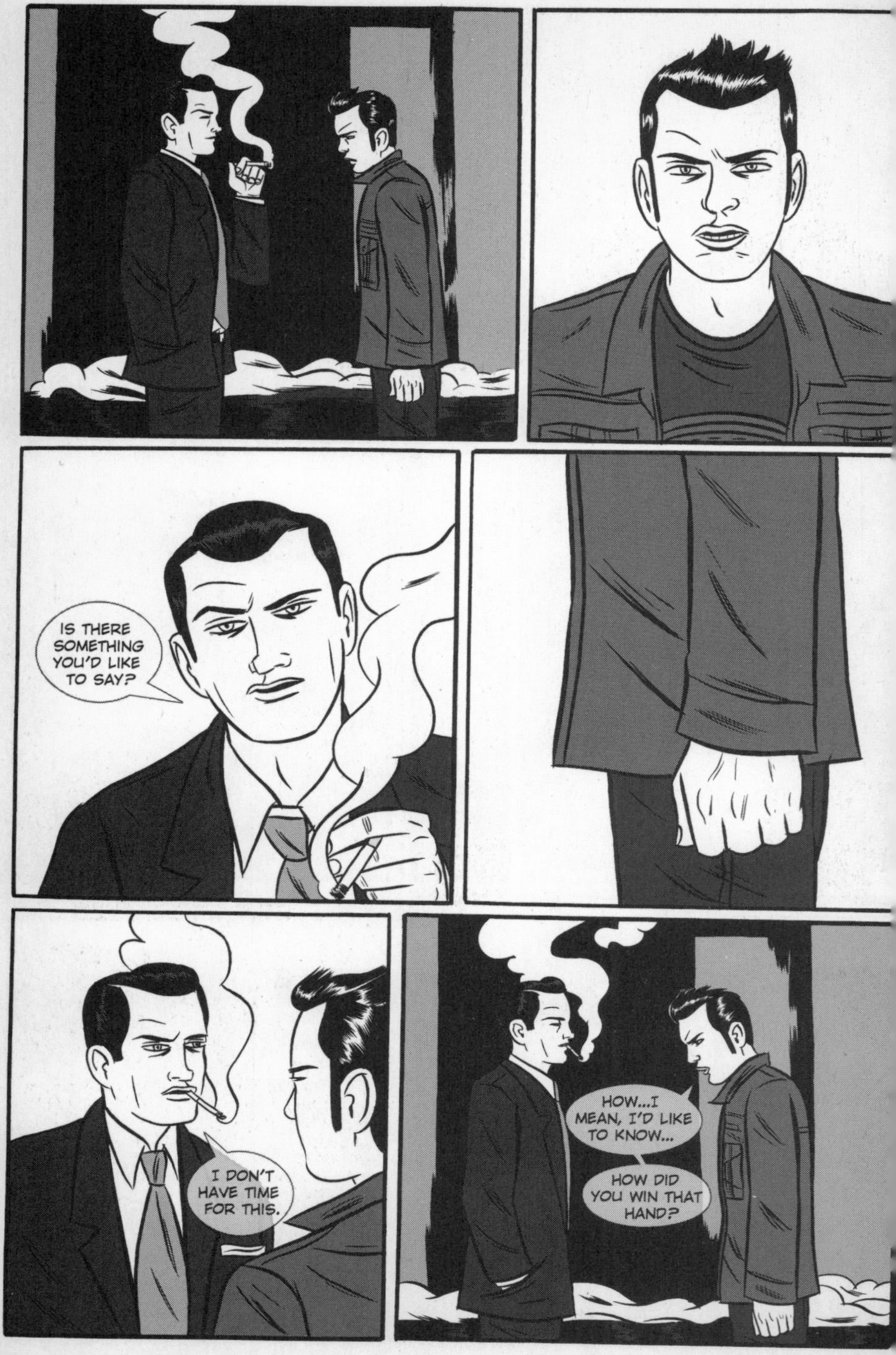
IS THERE SOMETHING YOU'D LIKE TO SAY?
I DON'T HAVE TIME FOR THIS.
HOW...I MEAN, I'D LIKE TO KNOW...
HOW DID YOU WIN THAT HAND?

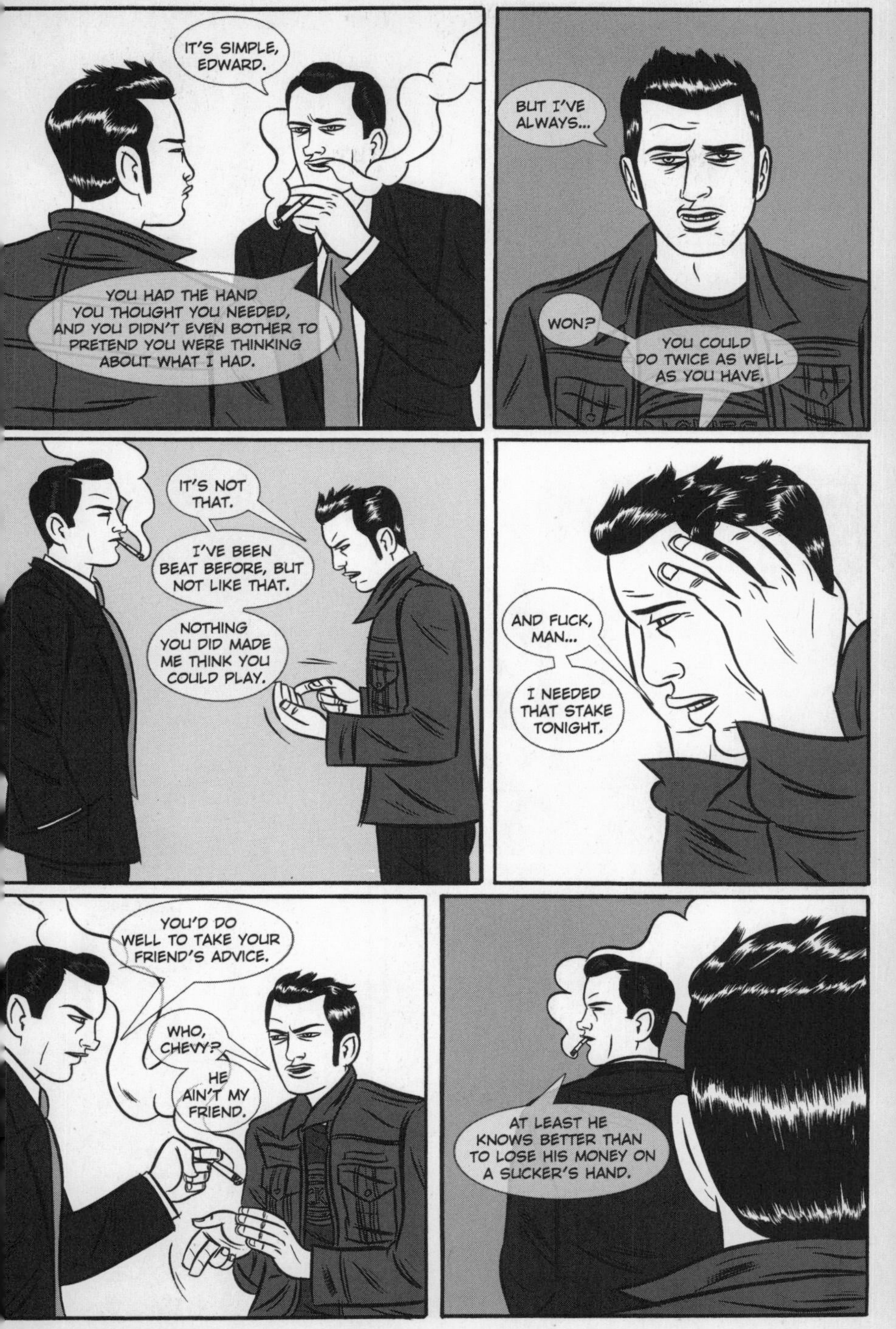
IT'S SIMPLE, EDWARD.
YOU HAD THE HAND YOU THOUGHT YOU NEEDED, AND YOU DIDN'T EVEN BOTHER TO PRETEND YOU WERE THINKING ABOUT WHAT I HAD.
BUT I'VE ALWAYS...
WON?
YOU COULD DO TWICE AS WELL AS YOU HAVE.
IT'S NOT THAT.
I'VE BEEN BEAT BEFORE, BUT NOT LIKE THAT.
NOTHING YOU DID MADE ME THINK YOU COULD PLAY.
AND FUCK, MAN...
I NEEDED THAT STAKE TONIGHT.
YOU'D DO WELL TO TAKE YOUR FRIEND'S ADVICE.
WHO, CHEVY?
HE AIN'T MY FRIEND.
AT LEAST HE KNOWS BETTER THAN TO LOSE HIS MONEY ON A SUCKER'S HAND.

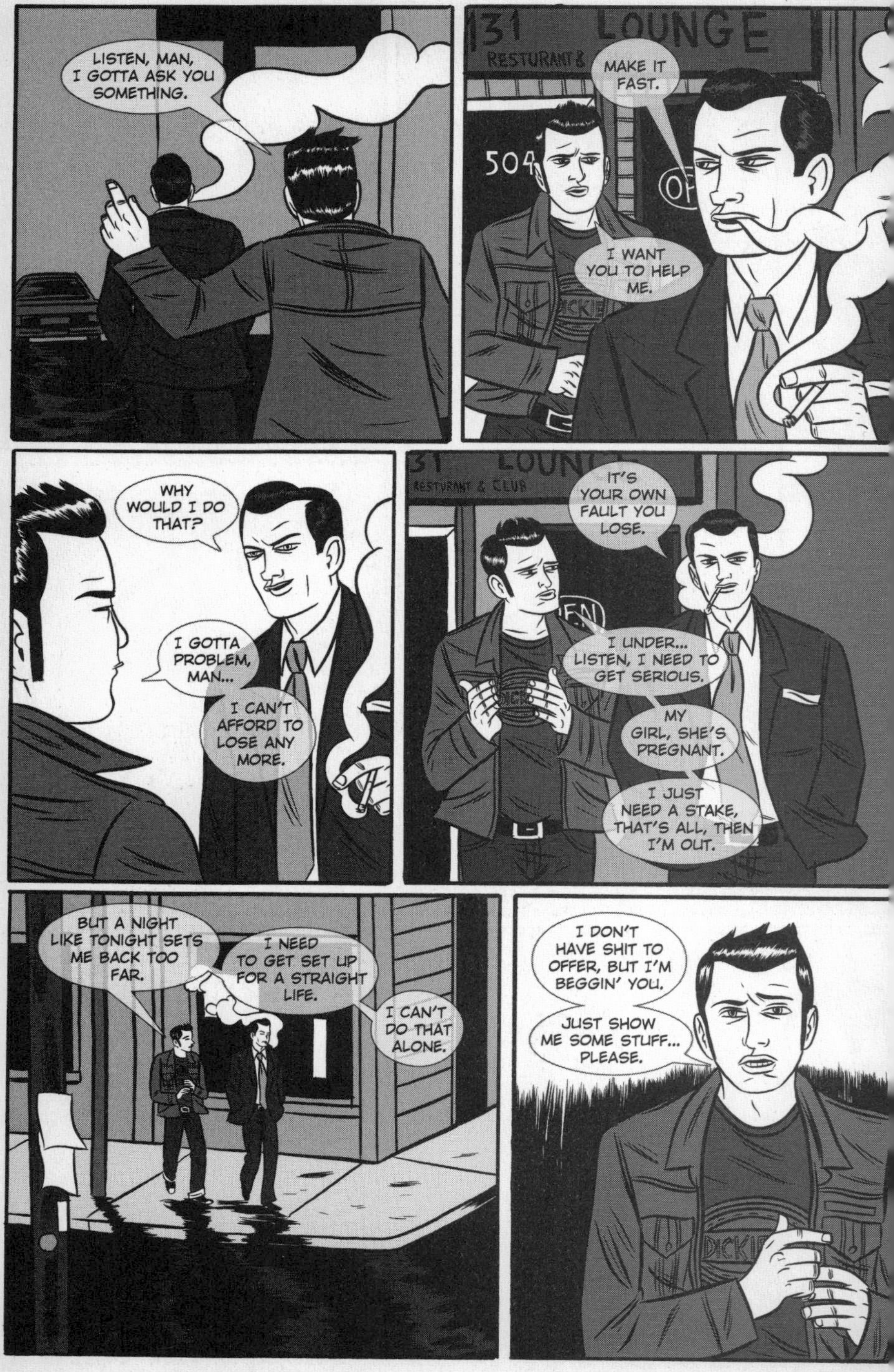
LISTEN, MAN, I GOTTA ASK YOU SOMETHING.
131 LOUNGE
RESTURANT &
MAKE IT FAST.
504
I WANT YOU TO HELP ME.
WHY WOULD I DO THAT?
I GOTTA PROBLEM, MAN...
I CAN'T AFFORD TO LOSE ANY MORE.
RESTURANT & CLUB
IT'S YOUR OWN FAULT YOU LOSE.
I UNDER... LISTEN, I NEED TO GET SERIOUS.
MY GIRL, SHE'S PREGNANT.
I JUST NEED A STAKE, THAT'S ALL, THEN I'M OUT.
BUT A NIGHT LIKE TONIGHT SETS ME BACK TOO FAR.
I NEED TO GET SET UP FOR A STRAIGHT LIFE.
I CAN'T DO THAT ALONE.
I DON'T HAVE SHIT TO OFFER, BUT I'M BEGGIN' YOU.
JUST SHOW ME SOME STUFF... PLEASE.

THAT'S NOT MY LINE OF WORK.

I FIGURED THAT. BUT WHAT THE HELL?

WHAT HAVE YOU GOT TO LOSE?

IF I HELP YOU, IT'S MY RULES FROM THE START. NO BULLSHIT.

YOU DO WHAT I SAY, AND YOU DON'T WORRY WHY I SAY IT.

I CAN'T DO IT WITHOUT YOU, SO WHY WOULD I FUCK WITH YOU?

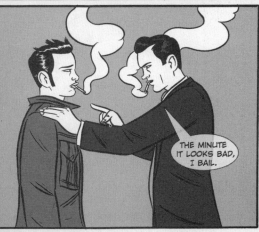

THE MINUTE IT LOOKS BAD, I BAIL.

SURE THING.

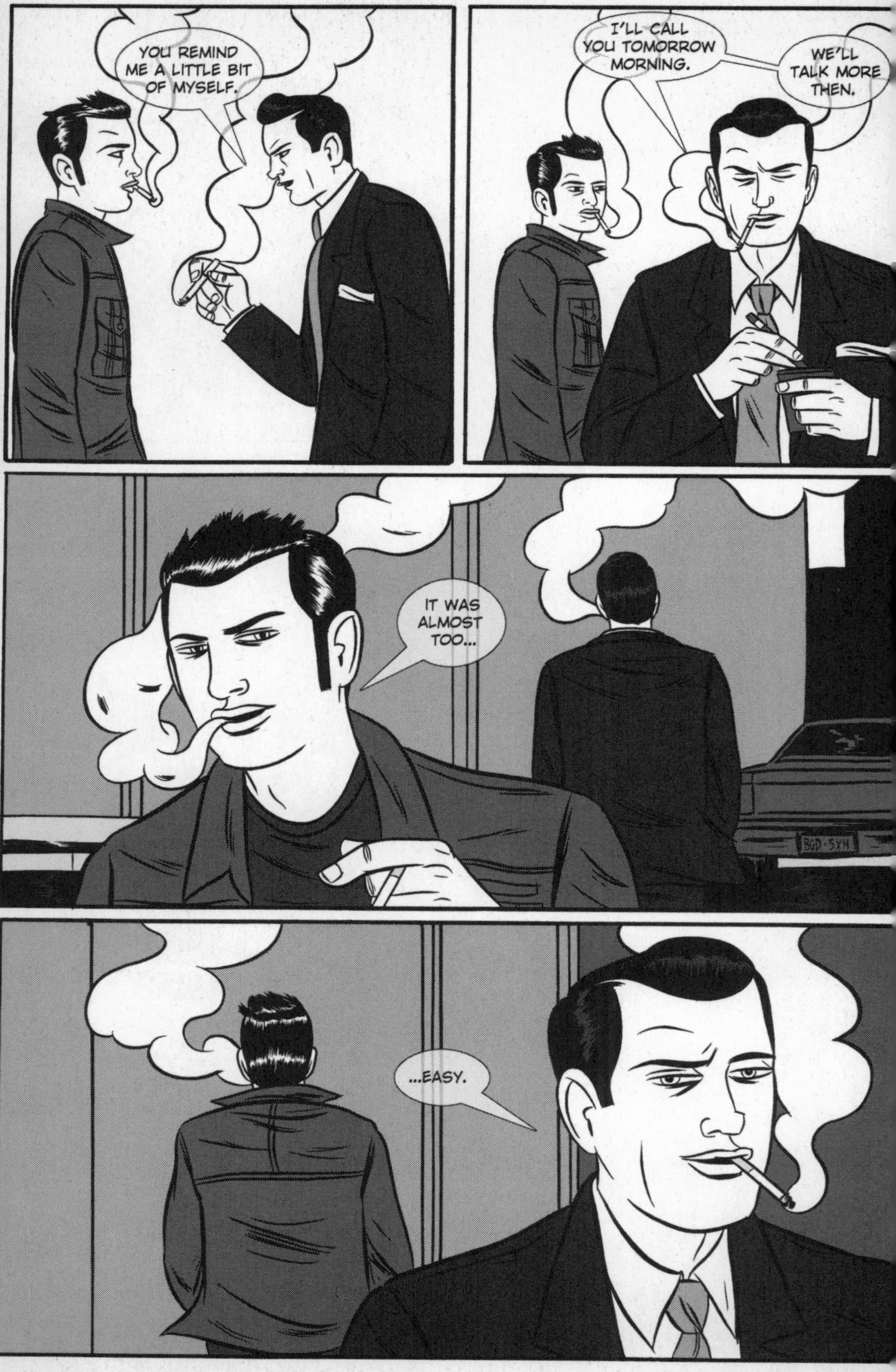
YOU REMIND ME A LITTLE BIT OF MYSELF.
I'LL CALL YOU TOMORROW MORNING.
WE'LL TALK MORE THEN.
IT WAS ALMOST TOO...
...EASY.

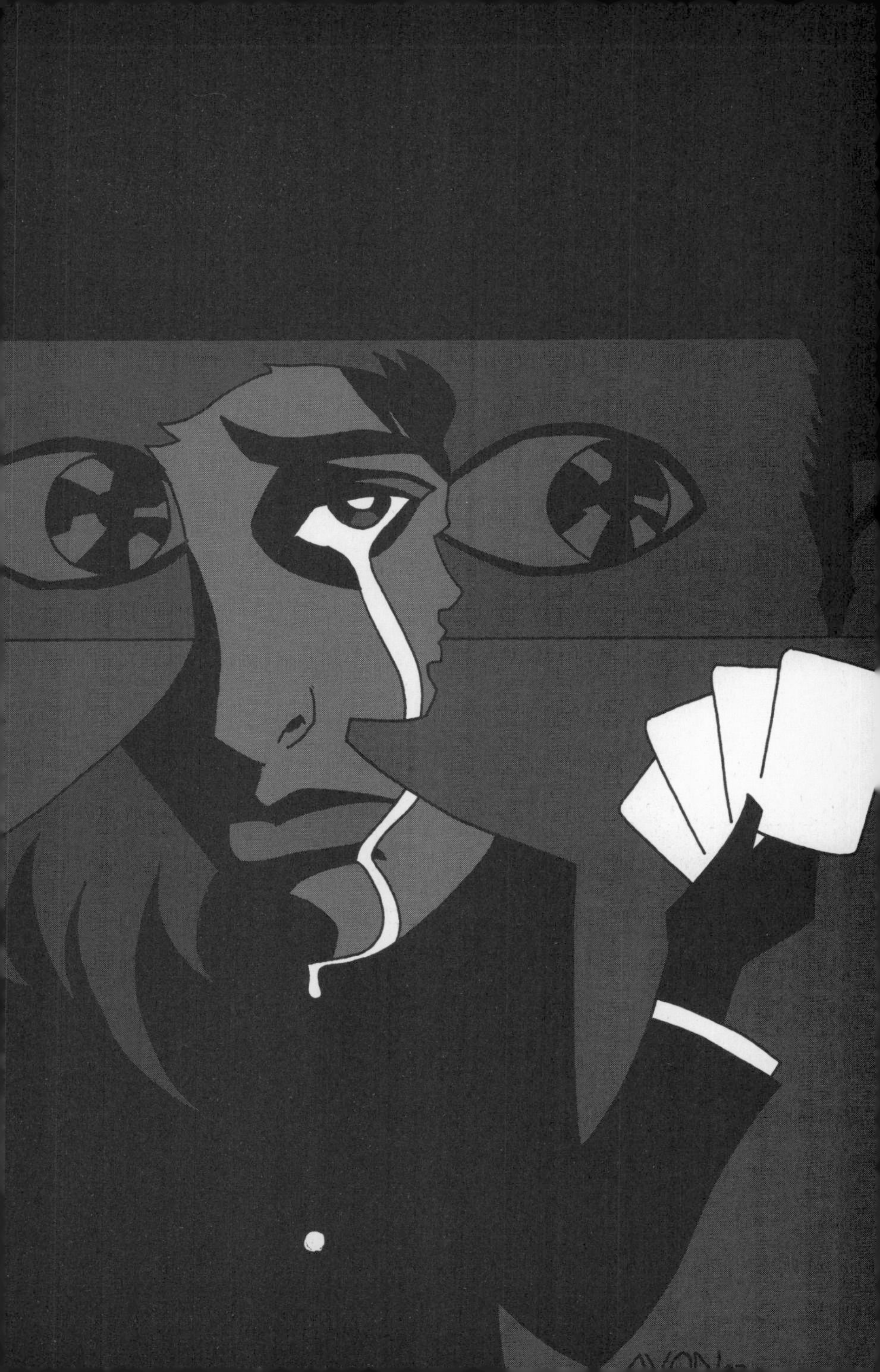

CHAPTER**THREE**

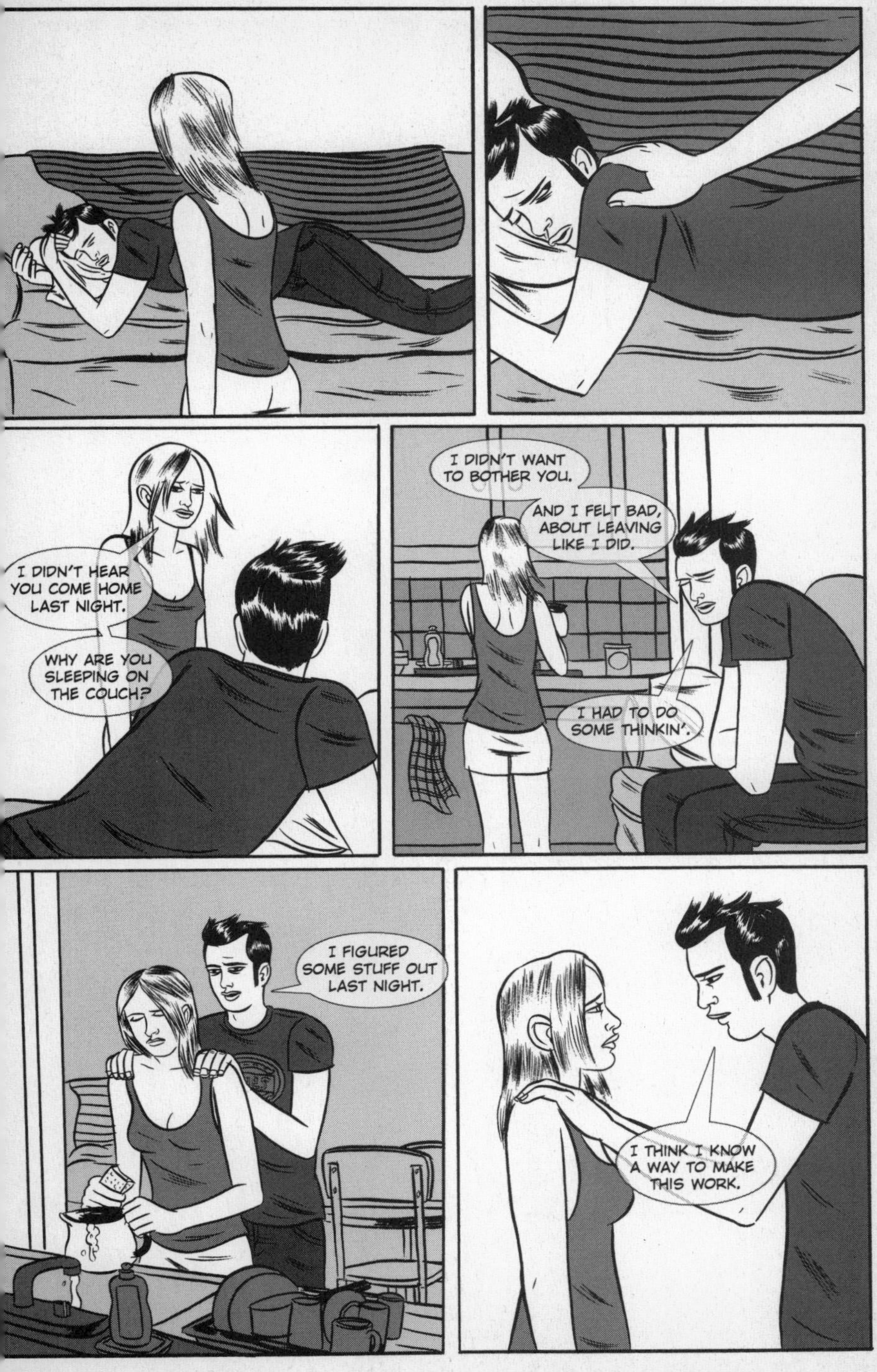
I DIDN'T HEAR YOU COME HOME LAST NIGHT.
WHY ARE YOU SLEEPING ON THE COUCH?
I DIDN'T WANT TO BOTHER YOU.
AND I FELT BAD, ABOUT LEAVING LIKE I DID.
I HAD TO DO SOME THINKIN'.
I FIGURED SOME STUFF OUT LAST NIGHT.
I THINK I KNOW A WAY TO MAKE THIS WORK.

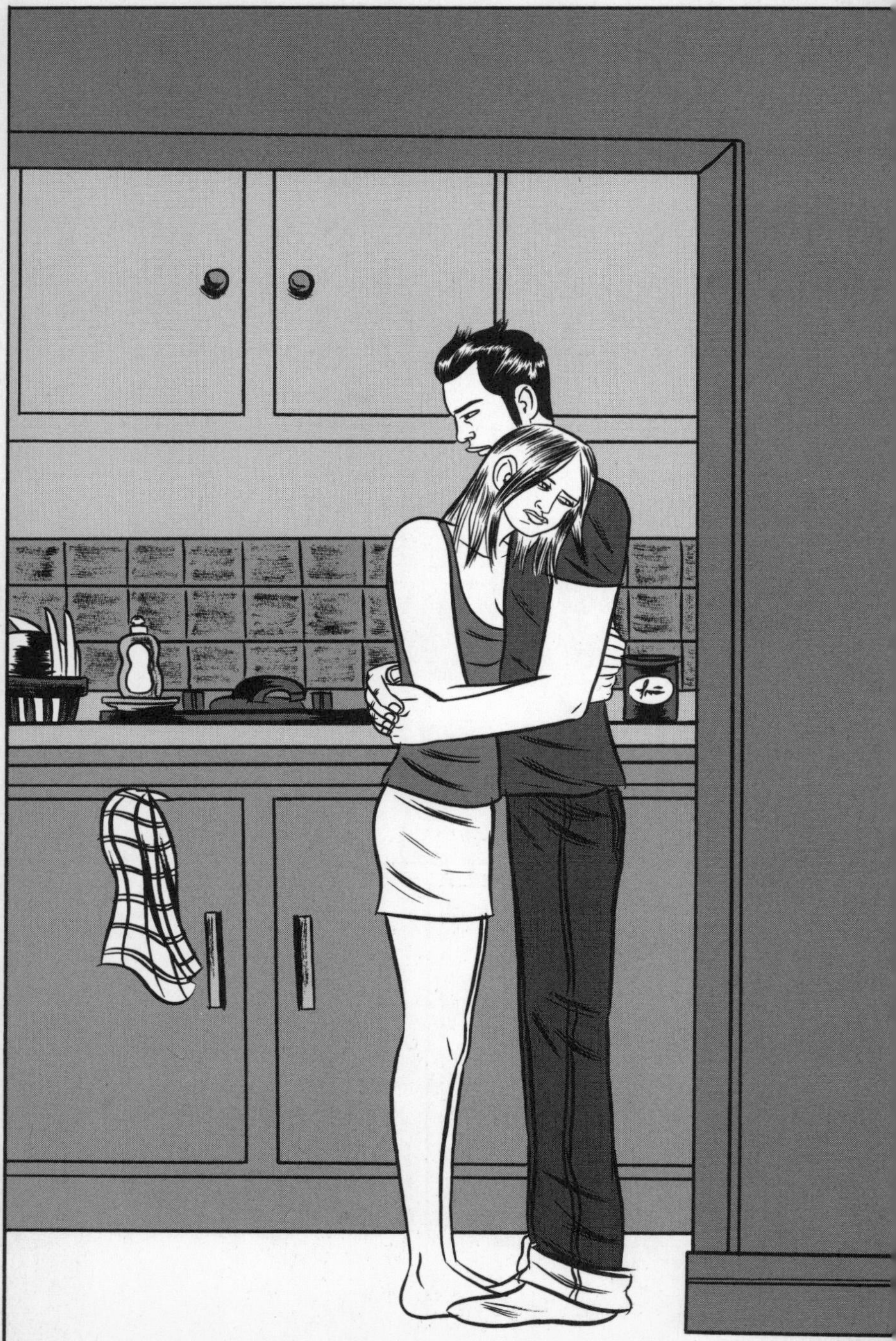

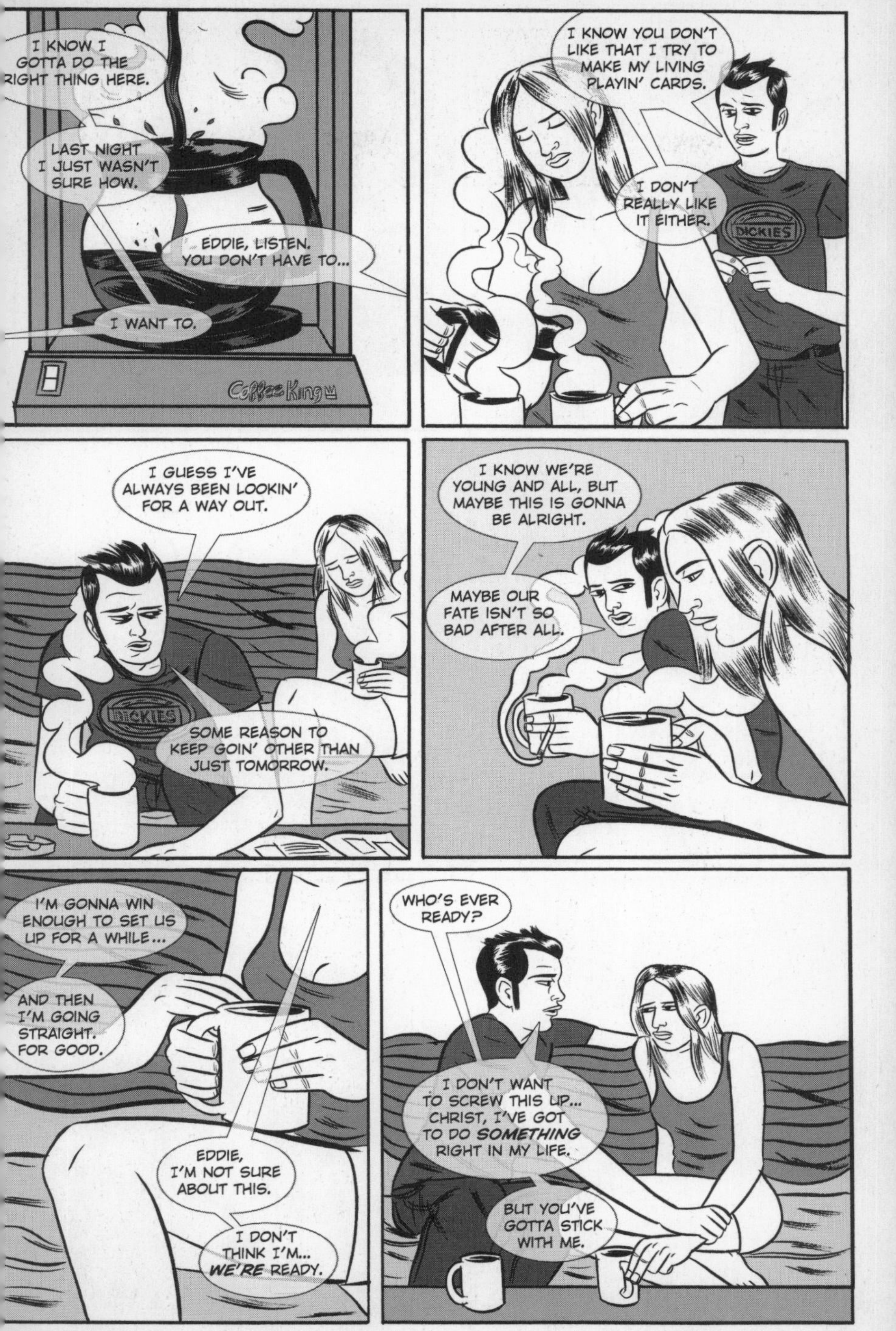
I KNOW I GOTTA DO THE RIGHT THING HERE.
LAST NIGHT I JUST WASN'T SURE HOW.
EDDIE, LISTEN. YOU DON'T HAVE TO...
I WANT TO.
Coffee King
I KNOW YOU DON'T LIKE THAT I TRY TO MAKE MY LIVING PLAYIN' CARDS.
I DON'T REALLY LIKE IT EITHER.
DICKIES
I GUESS I'VE ALWAYS BEEN LOOKIN' FOR A WAY OUT.
SOME REASON TO KEEP GOIN' OTHER THAN JUST TOMORROW.
DICKIES
I KNOW WE'RE YOUNG AND ALL, BUT MAYBE THIS IS GONNA BE ALRIGHT.
MAYBE OUR FATE ISN'T SO BAD AFTER ALL.
I'M GONNA WIN ENOUGH TO SET US UP FOR A WHILE...
AND THEN I'M GOING STRAIGHT. FOR GOOD.
EDDIE, I'M NOT SURE ABOUT THIS.
I DON'T THINK I'M... *WE'RE* READY.
WHO'S EVER READY?
I DON'T WANT TO SCREW THIS UP... CHRIST, I'VE GOT TO DO *SOMETHING* RIGHT IN MY LIFE.
BUT YOU'VE GOTTA STICK WITH ME.

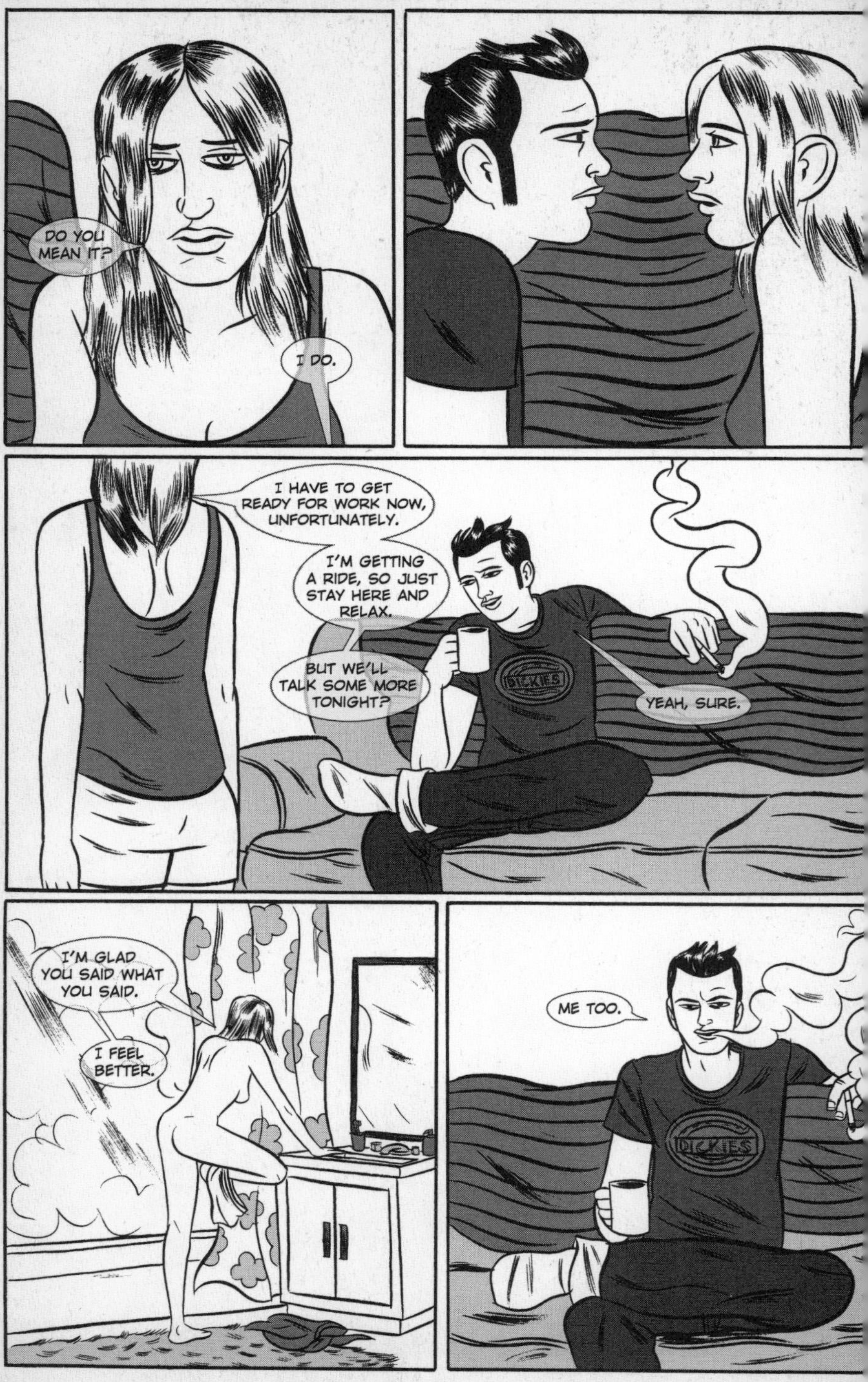
DO YOU MEAN IT?
I DO.
I HAVE TO GET READY FOR WORK NOW, UNFORTUNATELY.
I'M GETTING A RIDE, SO JUST STAY HERE AND RELAX.
BUT WE'LL TALK SOME MORE TONIGHT?
YEAH, SURE.
DICKIES
I'M GLAD YOU SAID WHAT YOU SAID.
I FEEL BETTER.
ME TOO.
DICKIES

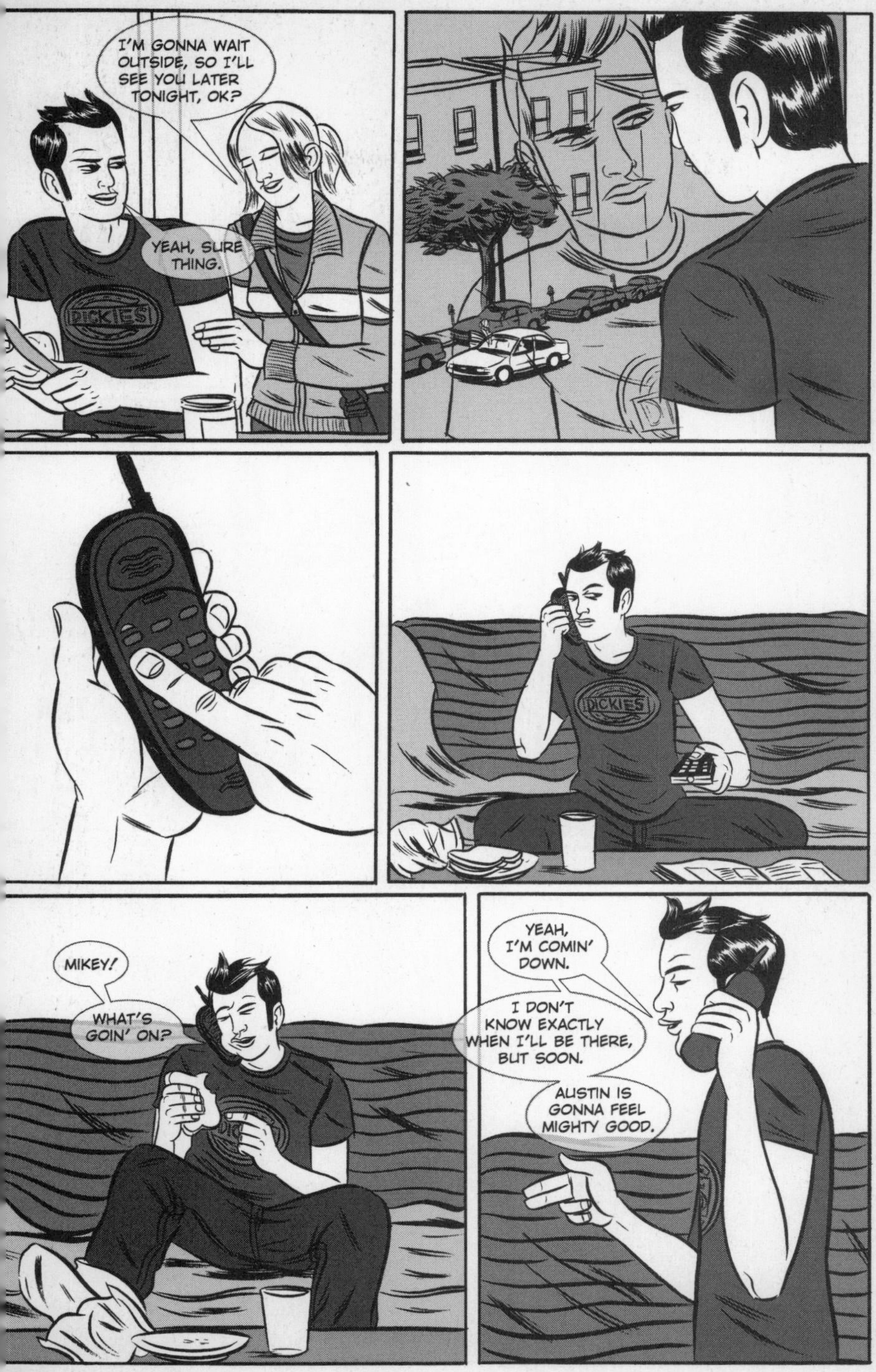
I'M GONNA WAIT OUTSIDE, SO I'LL SEE YOU LATER TONIGHT, OK?
YEAH, SURE THING.
DICKIES
MIKEY!
WHAT'S GOIN' ON?
YEAH, I'M COMIN' DOWN.
I DON'T KNOW EXACTLY WHEN I'LL BE THERE, BUT SOON.
AUSTIN IS GONNA FEEL MIGHTY GOOD.

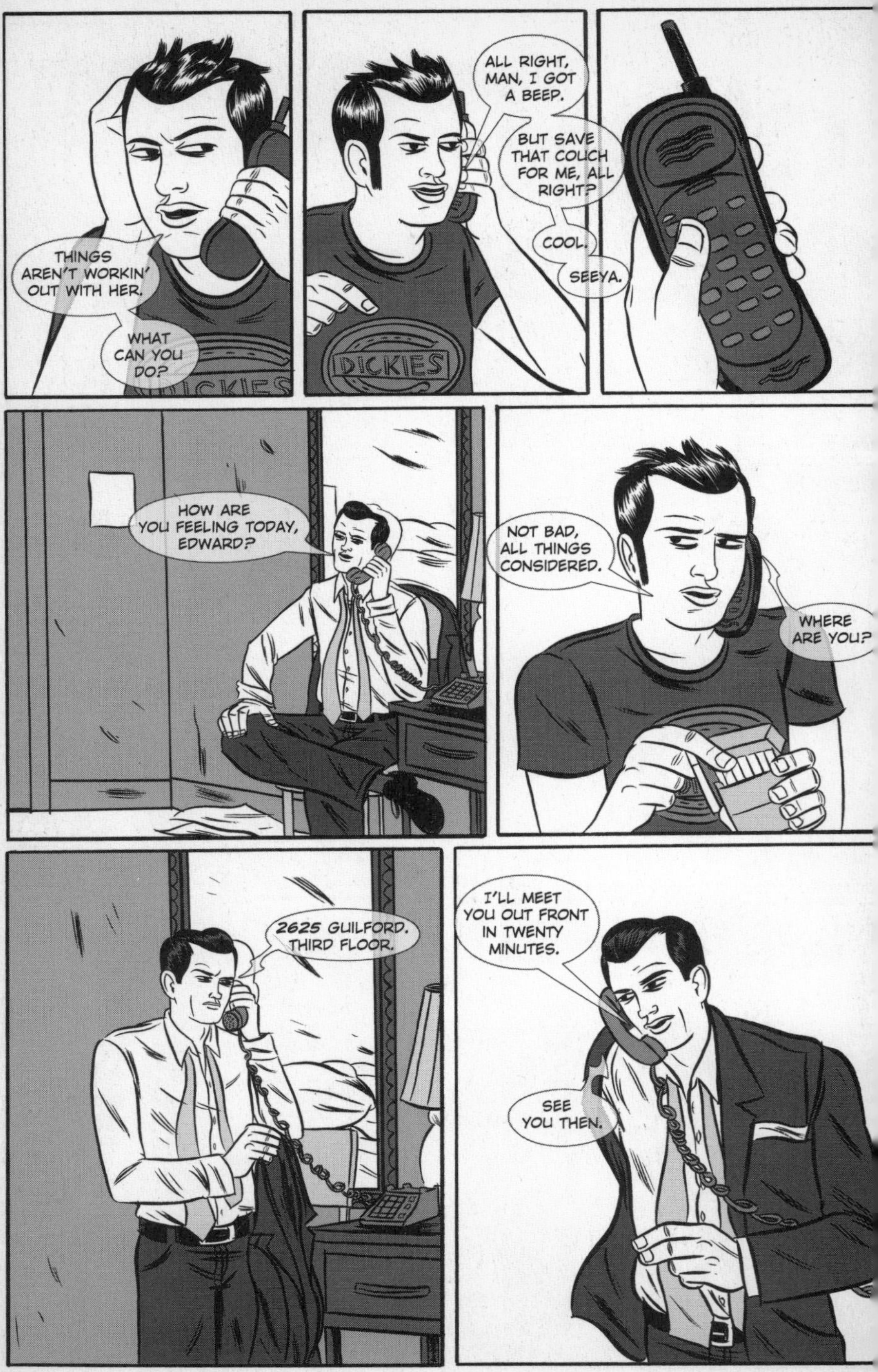
THINGS AREN'T WORKIN' OUT WITH HER.
WHAT CAN YOU DO?
DICKIES
ALL RIGHT, MAN, I GOT A BEEP.
BUT SAVE THAT COUCH FOR ME, ALL RIGHT?
COOL.
SEEYA.
DICKIES
HOW ARE YOU FEELING TODAY, EDWARD?
NOT BAD, ALL THINGS CONSIDERED.
WHERE ARE YOU?
2625 GUILFORD. THIRD FLOOR.
I'LL MEET YOU OUT FRONT IN TWENTY MINUTES.
SEE YOU THEN.

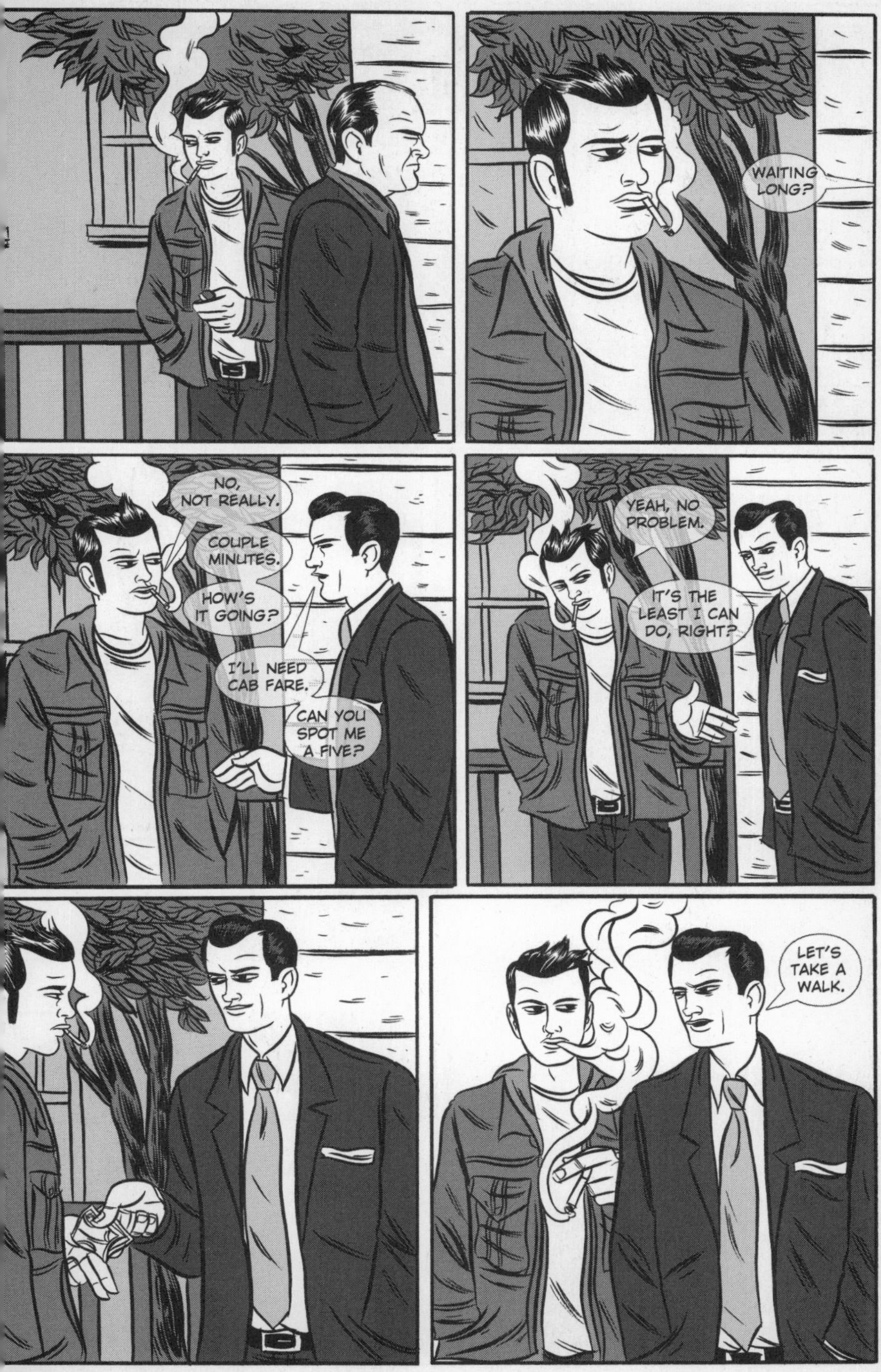
WAITING LONG?
NO, NOT REALLY.
COUPLE MINUTES.
HOW'S IT GOING?
I'LL NEED CAB FARE.
CAN YOU SPOT ME A FIVE?
YEAH, NO PROBLEM.
IT'S THE LEAST I CAN DO, RIGHT?
LET'S TAKE A WALK.

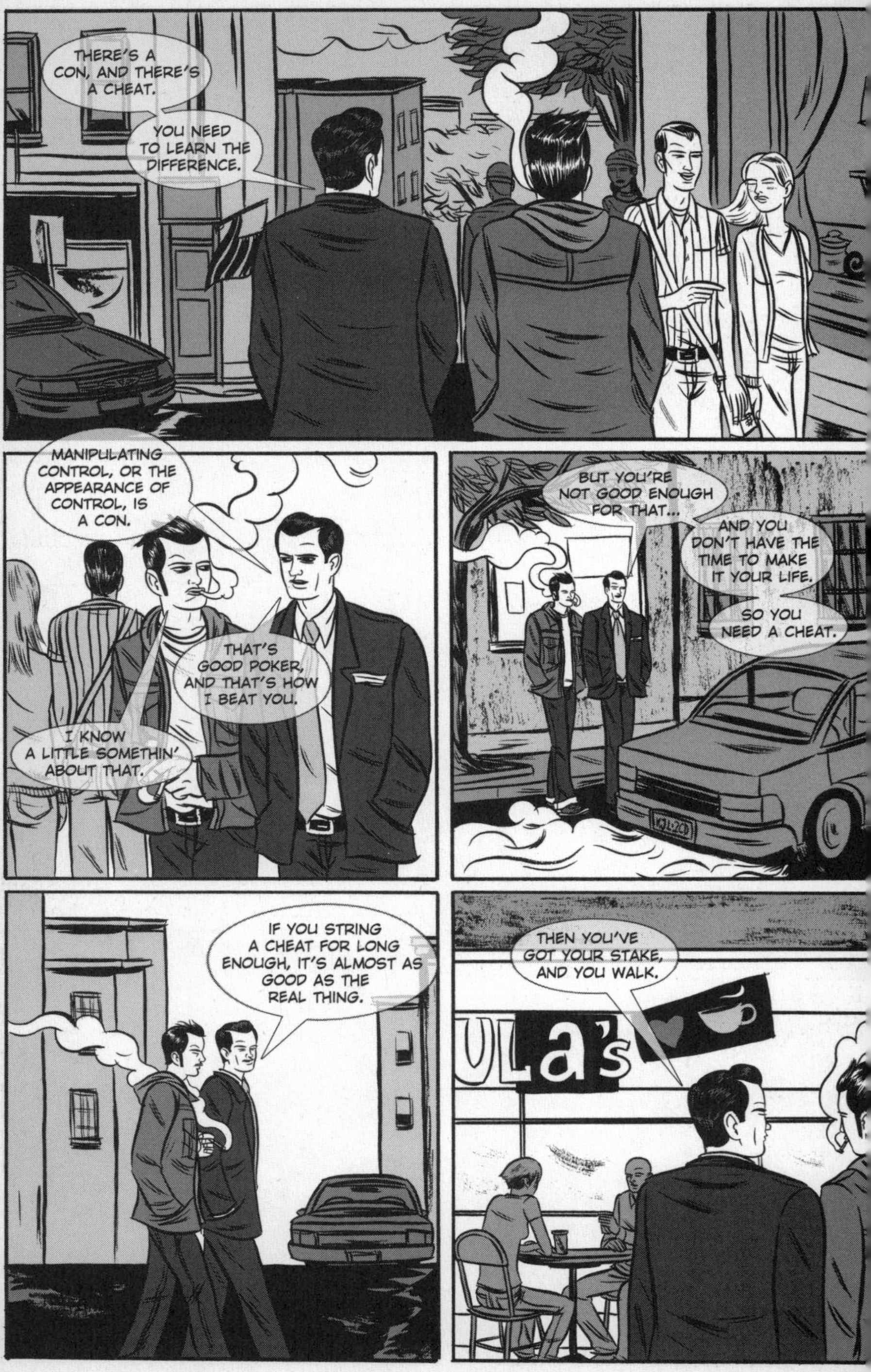
THERE'S A CON, AND THERE'S A CHEAT.
YOU NEED TO LEARN THE DIFFERENCE.
MANIPULATING CONTROL, OR THE APPEARANCE OF CONTROL, IS A CON.
THAT'S GOOD POKER, AND THAT'S HOW I BEAT YOU.
I KNOW A LITTLE SOMETHIN' ABOUT THAT.
BUT YOU'RE NOT GOOD ENOUGH FOR THAT...
AND YOU DON'T HAVE THE TIME TO MAKE IT YOUR LIFE.
SO YOU NEED A CHEAT.
IF YOU STRING A CHEAT FOR LONG ENOUGH, IT'S ALMOST AS GOOD AS THE REAL THING.
THEN YOU'VE GOT YOUR STAKE, AND YOU WALK.
ULA'S

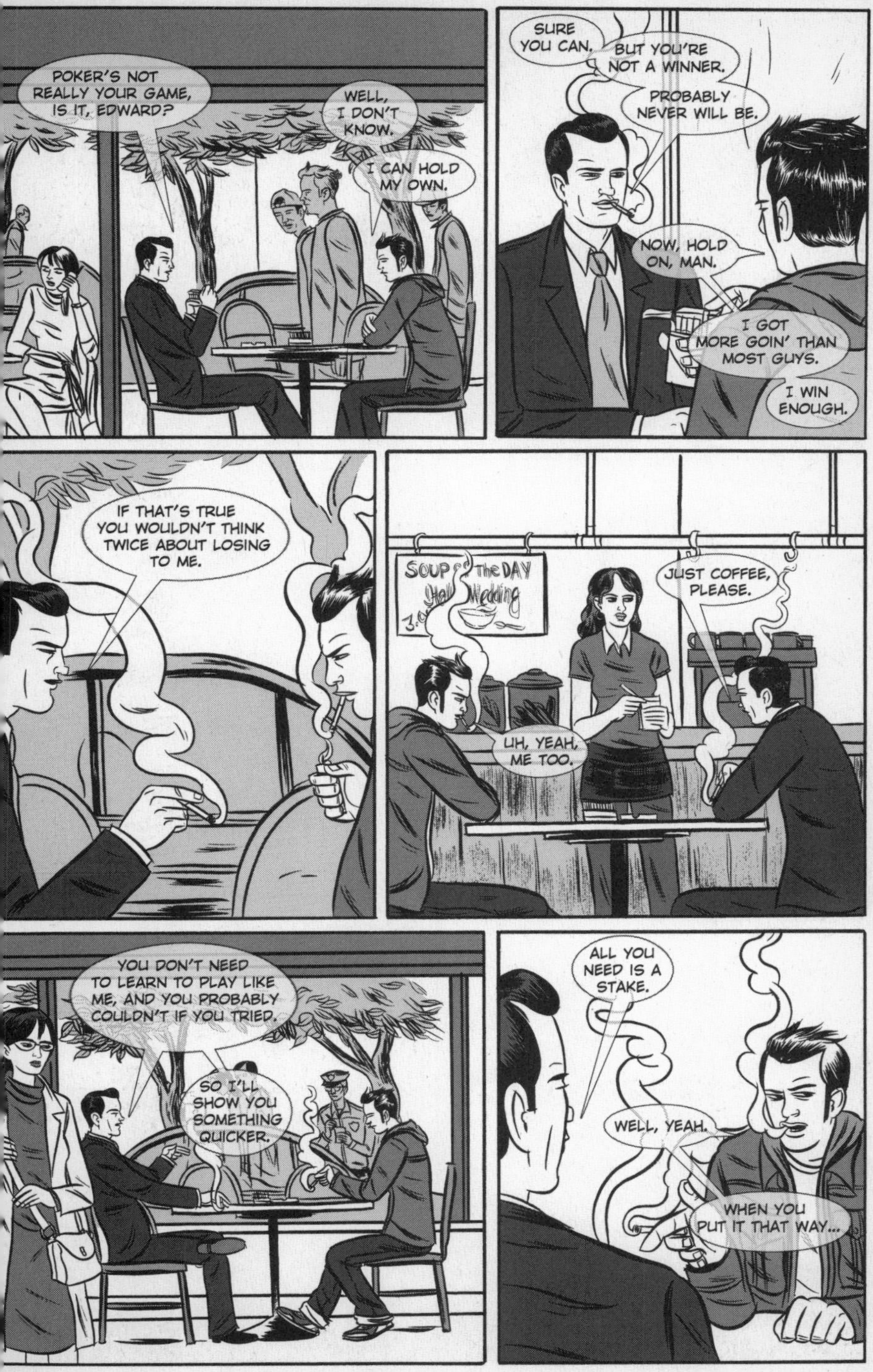
POKER'S NOT REALLY YOUR GAME, IS IT, EDWARD?
WELL, I DON'T KNOW.
I CAN HOLD MY OWN.
SURE YOU CAN.
BUT YOU'RE NOT A WINNER.
PROBABLY NEVER WILL BE.
NOW, HOLD ON, MAN.
I GOT MORE GOIN' THAN MOST GUYS.
I WIN ENOUGH.
IF THAT'S TRUE YOU WOULDN'T THINK TWICE ABOUT LOSING TO ME.
SOUP of the DAY
JUST COFFEE, PLEASE.
UH, YEAH, ME TOO.
YOU DON'T NEED TO LEARN TO PLAY LIKE ME, AND YOU PROBABLY COULDN'T IF YOU TRIED.
SO I'LL SHOW YOU SOMETHING QUICKER.
ALL YOU NEED IS A STAKE.
WELL, YEAH.
WHEN YOU PUT IT THAT WAY...

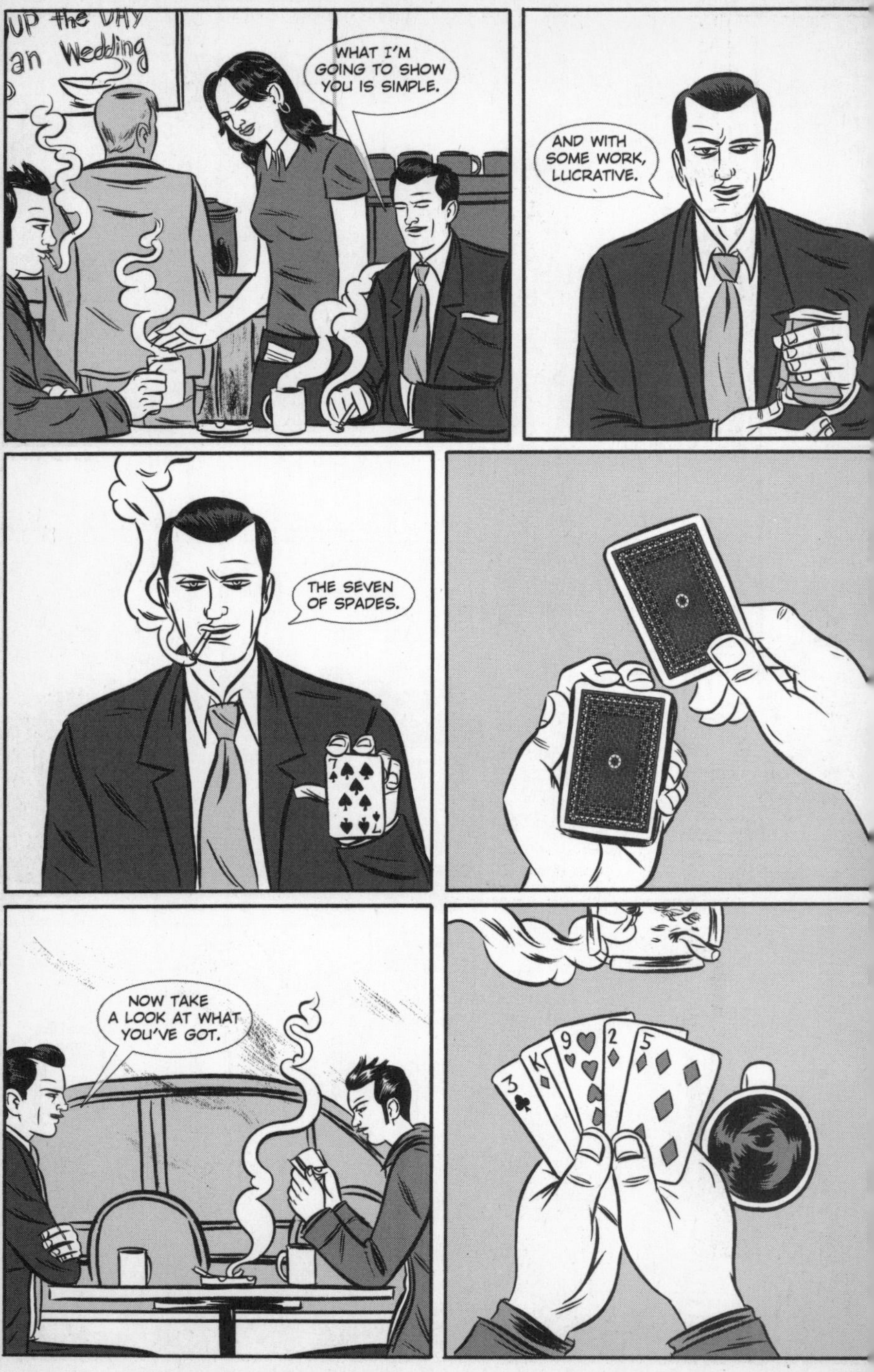
UP the DAY
an Wedding
WHAT I'M GOING TO SHOW YOU IS SIMPLE.
AND WITH SOME WORK, LUCRATIVE.
THE SEVEN OF SPADES.
NOW TAKE A LOOK AT WHAT YOU'VE GOT.

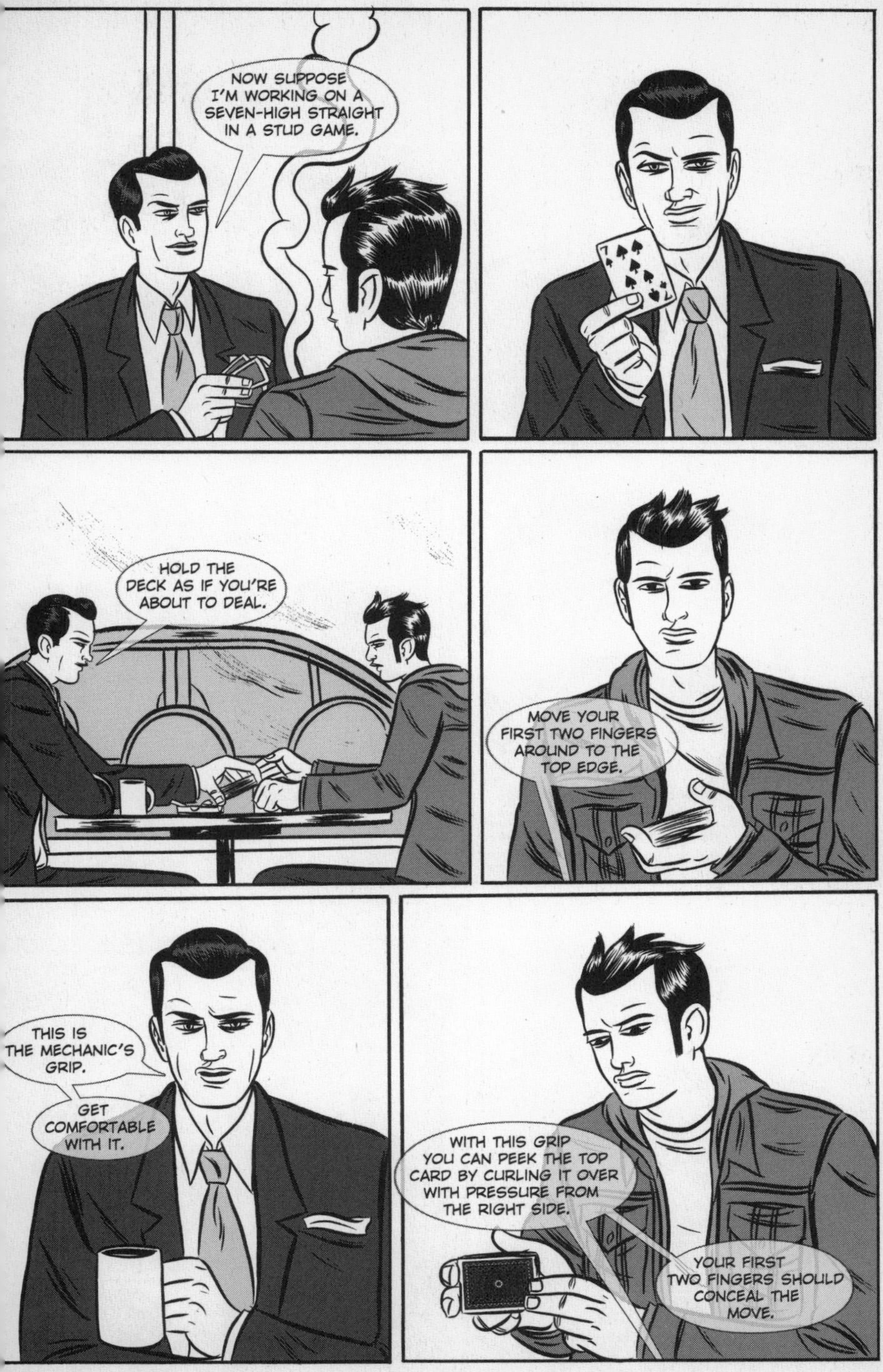
NOW SUPPOSE I'M WORKING ON A SEVEN-HIGH STRAIGHT IN A STUD GAME.
HOLD THE DECK AS IF YOU'RE ABOUT TO DEAL.
MOVE YOUR FIRST TWO FINGERS AROUND TO THE TOP EDGE.
THIS IS THE MECHANIC'S GRIP.
GET COMFORTABLE WITH IT.
WITH THIS GRIP YOU CAN PEEK THE TOP CARD BY CURLING IT OVER WITH PRESSURE FROM THE RIGHT SIDE.
YOUR FIRST TWO FINGERS SHOULD CONCEAL THE MOVE.

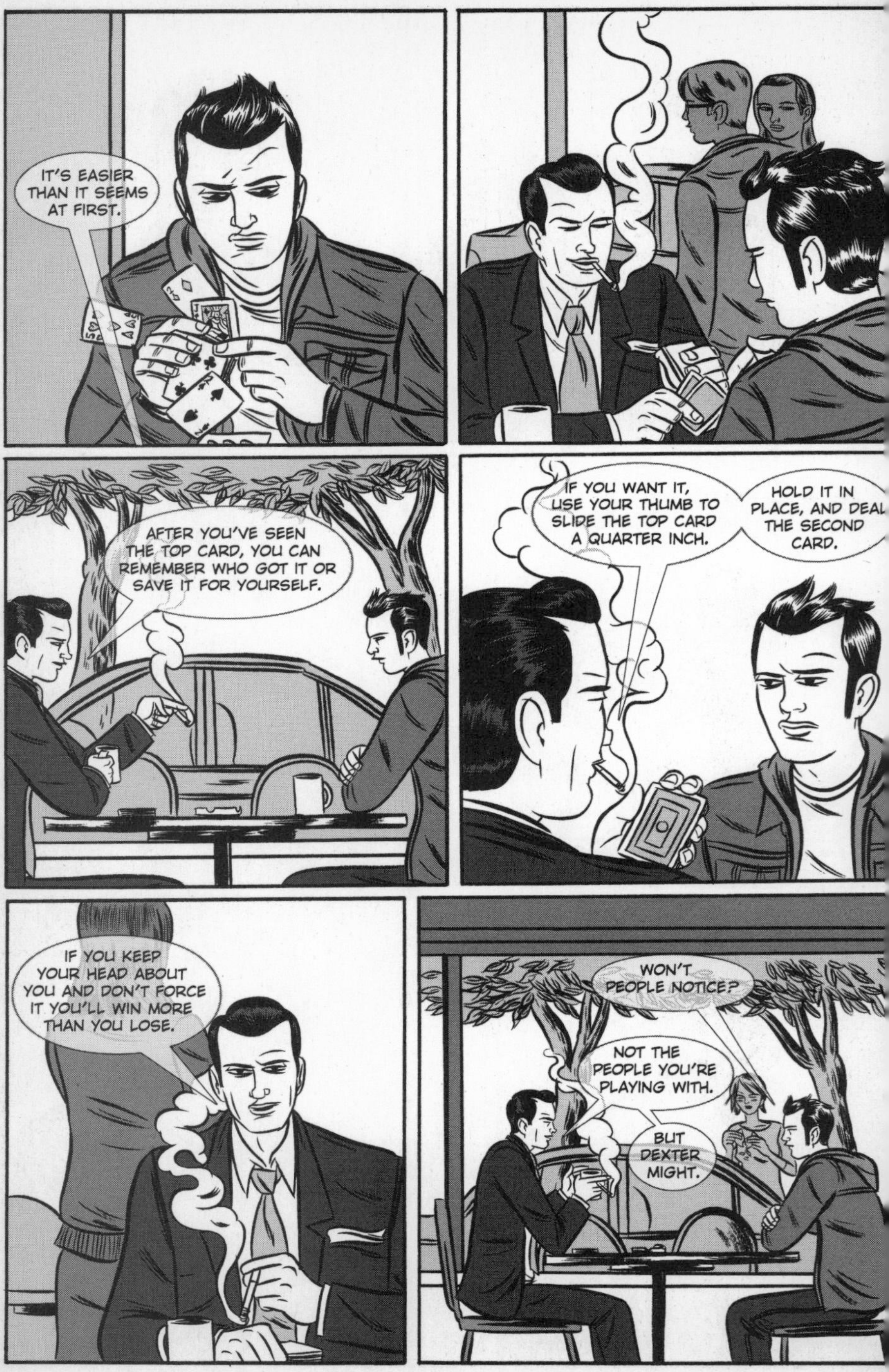
IT'S EASIER THAN IT SEEMS AT FIRST.
AFTER YOU'VE SEEN THE TOP CARD, YOU CAN REMEMBER WHO GOT IT OR SAVE IT FOR YOURSELF.
IF YOU WANT IT, USE YOUR THUMB TO SLIDE THE TOP CARD A QUARTER INCH.
HOLD IT IN PLACE, AND DEAL THE SECOND CARD.
IF YOU KEEP YOUR HEAD ABOUT YOU AND DON'T FORCE IT YOU'LL WIN MORE THAN YOU LOSE.
WON'T PEOPLE NOTICE?
NOT THE PEOPLE YOU'RE PLAYING WITH.
BUT DEXTER MIGHT.

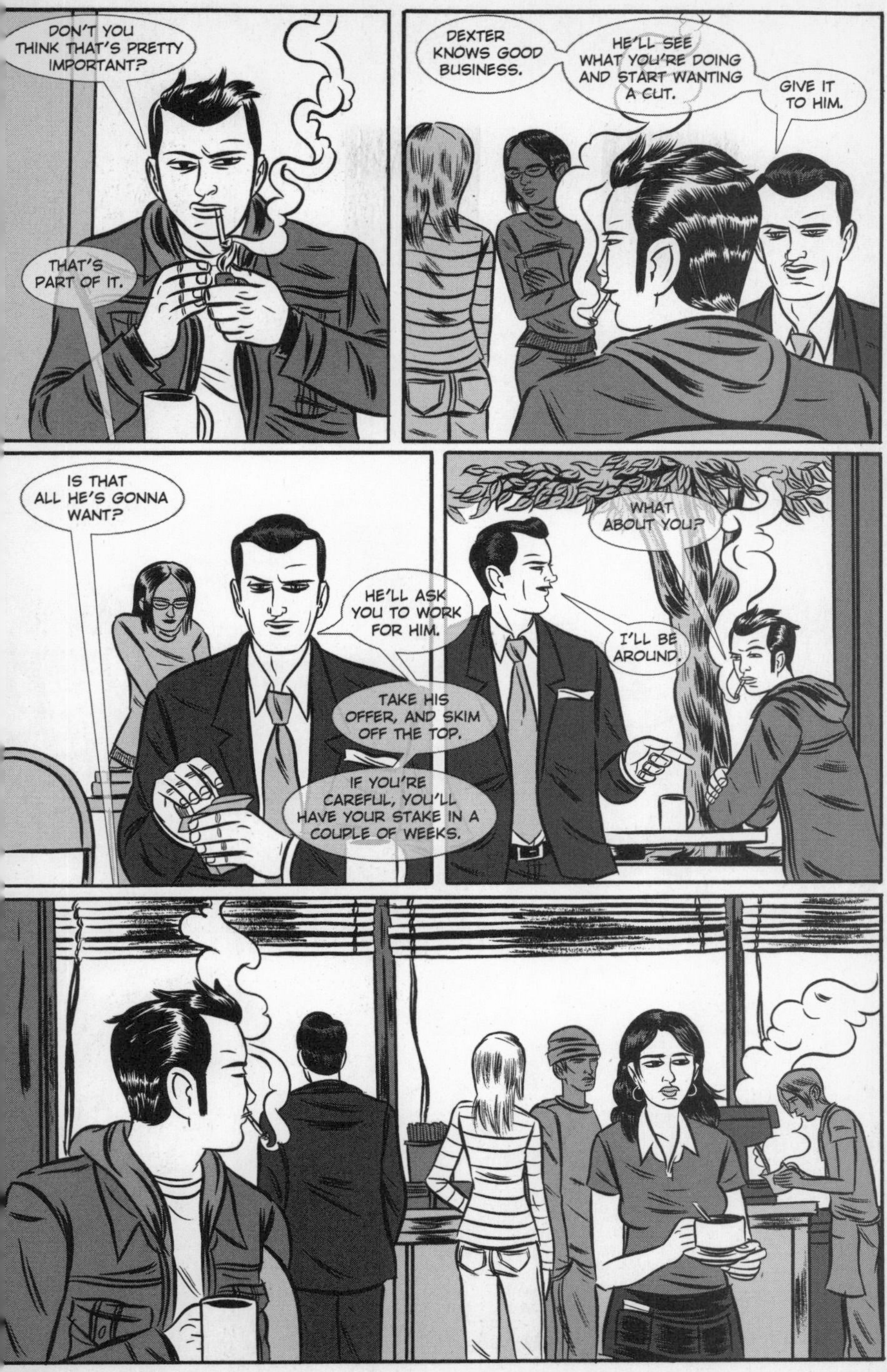
DON'T YOU THINK THAT'S PRETTY IMPORTANT?
THAT'S PART OF IT.
DEXTER KNOWS GOOD BUSINESS.
HE'LL SEE WHAT YOU'RE DOING AND START WANTING A CUT.
GIVE IT TO HIM.
IS THAT ALL HE'S GONNA WANT?
HE'LL ASK YOU TO WORK FOR HIM.
TAKE HIS OFFER, AND SKIM OFF THE TOP.
IF YOU'RE CAREFUL, YOU'LL HAVE YOUR STAKE IN A COUPLE OF WEEKS.
WHAT ABOUT YOU?
I'LL BE AROUND.

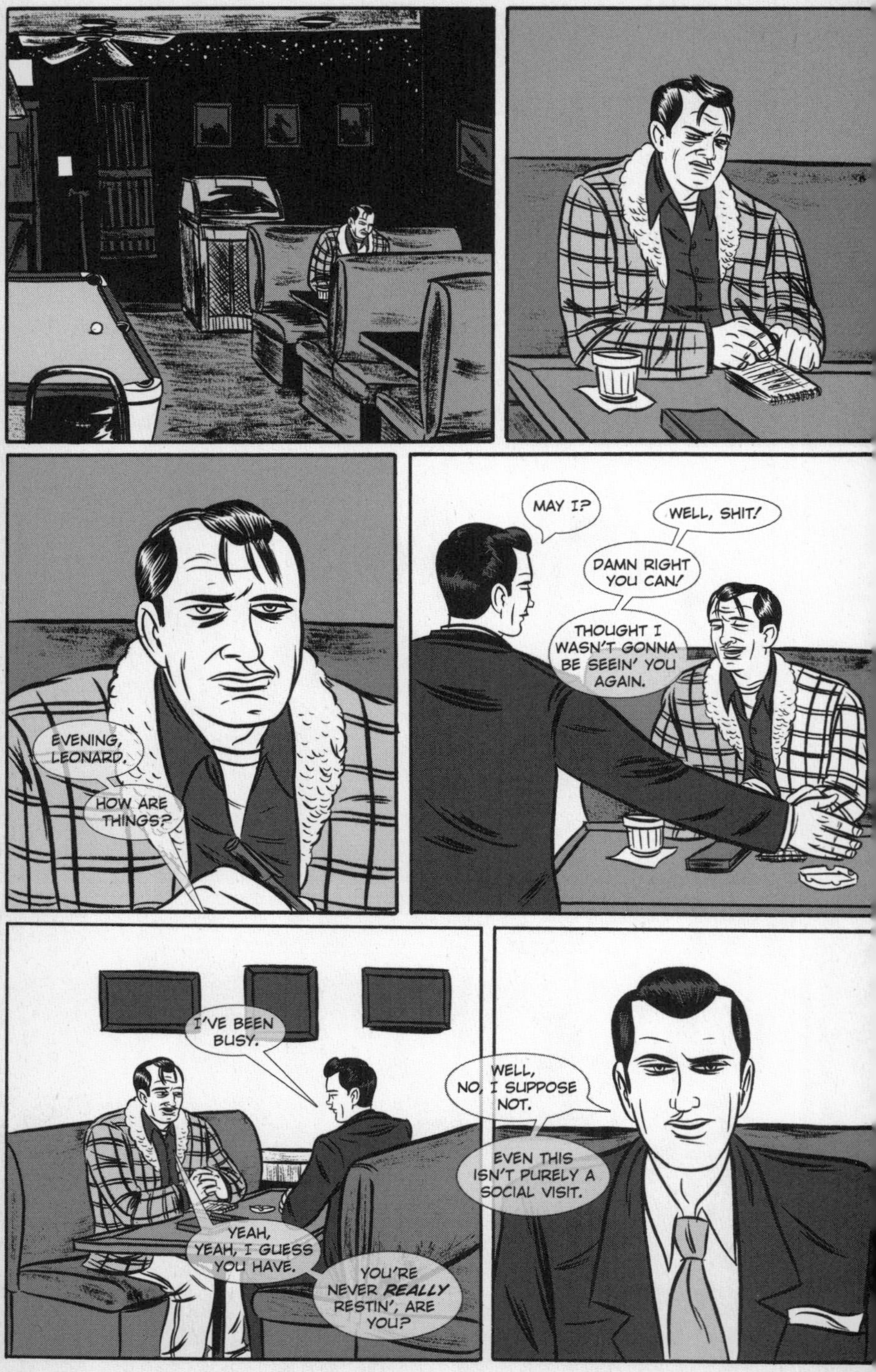
EVENING, LEONARD.
HOW ARE THINGS?
MAY I?
WELL, SHIT!
DAMN RIGHT YOU CAN!
THOUGHT I WASN'T GONNA BE SEEIN' YOU AGAIN.
I'VE BEEN BUSY.
YEAH, YEAH, I GUESS YOU HAVE.
YOU'RE NEVER REALLY RESTIN', ARE YOU?
WELL, NO, I SUPPOSE NOT.
EVEN THIS ISN'T PURELY A SOCIAL VISIT.

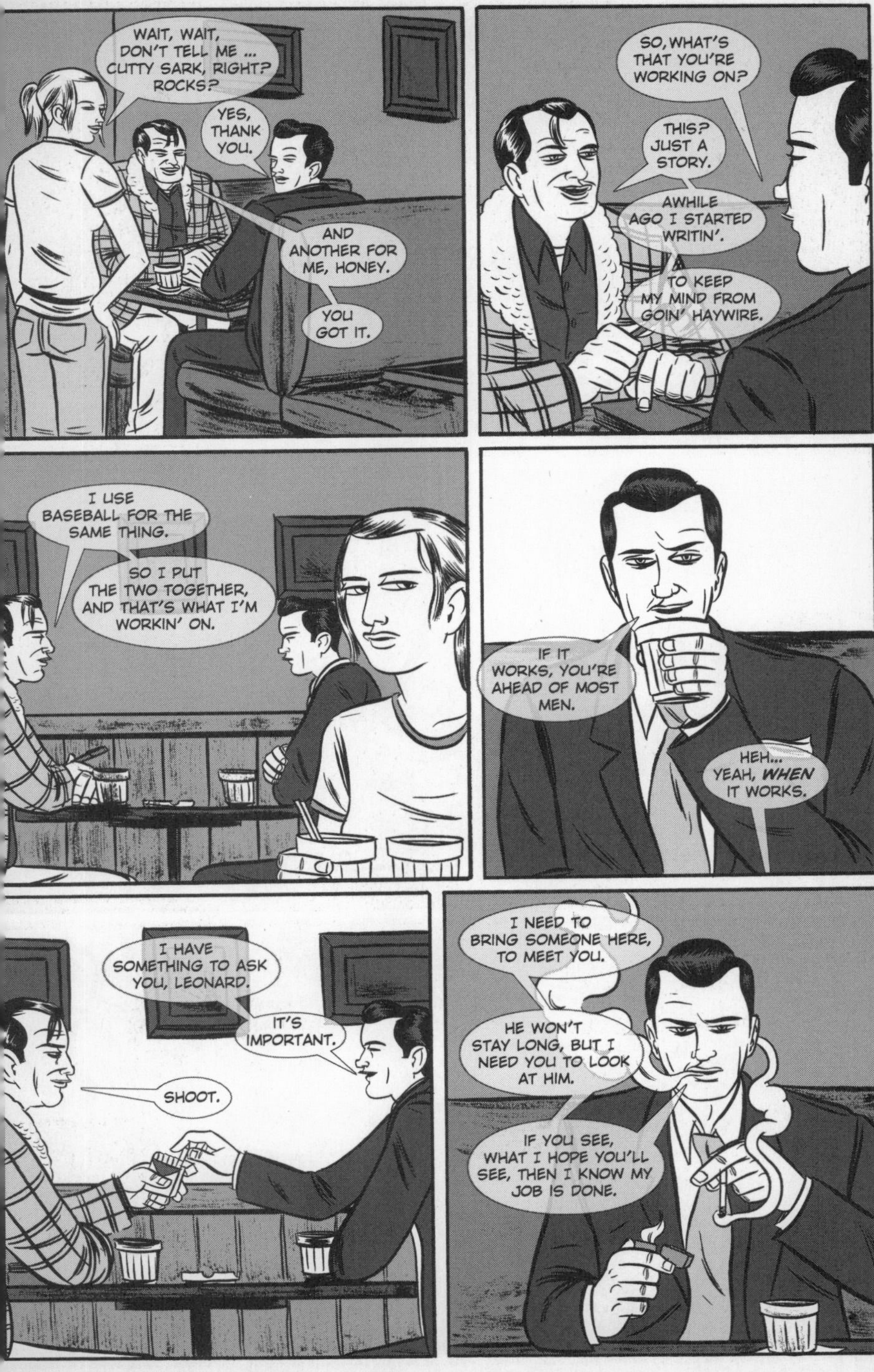
WAIT, WAIT, DON'T TELL ME ... CUTTY SARK, RIGHT? ROCKS?
YES, THANK YOU.
AND ANOTHER FOR ME, HONEY.
YOU GOT IT.
SO, WHAT'S THAT YOU'RE WORKING ON?
THIS? JUST A STORY.
AWHILE AGO I STARTED WRITIN'.
TO KEEP MY MIND FROM GOIN' HAYWIRE.
I USE BASEBALL FOR THE SAME THING.
SO I PUT THE TWO TOGETHER, AND THAT'S WHAT I'M WORKIN' ON.
IF IT WORKS, YOU'RE AHEAD OF MOST MEN.
HEH... YEAH, WHEN IT WORKS.
I HAVE SOMETHING TO ASK YOU, LEONARD.
IT'S IMPORTANT.
SHOOT.
I NEED TO BRING SOMEONE HERE, TO MEET YOU.
HE WON'T STAY LONG, BUT I NEED YOU TO LOOK AT HIM.
IF YOU SEE, WHAT I HOPE YOU'LL SEE, THEN I KNOW MY JOB IS DONE.

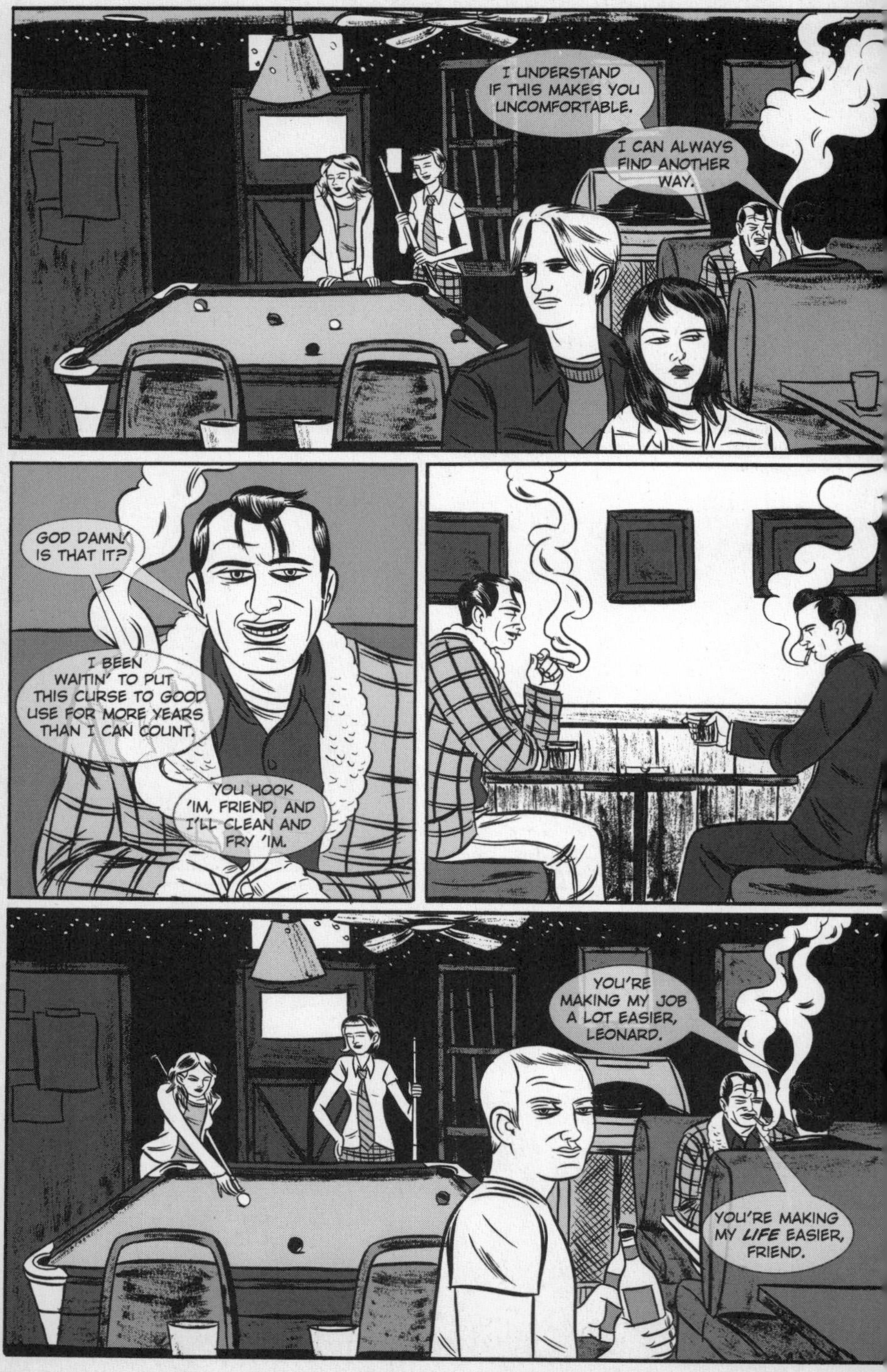
I UNDERSTAND IF THIS MAKES YOU UNCOMFORTABLE.
I CAN ALWAYS FIND ANOTHER WAY.
GOD DAMN! IS THAT IT?
I BEEN WAITIN' TO PUT THIS CURSE TO GOOD USE FOR MORE YEARS THAN I CAN COUNT.
YOU HOOK 'IM, FRIEND, AND I'LL CLEAN AND FRY 'IM.
YOU'RE MAKING MY JOB A LOT EASIER, LEONARD.
YOU'RE MAKING MY *LIFE* EASIER, FRIEND.

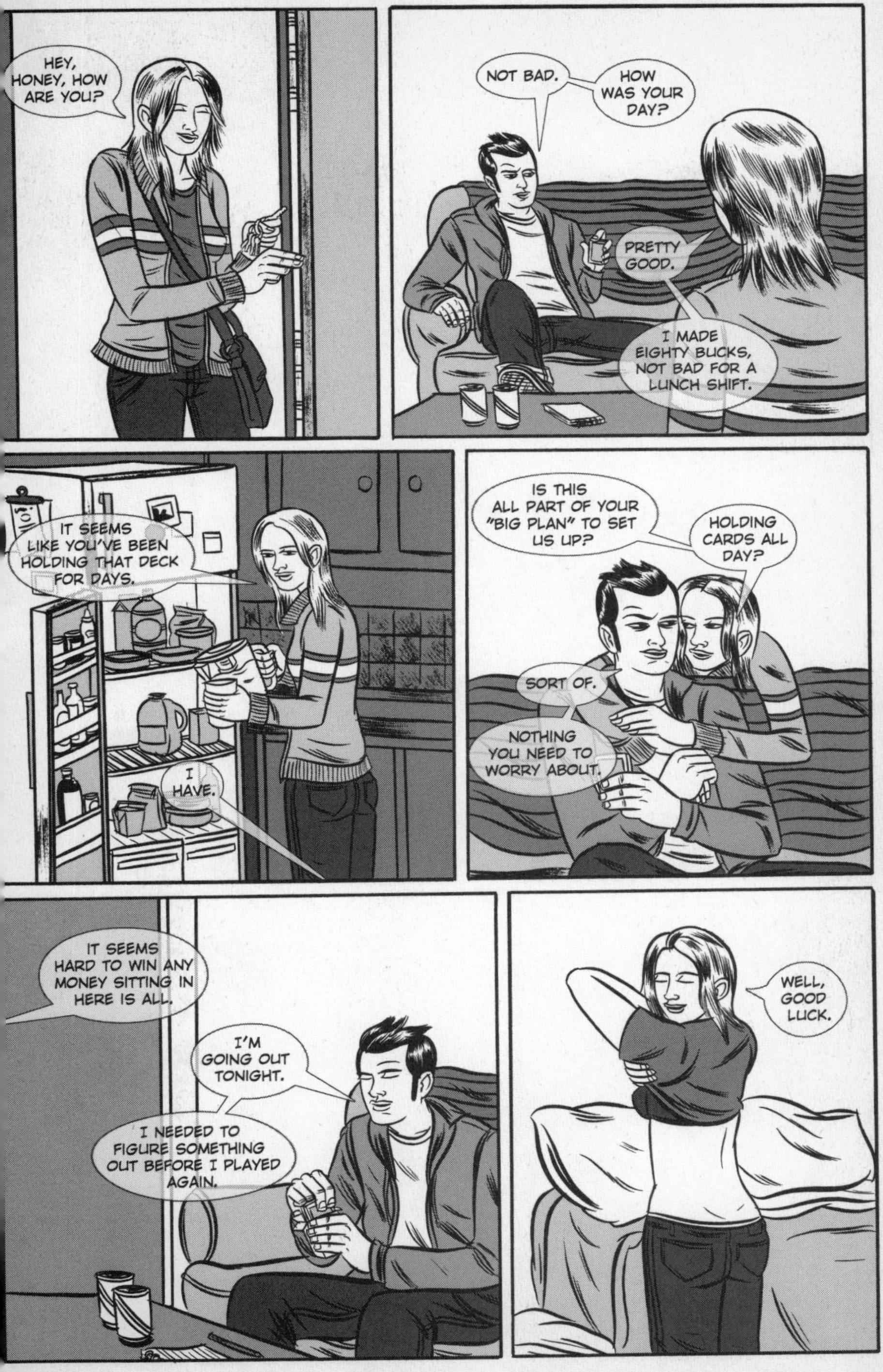
HEY, HONEY, HOW ARE YOU?
NOT BAD.
HOW WAS YOUR DAY?
PRETTY GOOD.
I MADE EIGHTY BUCKS, NOT BAD FOR A LUNCH SHIFT.
IT SEEMS LIKE YOU'VE BEEN HOLDING THAT DECK FOR DAYS.
I HAVE.
IS THIS ALL PART OF YOUR "BIG PLAN" TO SET US UP?
HOLDING CARDS ALL DAY?
SORT OF.
NOTHING YOU NEED TO WORRY ABOUT.
IT SEEMS HARD TO WIN ANY MONEY SITTING IN HERE IS ALL.
I'M GOING OUT TONIGHT.
I NEEDED TO FIGURE SOMETHING OUT BEFORE I PLAYED AGAIN.
WELL, GOOD LUCK.

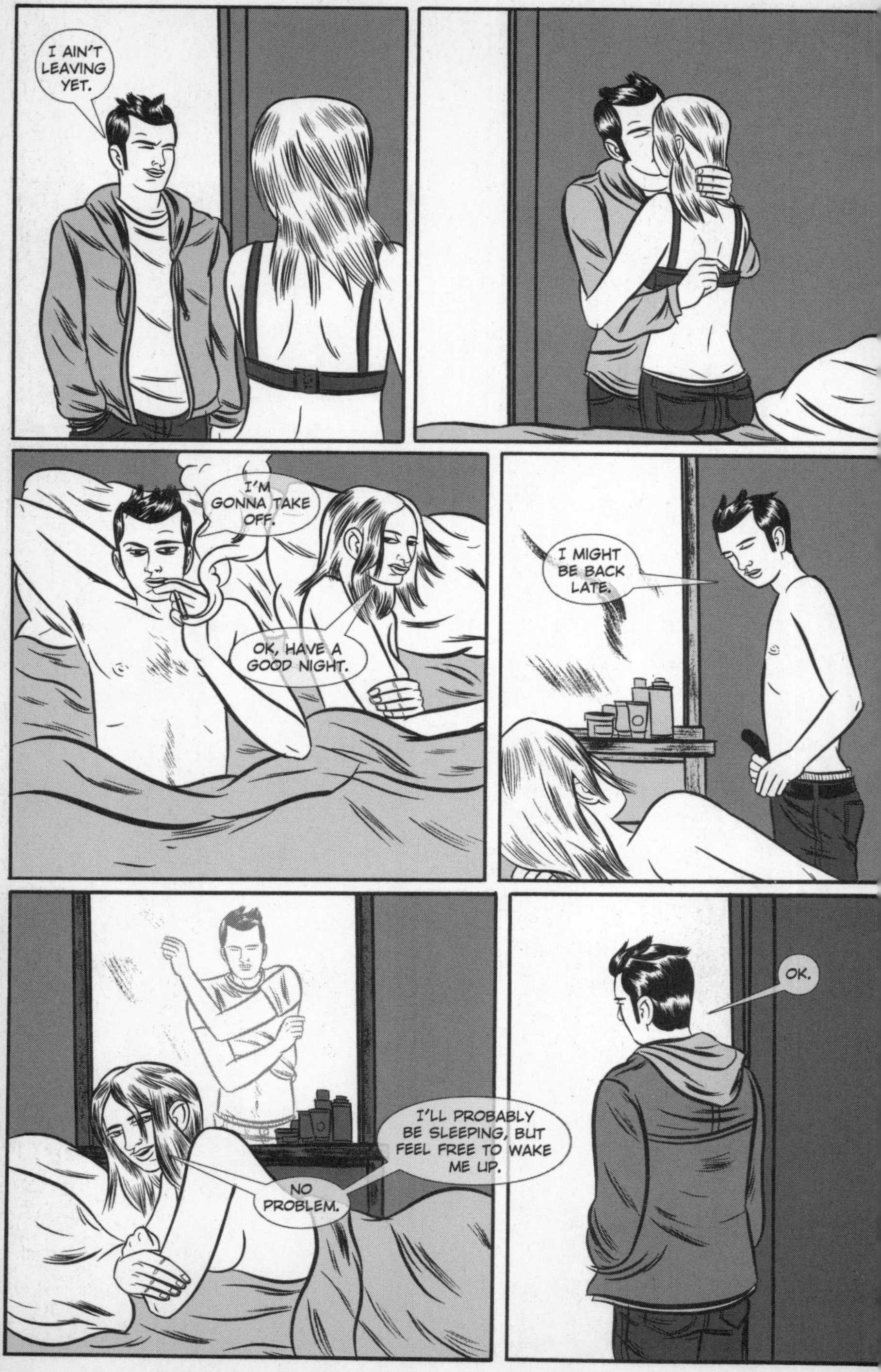
I AIN'T LEAVING YET.
I'M GONNA TAKE OFF.
OK, HAVE A GOOD NIGHT.
I MIGHT BE BACK LATE.
I'LL PROBABLY BE SLEEPING, BUT FEEL FREE TO WAKE ME UP.
NO PROBLEM.
OK.

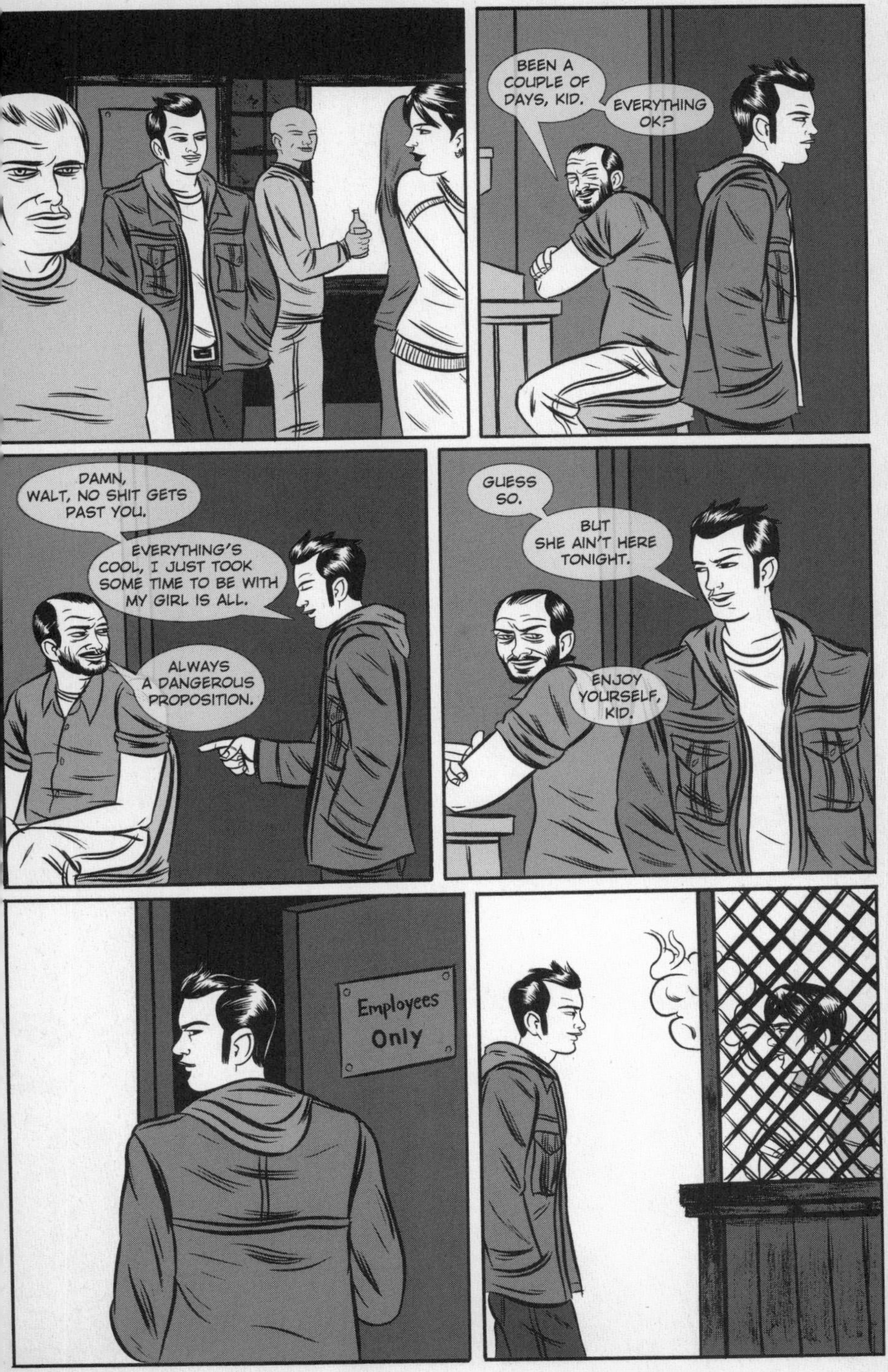
BEEN A COUPLE OF DAYS, KID.
EVERYTHING OK?
DAMN, WALT, NO SHIT GETS PAST YOU.
EVERYTHING'S COOL, I JUST TOOK SOME TIME TO BE WITH MY GIRL IS ALL.
ALWAYS A DANGEROUS PROPOSITION.
GUESS SO.
BUT SHE AIN'T HERE TONIGHT.
ENJOY YOURSELF, KID.
Employees Only

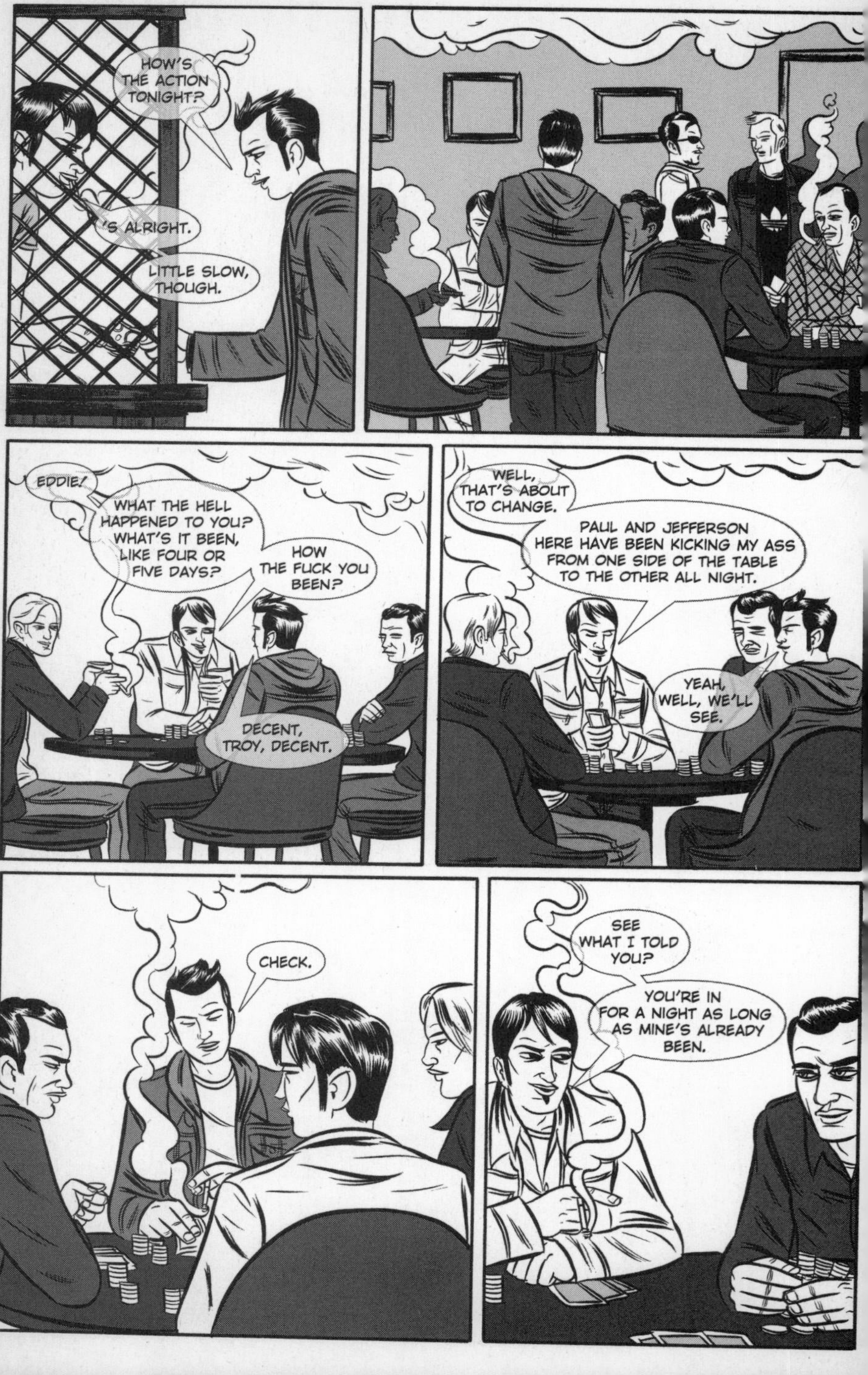
HOW'S THE ACTION TONIGHT?
'S ALRIGHT.
LITTLE SLOW, THOUGH.
EDDIE!
WHAT THE HELL HAPPENED TO YOU? WHAT'S IT BEEN, LIKE FOUR OR FIVE DAYS?
HOW THE FUCK YOU BEEN?
DECENT, TROY, DECENT.
WELL, THAT'S ABOUT TO CHANGE.
PAUL AND JEFFERSON HERE HAVE BEEN KICKING MY ASS FROM ONE SIDE OF THE TABLE TO THE OTHER ALL NIGHT.
YEAH, WELL, WE'LL SEE.
CHECK.
SEE WHAT I TOLD YOU?
YOU'RE IN FOR A NIGHT AS LONG AS MINE'S ALREADY BEEN.

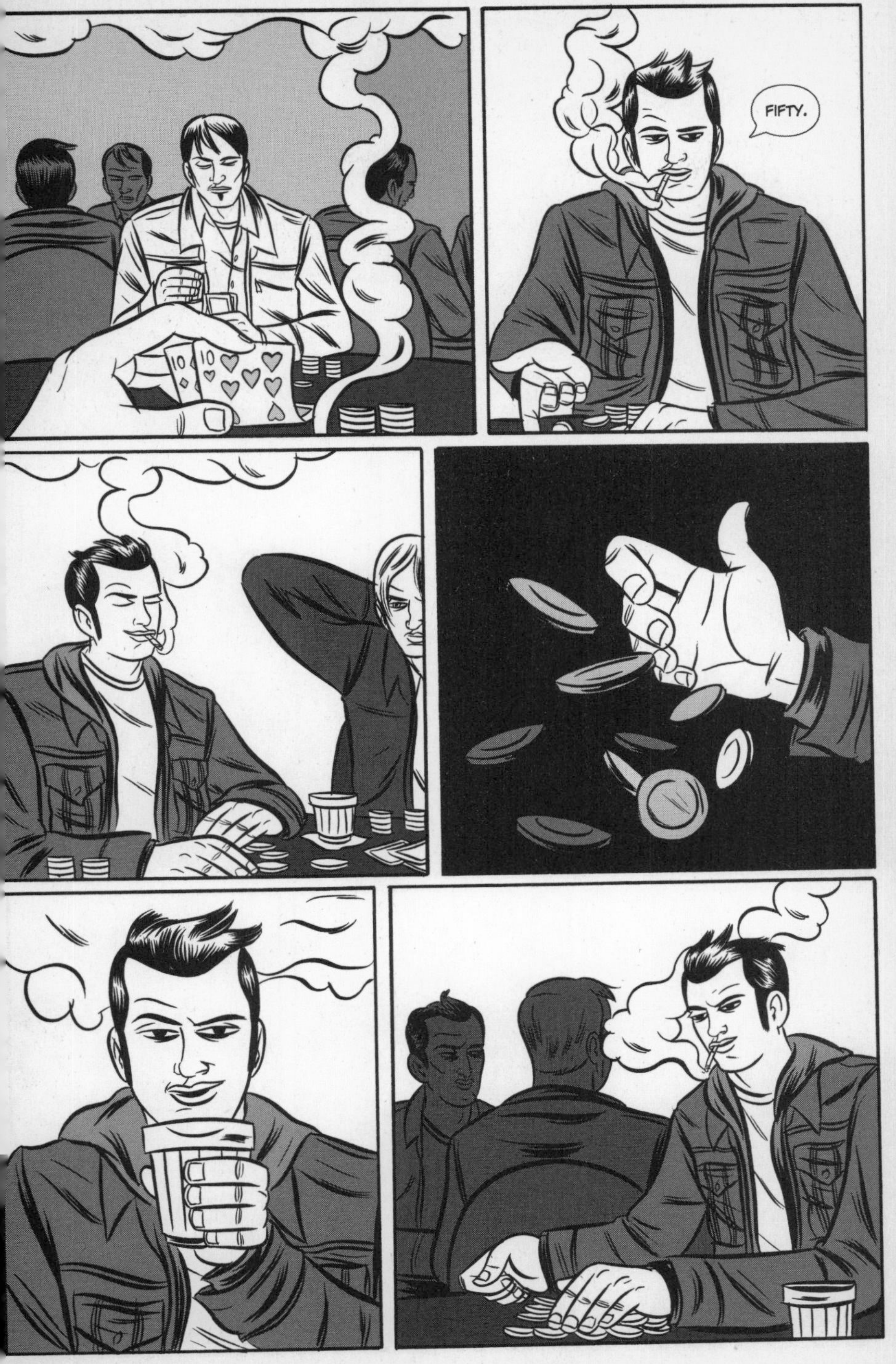
FIFTY.

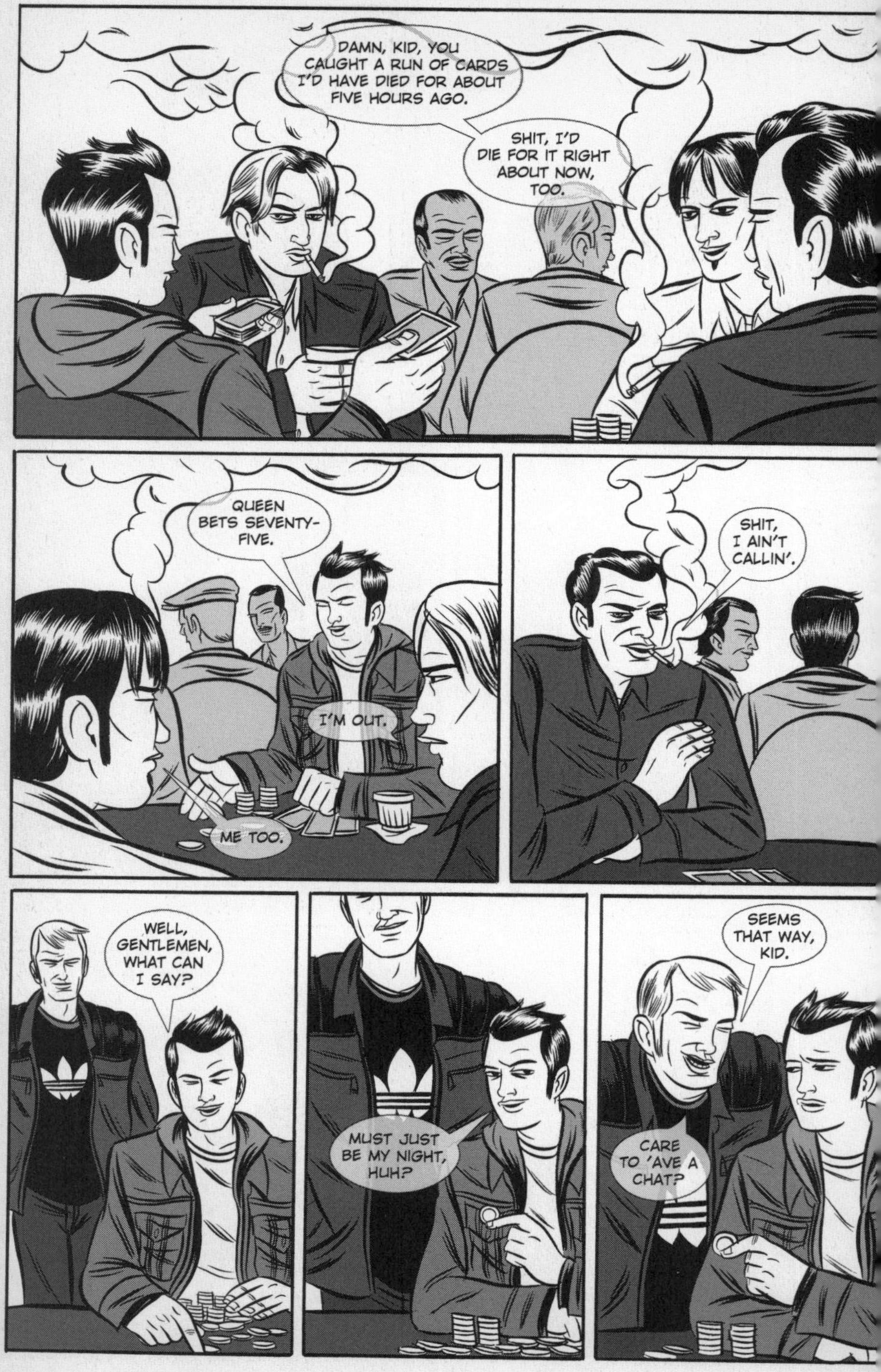
DAMN, KID, YOU CAUGHT A RUN OF CARDS I'D HAVE DIED FOR ABOUT FIVE HOURS AGO.
SHIT, I'D DIE FOR IT RIGHT ABOUT NOW, TOO.
QUEEN BETS SEVENTY-FIVE.
I'M OUT.
ME TOO.
SHIT, I AIN'T CALLIN'.
WELL, GENTLEMEN, WHAT CAN I SAY?
MUST JUST BE MY NIGHT, HUH?
SEEMS THAT WAY, KID.
CARE TO 'AVE A CHAT?

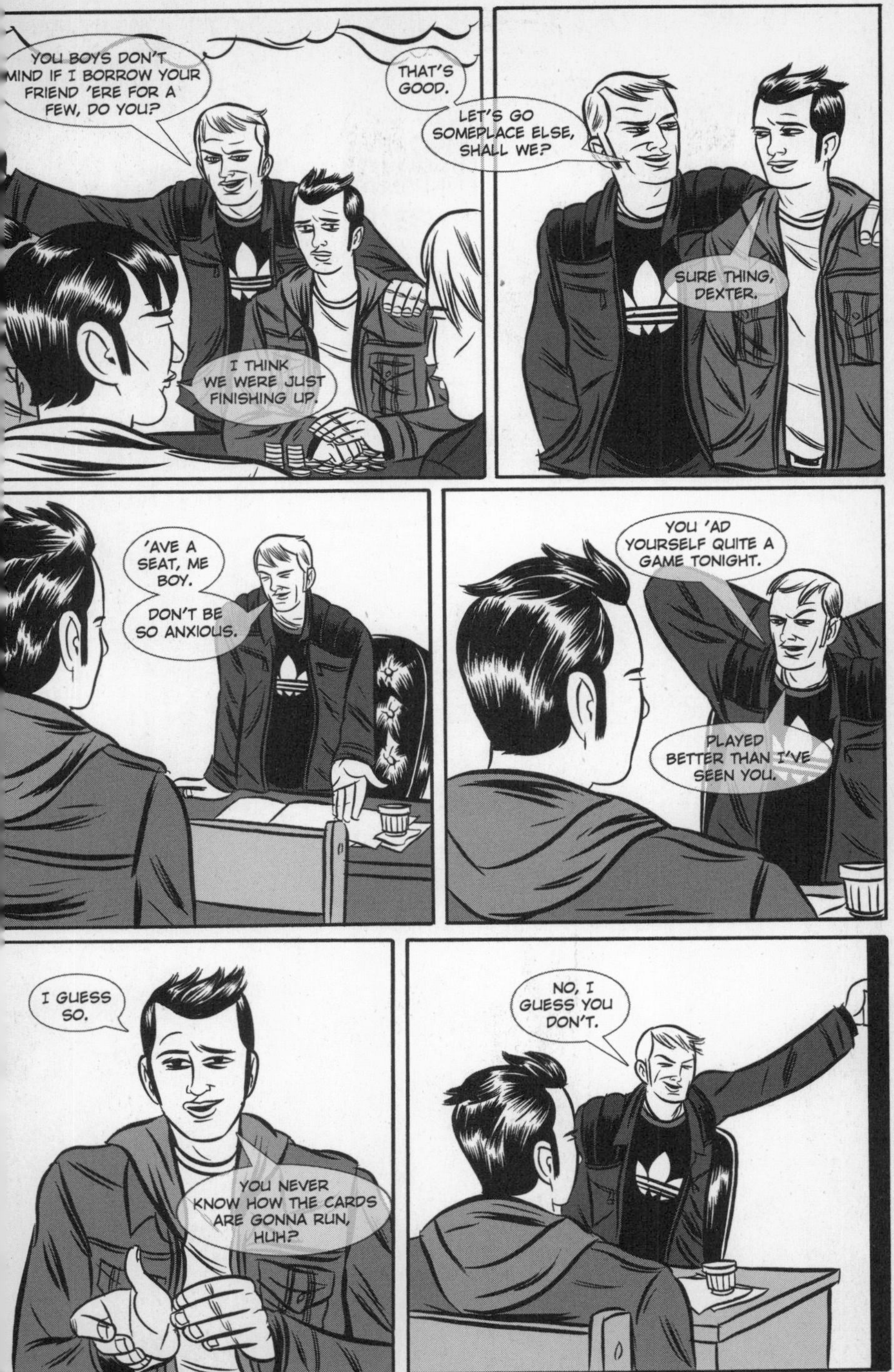
YOU BOYS DON'T MIND IF I BORROW YOUR FRIEND 'ERE FOR A FEW, DO YOU?
I THINK WE WERE JUST FINISHING UP.
THAT'S GOOD.
LET'S GO SOMEPLACE ELSE, SHALL WE?
SURE THING, DEXTER.
'AVE A SEAT, ME BOY.
DON'T BE SO ANXIOUS.
YOU 'AD YOURSELF QUITE A GAME TONIGHT.
PLAYED BETTER THAN I'VE SEEN YOU.
I GUESS SO.
YOU NEVER KNOW HOW THE CARDS ARE GONNA RUN, HUH?
NO, I GUESS YOU DON'T.

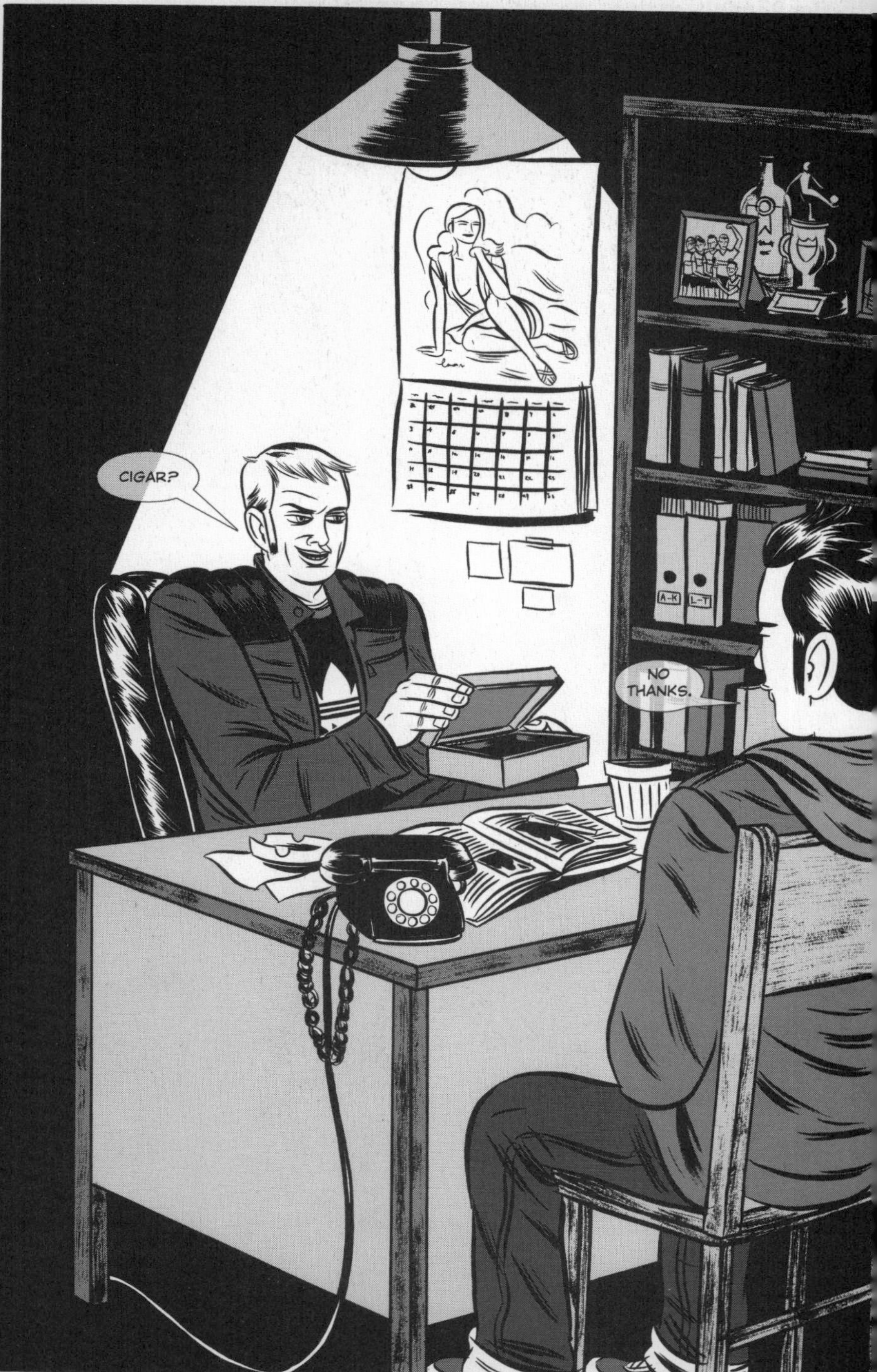
CIGAR?
NO THANKS.

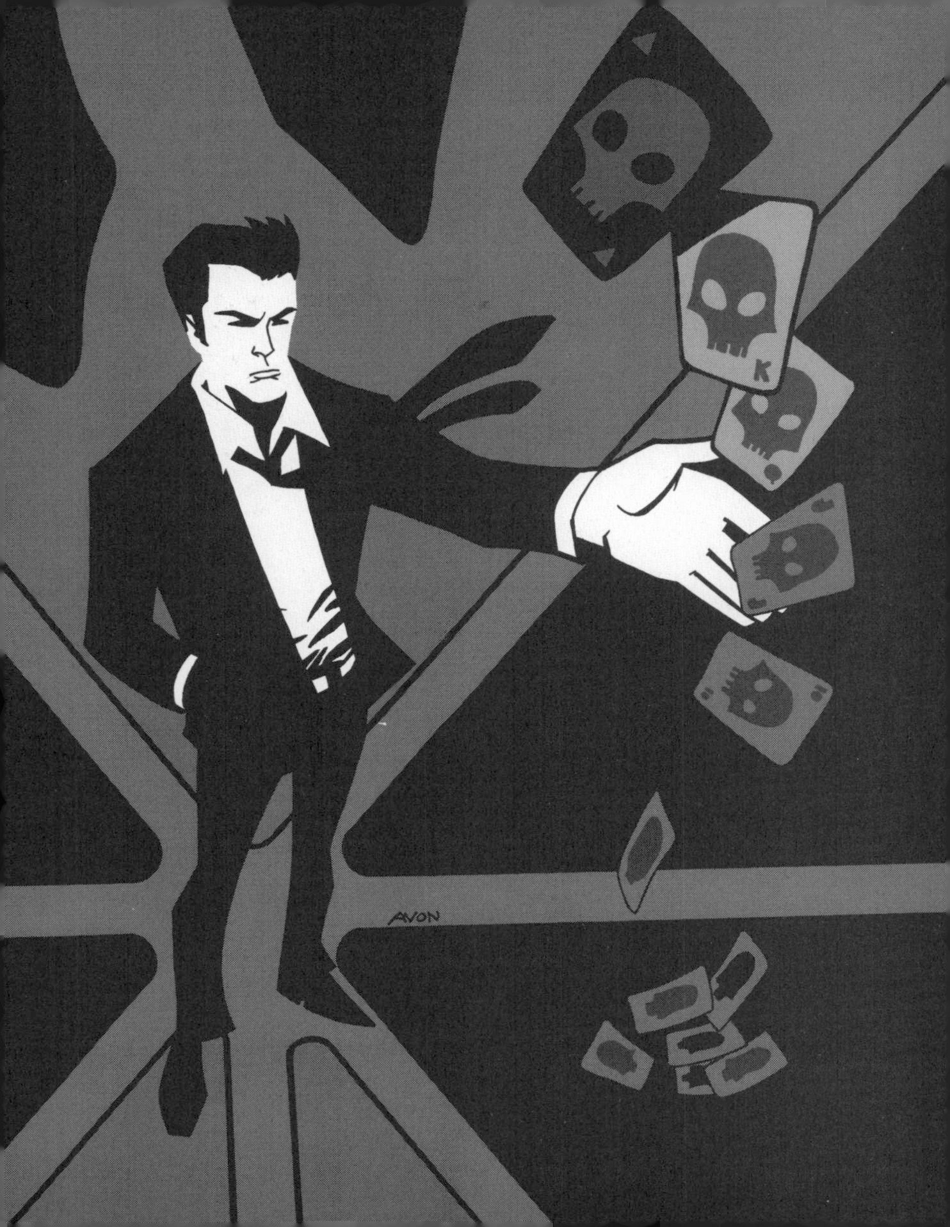
K
AVON

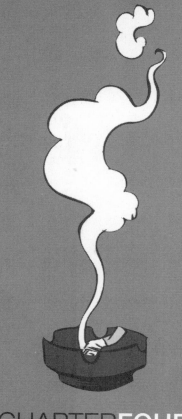

CHAPTER**FOUR**

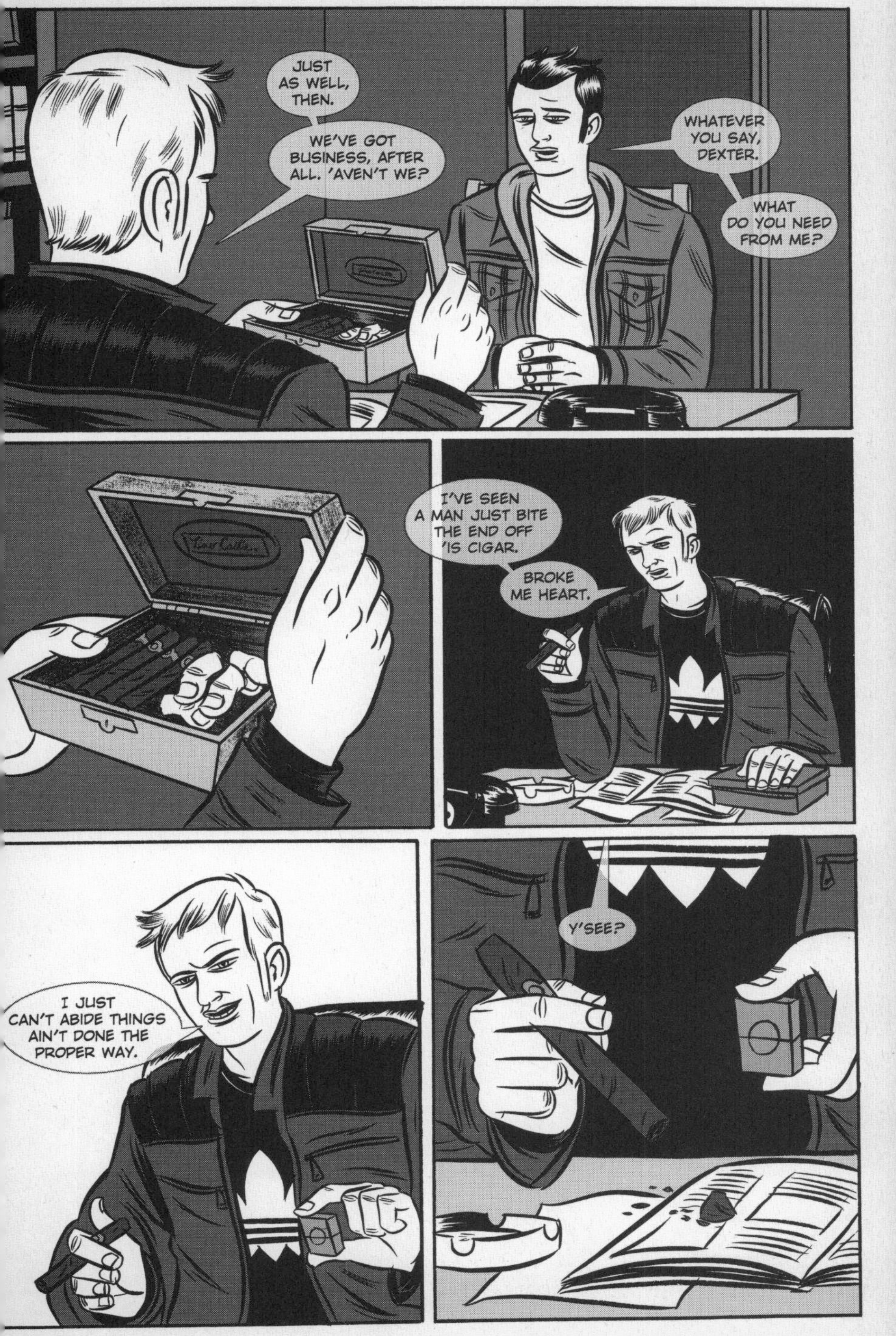

JUST AS WELL, THEN.
WE'VE GOT BUSINESS, AFTER ALL. 'AVEN'T WE?
WHATEVER YOU SAY, DEXTER.
WHAT DO YOU NEED FROM ME?
I'VE SEEN A MAN JUST BITE THE END OFF 'IS CIGAR.
BROKE ME HEART.
I JUST CAN'T ABIDE THINGS AIN'T DONE THE PROPER WAY.
Y'SEE?

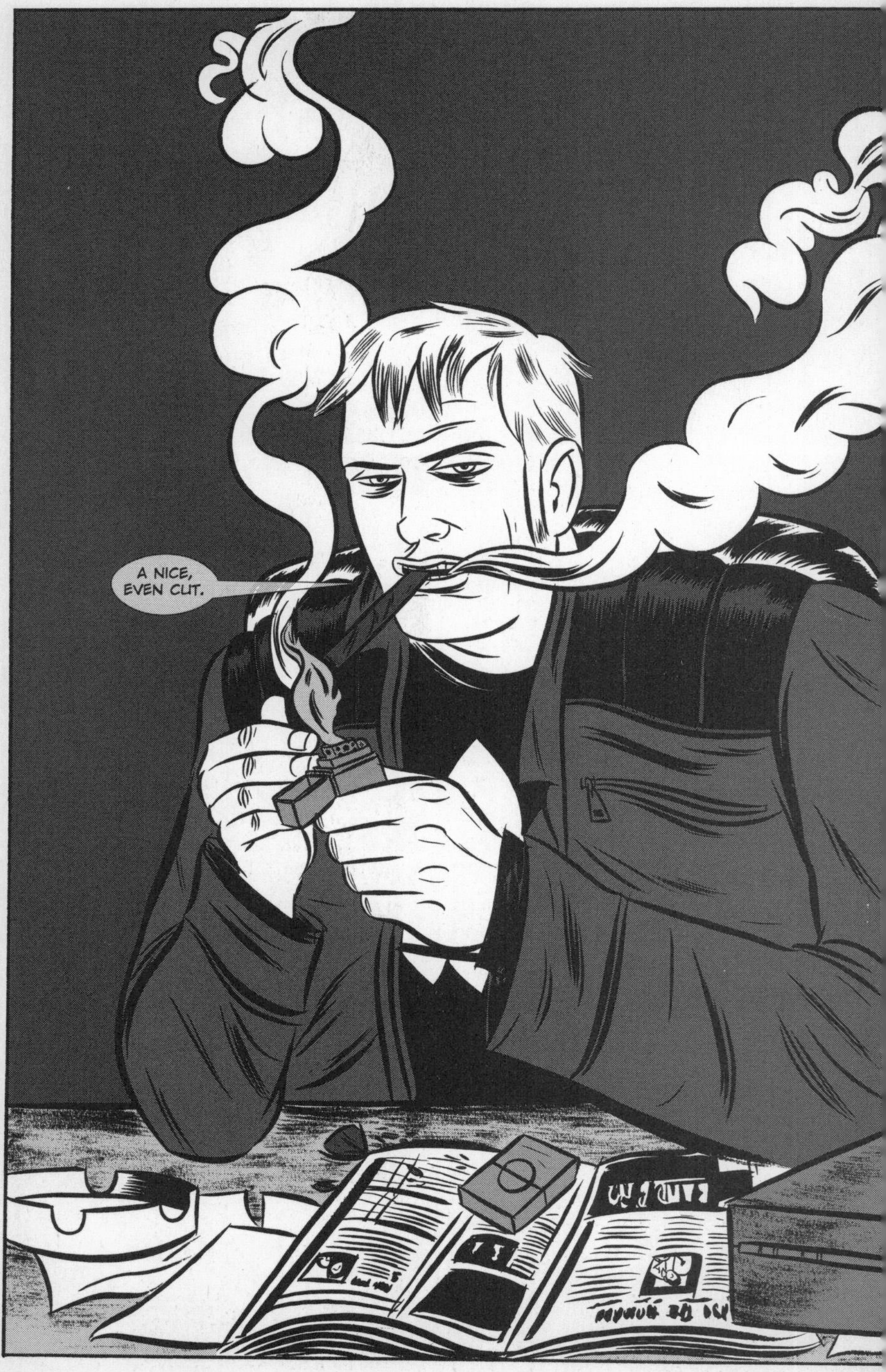
A NICE, EVEN CUT.

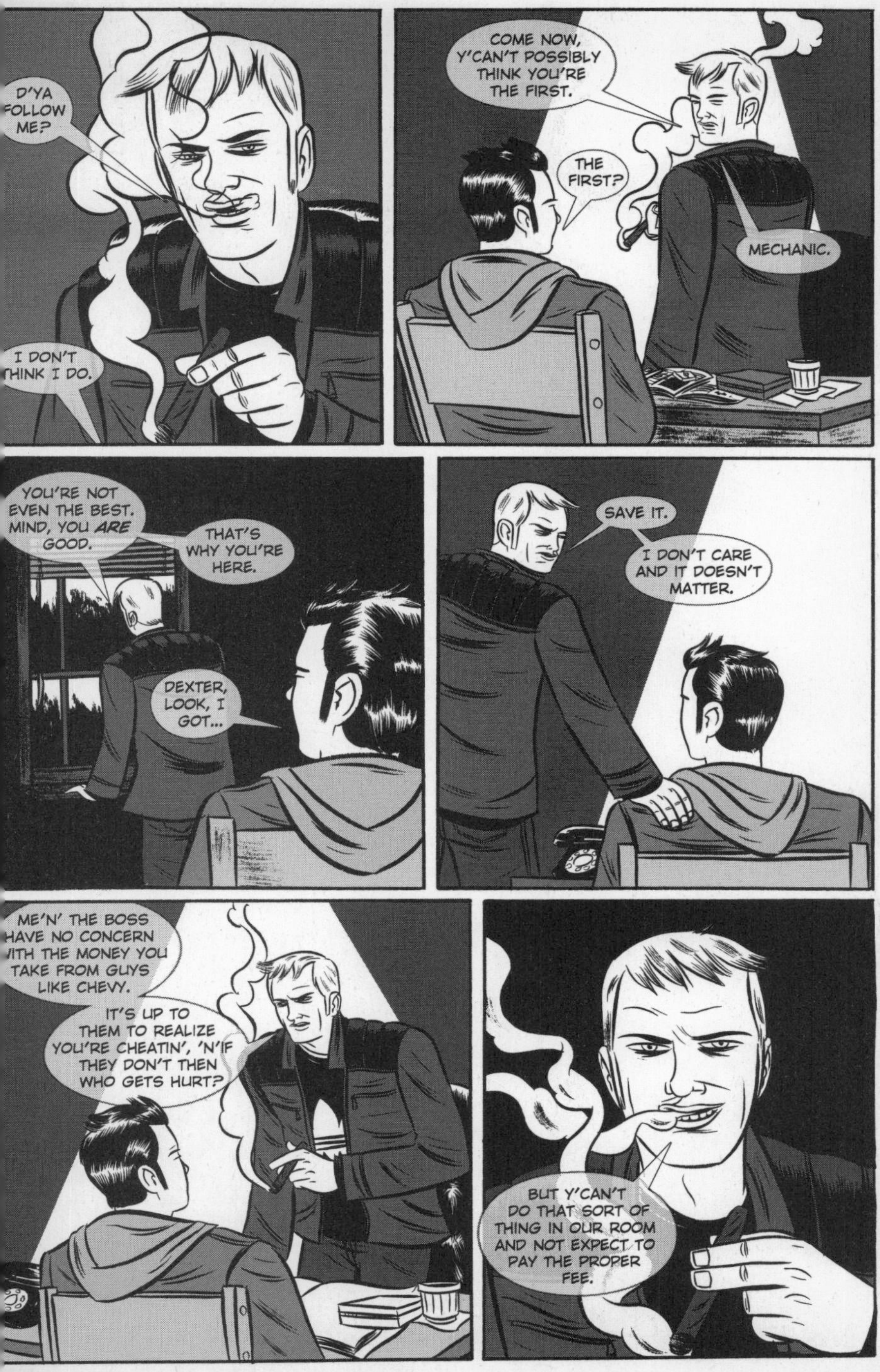
D'YA FOLLOW ME?
I DON'T THINK I DO.
COME NOW, Y'CAN'T POSSIBLY THINK YOU'RE THE FIRST.
THE FIRST?
MECHANIC.
YOU'RE NOT EVEN THE BEST. MIND, YOU *ARE* GOOD.
THAT'S WHY YOU'RE HERE.
DEXTER, LOOK, I GOT...
SAVE IT.
I DON'T CARE AND IT DOESN'T MATTER.
ME'N' THE BOSS HAVE NO CONCERN WITH THE MONEY YOU TAKE FROM GUYS LIKE CHEVY.
IT'S UP TO THEM TO REALIZE YOU'RE CHEATIN', 'N'IF THEY DON'T THEN WHO GETS HURT?
BUT Y'CAN'T DO THAT SORT OF THING IN OUR ROOM AND NOT EXPECT TO PAY THE PROPER FEE.

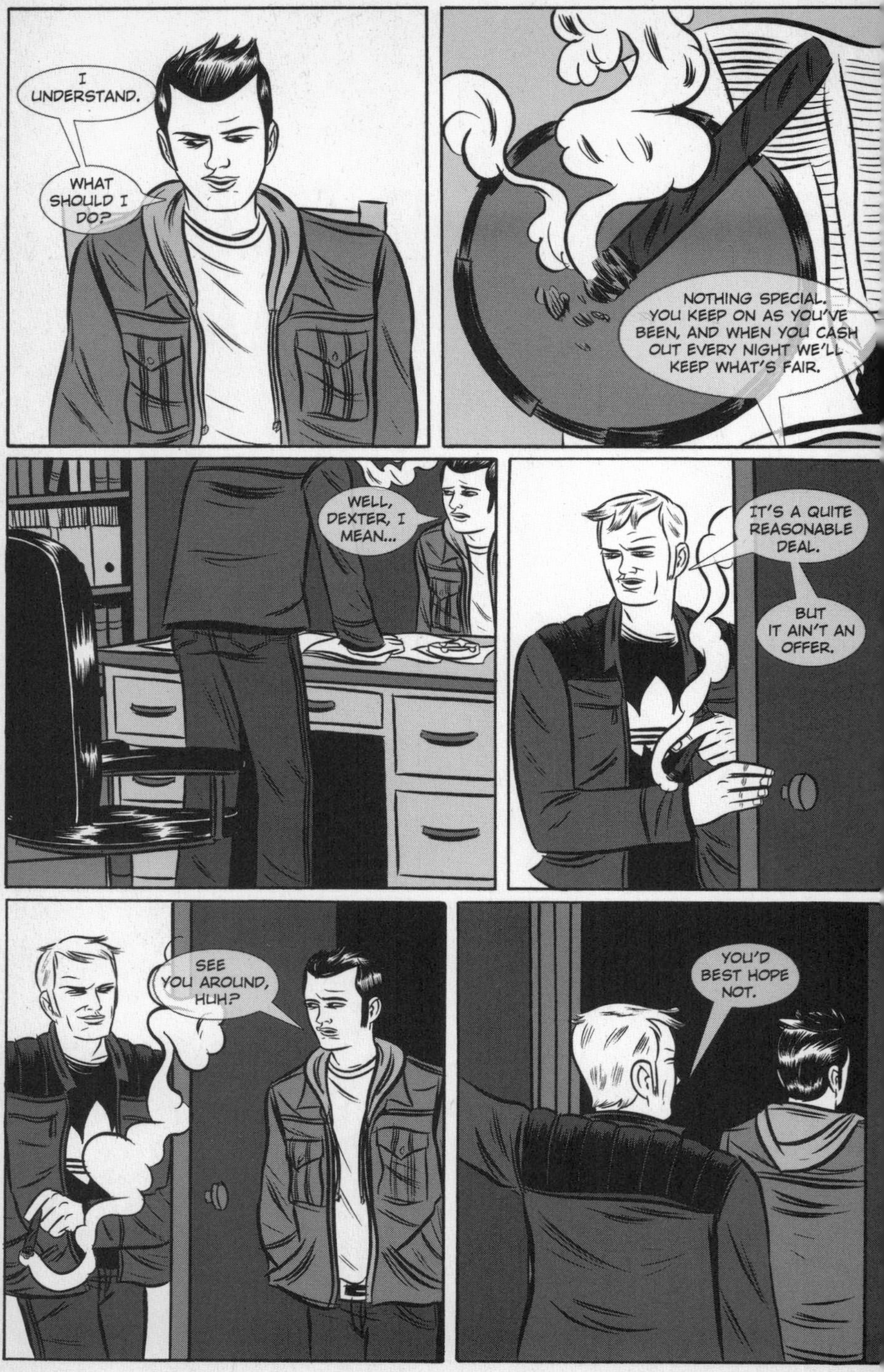
I UNDERSTAND.
WHAT SHOULD I DO?
NOTHING SPECIAL. YOU KEEP ON AS YOU'VE BEEN, AND WHEN YOU CASH OUT EVERY NIGHT WE'LL KEEP WHAT'S FAIR.
WELL, DEXTER, I MEAN...
IT'S A QUITE REASONABLE DEAL.
BUT IT AIN'T AN OFFER.
SEE YOU AROUND, HUH?
YOU'D BEST HOPE NOT.

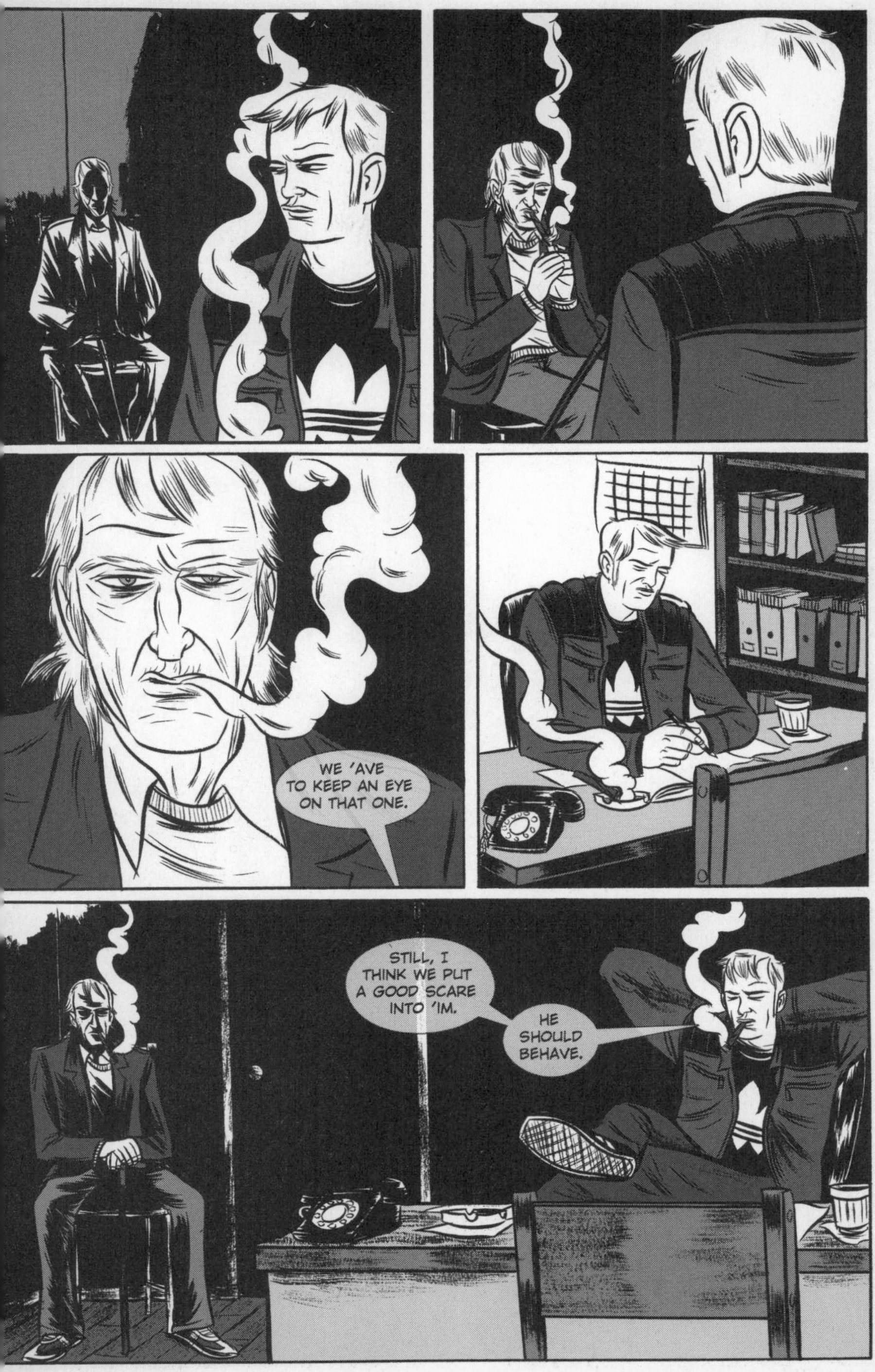
WE 'AVE TO KEEP AN EYE ON THAT ONE.
STILL, I THINK WE PUT A GOOD SCARE INTO 'IM.
HE SHOULD BEHAVE.

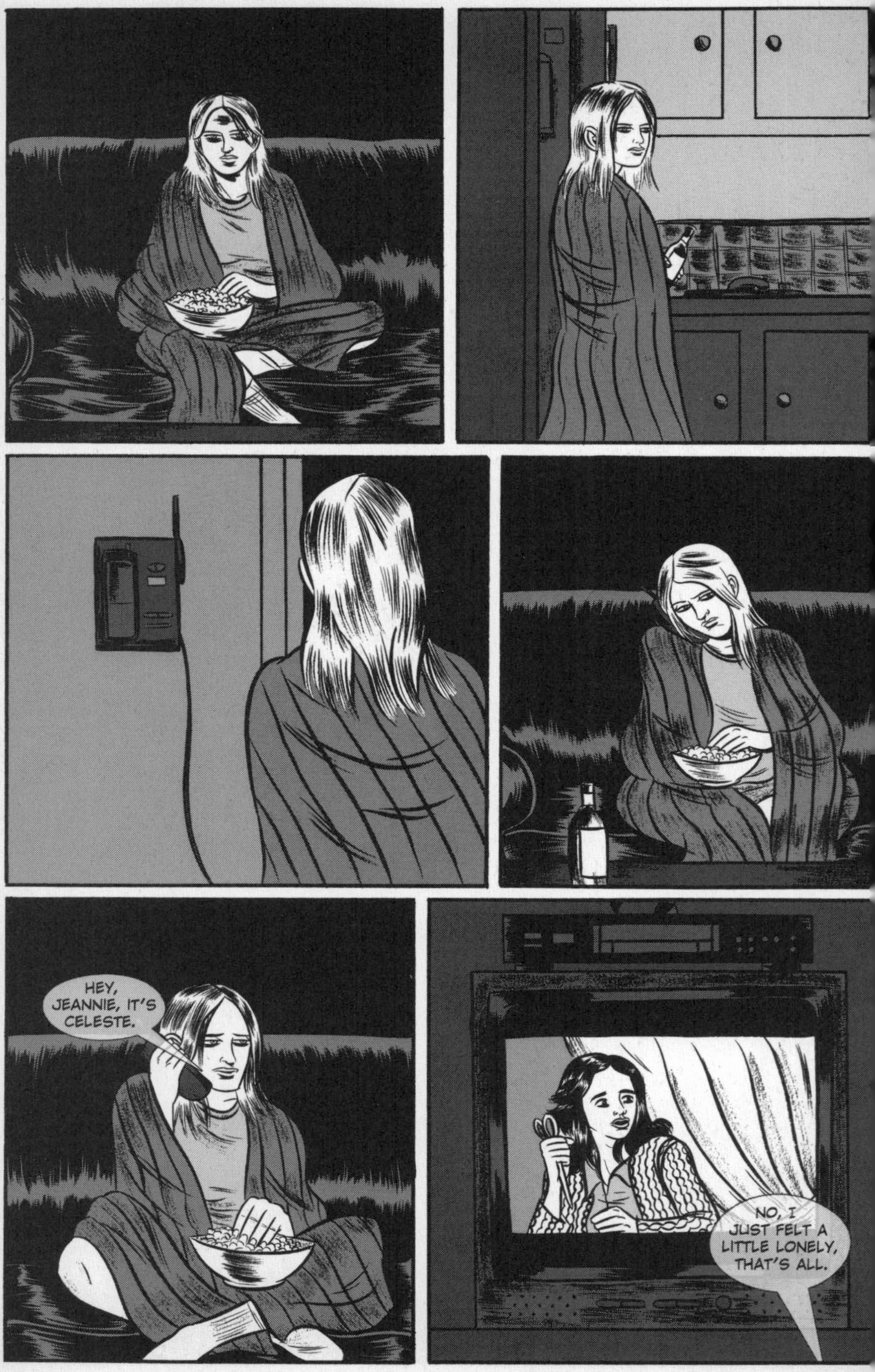
HEY, JEANNIE, IT'S CELESTE.
NO, I JUST FELT A LITTLE LONELY, THAT'S ALL.

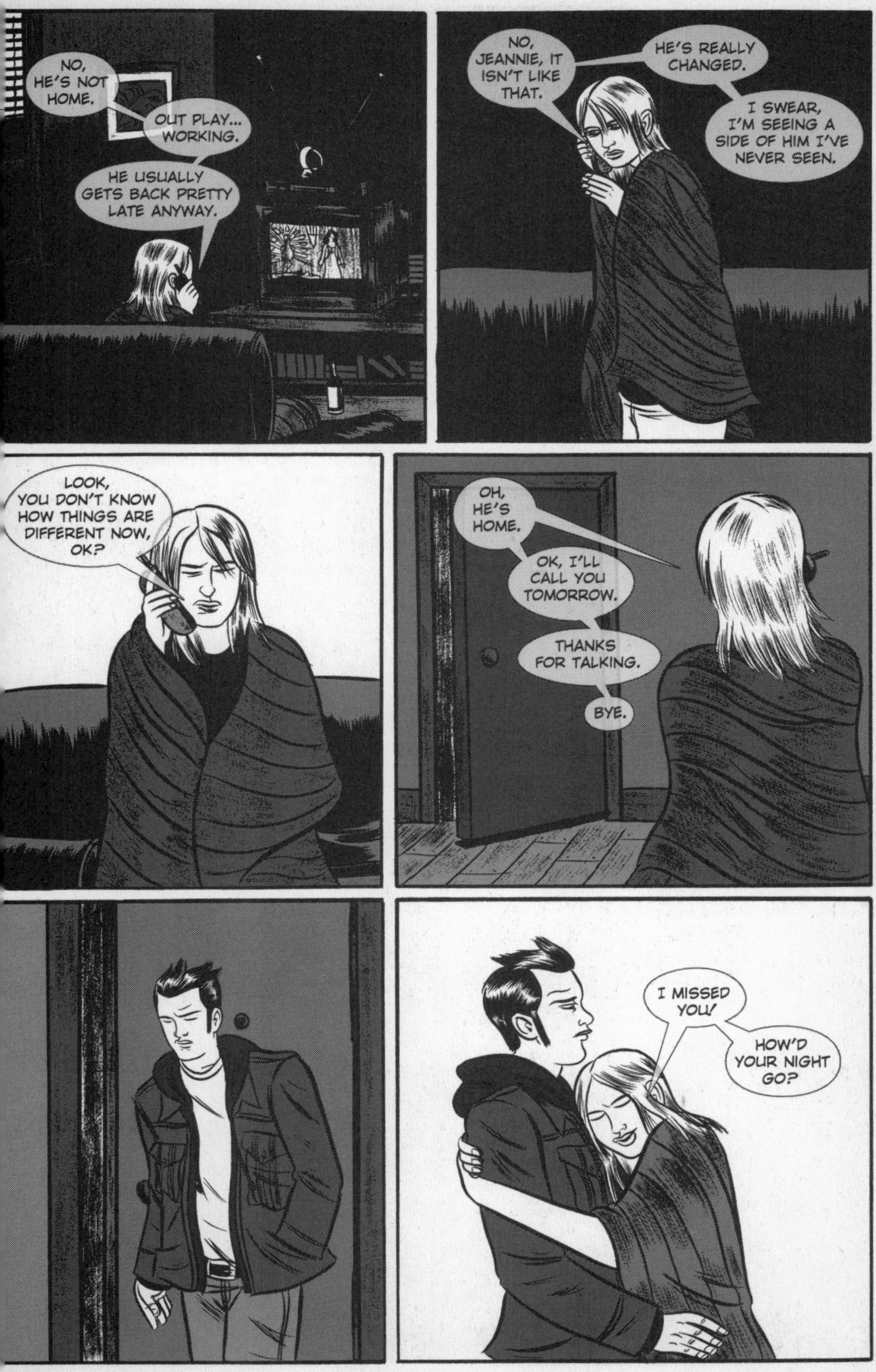
NO, HE'S NOT HOME.
OUT PLAY... WORKING.
HE USUALLY GETS BACK PRETTY LATE ANYWAY.
NO, JEANNIE, IT ISN'T LIKE THAT.
HE'S REALLY CHANGED.
I SWEAR, I'M SEEING A SIDE OF HIM I'VE NEVER SEEN.
LOOK, YOU DON'T KNOW HOW THINGS ARE DIFFERENT NOW, OK?
OH, HE'S HOME.
OK, I'LL CALL YOU TOMORROW.
THANKS FOR TALKING.
BYE.
I MISSED YOU!
HOW'D YOUR NIGHT GO?

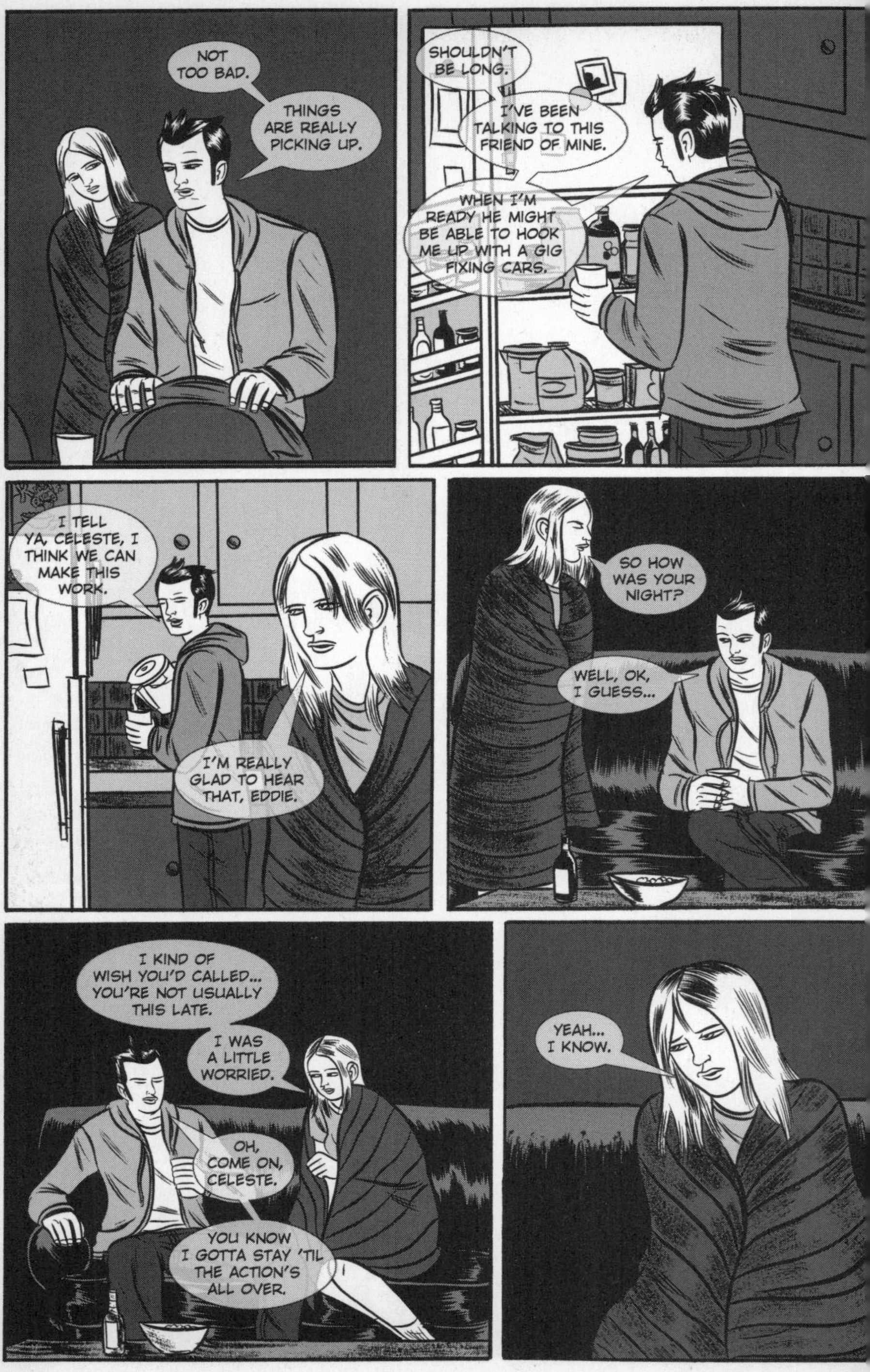
NOT TOO BAD.
THINGS ARE REALLY PICKING UP.
SHOULDN'T BE LONG.
I'VE BEEN TALKING TO THIS FRIEND OF MINE.
WHEN I'M READY HE MIGHT BE ABLE TO HOOK ME UP WITH A GIG FIXING CARS.
I TELL YA, CELESTE, I THINK WE CAN MAKE THIS WORK.
I'M REALLY GLAD TO HEAR THAT, EDDIE.
SO HOW WAS YOUR NIGHT?
WELL, OK, I GUESS...
I KIND OF WISH YOU'D CALLED... YOU'RE NOT USUALLY THIS LATE.
I WAS A LITTLE WORRIED.
OH, COME ON, CELESTE.
YOU KNOW I GOTTA STAY 'TIL THE ACTION'S ALL OVER.
YEAH... I KNOW.

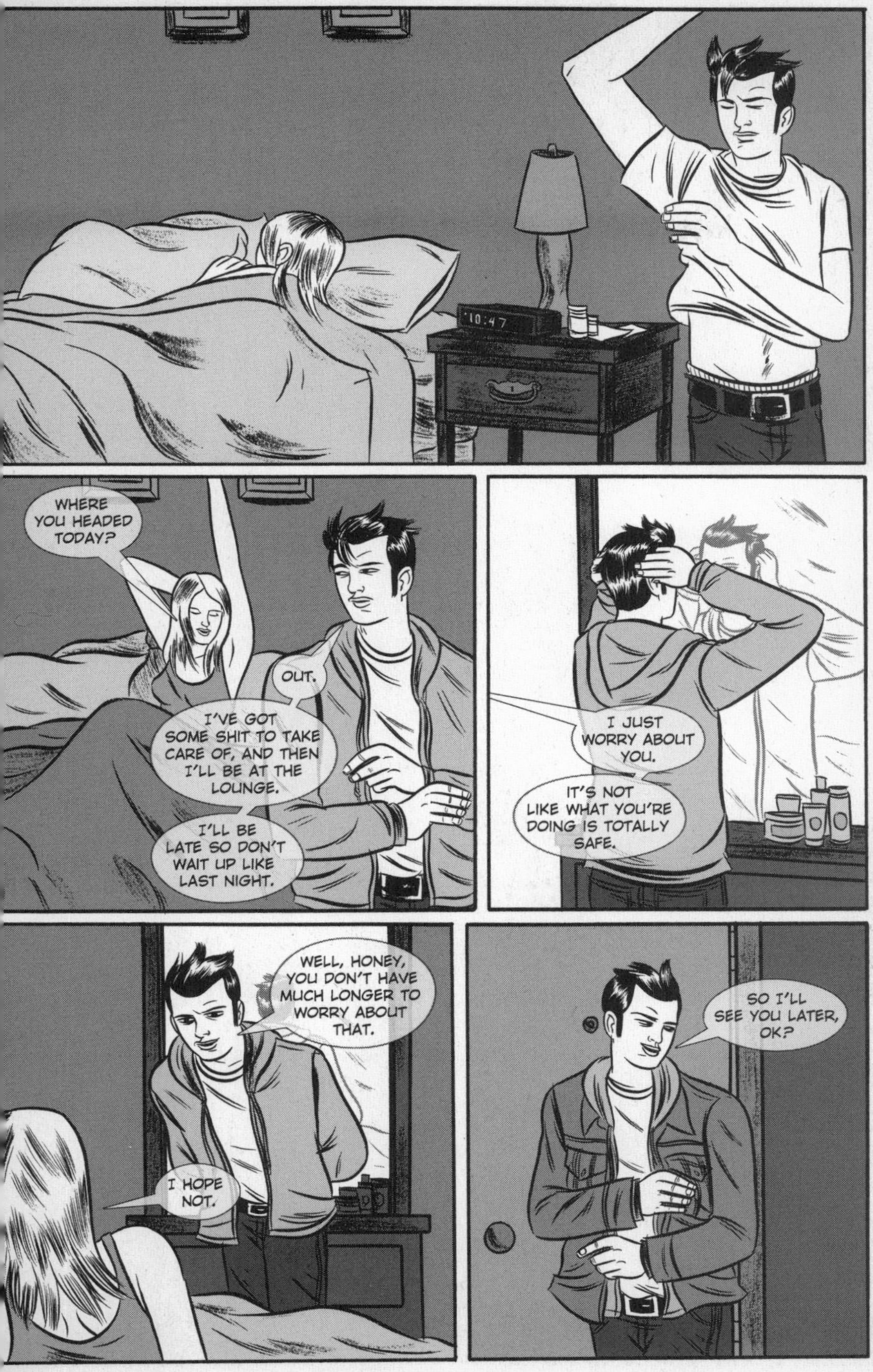
WHERE YOU HEADED TODAY?
OUT.
I'VE GOT SOME SHIT TO TAKE CARE OF, AND THEN I'LL BE AT THE LOUNGE.
I'LL BE LATE SO DON'T WAIT UP LIKE LAST NIGHT.
I JUST WORRY ABOUT YOU.
IT'S NOT LIKE WHAT YOU'RE DOING IS TOTALLY SAFE.
WELL, HONEY, YOU DON'T HAVE MUCH LONGER TO WORRY ABOUT THAT.
I HOPE NOT.
SO I'LL SEE YOU LATER, OK?

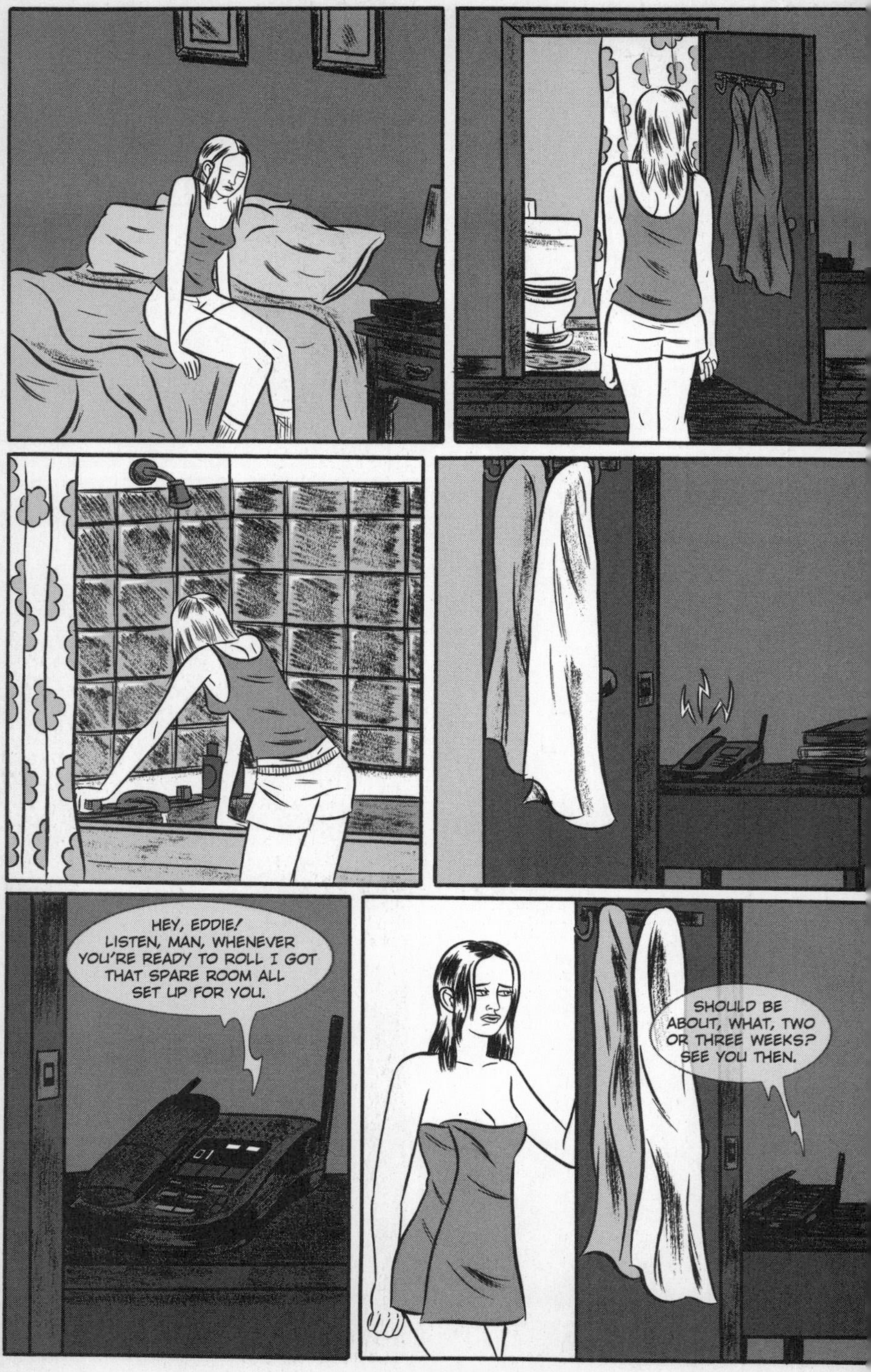
HEY, EDDIE! LISTEN, MAN, WHENEVER YOU'RE READY TO ROLL I GOT THAT SPARE ROOM ALL SET UP FOR YOU.
SHOULD BE ABOUT, WHAT, TWO OR THREE WEEKS? SEE YOU THEN.

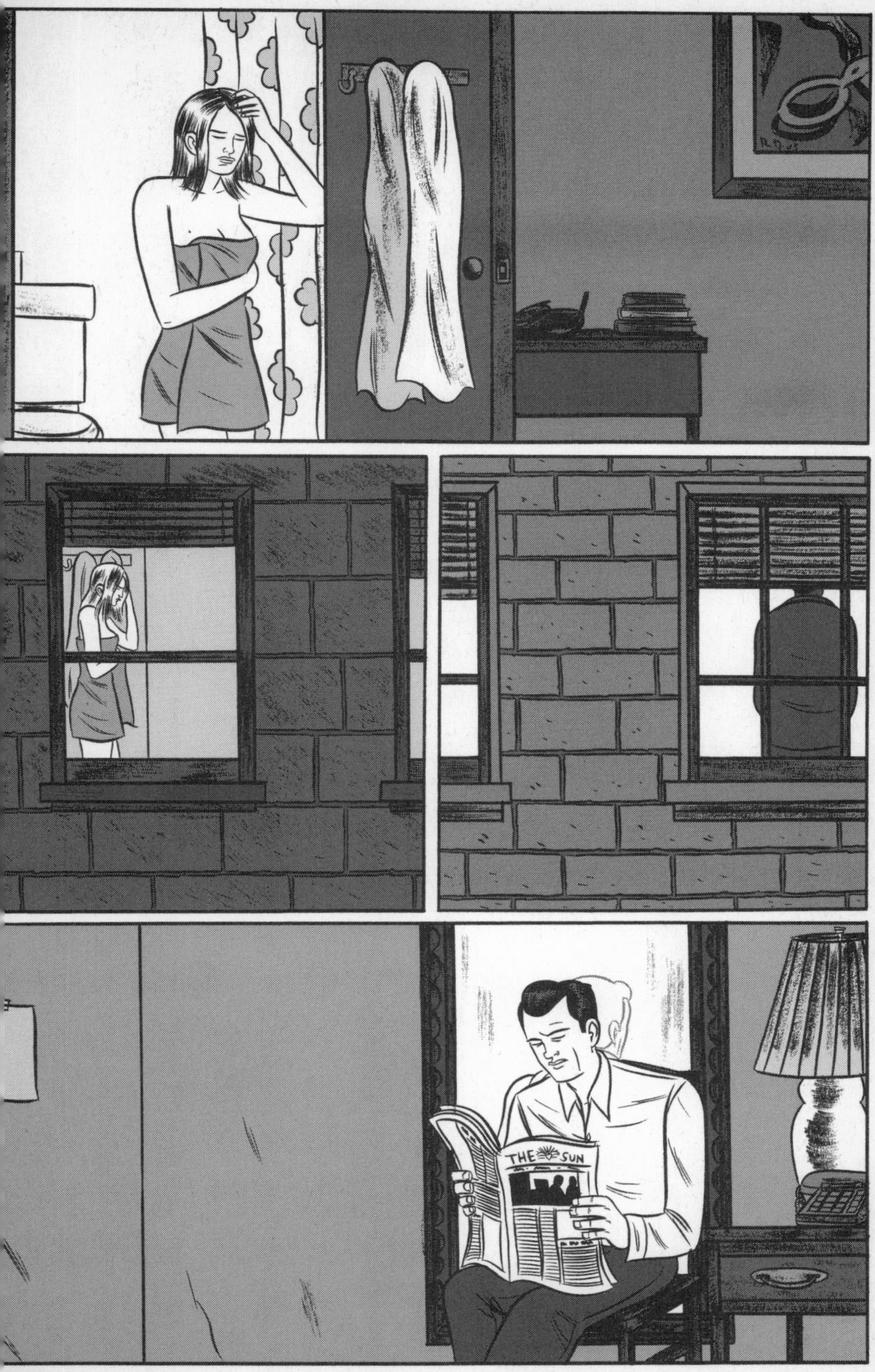
THE SUN

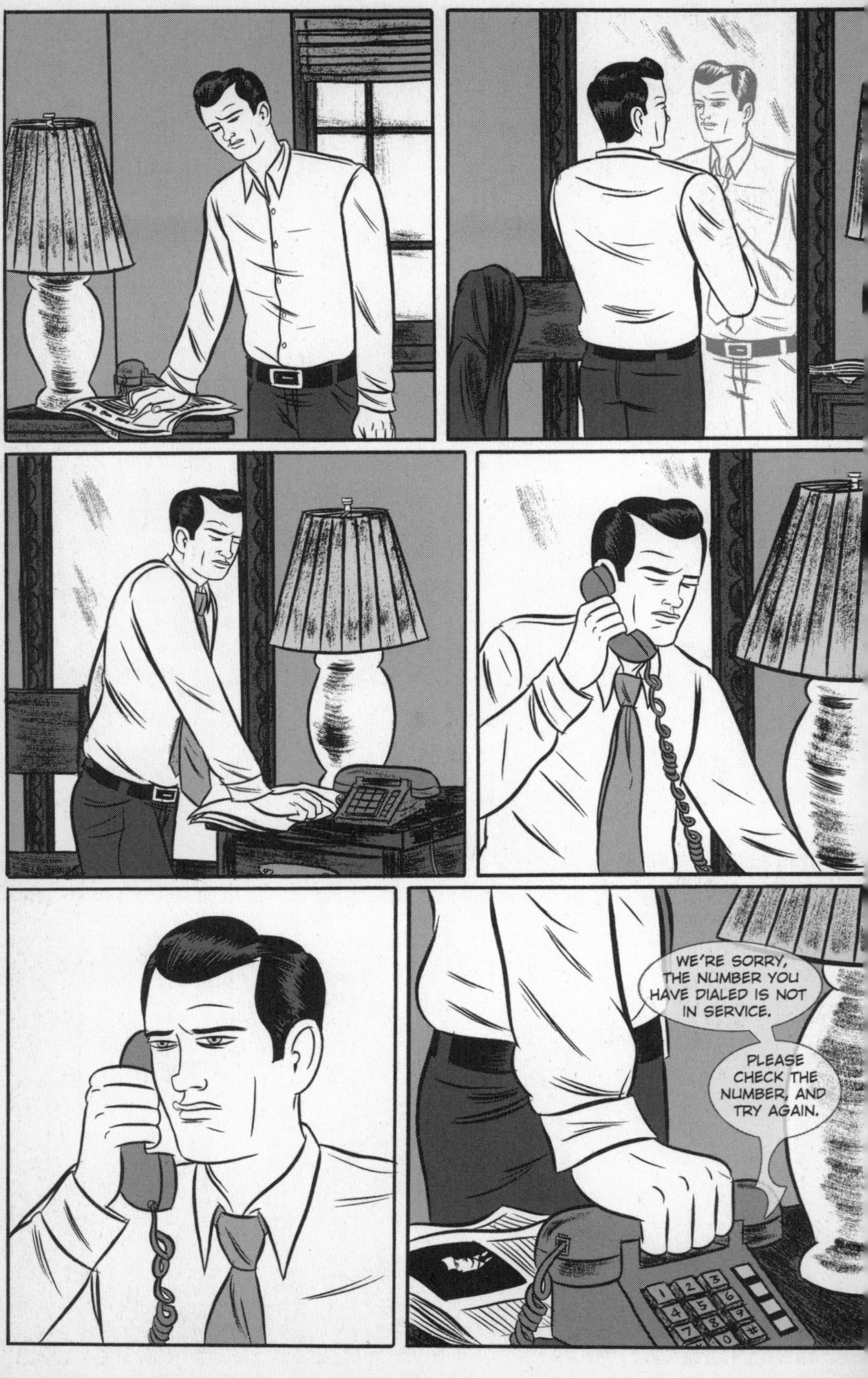
WE'RE SORRY, THE NUMBER YOU HAVE DIALED IS NOT IN SERVICE.
PLEASE CHECK THE NUMBER, AND TRY AGAIN.

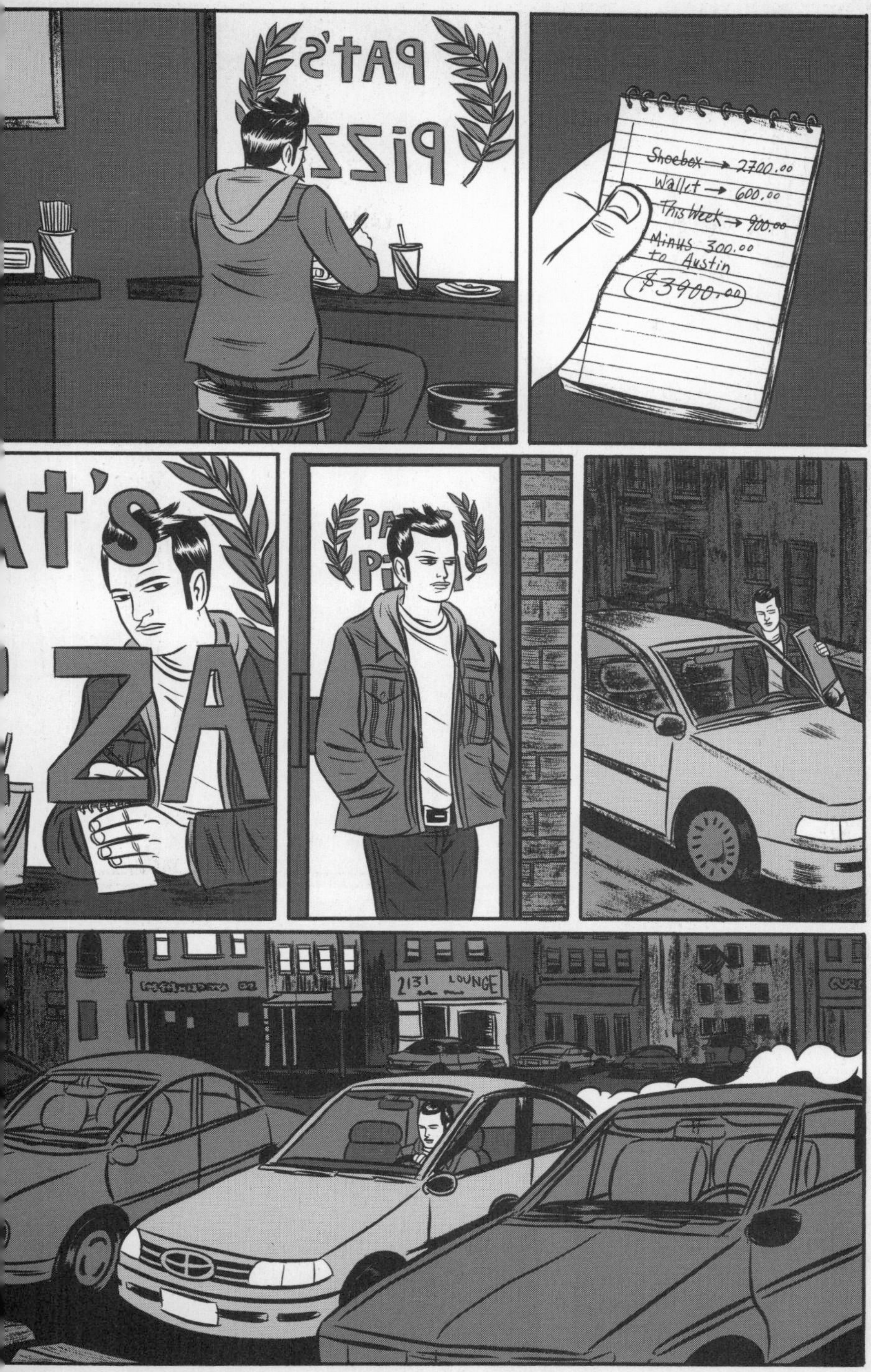
Shoebox → 2700.00
Wallet → 600.00
This Week → 900.00
Minus 300.00
to Austin
$3900.00
2131 LOUNGE

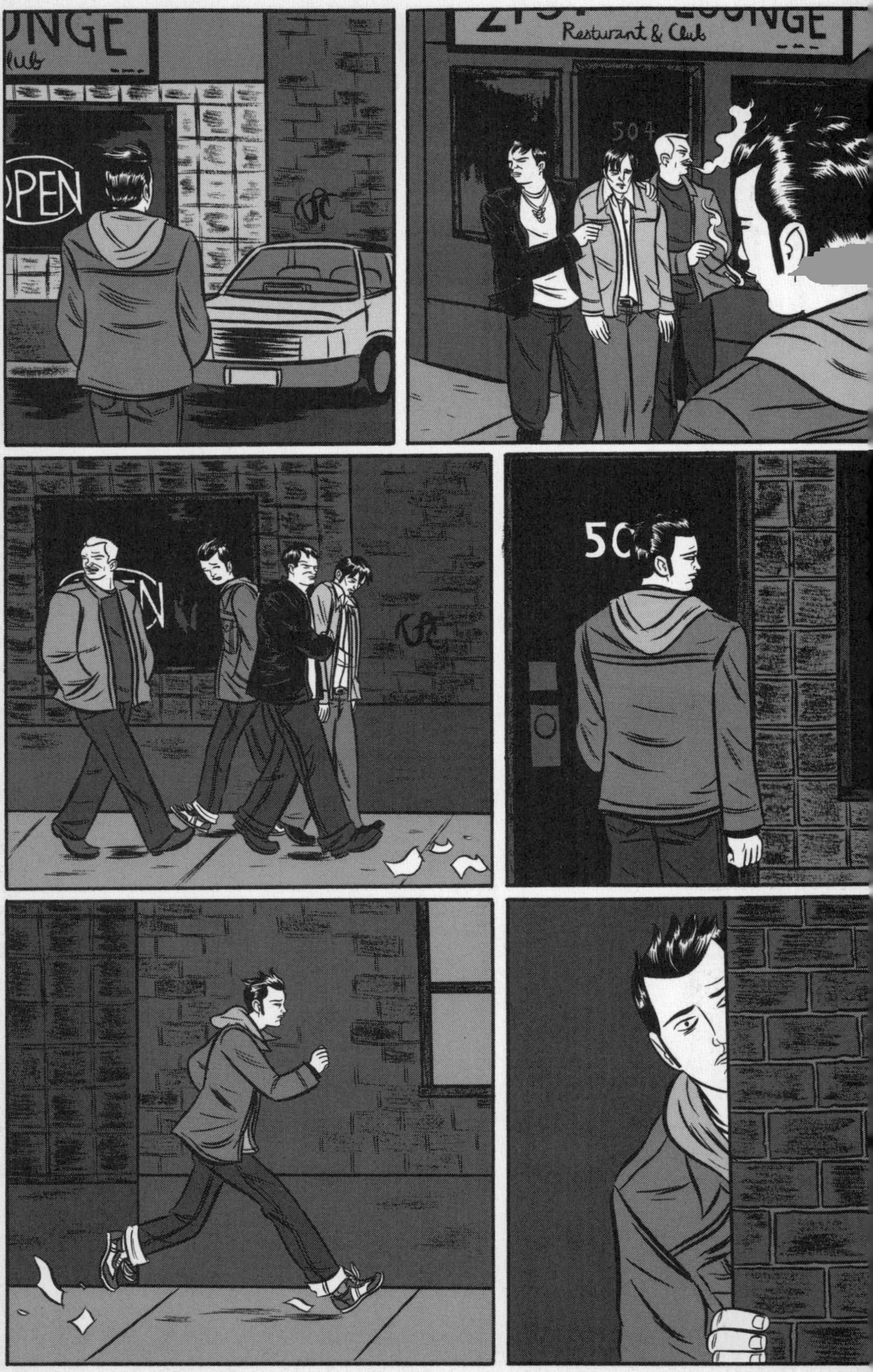

UNGE
lub
OPEN
LOUNGE
Resturant & Club
504
50

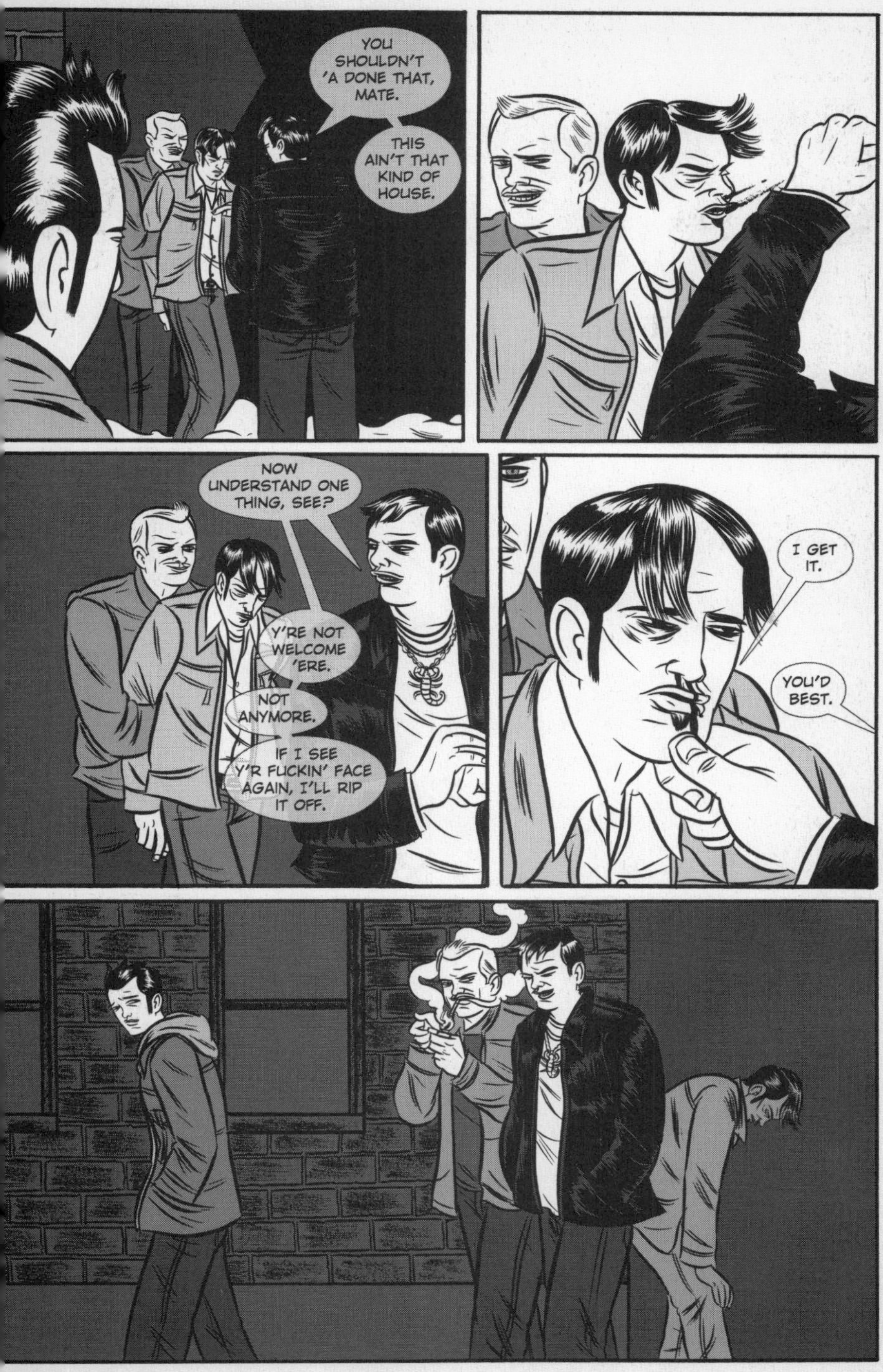
YOU SHOULDN'T 'A DONE THAT, MATE.
THIS AIN'T THAT KIND OF HOUSE.
NOW UNDERSTAND ONE THING, SEE?
Y'RE NOT WELCOME 'ERE.
NOT ANYMORE.
IF I SEE Y'R FUCKIN' FACE AGAIN, I'LL RIP IT OFF.
I GET IT.
YOU'D BEST.

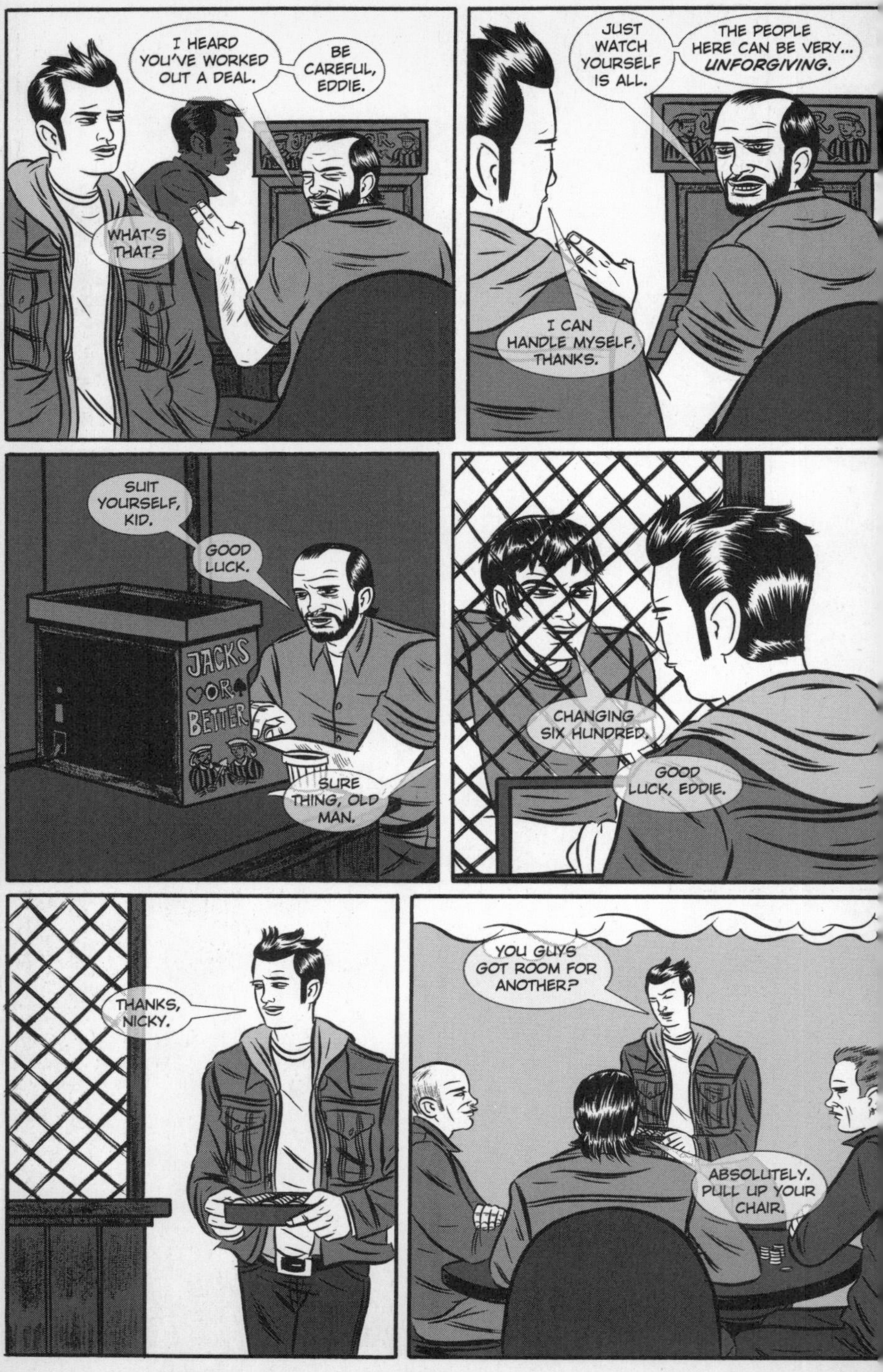
I HEARD YOU'VE WORKED OUT A DEAL.
BE CAREFUL, EDDIE.
WHAT'S THAT?
JUST WATCH YOURSELF IS ALL.
THE PEOPLE HERE CAN BE VERY... *UNFORGIVING.*
I CAN HANDLE MYSELF, THANKS.
SUIT YOURSELF, KID.
GOOD LUCK.
JACKS OR BETTER
SURE THING, OLD MAN.
CHANGING SIX HUNDRED.
GOOD LUCK, EDDIE.
THANKS, NICKY.
YOU GUYS GOT ROOM FOR ANOTHER?
ABSOLUTELY. PULL UP YOUR CHAIR.

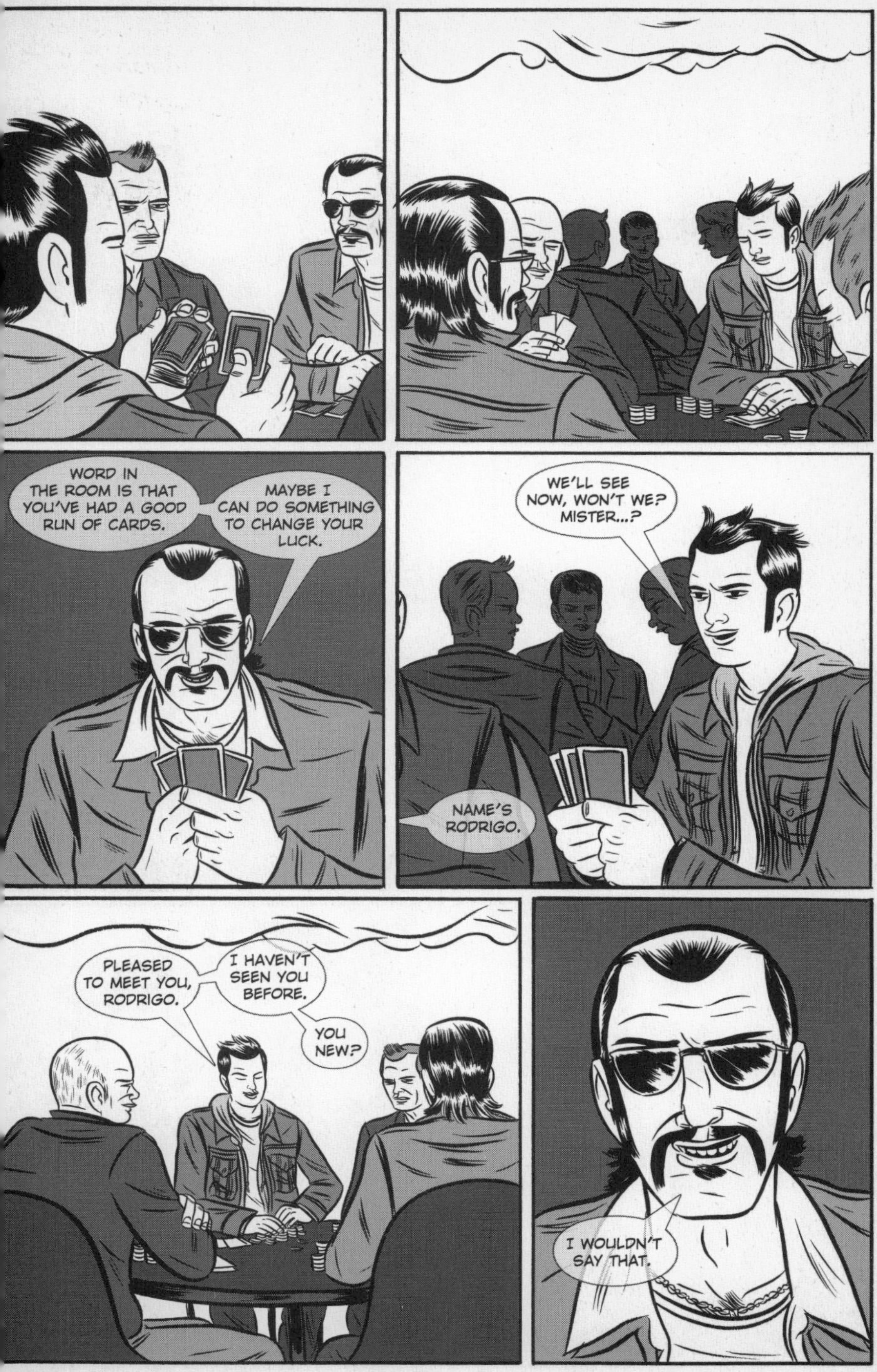

WORD IN THE ROOM IS THAT YOU'VE HAD A GOOD RUN OF CARDS.
MAYBE I CAN DO SOMETHING TO CHANGE YOUR LUCK.
WE'LL SEE NOW, WON'T WE? MISTER...?
NAME'S RODRIGO.
PLEASED TO MEET YOU, RODRIGO.
I HAVEN'T SEEN YOU BEFORE.
YOU NEW?
I WOULDN'T SAY THAT.

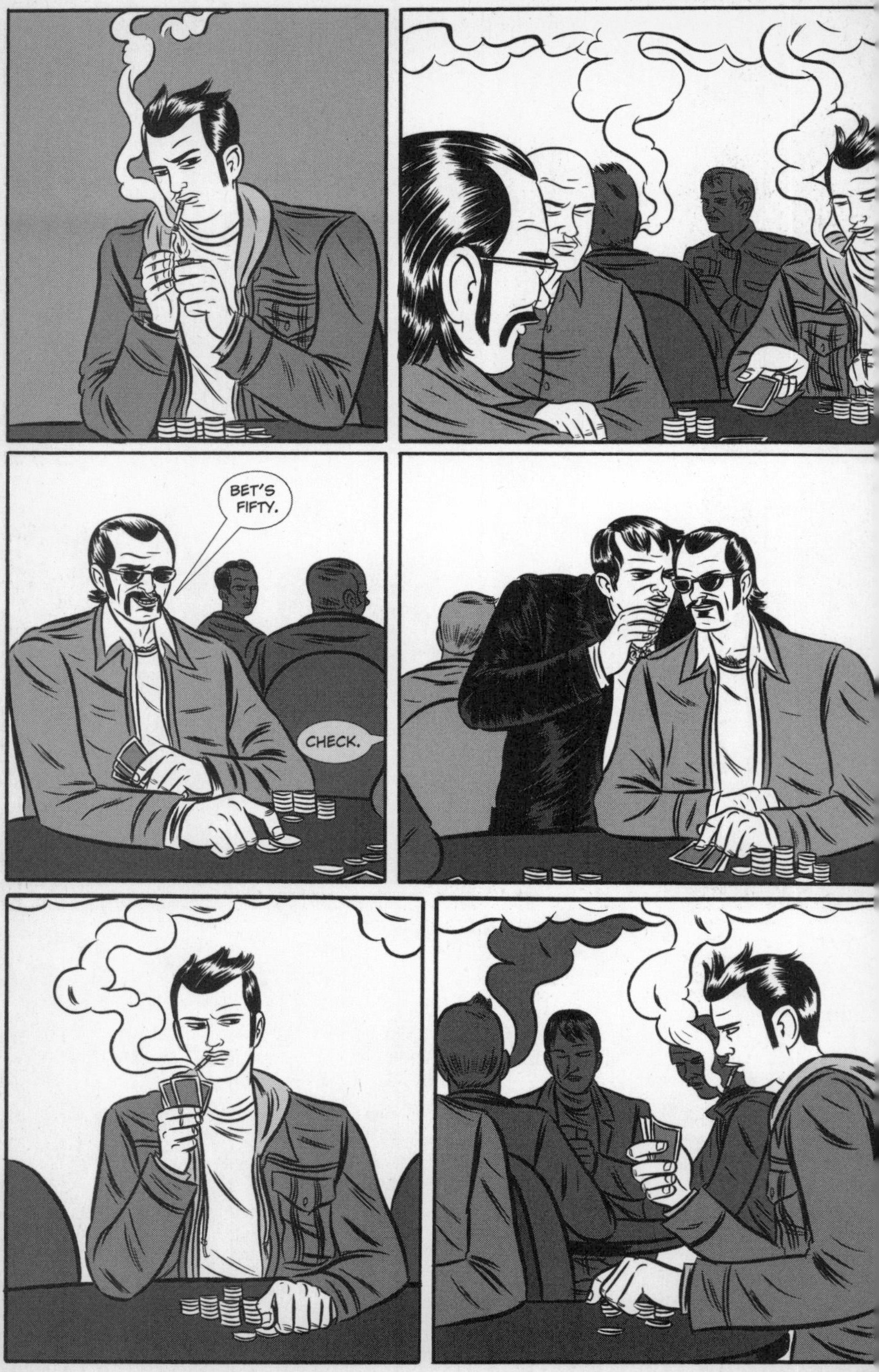
BET'S FIFTY.
CHECK.

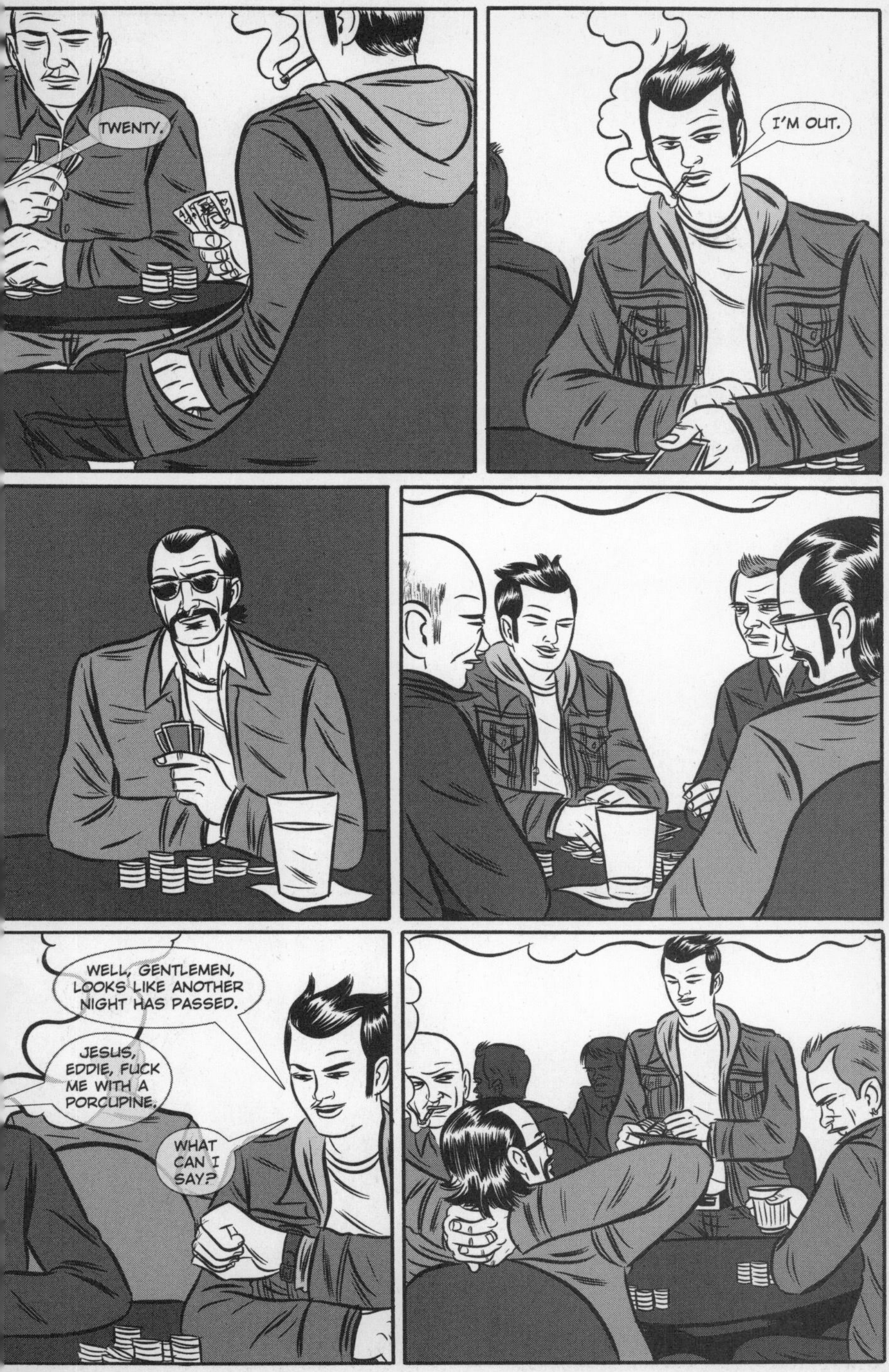
TWENTY.
I'M OUT.
WELL, GENTLEMEN, LOOKS LIKE ANOTHER NIGHT HAS PASSED.
JESUS, EDDIE, FUCK ME WITH A PORCUPINE.
WHAT CAN I SAY?

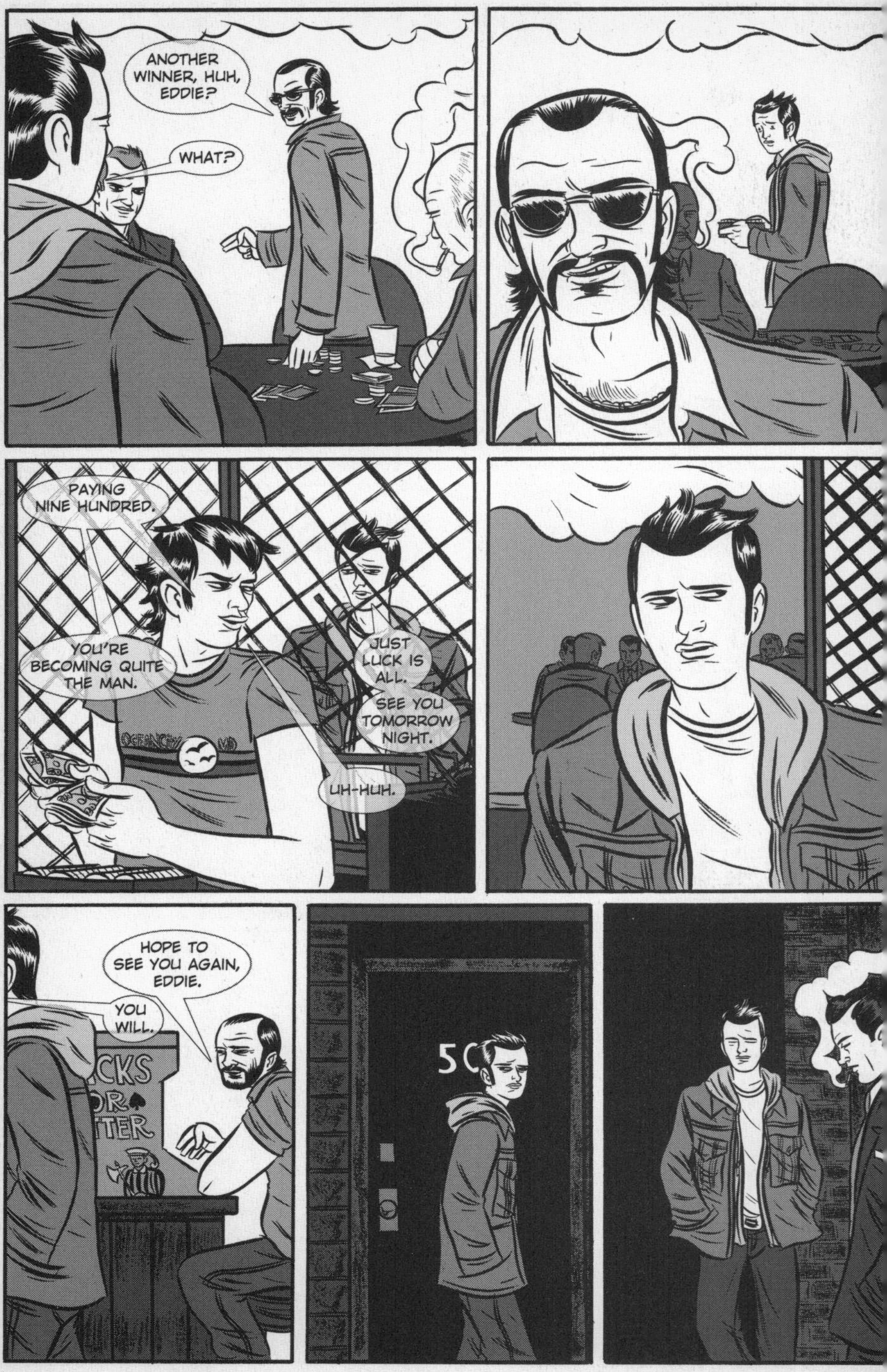
ANOTHER WINNER, HUH, EDDIE?
WHAT?
PAYING NINE HUNDRED.
YOU'RE BECOMING QUITE THE MAN.
JUST LUCK IS ALL.
SEE YOU TOMORROW NIGHT.
UH-HUH.
HOPE TO SEE YOU AGAIN, EDDIE.
YOU WILL.
50

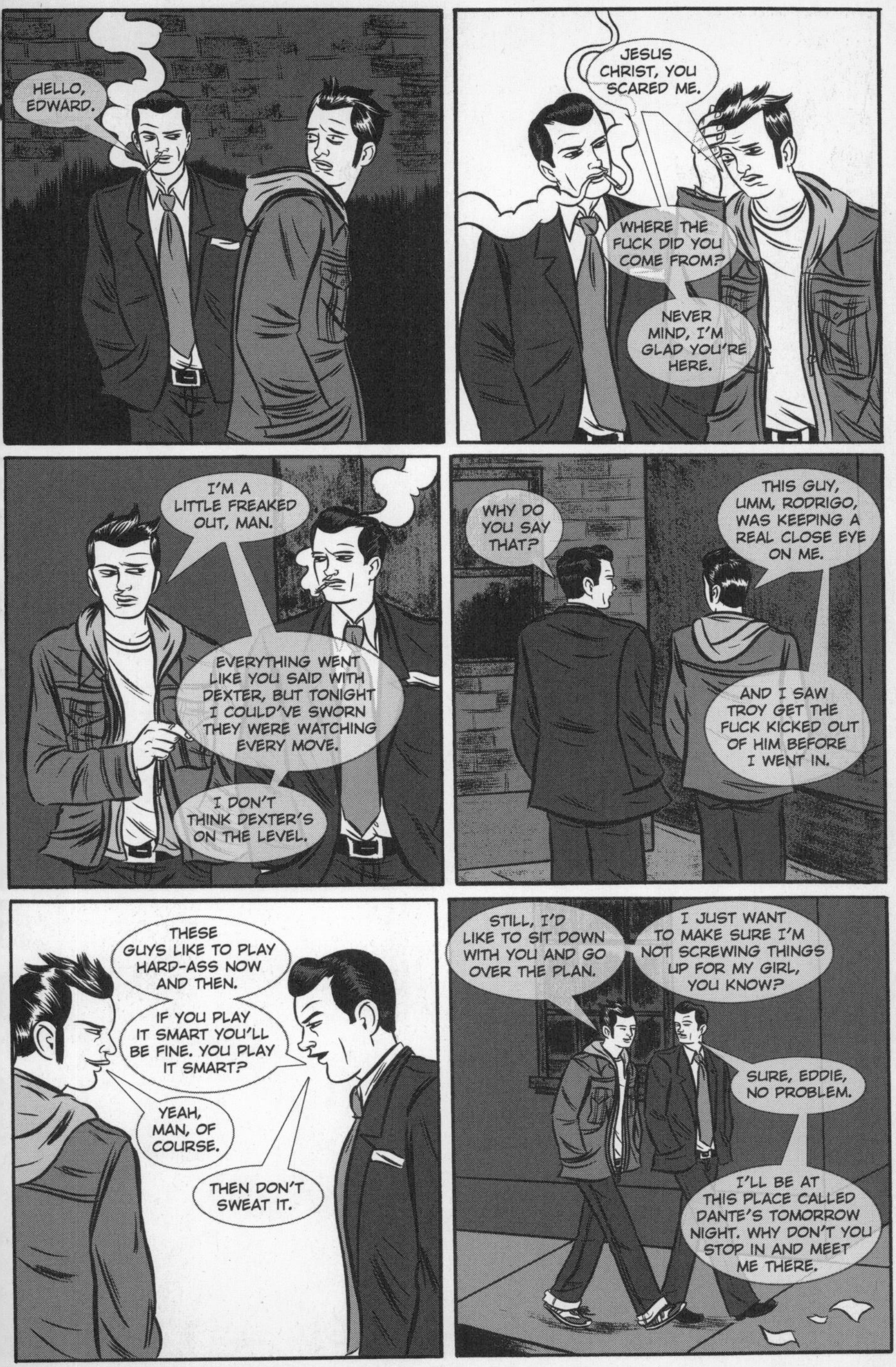
HELLO, EDWARD.
JESUS CHRIST, YOU SCARED ME.
WHERE THE FUCK DID YOU COME FROM?
NEVER MIND, I'M GLAD YOU'RE HERE.
I'M A LITTLE FREAKED OUT, MAN.
EVERYTHING WENT LIKE YOU SAID WITH DEXTER, BUT TONIGHT I COULD'VE SWORN THEY WERE WATCHING EVERY MOVE.
I DON'T THINK DEXTER'S ON THE LEVEL.
WHY DO YOU SAY THAT?
THIS GUY, UMM, RODRIGO, WAS KEEPING A REAL CLOSE EYE ON ME.
AND I SAW TROY GET THE FUCK KICKED OUT OF HIM BEFORE I WENT IN.
THESE GUYS LIKE TO PLAY HARD-ASS NOW AND THEN.
IF YOU PLAY IT SMART YOU'LL BE FINE. YOU PLAY IT SMART?
YEAH, MAN, OF COURSE.
THEN DON'T SWEAT IT.
STILL, I'D LIKE TO SIT DOWN WITH YOU AND GO OVER THE PLAN.
I JUST WANT TO MAKE SURE I'M NOT SCREWING THINGS UP FOR MY GIRL, YOU KNOW?
SURE, EDDIE, NO PROBLEM.
I'LL BE AT THIS PLACE CALLED DANTE'S TOMORROW NIGHT. WHY DON'T YOU STOP IN AND MEET ME THERE.

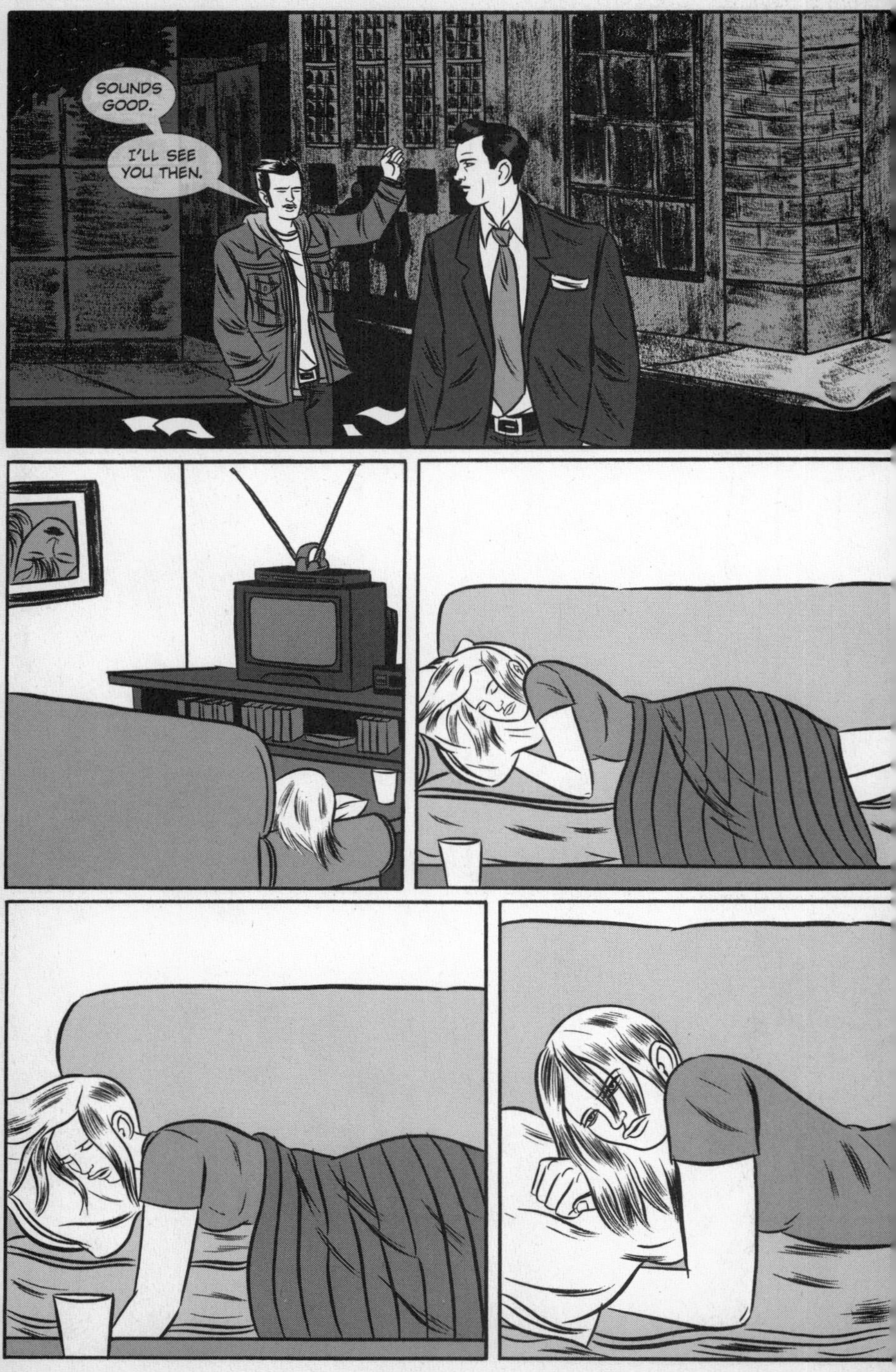
SOUNDS GOOD.
I'LL SEE YOU THEN.

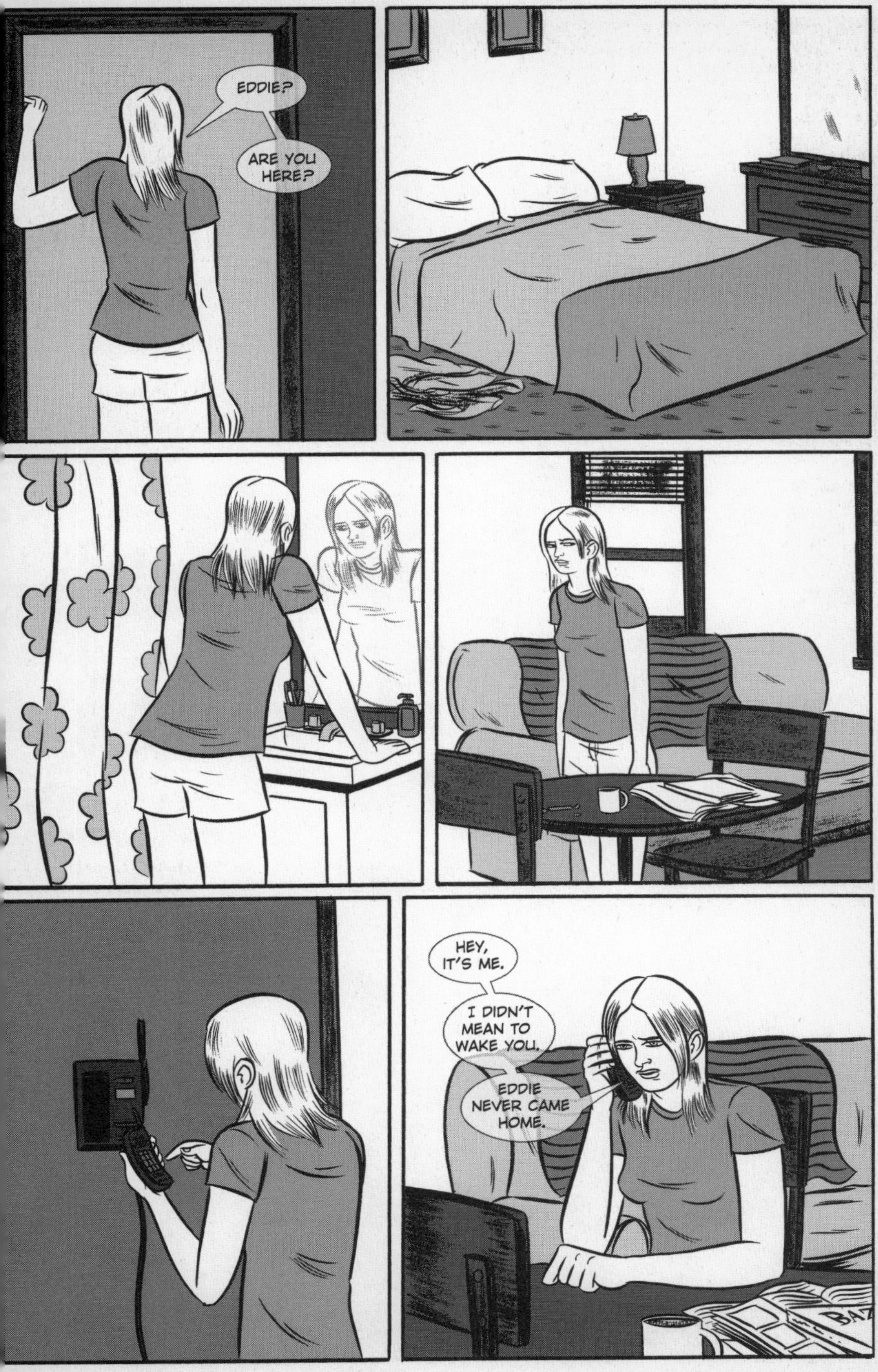
EDDIE?
ARE YOU HERE?
HEY, IT'S ME.
I DIDN'T MEAN TO WAKE YOU.
EDDIE NEVER CAME HOME.

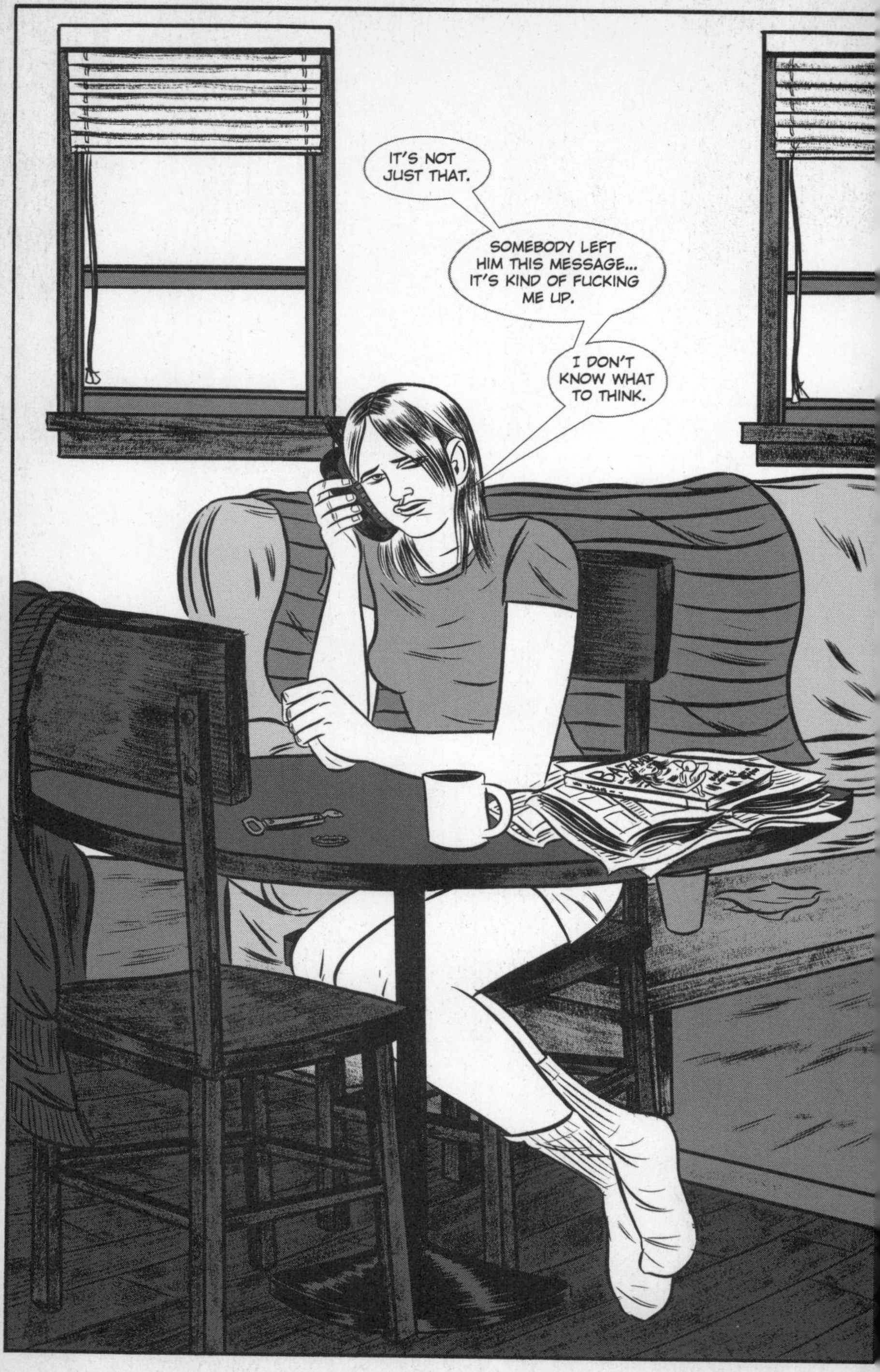
IT'S NOT JUST THAT.
SOMEBODY LEFT HIM THIS MESSAGE... IT'S KIND OF FUCKING ME UP.
I DON'T KNOW WHAT TO THINK.

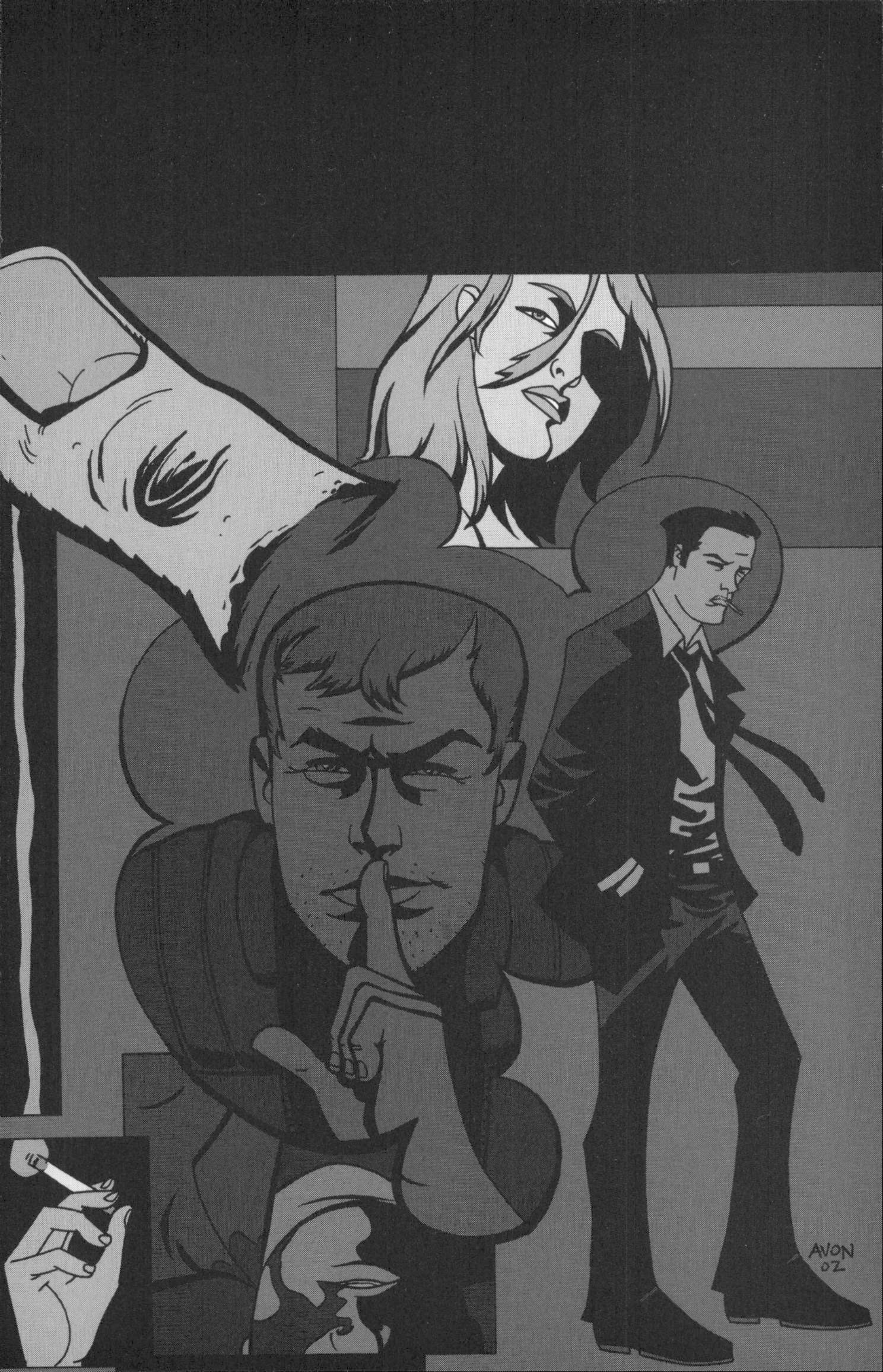
AVON
02

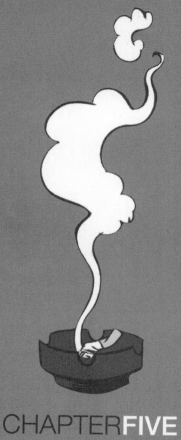

CHAPTER**FIVE**

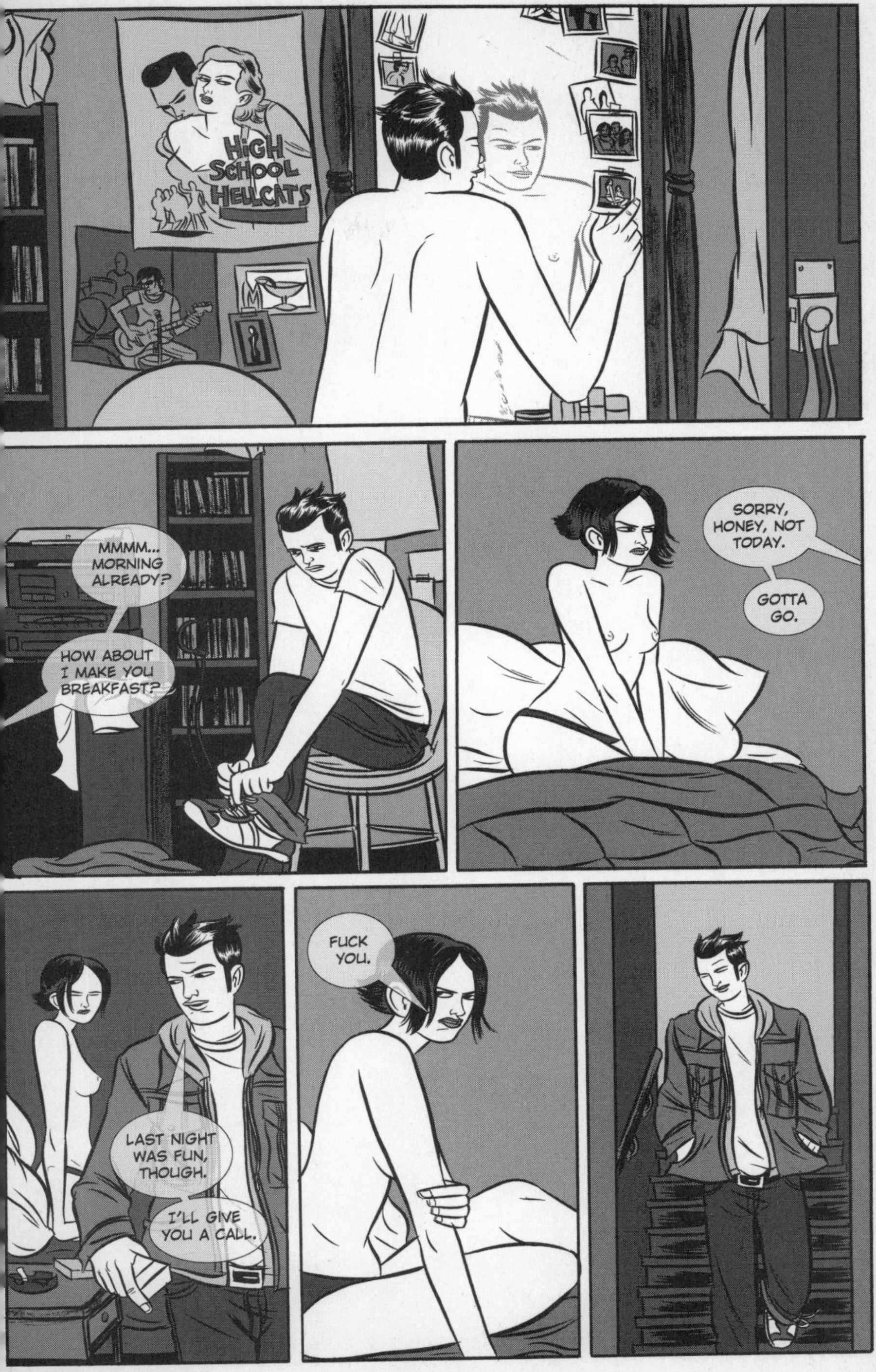
MMMM... MORNING ALREADY?
HOW ABOUT I MAKE YOU BREAKFAST?
SORRY, HONEY, NOT TODAY.
GOTTA GO.
LAST NIGHT WAS FUN, THOUGH.
I'LL GIVE YOU A CALL.
FUCK YOU.
HIGH SCHOOL HELLCATS

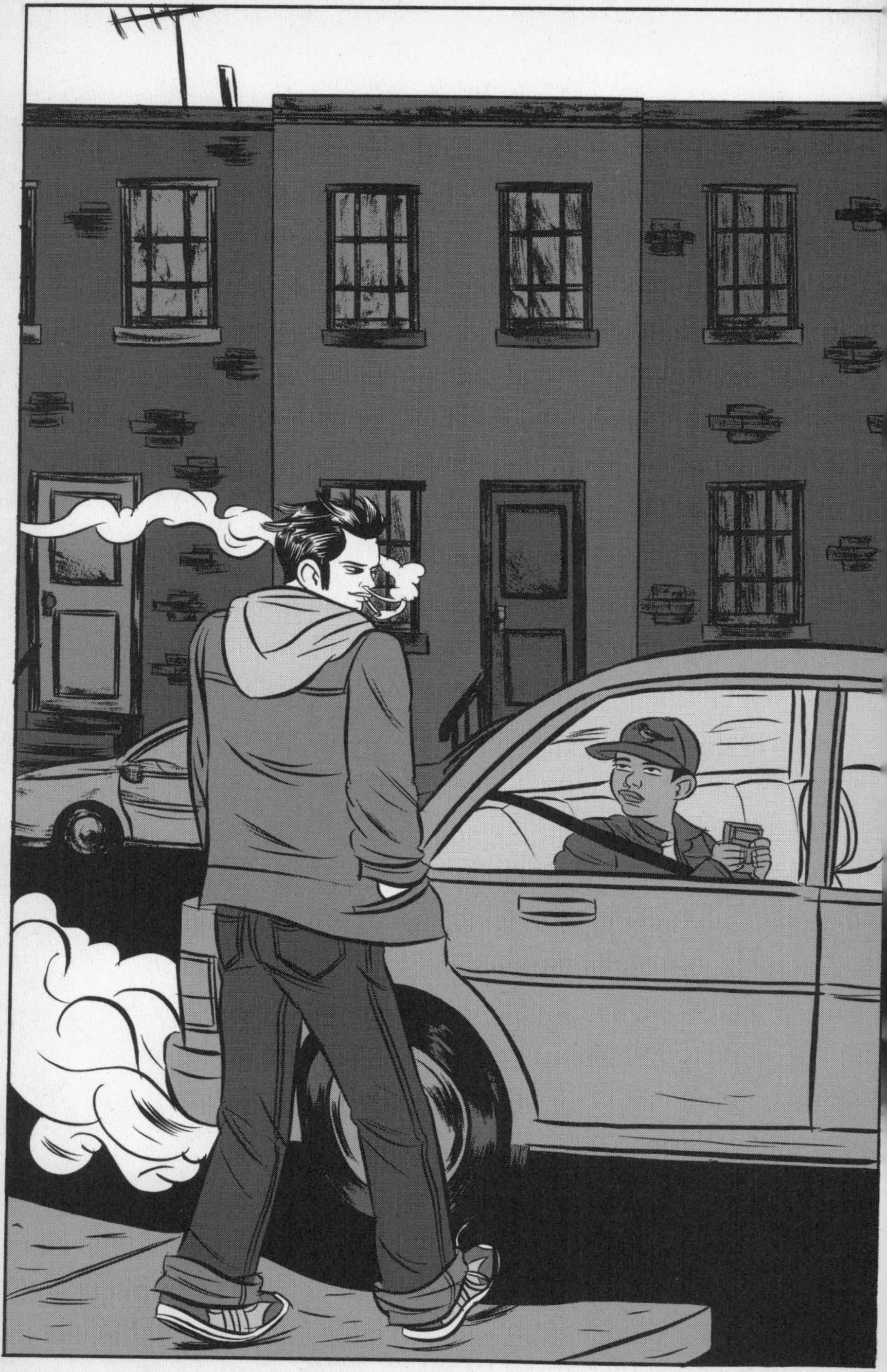

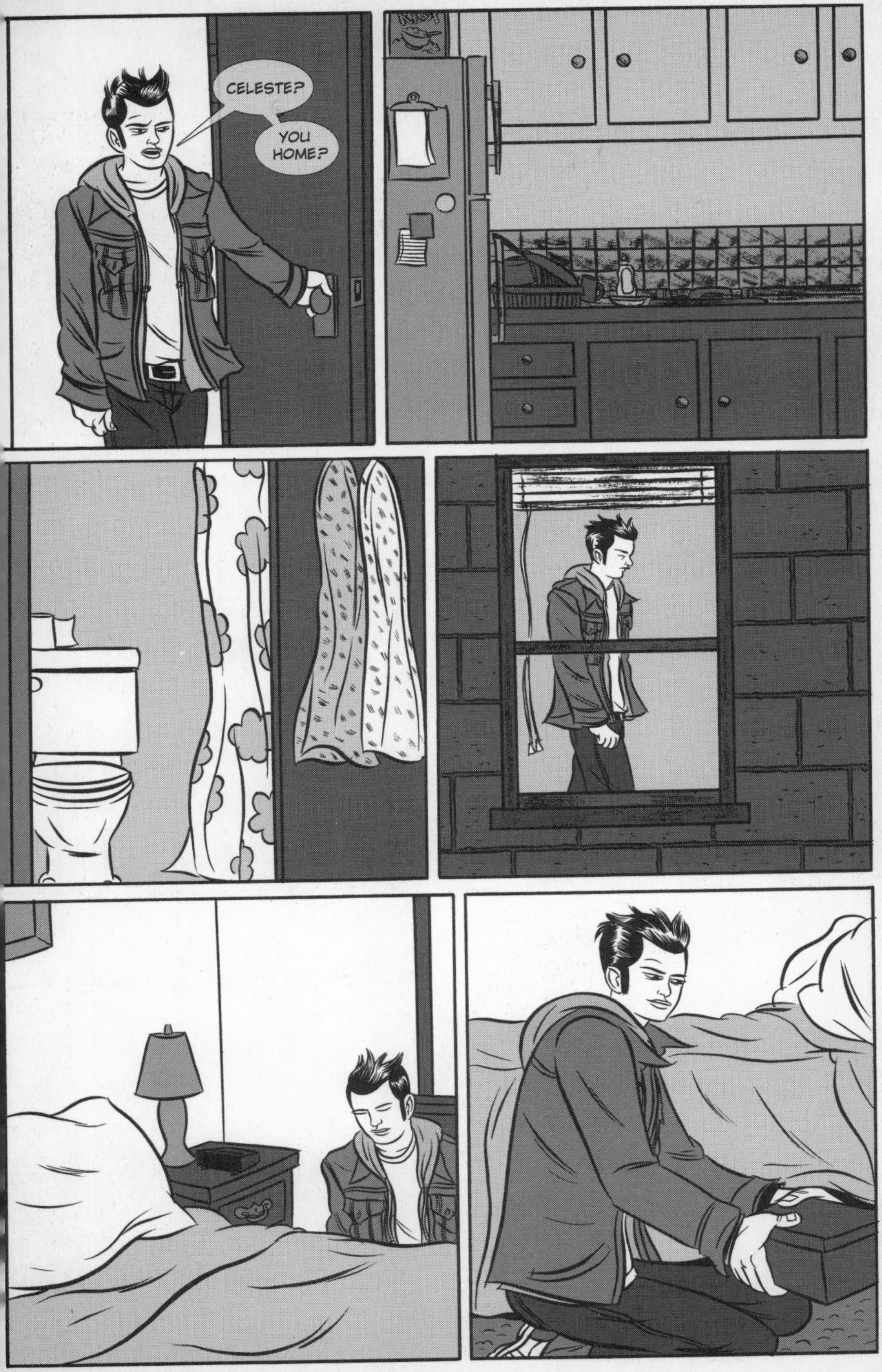
CELESTE?
YOU HOME?

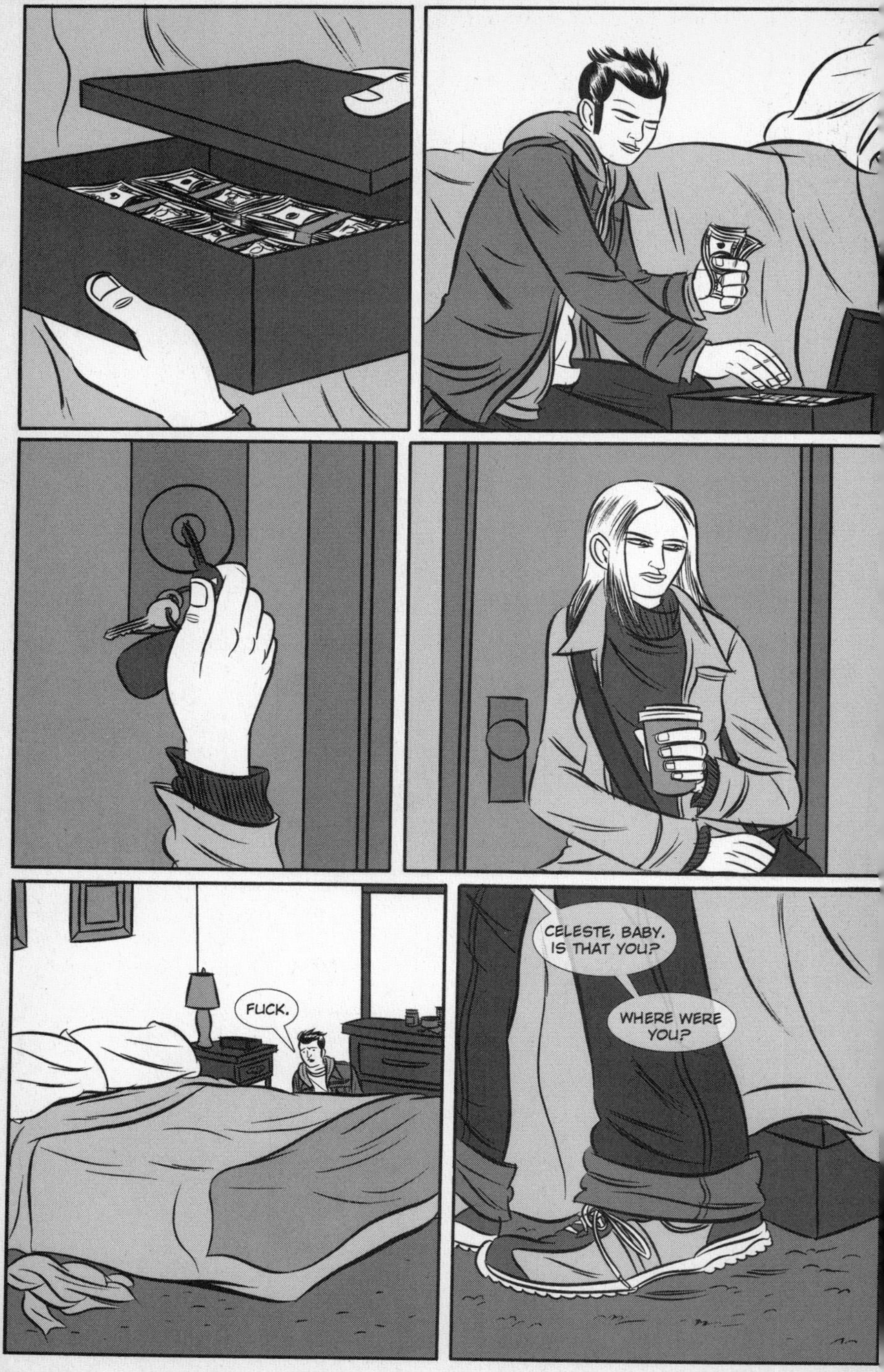
FUCK.
CELESTE, BABY. IS THAT YOU?
WHERE WERE YOU?

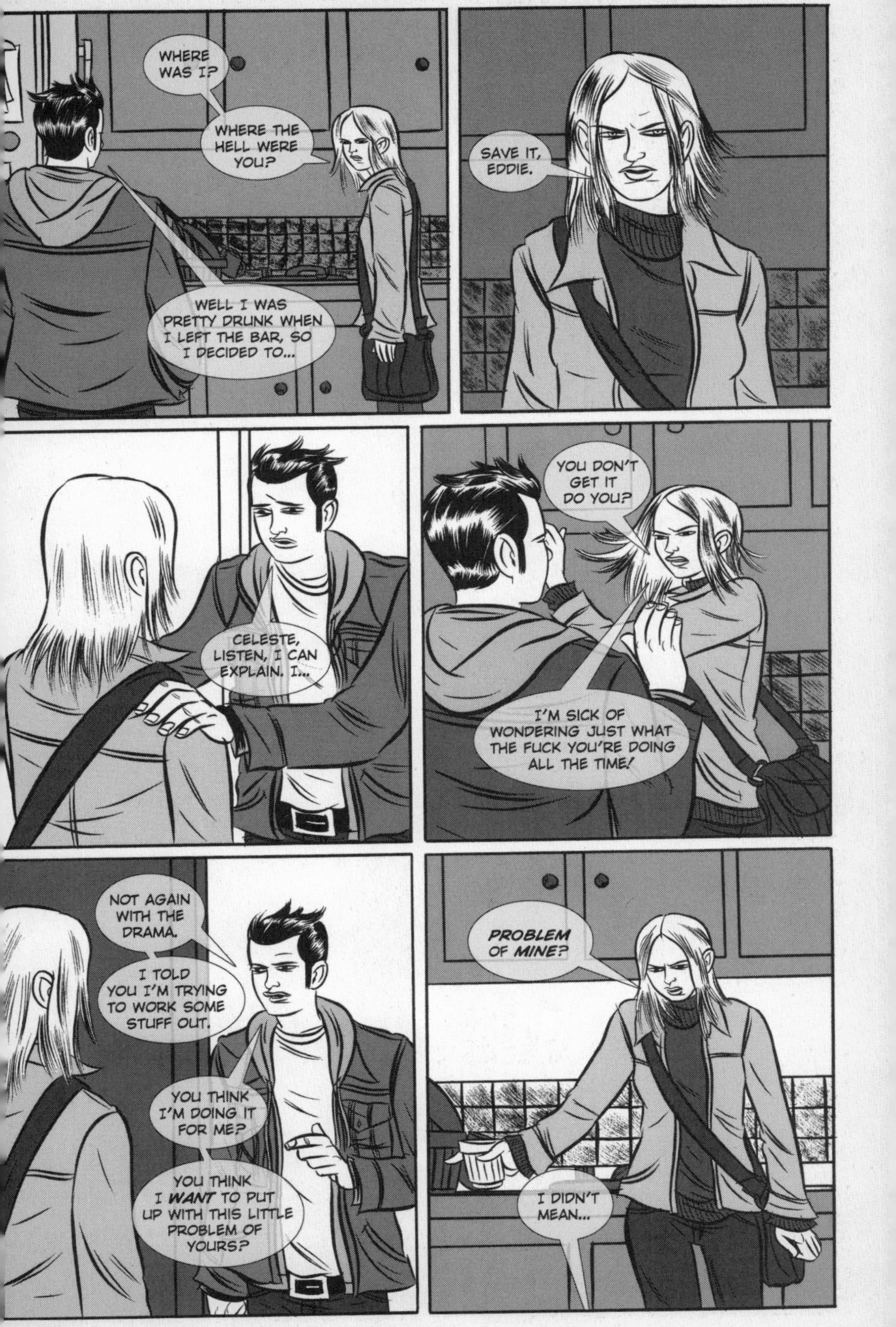
WHERE WAS I?
WHERE THE HELL WERE YOU?
WELL I WAS PRETTY DRUNK WHEN I LEFT THE BAR, SO I DECIDED TO...
SAVE IT, EDDIE.
CELESTE, LISTEN, I CAN EXPLAIN. I...
YOU DON'T GET IT DO YOU?
I'M SICK OF WONDERING JUST WHAT THE FUCK YOU'RE DOING ALL THE TIME!
NOT AGAIN WITH THE DRAMA.
I TOLD YOU I'M TRYING TO WORK SOME STUFF OUT.
YOU THINK I'M DOING IT FOR ME?
YOU THINK I *WANT* TO PUT UP WITH THIS LITTLE PROBLEM OF YOURS?
PROBLEM OF *MINE*?
I DIDN'T MEAN...

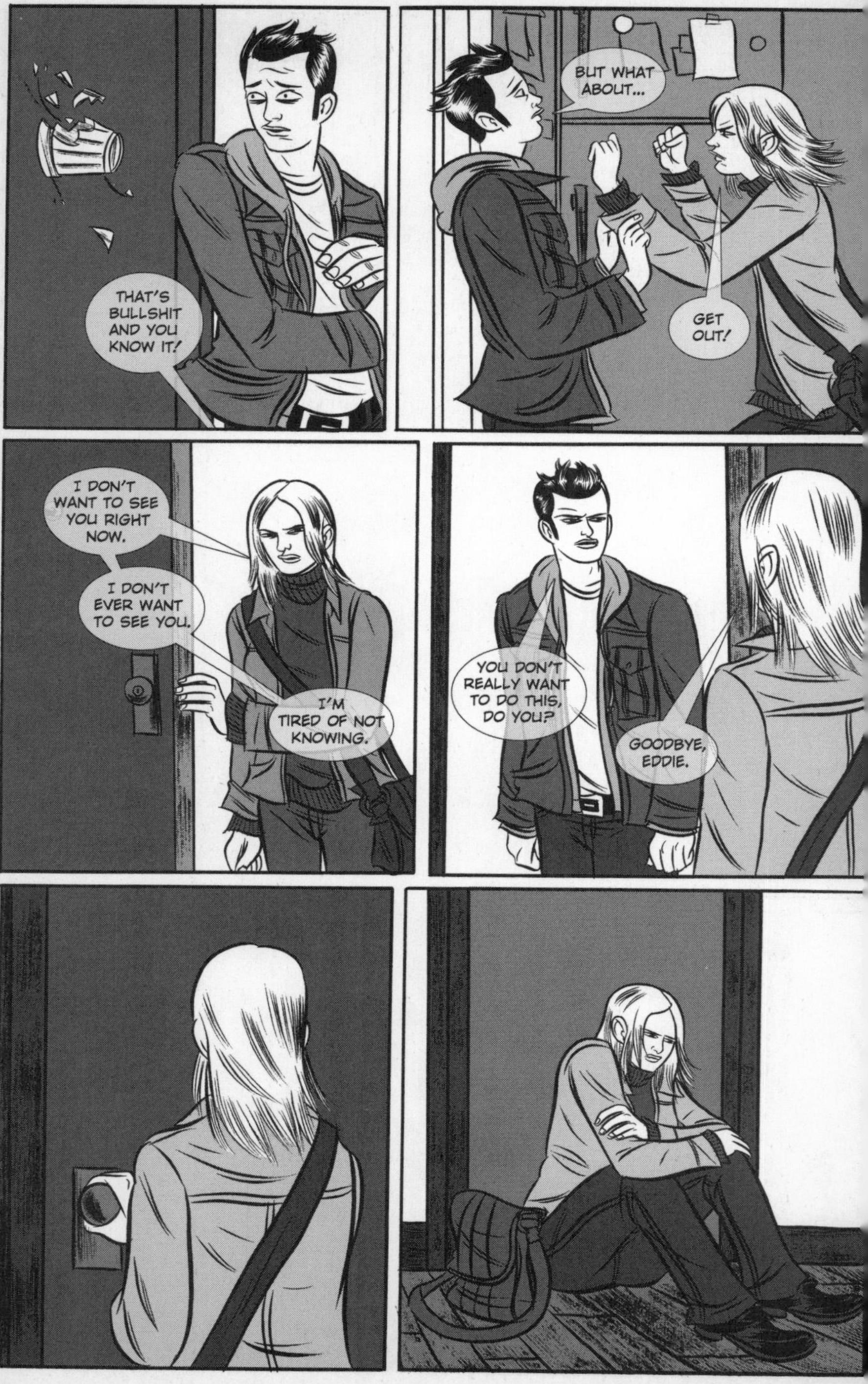
THAT'S BULLSHIT AND YOU KNOW IT!
BUT WHAT ABOUT...
GET OUT!
I DON'T WANT TO SEE YOU RIGHT NOW.
I DON'T EVER WANT TO SEE YOU.
I'M TIRED OF NOT KNOWING.
YOU DON'T REALLY WANT TO DO THIS, DO YOU?
GOODBYE, EDDIE.

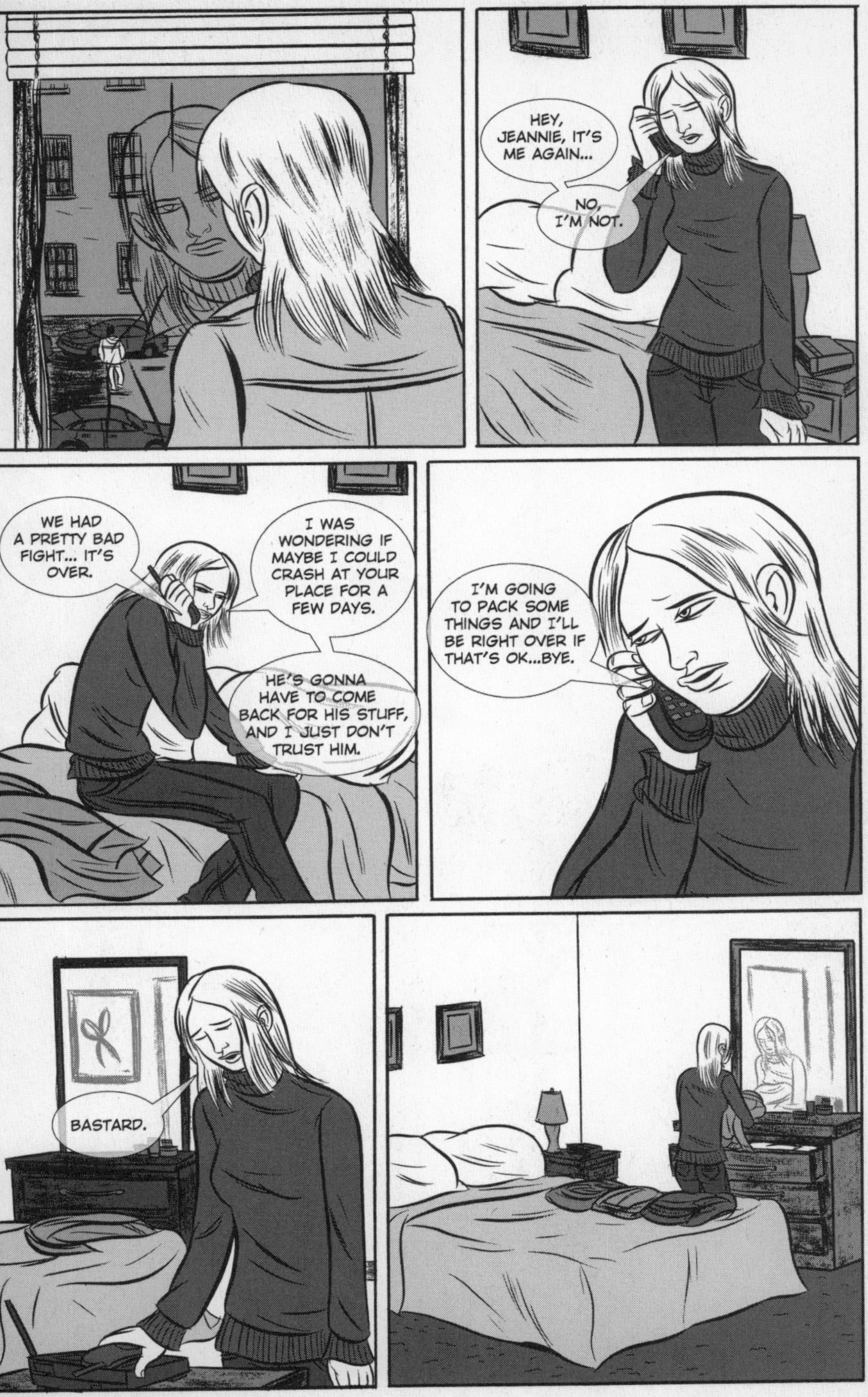
HEY, JEANNIE, IT'S ME AGAIN...
NO, I'M NOT.
WE HAD A PRETTY BAD FIGHT... IT'S OVER.
I WAS WONDERING IF MAYBE I COULD CRASH AT YOUR PLACE FOR A FEW DAYS.
HE'S GONNA HAVE TO COME BACK FOR HIS STUFF, AND I JUST DON'T TRUST HIM.
I'M GOING TO PACK SOME THINGS AND I'LL BE RIGHT OVER IF THAT'S OK...BYE.
BASTARD.

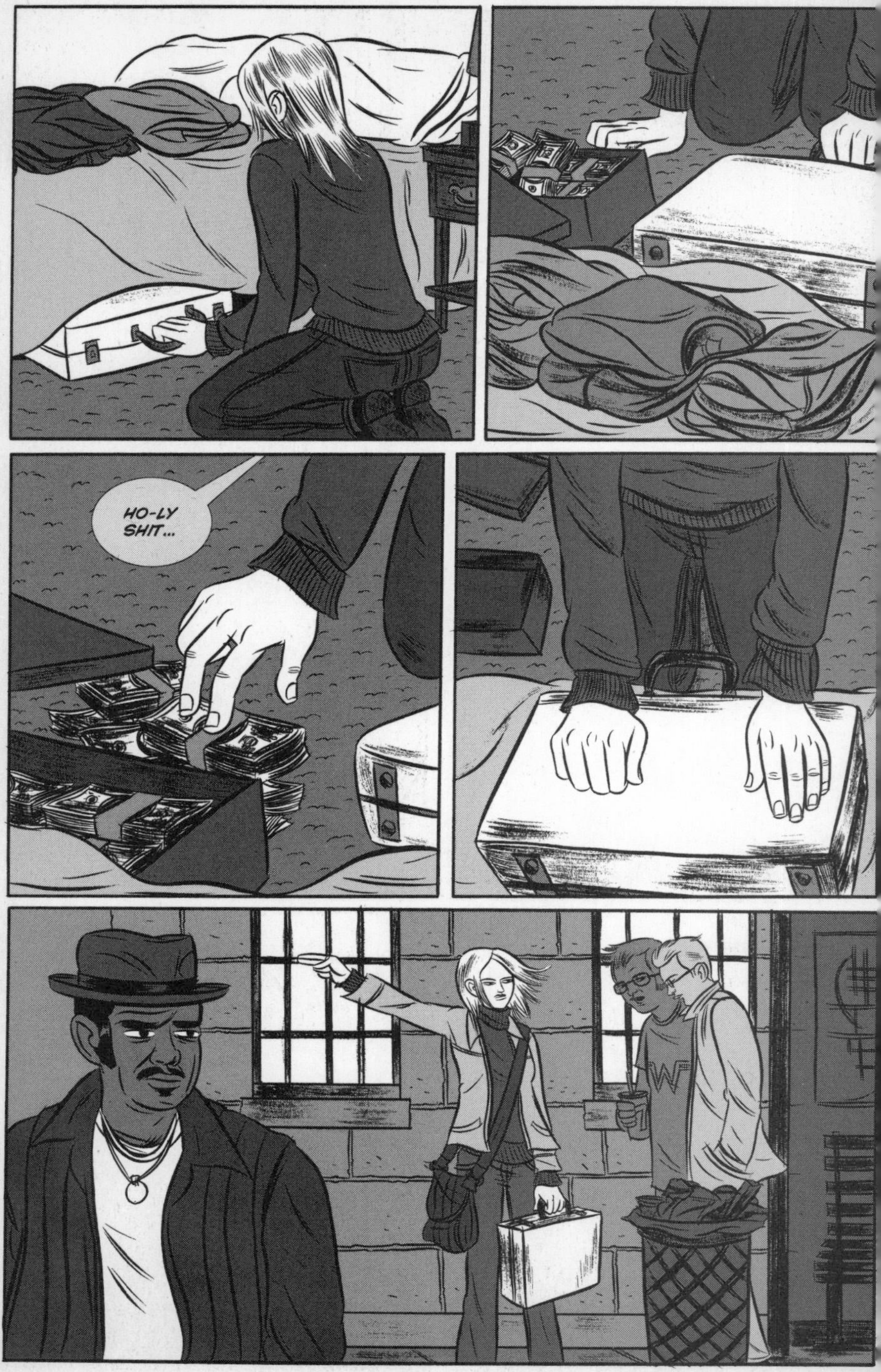
HO-LY SHIT...

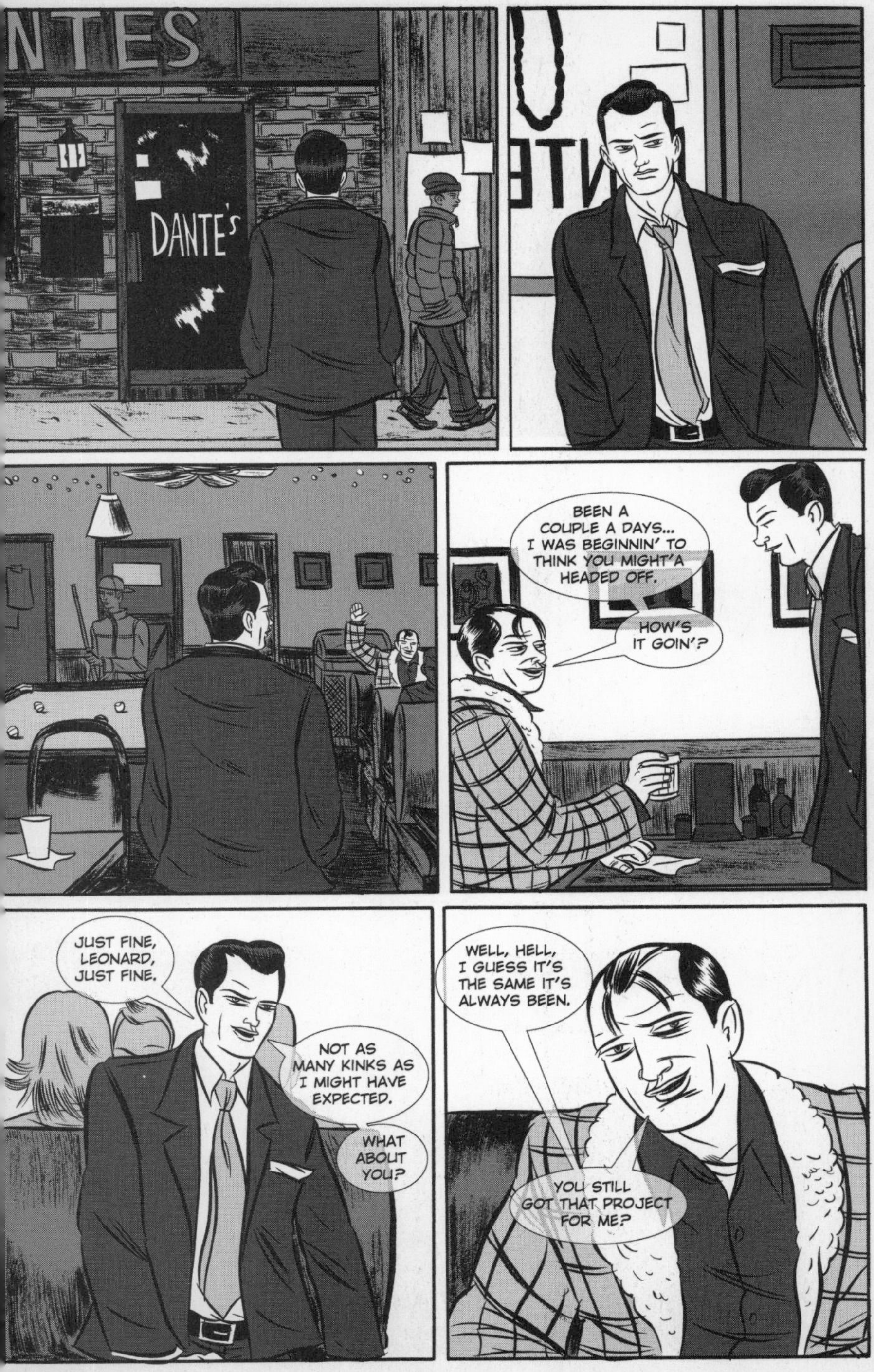
NTES
DANTE's
BEEN A COUPLE A DAYS... I WAS BEGINNIN' TO THINK YOU MIGHT'A HEADED OFF.
HOW'S IT GOIN'?
JUST FINE, LEONARD, JUST FINE.
NOT AS MANY KINKS AS I MIGHT HAVE EXPECTED.
WHAT ABOUT YOU?
WELL, HELL, I GUESS IT'S THE SAME IT'S ALWAYS BEEN.
YOU STILL GOT THAT PROJECT FOR ME?

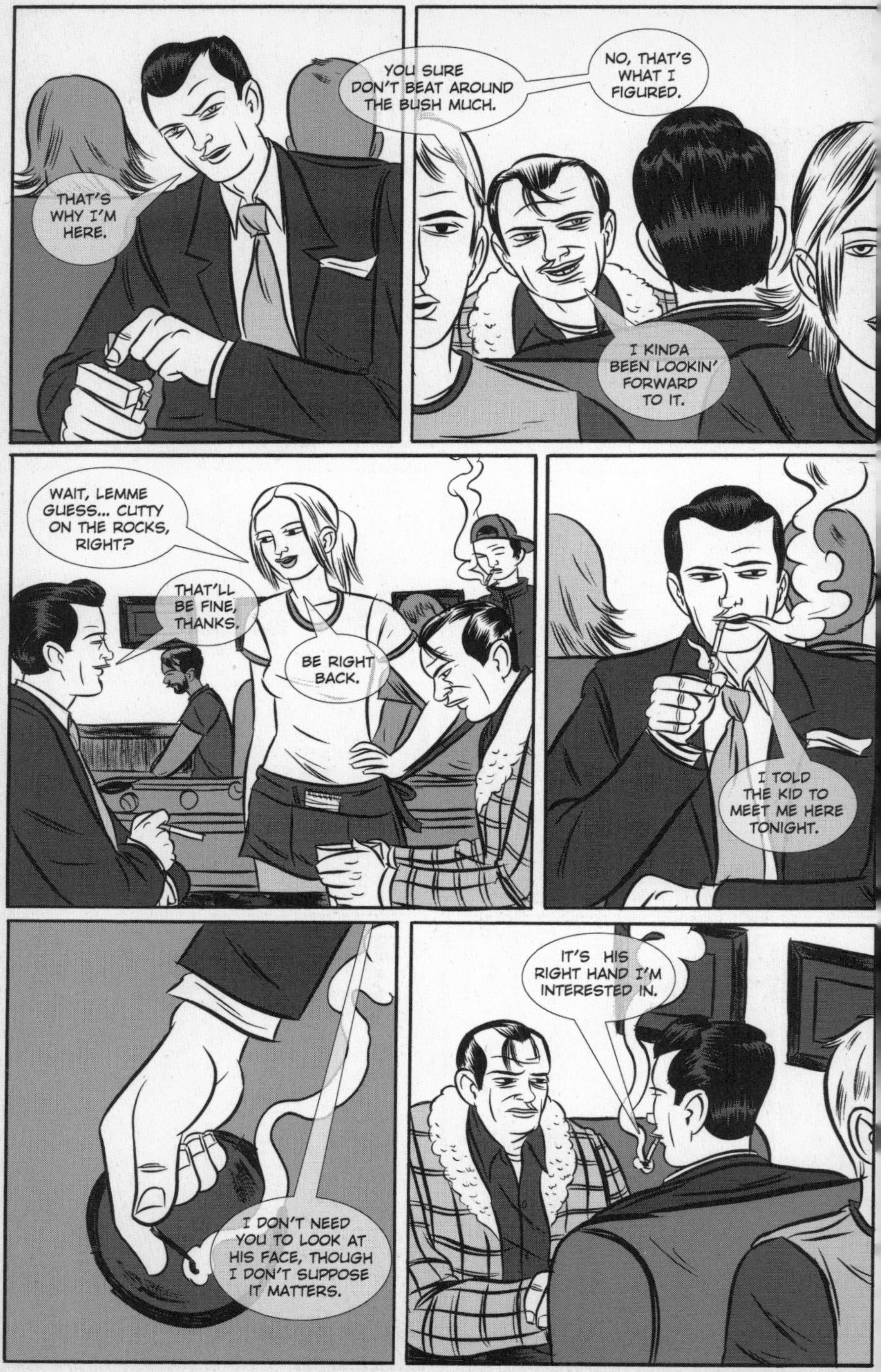
THAT'S WHY I'M HERE.
YOU SURE DON'T BEAT AROUND THE BUSH MUCH.
NO, THAT'S WHAT I FIGURED.
I KINDA BEEN LOOKIN' FORWARD TO IT.
WAIT, LEMME GUESS... CUTTY ON THE ROCKS, RIGHT?
THAT'LL BE FINE, THANKS.
BE RIGHT BACK.
I TOLD THE KID TO MEET ME HERE TONIGHT.
I DON'T NEED YOU TO LOOK AT HIS FACE, THOUGH I DON'T SUPPOSE IT MATTERS.
IT'S HIS RIGHT HAND I'M INTERESTED IN.

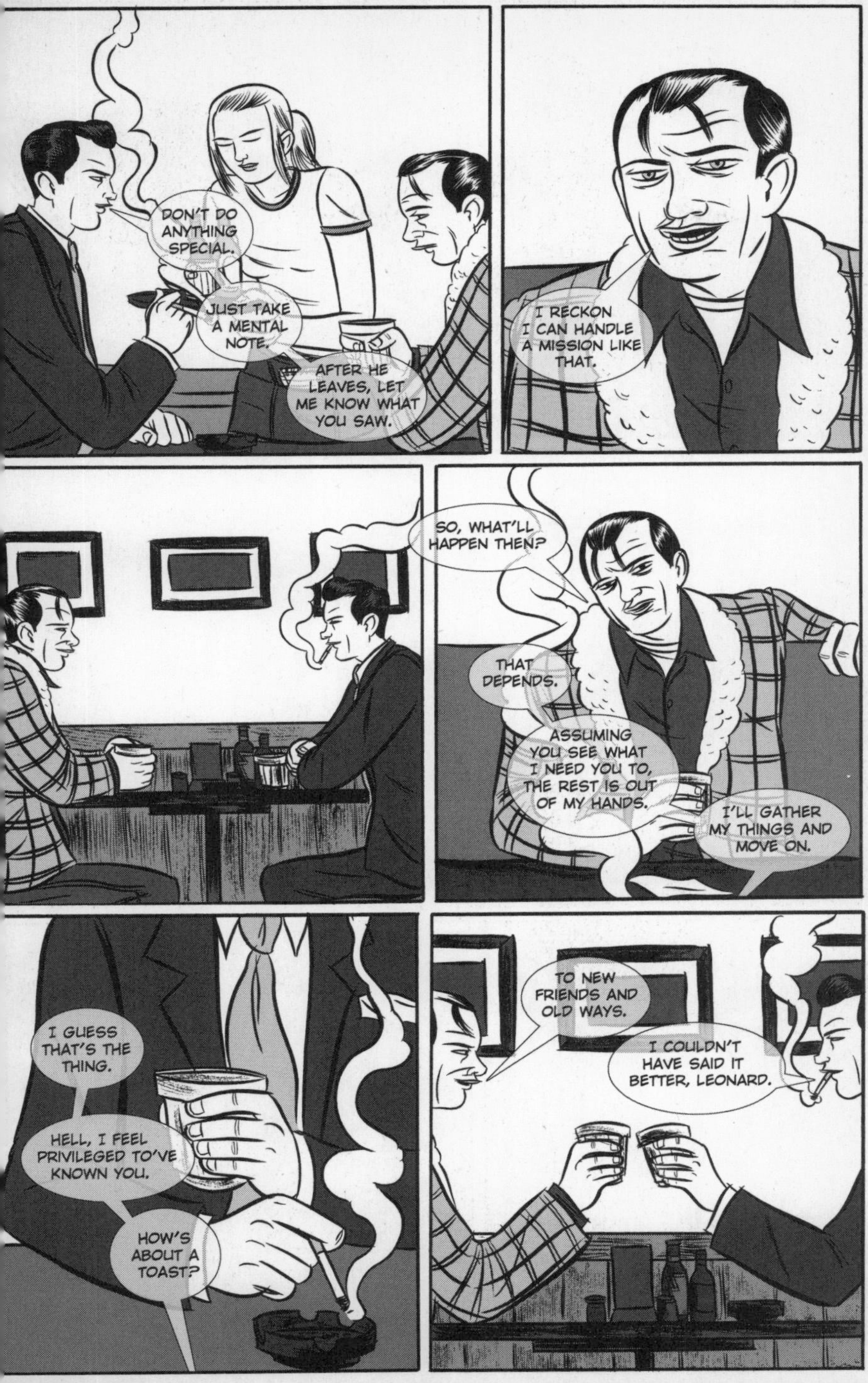
DON'T DO ANYTHING SPECIAL.
JUST TAKE A MENTAL NOTE.
AFTER HE LEAVES, LET ME KNOW WHAT YOU SAW.
I RECKON I CAN HANDLE A MISSION LIKE THAT.
SO, WHAT'LL HAPPEN THEN?
THAT DEPENDS.
ASSUMING YOU SEE WHAT I NEED YOU TO, THE REST IS OUT OF MY HANDS.
I'LL GATHER MY THINGS AND MOVE ON.
I GUESS THAT'S THE THING.
HELL, I FEEL PRIVILEGED TO'VE KNOWN YOU.
HOW'S ABOUT A TOAST?
TO NEW FRIENDS AND OLD WAYS.
I COULDN'T HAVE SAID IT BETTER, LEONARD.

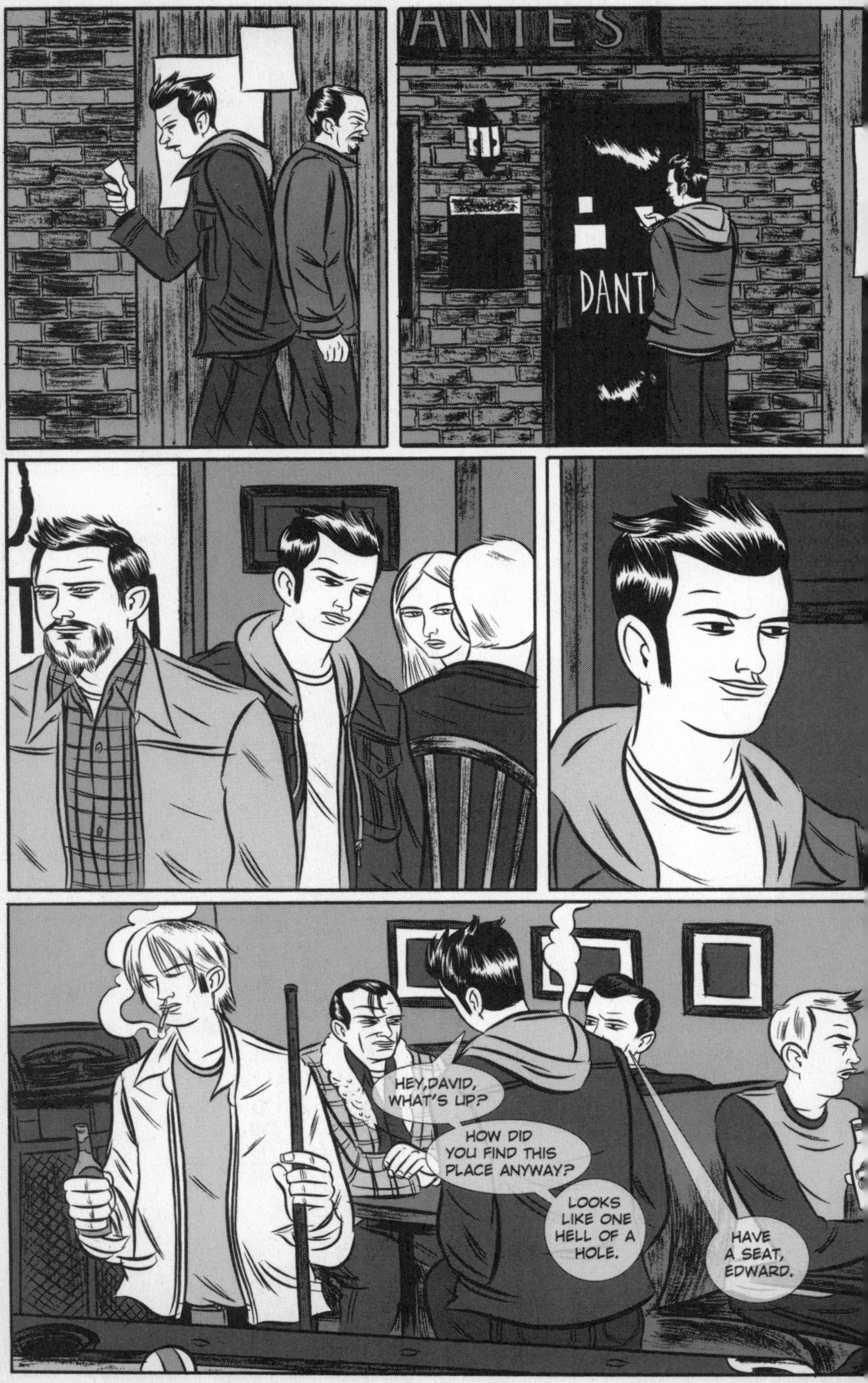
ANTES
DANT
HEY, DAVID, WHAT'S UP?
HOW DID YOU FIND THIS PLACE ANYWAY?
LOOKS LIKE ONE HELL OF A HOLE.
HAVE A SEAT, EDWARD.

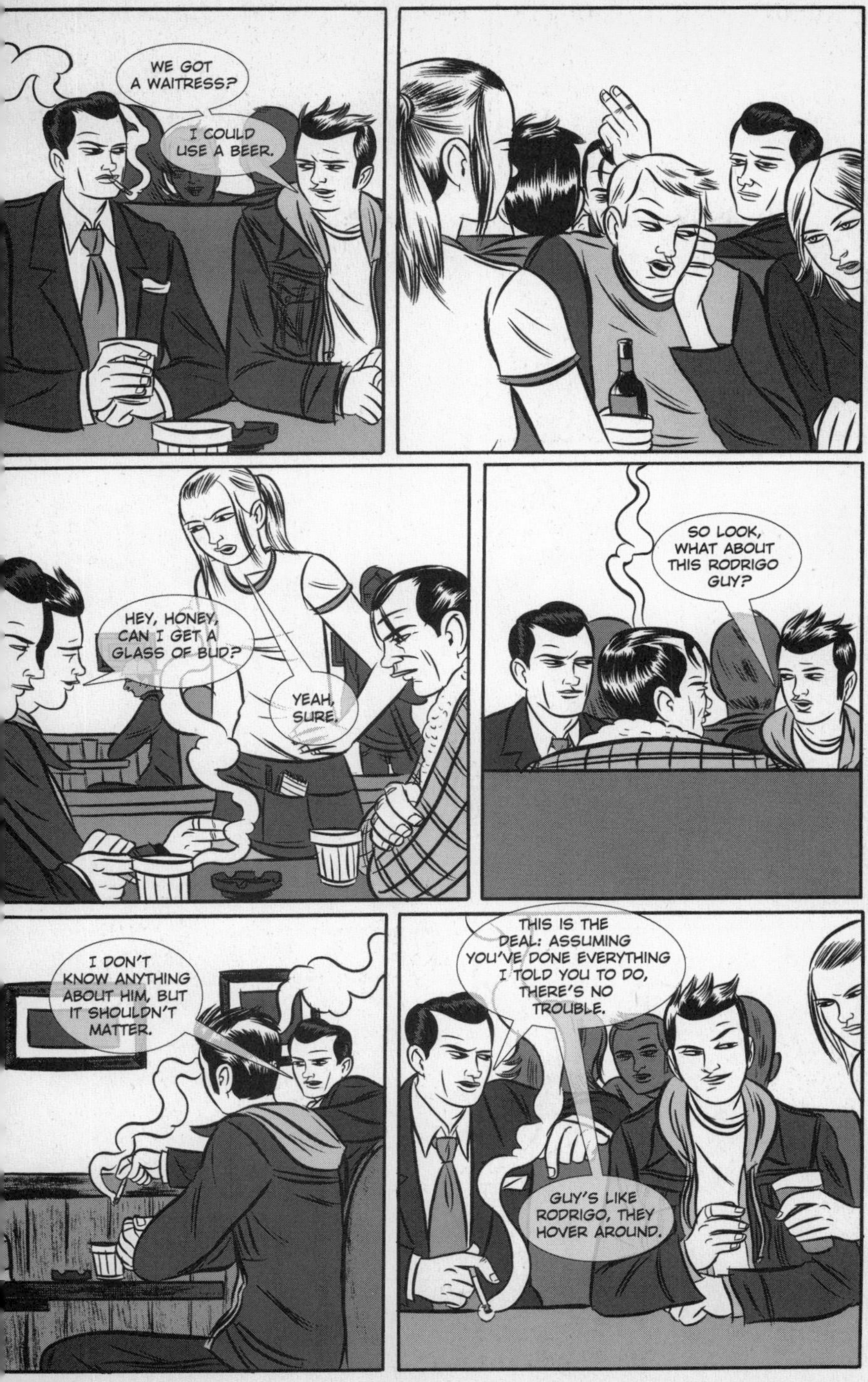
WE GOT A WAITRESS?
I COULD USE A BEER.
HEY, HONEY, CAN I GET A GLASS OF BUD?
YEAH, SURE.
SO LOOK, WHAT ABOUT THIS RODRIGO GUY?
I DON'T KNOW ANYTHING ABOUT HIM, BUT IT SHOULDN'T MATTER.
THIS IS THE DEAL: ASSUMING YOU'VE DONE EVERYTHING I TOLD YOU TO DO, THERE'S NO TROUBLE.
GUY'S LIKE RODRIGO, THEY HOVER AROUND.

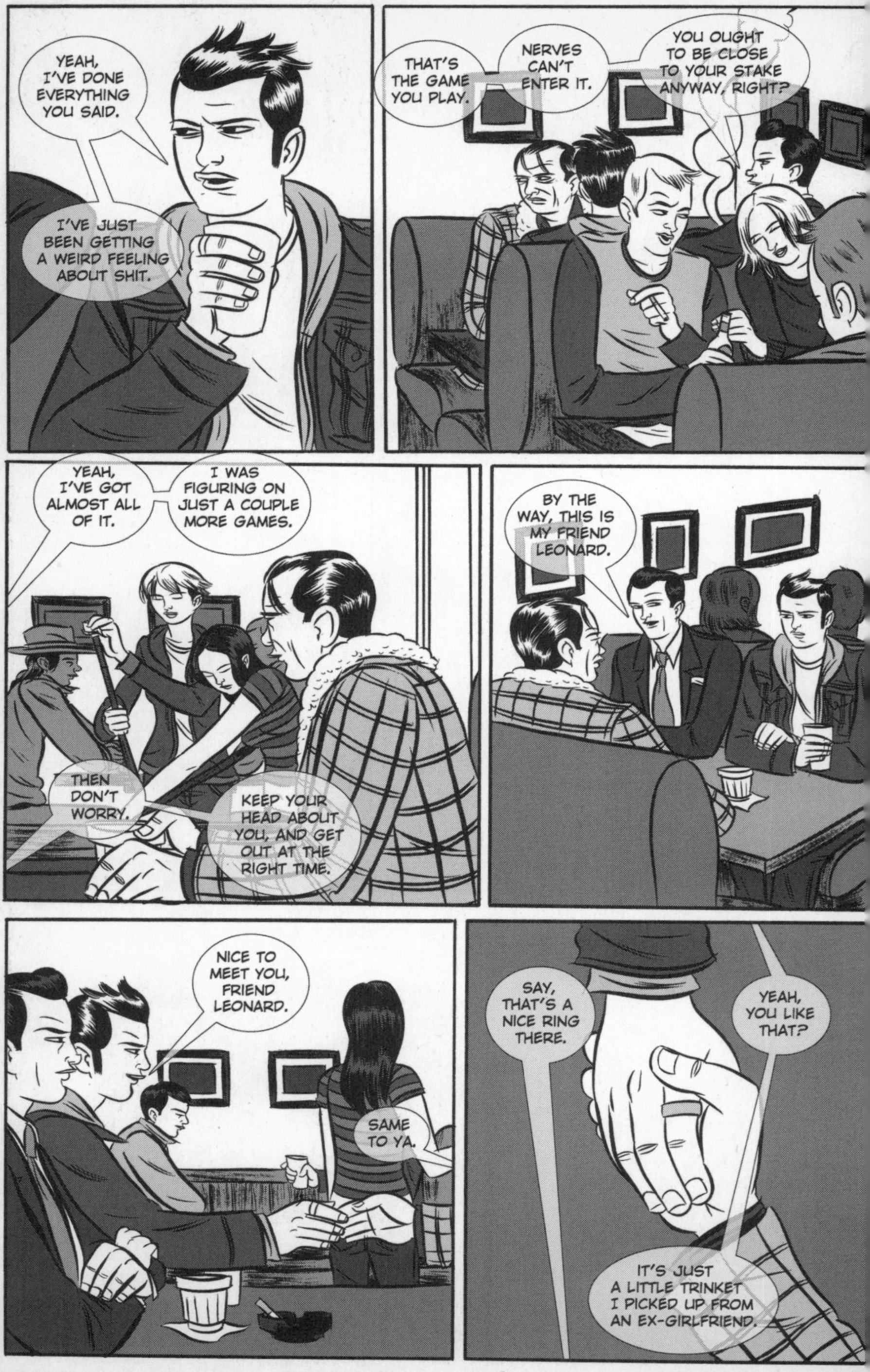
YEAH, I'VE DONE EVERYTHING YOU SAID.
I'VE JUST BEEN GETTING A WEIRD FEELING ABOUT SHIT.
THAT'S THE GAME YOU PLAY.
NERVES CAN'T ENTER IT.
YOU OUGHT TO BE CLOSE TO YOUR STAKE ANYWAY, RIGHT?
YEAH, I'VE GOT ALMOST ALL OF IT.
I WAS FIGURING ON JUST A COUPLE MORE GAMES.
THEN DON'T WORRY.
KEEP YOUR HEAD ABOUT YOU, AND GET OUT AT THE RIGHT TIME.
BY THE WAY, THIS IS MY FRIEND LEONARD.
NICE TO MEET YOU, FRIEND LEONARD.
SAME TO YA.
SAY, THAT'S A NICE RING THERE.
YEAH, YOU LIKE THAT?
IT'S JUST A LITTLE TRINKET I PICKED UP FROM AN EX-GIRLFRIEND.

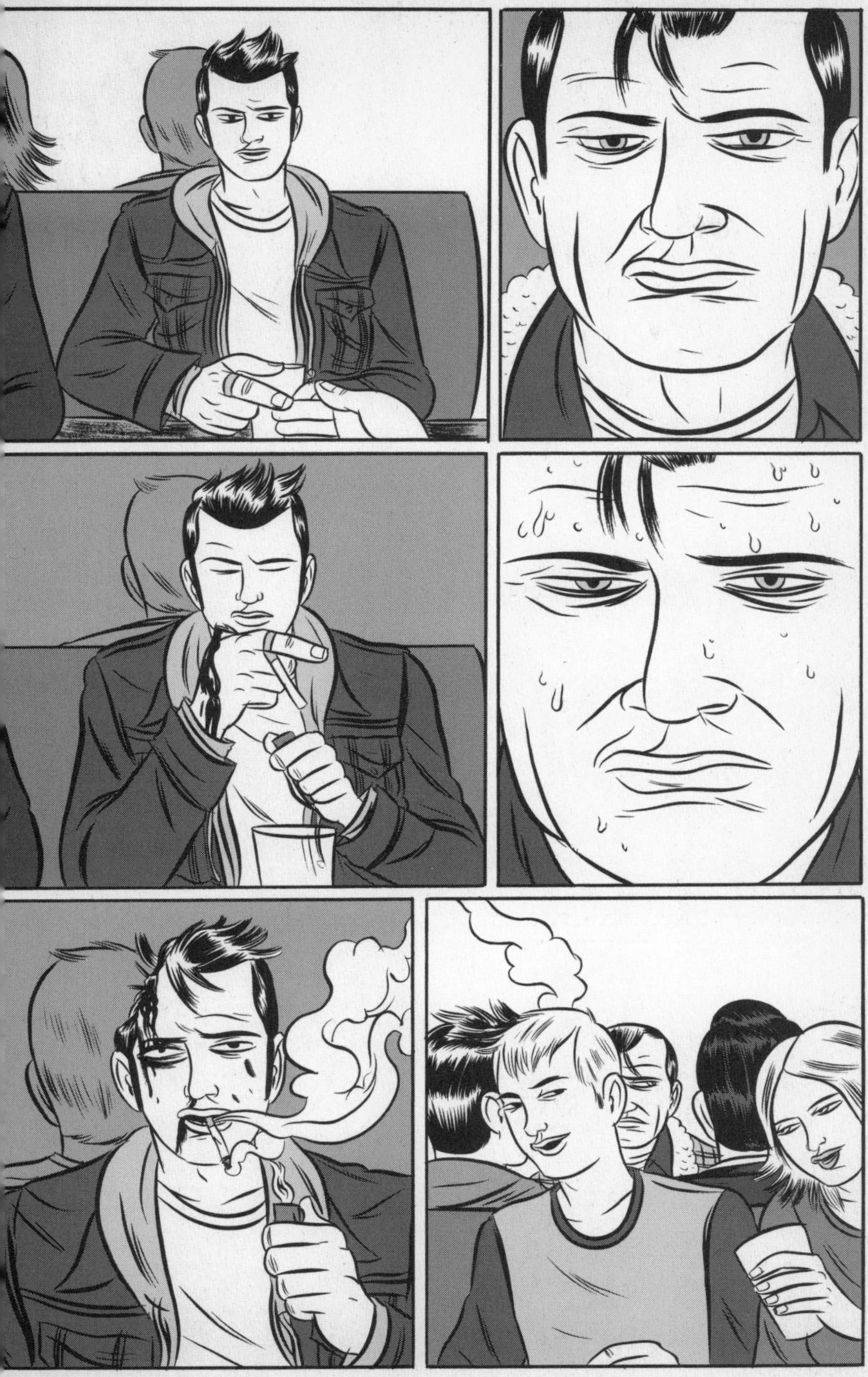

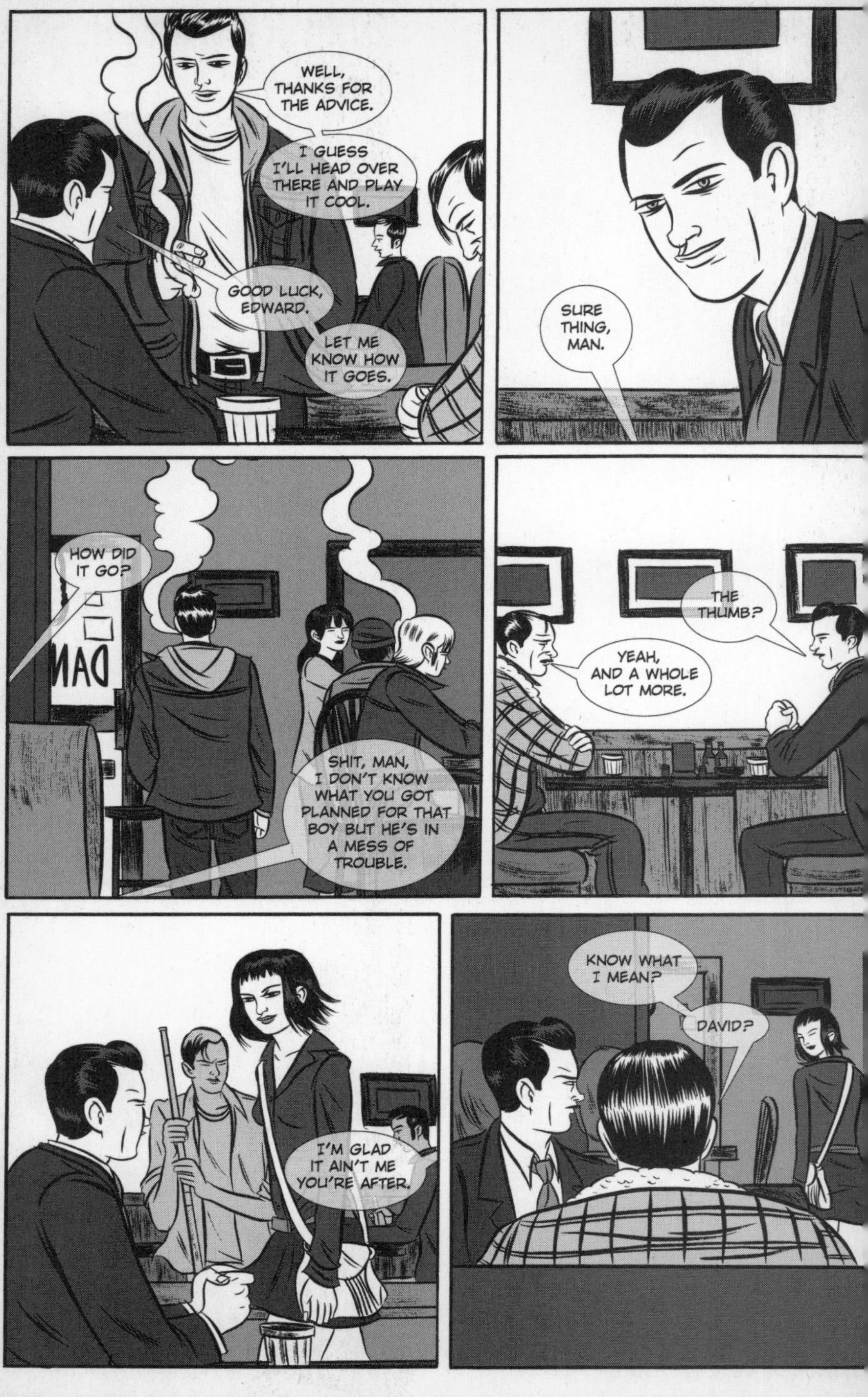

WELL, THANKS FOR THE ADVICE.
I GUESS I'LL HEAD OVER THERE AND PLAY IT COOL.
GOOD LUCK, EDWARD.
LET ME KNOW HOW IT GOES.
SURE THING, MAN.
HOW DID IT GO?
SHIT, MAN, I DON'T KNOW WHAT YOU GOT PLANNED FOR THAT BOY BUT HE'S IN A MESS OF TROUBLE.
THE THUMB?
YEAH, AND A WHOLE LOT MORE.
I'M GLAD IT AIN'T ME YOU'RE AFTER.
KNOW WHAT I MEAN?
DAVID?

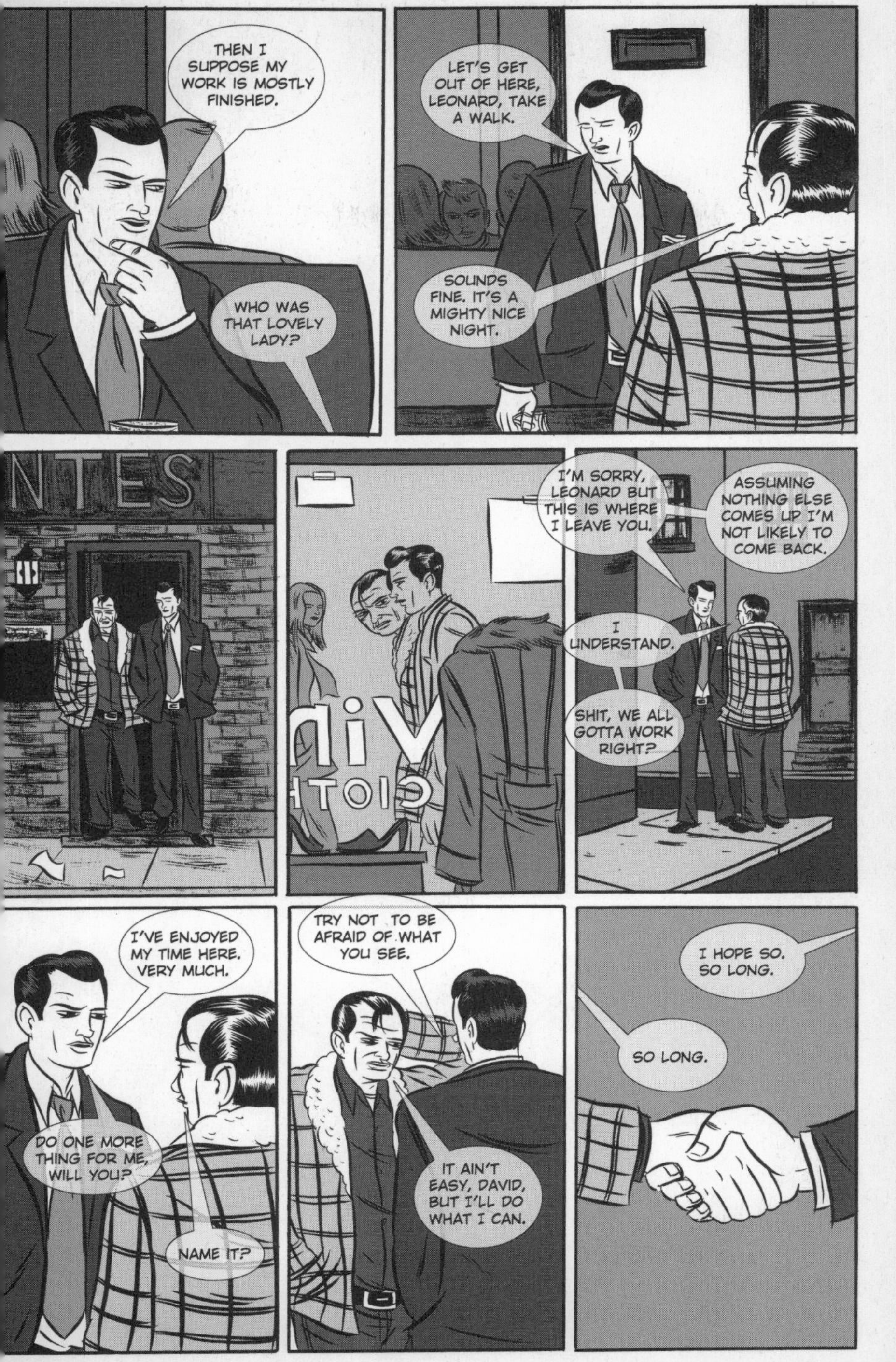
THEN I SUPPOSE MY WORK IS MOSTLY FINISHED.
WHO WAS THAT LOVELY LADY?
LET'S GET OUT OF HERE, LEONARD, TAKE A WALK.
SOUNDS FINE. IT'S A MIGHTY NICE NIGHT.
NTES
CLOTH
I'M SORRY, LEONARD BUT THIS IS WHERE I LEAVE YOU.
ASSUMING NOTHING ELSE COMES UP I'M NOT LIKELY TO COME BACK.
I UNDERSTAND.
SHIT, WE ALL GOTTA WORK RIGHT?
I'VE ENJOYED MY TIME HERE. VERY MUCH.
DO ONE MORE THING FOR ME, WILL YOU?
NAME IT?
TRY NOT TO BE AFRAID OF WHAT YOU SEE.
IT AIN'T EASY, DAVID, BUT I'LL DO WHAT I CAN.
I HOPE SO. SO LONG.
SO LONG.

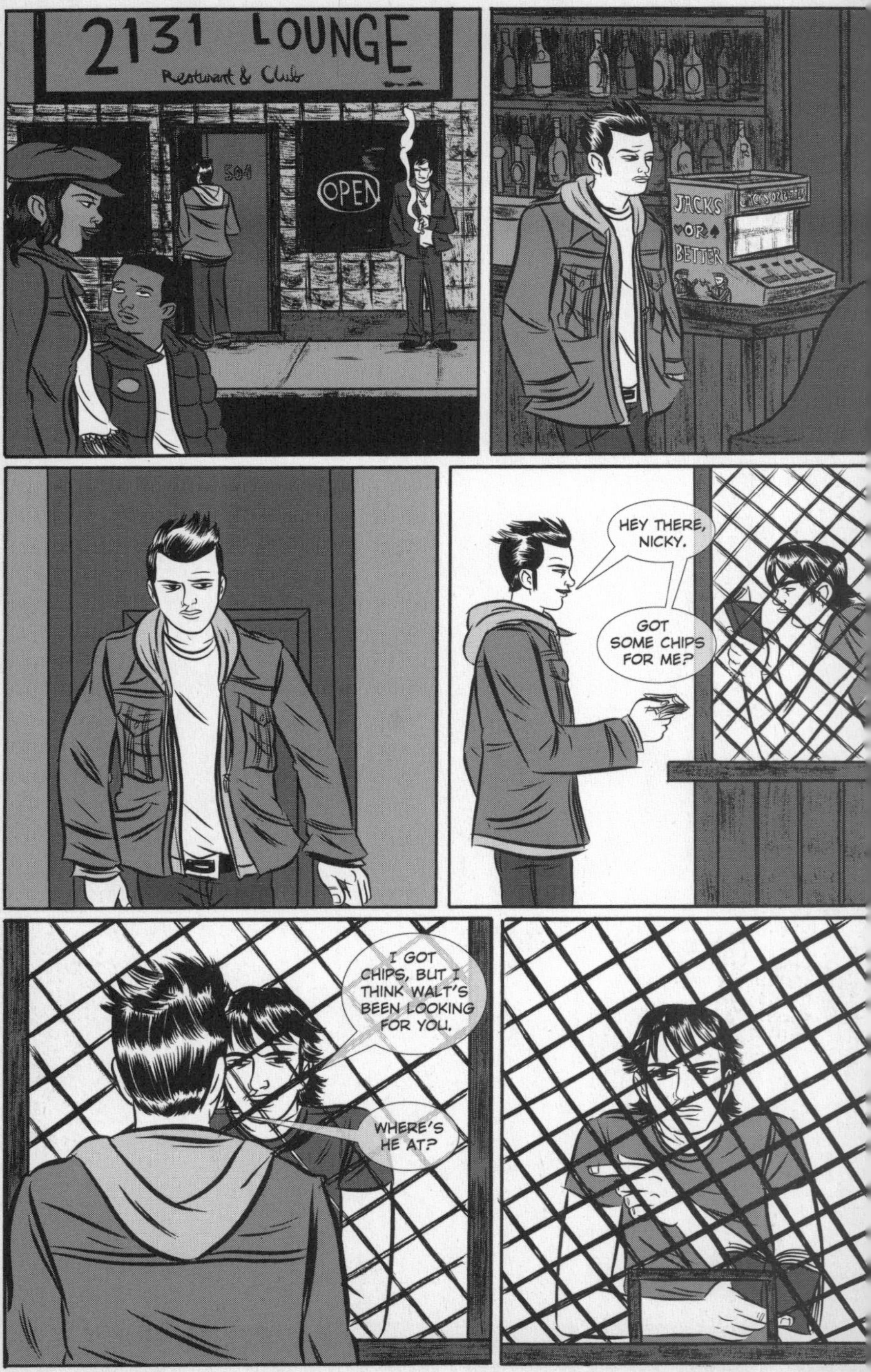
2131 LOUNGE
Restaurant & Club
501
OPEN
JACKS OR BETTER
HEY THERE, NICKY.
GOT SOME CHIPS FOR ME?
I GOT CHIPS, BUT I THINK WALT'S BEEN LOOKING FOR YOU.
WHERE'S HE AT?

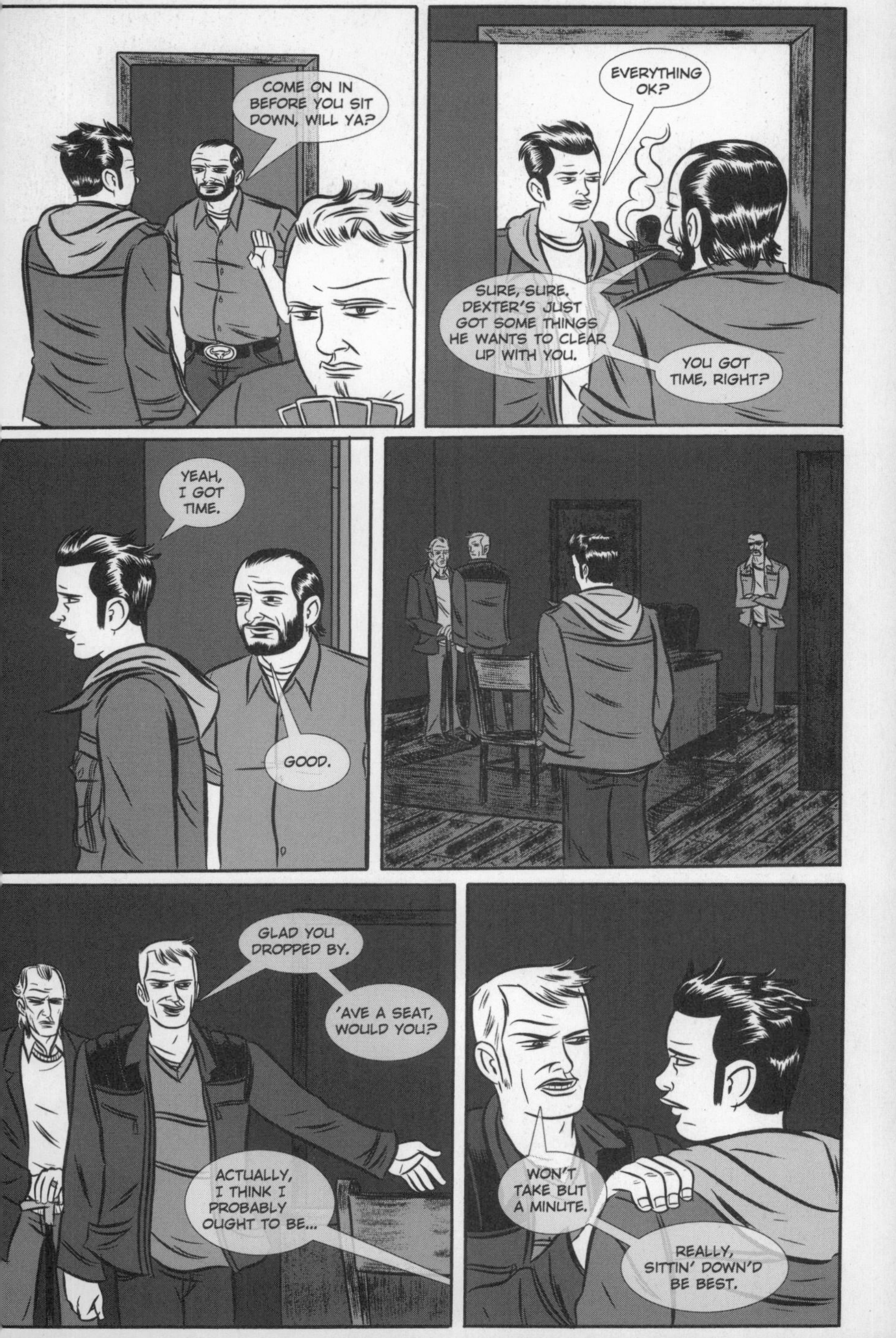
COME ON IN BEFORE YOU SIT DOWN, WILL YA?
EVERYTHING OK?
SURE, SURE. DEXTER'S JUST GOT SOME THINGS HE WANTS TO CLEAR UP WITH YOU.
YOU GOT TIME, RIGHT?
YEAH, I GOT TIME.
GOOD.
GLAD YOU DROPPED BY.
'AVE A SEAT, WOULD YOU?
ACTUALLY, I THINK I PROBABLY OUGHT TO BE...
WON'T TAKE BUT A MINUTE.
REALLY, SITTIN' DOWN'D BE BEST.

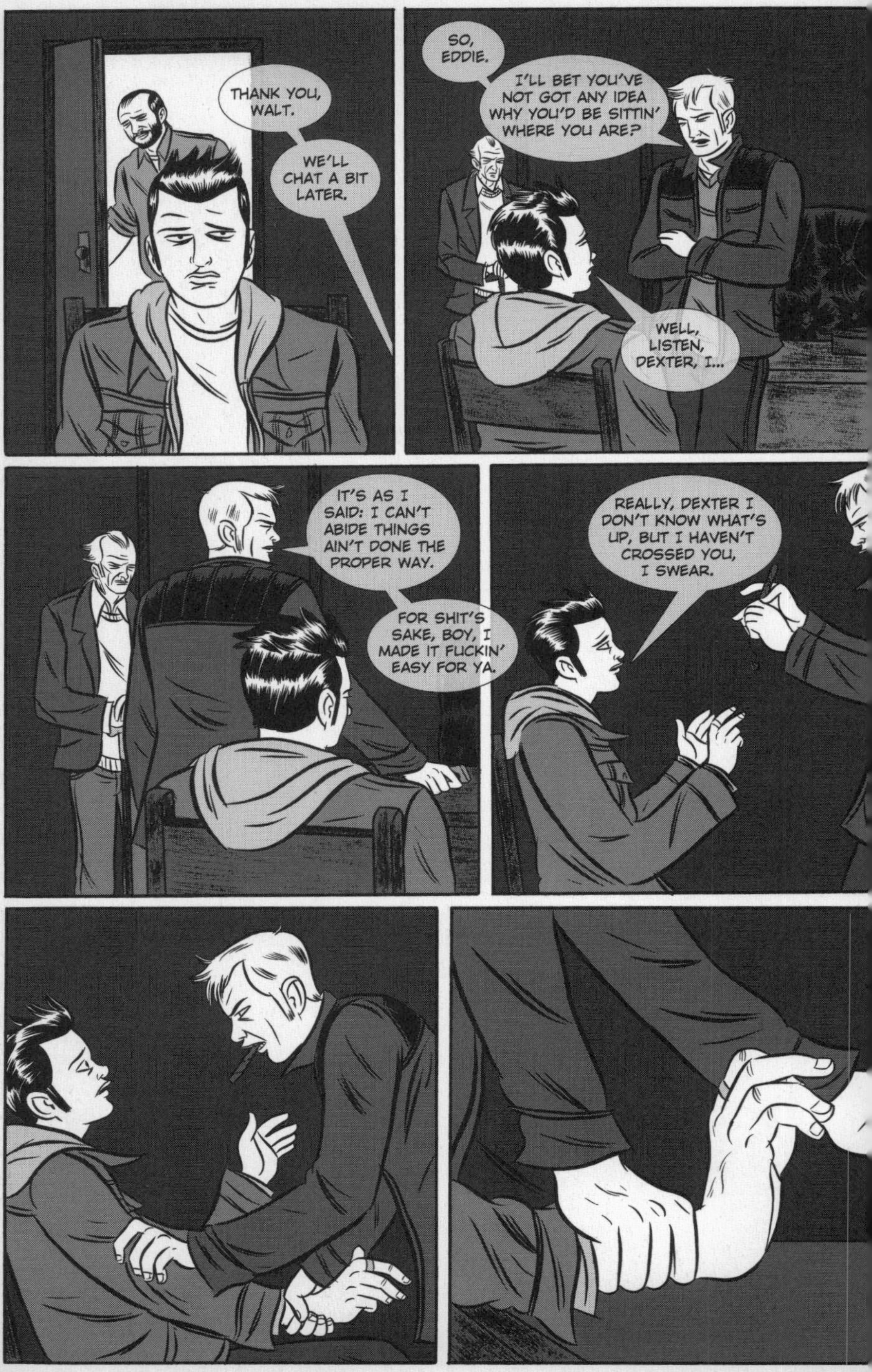
THANK YOU, WALT.
WE'LL CHAT A BIT LATER.
SO, EDDIE.
I'LL BET YOU'VE NOT GOT ANY IDEA WHY YOU'D BE SITTIN' WHERE YOU ARE?
WELL, LISTEN, DEXTER, I...
IT'S AS I SAID: I CAN'T ABIDE THINGS AIN'T DONE THE PROPER WAY.
FOR SHIT'S SAKE, BOY, I MADE IT FUCKIN' EASY FOR YA.
REALLY, DEXTER I DON'T KNOW WHAT'S UP, BUT I HAVEN'T CROSSED YOU, I SWEAR.

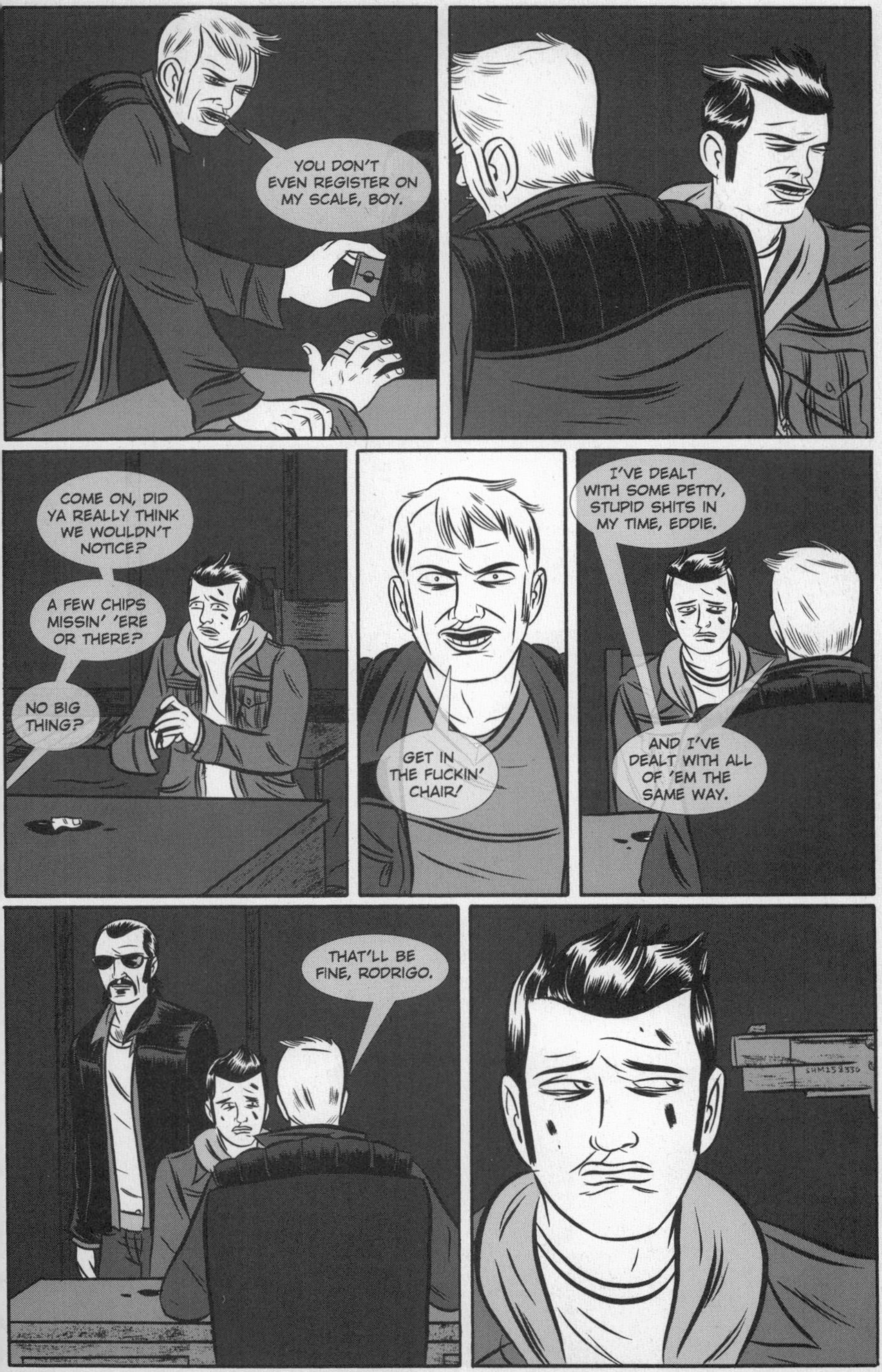

YOU DON'T EVEN REGISTER ON MY SCALE, BOY.
COME ON, DID YA REALLY THINK WE WOULDN'T NOTICE?
A FEW CHIPS MISSIN' 'ERE OR THERE?
NO BIG THING?
GET IN THE FUCKIN' CHAIR!
I'VE DEALT WITH SOME PETTY, STUPID SHITS IN MY TIME, EDDIE.
AND I'VE DEALT WITH ALL OF 'EM THE SAME WAY.
THAT'LL BE FINE, RODRIGO.

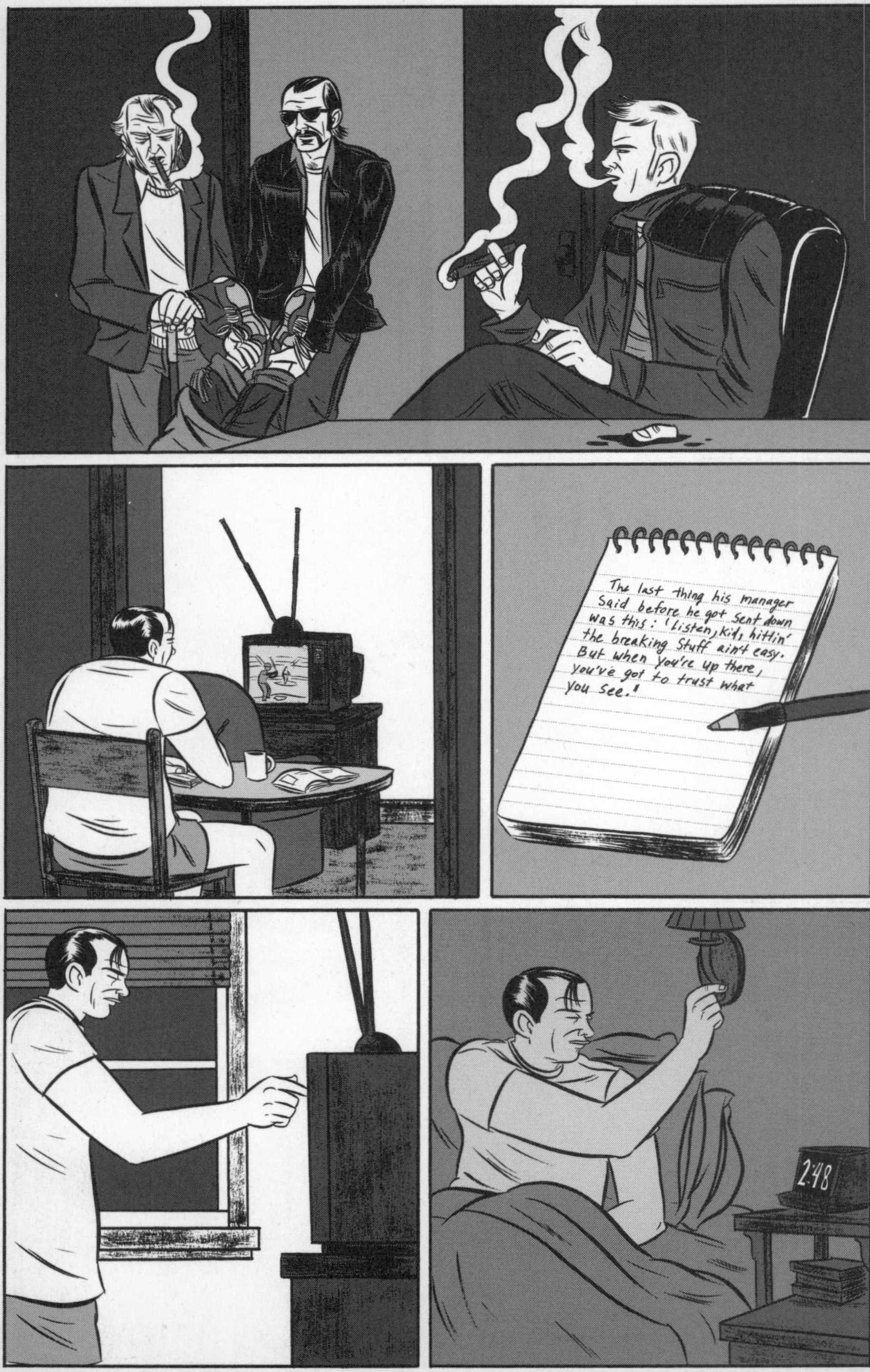
The last thing his manager Said before he got Sent down was this: 'Listen, kid, hittin' the breaking Stuff ain't easy. But when you're up there, you've got to trust what you see.'
2:48

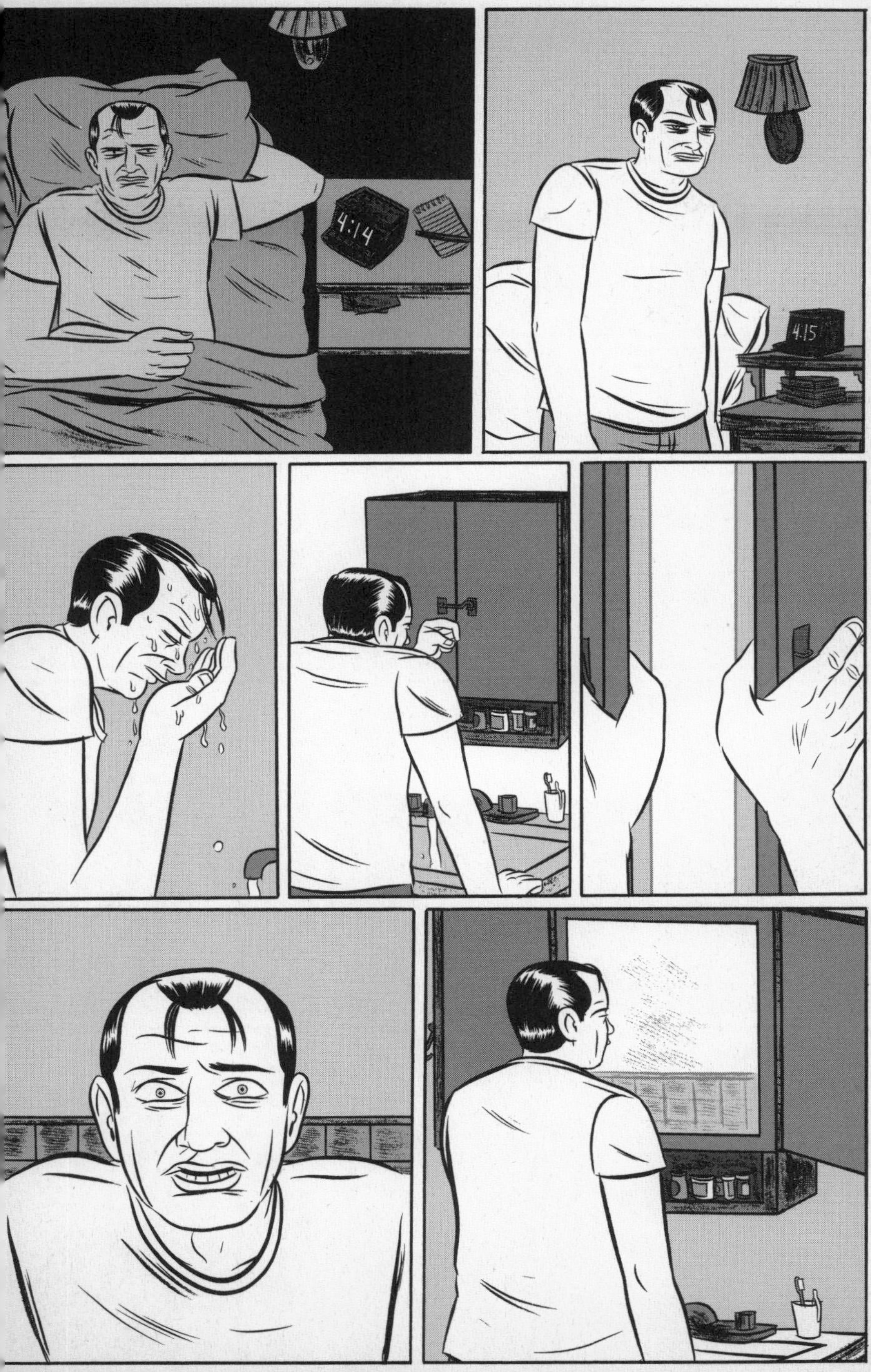
4:14
4:15

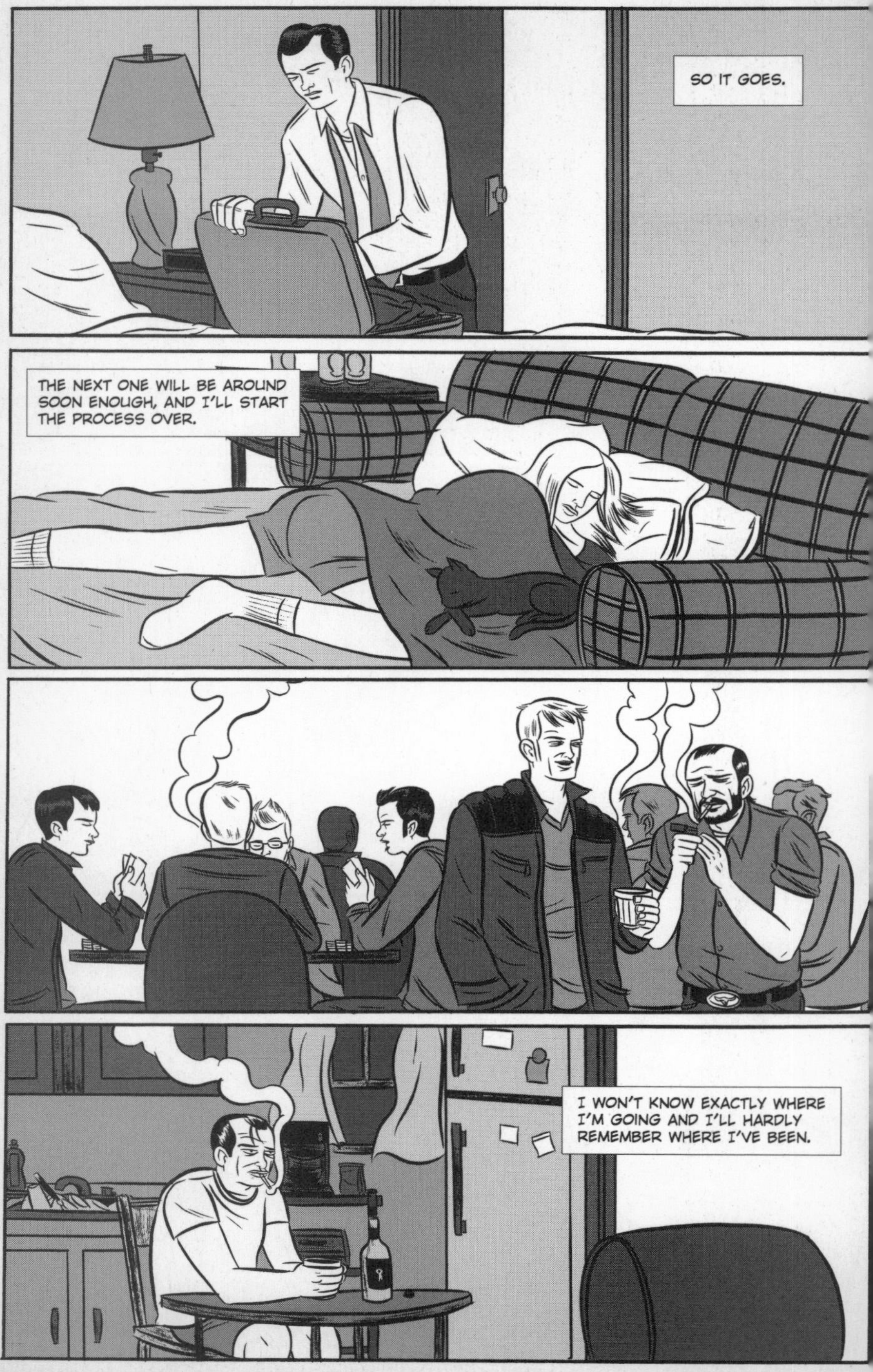
SO IT GOES.
THE NEXT ONE WILL BE AROUND SOON ENOUGH, AND I'LL START THE PROCESS OVER.
I WON'T KNOW EXACTLY WHERE I'M GOING AND I'LL HARDLY REMEMBER WHERE I'VE BEEN.

THE**EXTRAS**

The trade paperback collection is fast becoming the special edition DVD of the comics industry, and it's one of the best things that could have happened. The DVD boom has afforded film aficionados a chance to look into the process of filmmaking in ways unheard of only a few years ago, and now comics fans are getting their chance to do the same. It's particularly interesting for the latter group because there is no prescribed way to go about producing a comic book. The wide variety of styles in evidence on the shelf is emblematic of an equal number of approaches to creating the finished product. For fans, aspiring creators, and even, if we're lucky, academics, the trade paperback can be an invaluable resource.

The following pages contain a selection of materials that reveal something of the particular process that went into creating these first five issues of *One Plus One*.

The story that appeared in the *Oni Press Color Special 2002* was something of an experiment. With the first issue of the book not coming out for several months after the publication of the special, we were faced with a quandary. We only had four pages to work with, and we recognized that to try to fully introduce the characters in that time would be impossible. We opted instead for a short, self-contained story that was designed to be an unused excerpt from the story as a whole, a deleted scene.

Reaction to this approach was mixed. Most people said that it was interesting but that it made no sense. Now that the collection has arrived, the story has its context. In issue 5, page 17, David and Leonard leave Dante's in panels 2 and 3 to take a short walk. The story from the color special, reprinted on the following pages, is the conversation that takes place between the two men as they are walking. It is the missing action from panel 4, when we observe them from behind a glass storefront. The woman in the story is Evelyn Carver, a character who will play an interesting role in the next *One Plus One* story arc. *Art on this page by Mike Allred.*

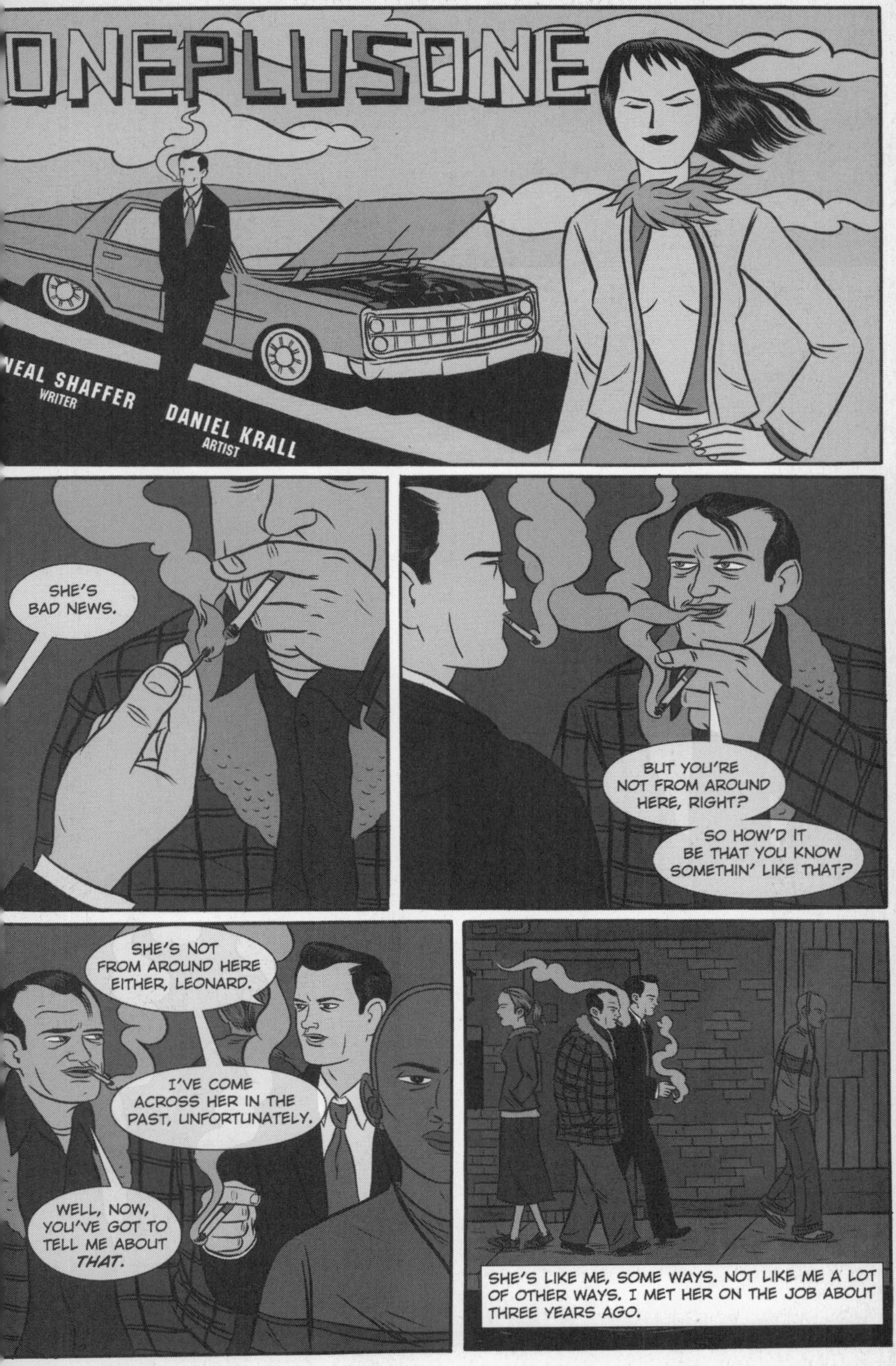
ONEPLUSONE
NEAL SHAFFER
WRITER
DANIEL KRALL
ARTIST
SHE'S BAD NEWS.
BUT YOU'RE NOT FROM AROUND HERE, RIGHT?
SO HOW'D IT BE THAT YOU KNOW SOMETHIN' LIKE THAT?
SHE'S NOT FROM AROUND HERE EITHER, LEONARD.
I'VE COME ACROSS HER IN THE PAST, UNFORTUNATELY.
WELL, NOW, YOU'VE GOT TO TELL ME ABOUT *THAT*.
SHE'S LIKE ME, SOME WAYS. NOT LIKE ME A LOT OF OTHER WAYS. I MET HER ON THE JOB ABOUT THREE YEARS AGO.

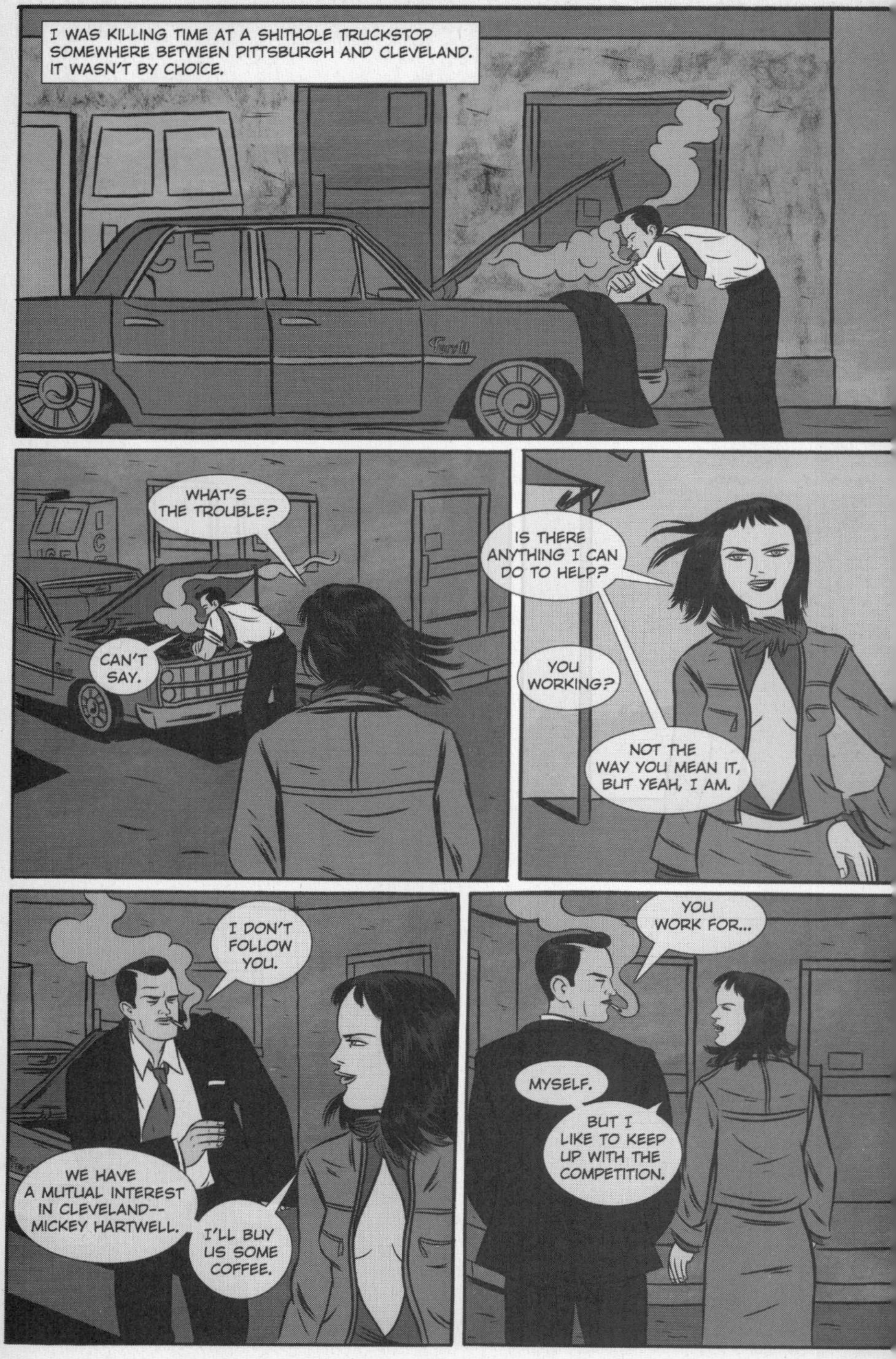
I WAS KILLING TIME AT A SHITHOLE TRUCKSTOP SOMEWHERE BETWEEN PITTSBURGH AND CLEVELAND. IT WASN'T BY CHOICE.
WHAT'S THE TROUBLE?
CAN'T SAY.
IS THERE ANYTHING I CAN DO TO HELP?
YOU WORKING?
NOT THE WAY YOU MEAN IT, BUT YEAH, I AM.
I DON'T FOLLOW YOU.
WE HAVE A MUTUAL INTEREST IN CLEVELAND-- MICKEY HARTWELL.
I'LL BUY US SOME COFFEE.
YOU WORK FOR...
MYSELF.
BUT I LIKE TO KEEP UP WITH THE COMPETITION.

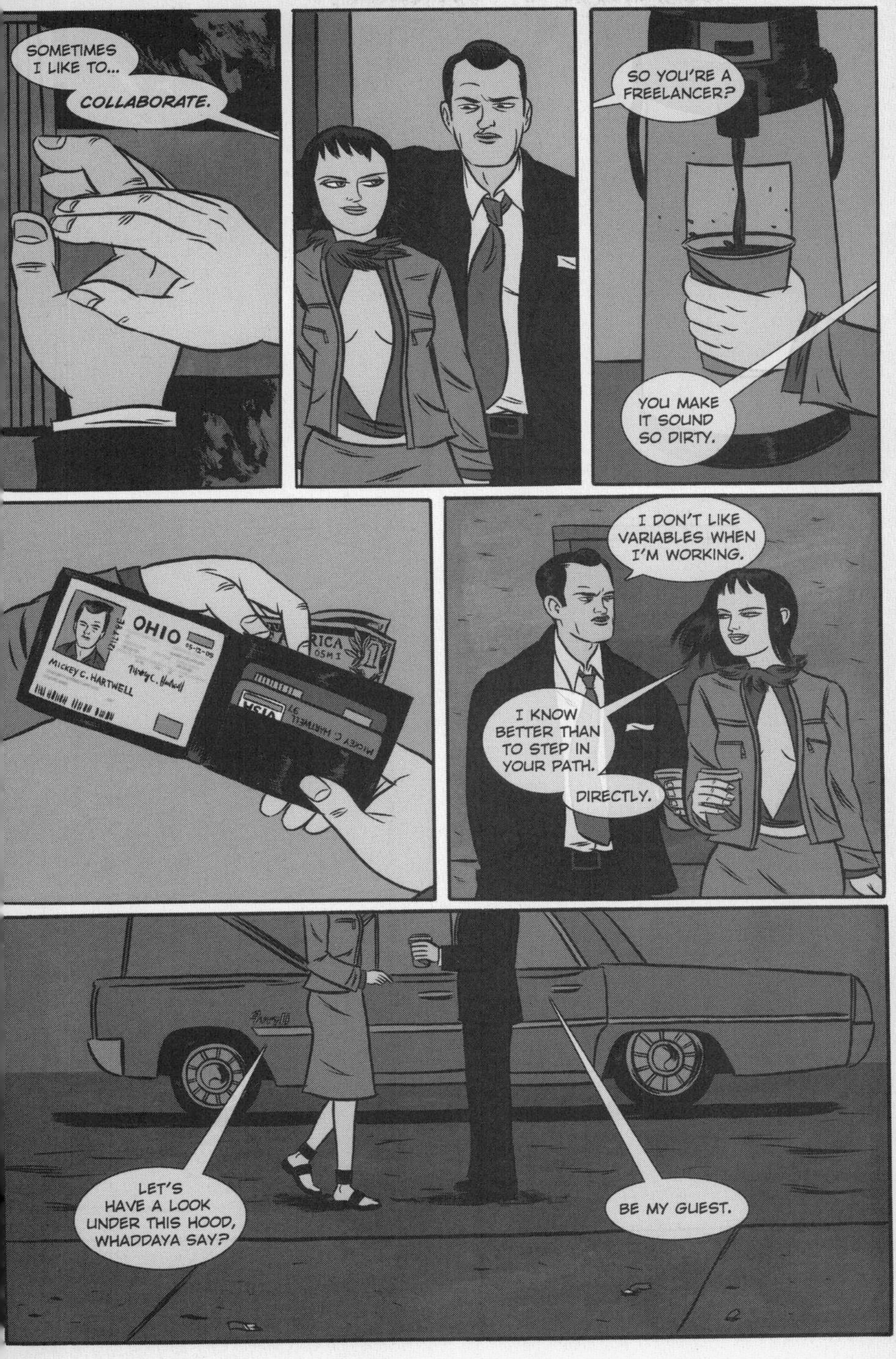
SOMETIMES I LIKE TO...
COLLABORATE.
SO YOU'RE A FREELANCER?
YOU MAKE IT SOUND SO DIRTY.
OHIO
MICKEY C. HARTWELL
VISA
I DON'T LIKE VARIABLES WHEN I'M WORKING.
I KNOW BETTER THAN TO STEP IN YOUR PATH.
DIRECTLY.
LET'S HAVE A LOOK UNDER THIS HOOD, WHADDAYA SAY?
BE MY GUEST.

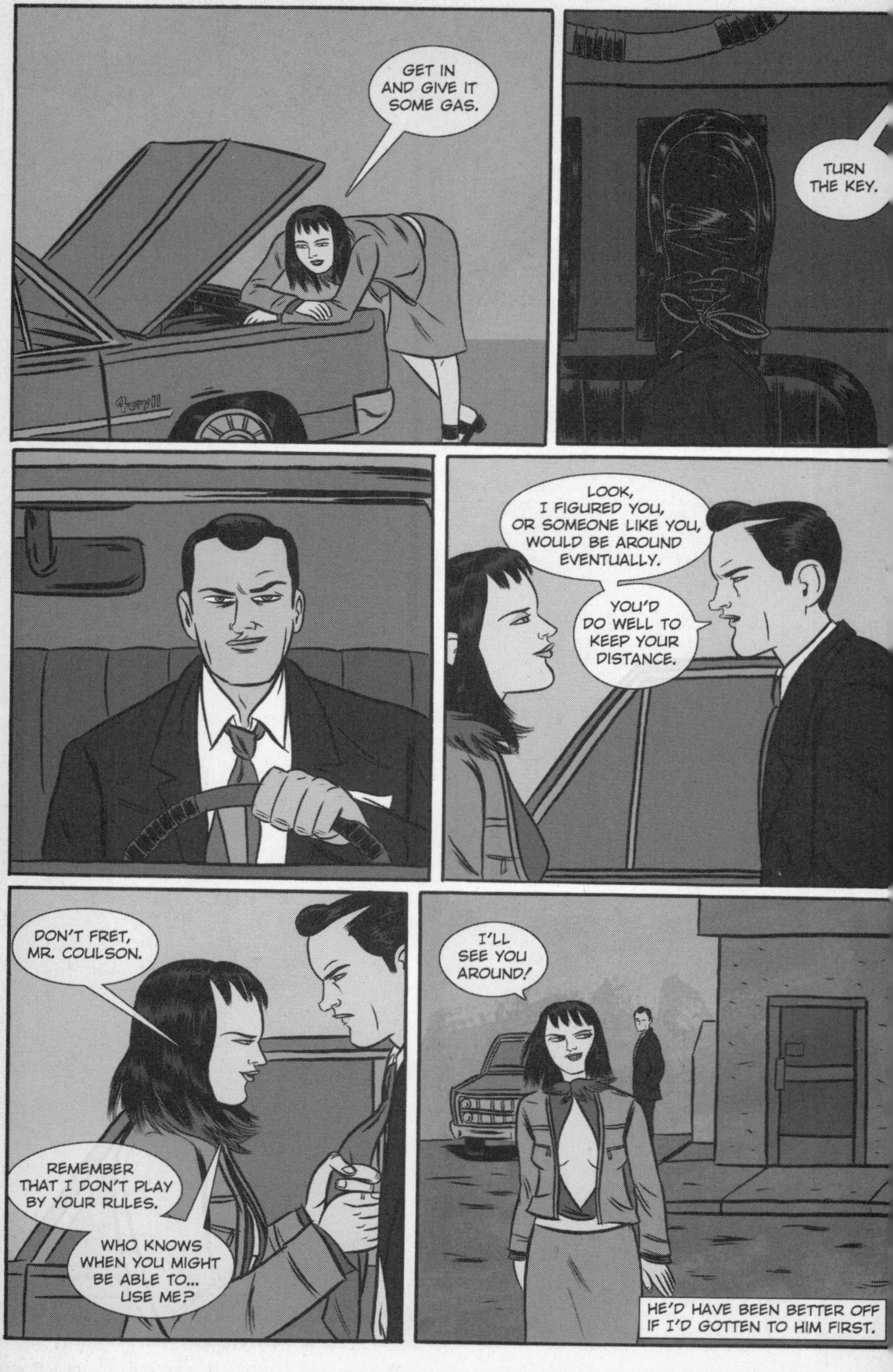

GET IN AND GIVE IT SOME GAS.
TURN THE KEY.
LOOK, I FIGURED YOU, OR SOMEONE LIKE YOU, WOULD BE AROUND EVENTUALLY.
YOU'D DO WELL TO KEEP YOUR DISTANCE.
DON'T FRET, MR. COULSON.
REMEMBER THAT I DON'T PLAY BY YOUR RULES.
WHO KNOWS WHEN YOU MIGHT BE ABLE TO... USE ME?
I'LL SEE YOU AROUND!
HE'D HAVE BEEN BETTER OFF IF I'D GOTTEN TO HIM FIRST.

THE PITCH

Just as there is no prescribed way to create a comic book, there is no prescribed way to go about getting one published. Luck will, as ever, play a role, but there are certain things that seem to work. It's important to know your story and have confidence in it, and it's equally important to know which companies might be interested, based on books they've already published.

The following pages are reproductions of the pitch that we took with us to San Diego Comic-Con 2001. We were very fortunate to arouse the interest of Oni Press, an outstanding place to work. But we also felt, before we left, that Oni would be a perfect place for us. There's no way to say if our approach would work for anyone else, but it did work for us. All of the guys at Oni made mention of the fact that they found our pitch impressive. So, we're printing these reproductions as a favor to anyone who might be trying to do the same thing and as added content for anyone who enjoys the book. It can't hurt.

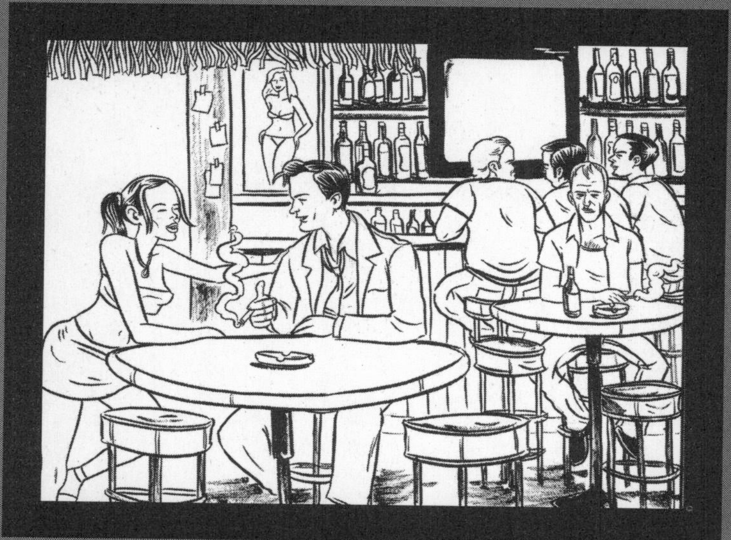

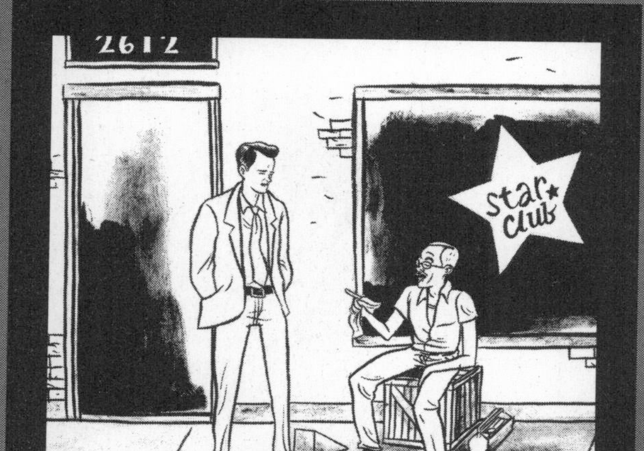
2612
star club

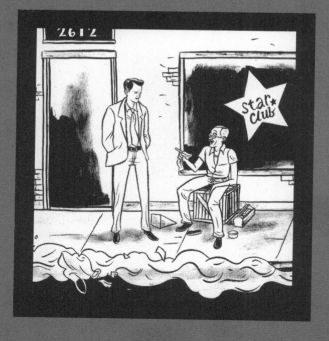

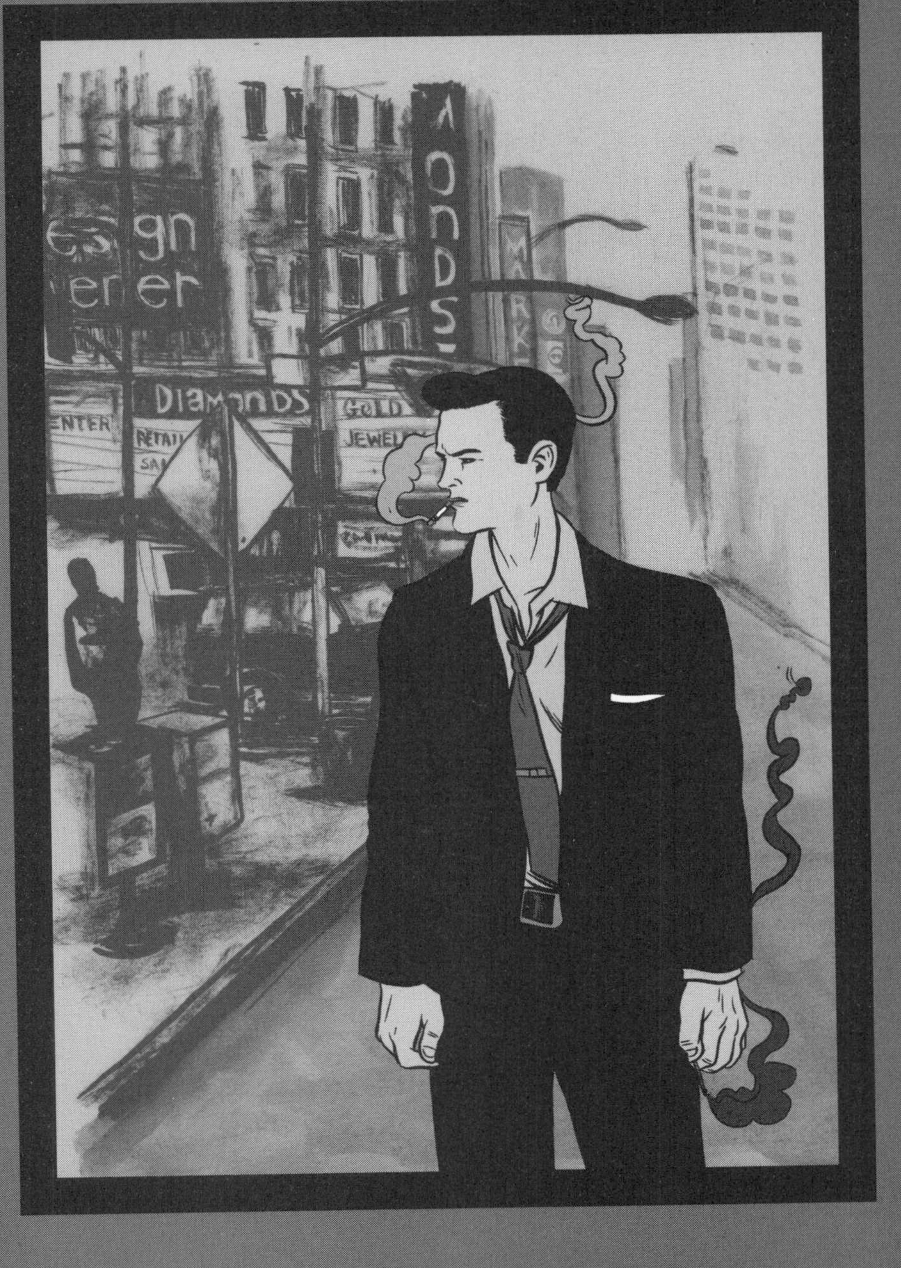
DIAMONDS
GOLD
JEWEL
ENTER
RETAIL

CARD GAME

The following is one sequence that we, and others, particularly enjoy. We're providing the original script and the initial thumbnail sketches as a way to peek into what *One Plus One* resembled in its fetal stages.

The script is written using Final Draft, a screenwriting program. Since there is no universal format for comic scripts, Final Draft is an easy (and relatively economical) way to go about it. It isn't, however, necessary. Word, or even a typewriter, would be just as functional. As long as the editor and the co-creators are happy, the script works.

The thumbnail step is unique to every artist, and most artists do not use thumbnails as detailed as those that Daniel creates. Some don't use them at all, opting to start with pencils. This level of detail, however, makes the layout and pencilling stages that much easier.

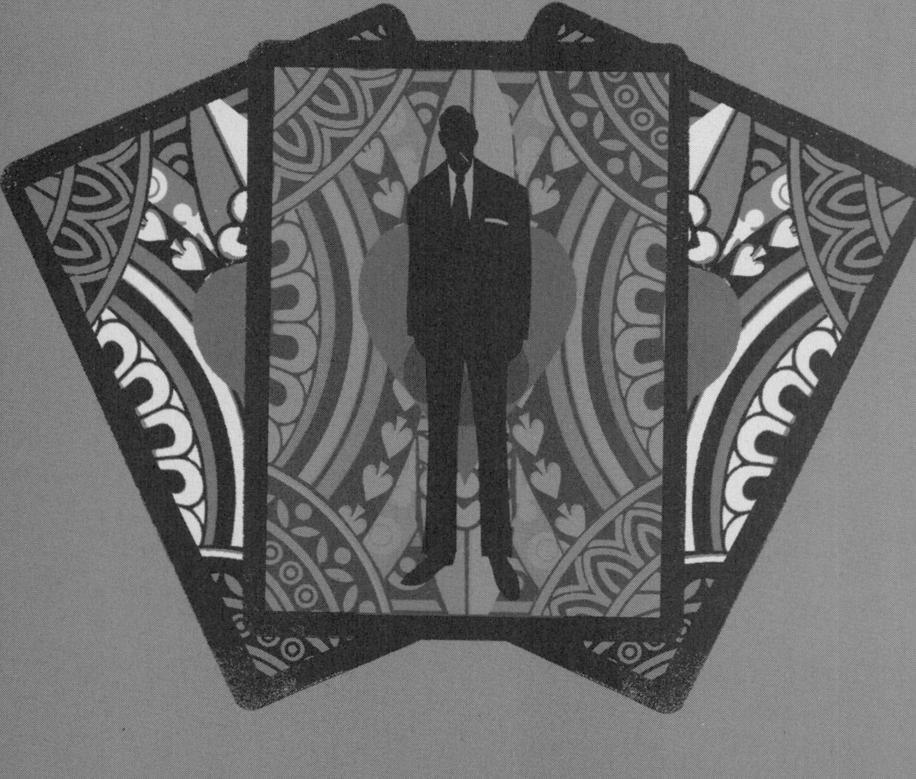

PAGE NINE

PANEL ONE

David and Eddie, taking a seat in a cafe. It's a typically hip, modern, and urban coffee joint with tables by the window. It is at one such table that David and Eddie are now seated. Our angle shows the activity on the street.

As David speaks, he is pulling a cigarette out of a pack.

DAVID
Poker's not really your game, is it, Edward?

EDDIE
Well, I don't know. I can hold my own.

PANEL TWO
David, cigarette hanging from his lips, holding the pack out for Eddie, who is grabbing one for himself.

DAVID
Sure you can. But you're not a winner. Probably never will be.

EDDIE
Now, hold on, man. I got more goin' than most guys. I win enough.

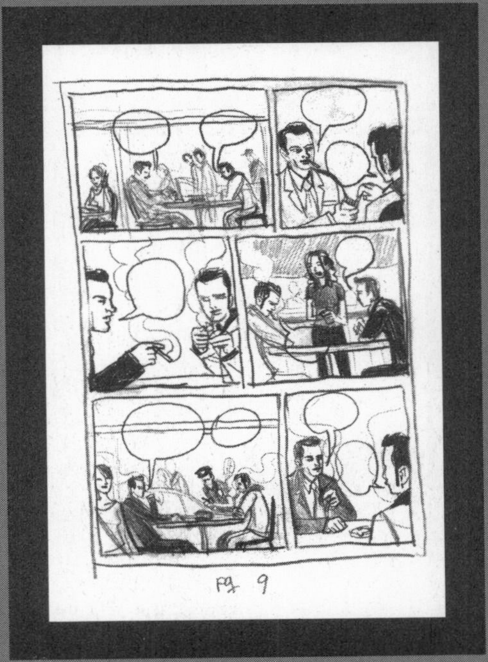
pg 9

PANEL THREE
David is now pointing at Eddie.

DAVID
If that's true you wouldn't think twice about losing to me.

PANEL FOUR

There is now a waitress at the table.

DAVID
Just coffee, please.

EDDIE
Uh, yeah, me too.

PANEL FIVE

The waitress is now gone, and we are still with them. Our angle once again shows the street activity. There is a cop putting a ticket onto a windshield.

DAVID
You don't need to learn to play like me, and you probably couldn't if you tried. So I'll show you something quicker.

PANEL SIX

Same situation, different angle.

DAVID
All you need is a stake.

EDDIE
Well, yeah. When you put it that way...

PAGE TEN

PANEL ONE

David, reaching into his inside coat pocket. The waitress has just placed their coffee on the table.

DAVID
What I'm going to show you is simple.

PANEL TWO

David, removing cards from a pack.

DAVID
And with some work, lucrative.

PANEL THREE

David is holding the deck in one hand and showing the top card to Eddie.

DAVID
The seven of spades.

PANEL FOUR

Close on David's hands, dealing. He is holding the deck in his left hand. His thumb is on top of the deck, his first two fingers are on the short (far) edge, and his third finger and pinky are on the right edge. His right hand is flipping a card to Eddie's side of the table.

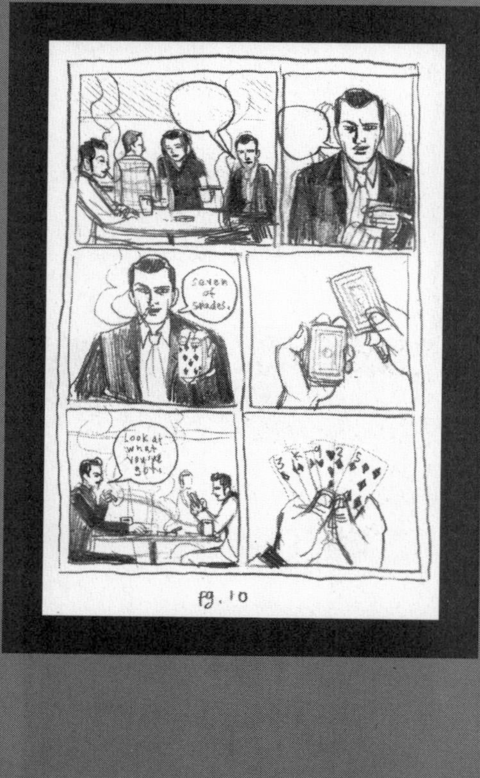

Seven of spades.
Look at what you've got.
pg. 10

PANEL FIVE
David has set the pack down on the table.

DAVID
Now take a look at what you've got.

PANEL SIX

Eddie's cards. There is no seven of spades.

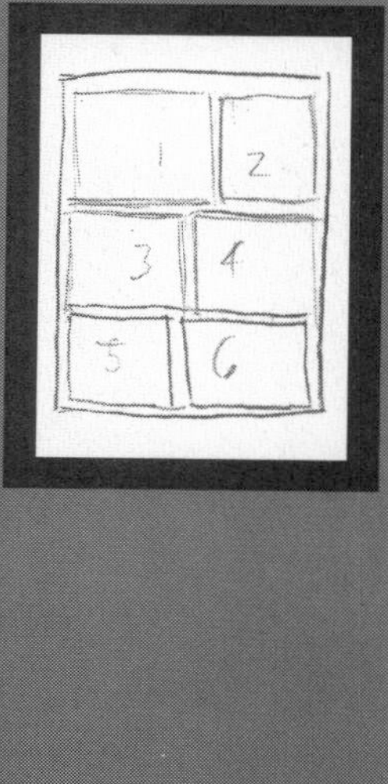

1
2
3
4
5
6

PAGE ELEVEN

PANEL ONE

David, pulling one card from the pile he has dealt to himself.

> DAVID
> Now suppose I'm working on a seven-high straight in a stud game.

PANEL TWO

David, holding the seven of spades up for Eddie.

PANEL THREE

David handing Eddie the deck.

> DAVID
> Hold the deck as if you're about to deal.

PANEL FOUR

Eddie is holding the deck. His thumb, as David's was, is on top of the deck. His other four fingers all rest along the opposite, long edge.

> DAVID (o.s.)
> Move your first two fingers around to the top edge.

PANEL FIVE

On David.

> DAVID
> This is the mechanic's grip. Get comfortable with it.

PANEL SIX

Straight ahead on Eddie, who is looking down at his hand quizzically.

> DAVID (o.s.)
> With this grip you can peek the top card by curling it over with pressure from the right side. Your first two fingers should conceal the move.

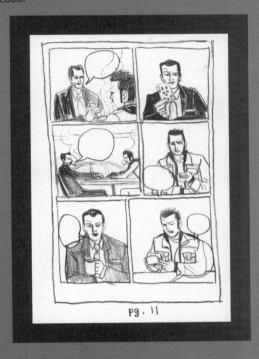

pg. 11

PAGE TWELVE

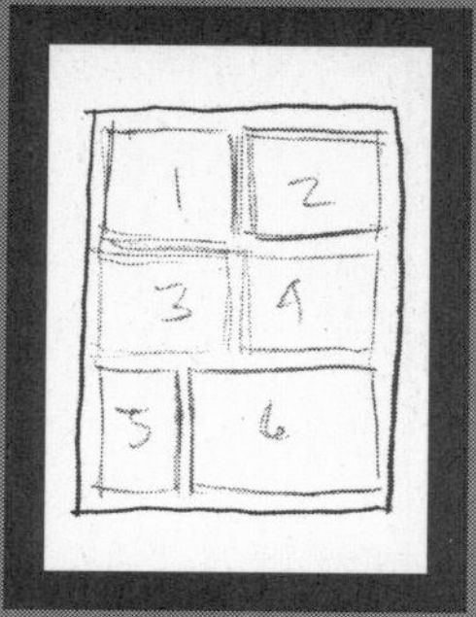
1
2
3
4
5
6

PANEL ONE

Eddie, surprised, as the cards spill out of his hand.

DAVID
It's easier than it seems at first.

PANEL TWO

David is now gathering the cards.

PANEL THREE

David is once again holding the pack.

DAVID
After you've seen the top card, you can remember who got it or save it for yourself.

PANEL FOUR

Same situation, different angle.

DAVID
If you want it, use your thumb to slide the top card a quarter inch. Hold it in place, and deal the second card.

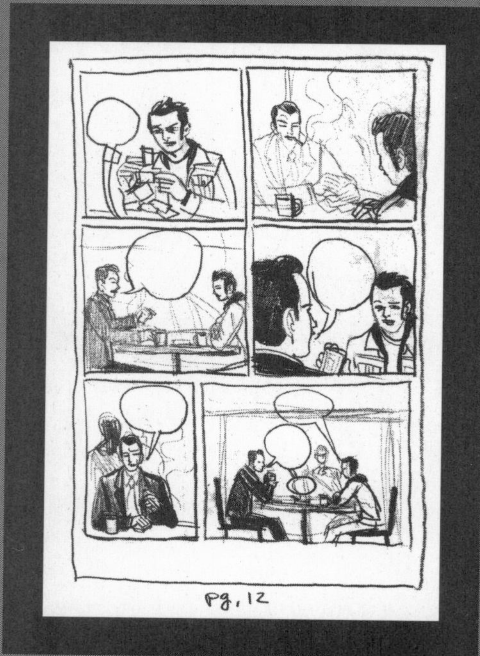
Pg. 12

PANEL FIVE

David, setting the deck down on the table.

DAVID
If you keep your head about you and don't force it you'll win more than you lose.

PANEL SIX

From the side again, looking out. We see a young woman tearing up that parking ticket.

EDDIE
Won't people notice?

DAVID
Not the people you're playing with. But Dexter might.

PAGE THIRTEEN

PANEL ONE

Eddie, lighting another smoke and speaking through it.

> EDDIE
> Don't you think that's pretty important?

> DAVID
> That's part of it.

PANEL TWO

David, from over Eddie's shoulder. Eddie's head is cocked slightly as he stares at a woman's ass as she walks by.

> DAVID
> Dexter knows good business. He'll see what you're doing and start wanting a cut. Give it to him.

PANEL THREE

Close on David's hand sliding the cards back into their box.

> EDDIE (o.s.)
> Is that all he's gonna want?

> DAVID (o.s.)
> He'll ask you to work for him. Take his offer, and skim off the top. If you're careful, you'll have your stake in a couple of weeks.

PANEL FOUR

David has stood up.

> EDDIE
> What about you?

> DAVID
> I'll be around.

PANEL FIVE

Panoramic of the cafe with David headed toward the door.

pg. 13

THESKETCHES

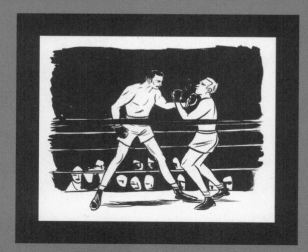

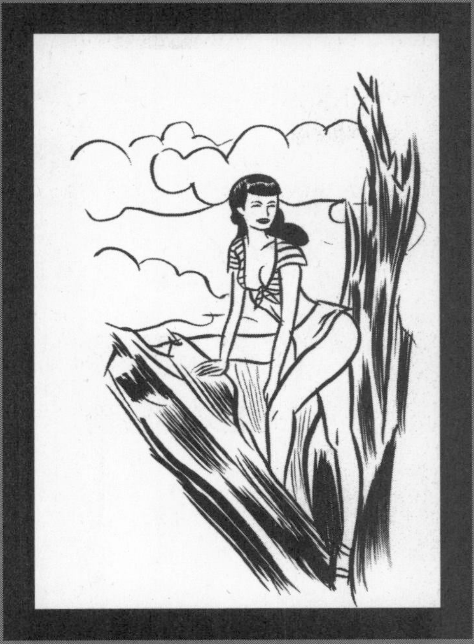

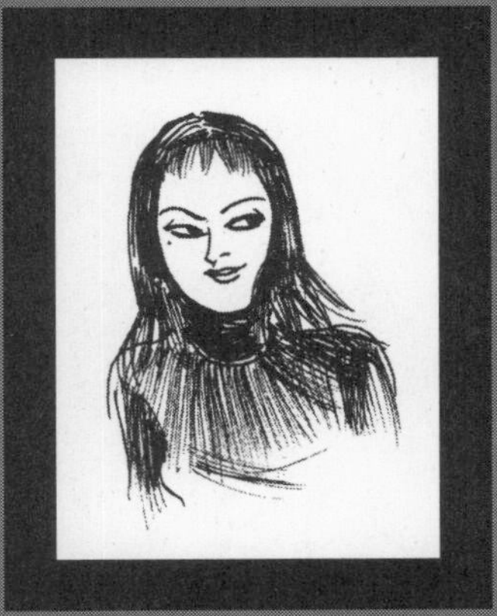

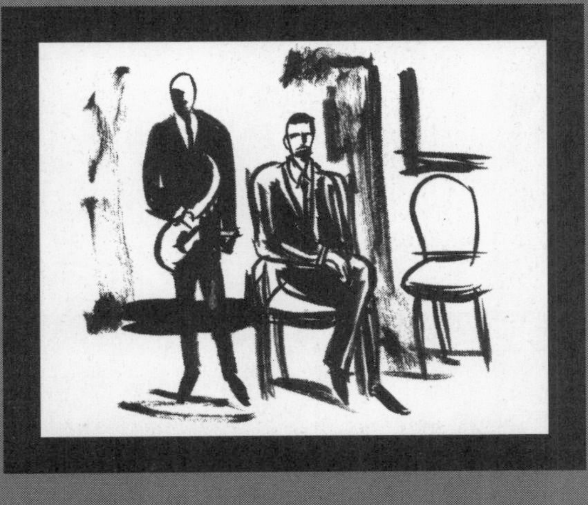

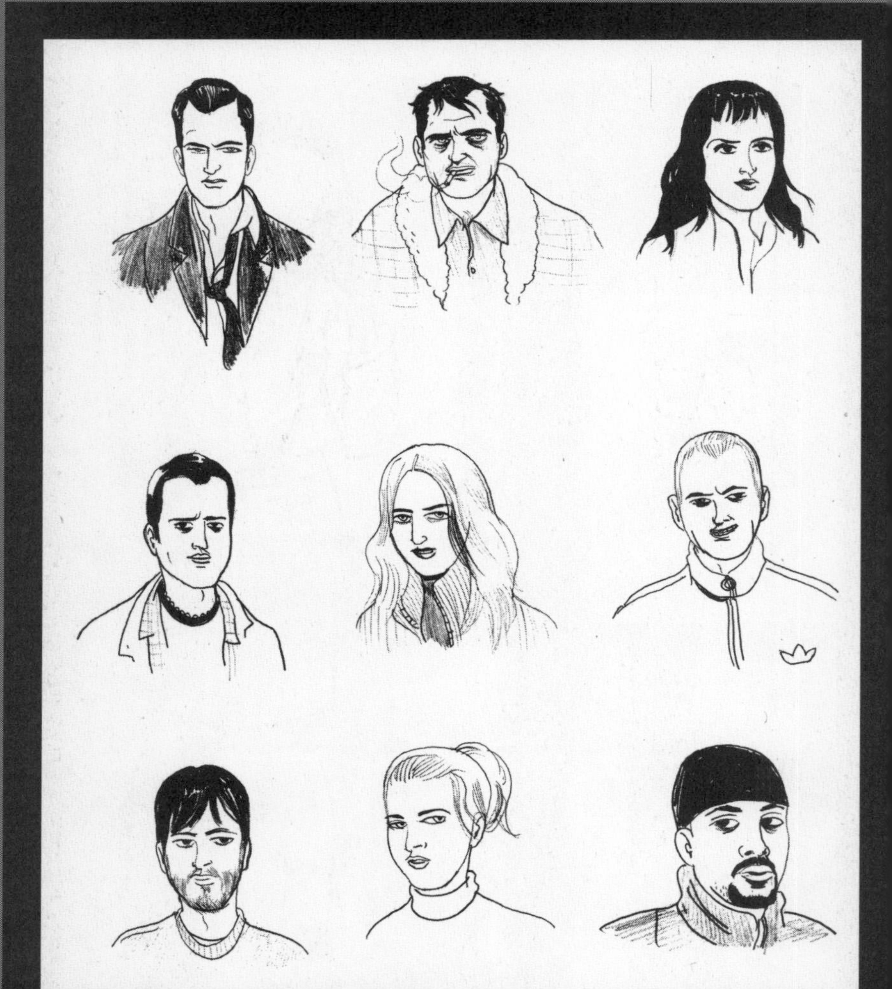

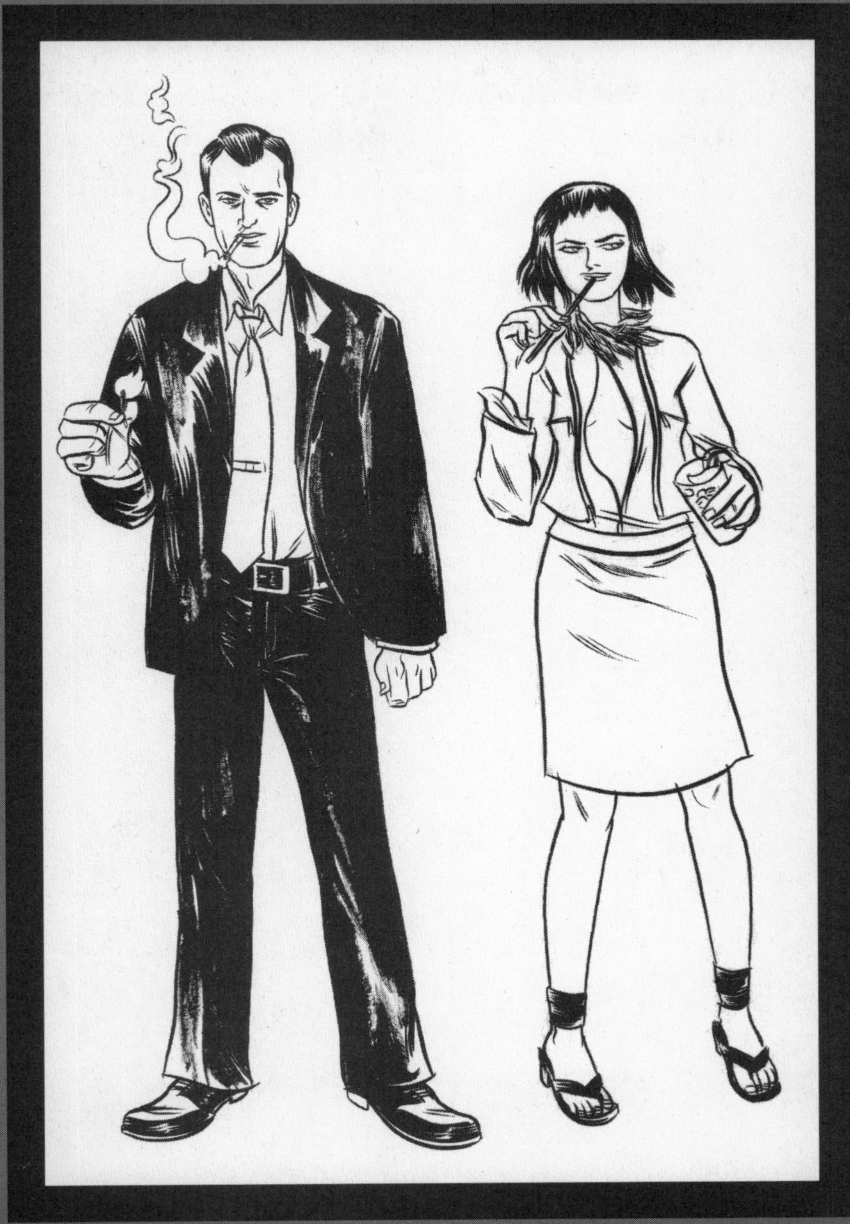

Neal Shaffer would like to thank the following, in no particular order, without whom *One Plus One* and all other works would not be possible:

Mom, Dad, Kim, Grandma, Grandpa, Lynn K., George F., John M., Steve I., John W., Jayson and John Whitehead, Chip M., Joe N., Jamie R., James L.J., Louis U., Daniel K., Dawn P., R.J.R. Nabisco, Miller Brewing Co., Frazier's on the Avenue, Fletcher's, the Baltimore Orioles, and any other entity, human or inanimate, living or dead, who may have been inadvertently omitted.

Extra special thanks are due to Greg Metcalf, a true friend who will never take as much credit as he deserves.

Daniel Krall thanks:

My Mom and Dad, for teaching me all the important stuff and always loving and supporting me; Ma, who I miss every day; all the rest of my family (including Kreiders, Kralls, and Pietruskos); my good pals from all over, like Joe M., Jeff, Shannon, Rama, Simon, Mark, Trey, Peat, Sean, Louis, Amy, Brian T., Joe K., Jenny (thanks so much, Jenny); fellow comic book folks, like Christine, Bone, Brian, Arthur, Chip, Scott, Mike A., Mike H., Jim, Steve R., Mark R., Jose, Chynna, Keith W., Jeff V., Mark W. (special thanks for the words of wisdom), Marc H., Frank C., Mike O. (of course for the awsome covers); teachers, like Ken, Warren, Julian, Whitney, Less, Howie, Chris S., Steven, Jose, Brian R., R. Dehaven, J. Barker, and D. Schade.

Outstanding super thanks to Dawn for bailing me out and being a terrific lady; Neal, for being a good pal and partner; and Jamie, James, and Joe for being the best guys to work with and for... ever. If I've forgotten anyone, I'll be sure to thank you in person.

Neal Shaffer writes from Baltimore, MD. In addition to his comics scripts, his work has included political and cultural essays, music journalism, sports columns, and book and movie reviews for a variety of print and web sources. His next scheduled comics work is *Last Exit Before Toll,* an original graphic novel collaboration with penciller Christopher Mitten and digital colorist Dawn Pietrusko, coming in November, 2003, from Oni Press.

Daniel Krall is a painter and freelance illustrator, contributing to various newspapers and fashion/entertainment magazines, including *Details* and *YM*. He is currently working on his debut solo comics project, *Follow Me Closely*, for Oni Press, while inking Christine Norrie on DC Comics' *Bad Girls* series. He lives in Baltimore in a house that, according to his landlord, is over a hundred years old. He has very patient parents.

OTHER BOOKS FROM ONI PRESS...

LAST EXIT BEFORE TOLL™
by Neal Shaffer, Christopher Mitten,
& Dawn Pietrusko
96 pages, black-and-white interiors
$9.95 US
ISBN 1929998-70-8

**MADMAN KING-SIZE SUPER
GROOVY SPECIAL™**
by Mike Allred
w/ Daniel Krall, Nick Derington, &
Steven Weissman
56 pages, full color interiors
$6.95 US
ISBN 1929998-63-5

CHEAT™
by Christine Norrie
72 pages,
black-and-white interiors
$5.95 US
ISBN 1929998-47-3

THE COMPLETE GEISHA™
by Andi Watson
152 pages, black-and-white interiors
$15.95 US
ISBN 1929998-51-1

KISSING CHAOS™
vol. 1
by Arthur Dela Cruz
196 pages, black-and-white interiors
$17.95 US
ISBN 1929998-32-5

**KISSING CHAOS:
NONSTOP BEAUTY™**
vol. 2
by Arthur Dela Cruz
128 pages, black-and-white interiors
$11.95 US
ISBN 1929998-64-3

ONE BAD DAY™
by Steve Rolston
120 pages, black-and-white interiors
$9.95 US
ISBN 1-929998-50-3

SKINWALKER™
by Nunzio DeFilippis, Christina Weir,
Brian Hurtt, & Arthur Dela Cruz
128 pages, black-and-white interiors
$11.95 US
ISBN 1929998-45-7

UNION STATION™
by Ande Parks & Eduardo Barretto
112 pages, black-and-white interiors
$11.95 US
ISBN 1929998-69-4
Available October 2003!

VISITATIONS™
by Scott Morse
88 pages, black-and-white interiors
$8.95 US
ISBN 1-929998-34-1